The Two Mrs Robinsons

The Two Mrs Robinsons

DONNA HAY

First published in Great Britain in 2007 by Orion Books,
an imprint of The Orion Publishing Group Ltd
Orion House, 5 Upper Saint Martin's Lane
London WC2H 9EA

1 3 5 7 9 10 8 6 4 2

A CIP catalogue record for this book is
available from the British Library.

ISBN-13 978 0 7528 7452 4 (Hardback)
ISBN-13 978 0 7528 7453 1 (Trade Paperback)

Typeset by Deltatype Ltd, Birkenhead, Merseyside

Printed in Great Britain by Clays Ltd, St Ives plc

The Orion Publishing Group's policy is to use papers that are natural,
renewable and recyclable products and made from wood grown in sustainable
forests. The logging and manufacturing processes are expected to
conform to the environmental regulations of the country of origin.

www.orionbooks.co.uk

Dedicated to the memory
of my mother-in-law,
Ellen Veronica Hay.

Chapter 1

DECEMBER

Eve Robinson remembered how Christmas used to be. Before dawn, she and Oliver would be sitting in bed amid a sea of discarded wrapping paper as Matt and Georgia opened their presents, squealing with excitement at each uncovered treasure.

Later, there would be a crisp, cold walk by the river before coming home to a crackling fire and the smell of roast turkey filling the air.

Five years later, it was all different. Oliver was off playing happy families with his girlfriend, Georgia was locked in her bedroom with her new MP3 player, and Matt was sleeping off his hangover after stumbling home at dawn and drunkenly felling the Christmas tree.

It was hardly the stuff Bing Crosby had been dreaming of.

'Looks like it's just you and me,' she sighed to Benson the Labrador, who lay at her feet by the fire, looking ill after scoffing most of the chocolate decorations off the fallen tree.

At least she still had some presents to open. Matt had given her a set of oven gloves and a novelty tea towel in a BHS carrier bag, while Georgia had splashed out on a jar of anti-wrinkle cream.

'The woman in the shop said it's better than Botox,' she'd said, as she ripped the plastic packaging off her MP3 headphones.

'Lovely.' Eve thought about the hair colourant Georgia had bought her for her birthday, one that guaranteed to get rid of grey, and wondered if her daughter was trying to tell her something.

She wondered what Oliver's girlfriend, Anna, might be

unwrapping at this very moment. Whatever it was, she was sure it wasn't a novelty tea towel.

Oliver had always been brilliant at giving presents. Way too extravagant, of course – Eve had often fretted over their post-Christmas credit-card bill – but somehow he always seemed to get it absolutely right. His gifts were quirky, fun and unpredict-able, just like him.

The phone rang. For a fraction of a second before she picked it up, Eve thought it might be her mother. Vanessa was spend-ing a month among the yurt makers of Kyrgysztan, but surely it wasn't too much to hope she'd remembered her only child at Christmas?

But it was her friend Jan. 'Just calling to wish you a happy Christmas,' she shouted, against a din of shrieking children. Although they were the same age, Jan had put off having babies until she'd turned thirty and established herself in her teaching career. At the time it seemed like a sensible move, but listening to the chaos on the other end of the line now, Eve was pleased her children had arrived unplanned in her early twenties while she still had the energy to cope.

'Happy Christmas to you, too. Sounds like Armageddon there?'

'Oh God, I know. I told Peter we shouldn't give them those selection boxes for breakfast. So what did Santa bring you?'

'The dog bought me a Chocolate Orange. But he's eaten it.' She nudged Benson's podgy flank with her toe. He opened his eyes, groaned and closed them again. 'How about you? Did Pete buy you nipple clamps again?'

'Funnily enough, no. It was Chanel No. 5 this year.'

'Wow, I'm impressed.'

'Don't be, I bought it for myself. And wrapped it. I even wrote out my own gift tag. Why are men so crap at buying presents?'

'Oliver wasn't.' She heard Jan's sigh, but ignored it. They both knew what she was going to say next. 'I wonder what he's got Anna for Christmas ...'

'Eve, don't.'

'A Barbie annual, I expect. That's the kind of thing she'd want at her age.'

'Eve!' Jan laughed, while trying to be stern. 'Stop it. You know I'm in a difficult position here.'

She and Peter had been friends of Eve and Oliver's since university, and they were trying to stay friends with them both despite the break-up. Eve didn't mind Jan's double-dealing, if it meant she could pass on juicy gossip about Oliver's girlfriend.

'No, seriously, what did he get her?'

'I don't know.'

'Liar. It's underwear, isn't it? Something dead sexy, but very tasteful at the same time. And expensive.' She could just imagine it. A frivolous concoction of La Perla lace, or something saucy from Agent Provocateur. Anna probably wore underwear like dental floss, unlike the M&S economy packs Eve always ended up buying. No wonder Oliver had dumped her.

'I told you, I don't know, and I wouldn't tell you anyway. TASHA! Stop that right now! Hang on a minute.' Eve listened to Jan dishing out some stern words on the other end of the line. Then she came back. 'How come I can control a class of five-year-olds but not my own kids? Now, what were we saying?'

'We were talking about what Britney Spears got for Christmas.'

'No, we weren't.'

'Suit yourself. If you won't tell me I'll just have to ask her myself when I see her tonight.'

There was an uncomfortable silence. 'You're not going to Oliver's party?'

'Why not? We always go. Matt and Georgia like to see their dad on Christmas Day, especially as it's his birthday as well.'

'Wouldn't it be better to let them go on their own?'

'What, and spend Christmas night alone with a turkey sandwich, watching a twenty-year-old *Only Fools and Horses* special while Anna Bowman plays happy families with my kids? No thanks.'

'But you're not supposed to go to your ex's parties when you're divorced.'

'We're not divorced,' Eve reminded her tartly.

'I don't care, it's still all wrong. You're supposed to wish him dead and communicate through solicitors. You get on better than me and Peter, and we're married.'

Eve smiled to herself. 'Surely it's better for the children if we can all be civilised about it.'

'You're not very civilised to Anna. Don't you remember what it was like last year?'

'I didn't say a word to her.'

'Exactly. You spent the whole evening giving each other evil death-stares.'

'Look, I can't help it if she's not grown-up enough to accept that Oliver and I are still friends, can I? We're not going to fall out with each other just because she doesn't like it.'

'So you're not just going to this party to wind her up?'

'The thought hadn't crossed my mind,' Eve said piously.

Jan laughed. 'Yeah, right. And those are real reindeer tracks on our patio.'

'Is that new?'

Georgia Robinson stood in the bedroom doorway, watching her mother struggle with the zip on her dress.

'As a matter of fact, it is.' With a giant sucked-in breath, she managed to wrench the zip up the last two inches. She smoothed the fabric over her hips and looked at her reflection in the mirror. 'Do you like it?'

'Where did you buy it?' She caught her mother's evasive look. 'Oh God, you got it from Top Shop, didn't you? How many times do I have to tell you not to go in there?'

'But it was on the sale rail.'

'I don't care. It's just wrong. You're nearly forty, for heaven's sake. Why can't you start acting your age?'

Her mother pulled a face at her in the mirror. 'So I suppose this isn't the right time to show you my new body piercing?'

Georgia shuddered. 'Don't even joke about it.' She wouldn't put any kind of embarrassing behaviour past her mother. She already insisted on singing along to Georgia's Arctic Monkeys

4

CD, and using the word 'wicked' in front of her friends, like she was down with the kids or something. 'I thought you were going to wear your black trousers?'

'I fancied a change.' She did a little twirl in front of the mirror. 'It's not that bad, is it?'

Her daughter studied Eve carefully. She hated to admit it, but it looked quite good. The deep red swirly print suited her honey-gold hair, and the soft jersey fabric hid all her flabby bits.

It was what it meant that troubled Georgia. There was only one reason why she'd want to wear a dress like that.

Dad.

Georgia despaired of her mum ever getting over him. She did this big thing about them being good friends, but it was obvious she was still mad about him. She almost wished they didn't get on so well. Why couldn't Eve be more like Stacey's mum next door? She couldn't stand her ex-husband; Stacey told her that she'd once tried to run him over in her Fiat Punto on Green Lane. Exes always hated each other, you only had to watch *EastEnders* to know that. Life got too confusing otherwise.

Her mum had no trouble hating Anna, which was a shame because Georgia quite liked her. It wasn't Anna's fault her parents had split up. It was a bit embarrassing at first, her dad having a girlfriend only seven years older than her brother, but Anna wasn't really like a stepmum. She was cool, and funny, more like a big sister really. And she made Dad happy. Although Georgia could never tell her mum that.

She'd tried to talk to Matt about the Mum situation, but all he did was shrug and say, 'It's no big deal.' He said that about everything except his stupid A levels and his crappy band. And he was supposed to be the genius of the family.

But Georgia knew better. Her mum could be annoying but she loved her, and she worried about her ending up lonely and bitter, spending her whole life waiting for her one true love to return, like that mentalist in the wedding dress in that Dickens novel they'd had to read for English.

If only she could find a man – or several men, like Stacey's mum next door.

She closed the door and went back to her own room to get changed. Who listened to her, anyway? She was only fifteen years old, she wasn't supposed to know anything.

Oliver's restaurant was in Fossgate, the road that led down from bustling, touristy Coppergate to the humped bridge over the river Foss, and beyond to the imposing Walmgate Bar. Once, the area had been part of the dark underbelly of York, home to the penniless Irish immigrants that flooded in during the famine. It still had an edgy feel about it, with its higgledy-piggledy black and white Tudor buildings rubbing up alongside Victorian terraces and drab 1960s council blocks, like dispossessed people thrown together by circumstance.

Its quirkiness was one of the things Oliver loved about it, and the reason why he'd first bought the failing restaurant fifteen years ago. That, and the fact that it was cheap because the area was so down at heel. It had smartened up a bit since then, with several classy restaurants joining the shabby secondhand bookshops, vintage clothing emporia and cheap furniture stores. But with its warren of narrow passageways leading off to hidden courtyards, and the dark ribbon of the river running through a deep gorge below it, Fossgate still felt as shady as its most famous resident, the highwayman Dick Turpin, who was buried in a corner of St George's churchyard.

Walking in to Oliver's felt like coming home to Eve. The place had hardly changed since they first opened the doors all those years ago. The atmosphere was cosy French bistro, dark and intimate, with low beamed ceilings, red checked tablecloths, and candles in wax-encrusted wine bottles.

It was bittersweet for her, coming back here. Everything had a memory imprinted on it, from the polished floorboards they'd sanded for hours on their hands and knees because they couldn't afford to hire professional equipment, to the old lamps hanging from the blackened beams, which they'd picked up in a fleamarket on one of their shoestring holidays to France when Matt was a baby. Oliver hadn't even had a restaurant then, but Eve was so sure his dream would happen she'd let him buy them anyway,

6

even though it cleaned out their spending money for the rest of the week.

The whole place was like a photo album of their lives together. Among the empty vintage bottles displayed on the shelves behind the bar, he'd even kept the Moët they'd cracked to celebrate their opening night. Eve could never taste the sharp, dry fizz of champagne without remembering how they had all gathered around the bar after closing time, tired but euphoric, laughing as Oliver tried to make an emotional speech.

Tonight, the place was already crowded with guests. Eve waved at Jan, who smiled apprehensively back from the other side of the room where she was talking to Frankie the chef.

She helped herself to a glass of wine from the bar and gave one to Georgia.

'Make it last,' she warned. 'It's the only one you're getting.'

'You don't say that to *him*.' Georgia shot a filthy look at Matt, who was checking his texts, his shaggy dark hair falling into his eyes.

'He's old enough to know better.'

'Is that why he threw up in the flowerbed last night?'

'Just the one,' Eve restated firmly. She scanned the crowd. 'I can't see your dad anywhere.'

'You know Oliver. He loves to make an entrance,' said a voice behind her. 'He's probably lurking round the corner, waiting for everyone else to arrive.'

Eve turned round, coming face to shoulder with Adam, Oliver's cousin. He had a new woman with him, a cool brunette this time.

'Are you saying my estranged husband is an attention seeker?' she said, mock stern.

'Oliver doesn't have to seek attention. He only has to appear and it comes his way. It's the rest of us poor mortals who have to jump up and down to get noticed.'

Eve smiled. There was no way Adam would have wanted to be noticed. He was just about the shyest person she knew.

He and Oliver, both tall and dark with warm grey eyes, could have been brothers. But while Oliver held himself confidently upright, Adam seemed apologetic about his height, his shoulders permanently stooped.

'I'd notice you,' said the woman with him.

'You say that now, but you haven't met my cousin. I'm telling you, it was no accident he was born on Christmas Day.'

'Take no notice of him, he adores Oliver really.' Eve held out her hand. 'I'm Eve Robinson.'

'Imogen Walsh.' The woman's eyes widened. 'So you're Oliver's ex? Wow, I'm surprised you're here.'

'Are you kidding? This is the highlight of my social calendar.' She was only half joking. The only dates marked in her diary were the days when she had to put out the recycling bin.

'I think you're amazing. When I split up with a man, all I ever want to do is take a pair of scissors to his suits.'

'I don't own a suit, but I'll take that as a warning,' Adam said solemnly.

Imogen smiled up at him and stroked his chest. 'Oh no, I'm not letting you go for a while,' she purred.

How did he do it? Eve wondered. He was so quiet and self-effacing, he went out of his way not to draw attention to himself. And yet he always seemed to have a new woman in tow.

She knew that underneath that shy exterior lurked a sharp sense of humour and a warm, caring heart, but it had taken a long time for her to find that out. She'd been seeing Oliver for months before Adam even looked her in the eye.

She felt slightly sorry for Imogen. She thought she had him now, but in a few weeks one or other of them would have lost interest. Adam's only real passion was for his work. He'd inherited the family's market-garden business when Oliver's father died seven years before. Since then, he'd worked hard and turned it into a thriving concern, taking on more land, opening a farm shop and breaking into the organic market.

Maybe that was why he couldn't hang on to a woman for long, she thought. No one wanted to come second to a sack of potatoes.

'You haven't met Oliver,' he said. 'You never know, you could be swept off your feet by his sheer charisma.'

'I doubt it.'

'We'll soon find out, won't we? Here he is now.'

Eve had her back to the door, but she didn't need to be told that Oliver had walked into the room. She could feel the tell-tale prickle on the nape of her neck, just as she'd felt it that night he'd strolled into the Student Union bar more than twenty years ago.

'Is that his girlfriend?' Imogen whispered. 'She's very—'

'Young?' Eve finished for her.

She looked at Anna, running through the usual envious inventory of her youthful features. Twenty-four years old, skinny and sexy, she wore a short black shift dress that showed off her schoolgirl-slender legs. Shiny, spiky dark hair framed her elfin face, making her big chocolate-brown eyes look even bigger and more doe-like.

Eve felt her bulges oozing over her control pants just looking at her. Anna was everything she wasn't. Not just thin and young and pretty, but cool and confident with it. Eve had waited nearly forty years for that kind of serene self-possession, and it still hadn't arrived.

'Eve?' She hadn't realised she was gawping until Adam spoke to her.

She pinned a smile on her face and grabbed the nearest empty wine bottle. 'Oops, looks like we're running low. I'll just go and get another couple of bottles from the kitchen.'

It was a relief to be able to escape and lose her fixed smile for a minute or two. Everyone was right, she shouldn't have come. She didn't belong here, she was just making a fool of herself. She wished she could have had more pride and kept her distance but she couldn't resist it; it was like probing an aching tooth.

How many people had guessed she still had a massive, hopeless crush on her almost-ex-husband? Everyone, probably. They were all watching her – no doubt feeling sorry for her – and not believing for a moment all her talk of staying friends for the sake of the children. At least Oliver had no idea how she still felt about him. She would have died of shame if he'd found out.

She was coming out of the storeroom with an armful of bottles when he walked into the kitchen. Seeing him standing in the doorway, Eve felt the familiar, treacherous tug of attraction.

'Adam said you were in here.' He came towards her, arms outstretched, and for a panicky moment Eve thought he was going to hug her, until he said, 'Here, let me take those for you.'

She handed the bottles over, keeping a Rioja in her hand. 'Happy birthday, by the way.'

'Thanks.' He grimaced. 'Just think, next year it'll be the big Four-O.'

'I don't want to think about it, thanks very much. Georgia will probably have me wearing a burkha by then.'

'You'll still look gorgeous.'

She fiddled with the label on the bottle to hide her confusion, and said, 'We were beginning to think you weren't coming tonight?'

'We had a bit of a domestic crisis.'

'Oh?'

'Charlie was poorly this afternoon. Throwing up all over the place.'

'Over-excitement, I expect.'

'That's what I tried to tell Anna, but she wouldn't listen. She was convinced he had meningitis at least.'

Eve bit back the caustic comment. 'It's only natural for a mother to worry. Don't you remember what I was like when Matt and Georgia were babies? Every time they hiccuped I was on the phone to the health visitor.'

'I know. I'd just forgotten how exhausting it can be.'

He looked tired, Eve thought. Maybe the strain of having a young girlfriend and a toddler was beginning to tell on him at last. There were visible lines fanning out from the corners of his eyes that she hadn't noticed before.

'How is he now?' she asked.

'Absolutely fine, just like I said he would be. Anna's mum's looking after him, but it took ages to persuade her to leave him.' He nodded towards the bottle. 'Are you going to open that?'

'Shouldn't we go back to the party?'

'In a minute. Let's have a quiet drink and catch up first.'

'I don't think Anna would like that, do you?'

'Why not?' He looked genuinely puzzled. That was Oliver, oblivious to everything. Including the effect he had on other people.

'I just don't think she'd appreciate us being alone together.' She put the bottle down and opened the drawer, rummaging for a corkscrew.

'Anna's fine about it. Anyway, you're family.'

'I'm not sure I qualify as that any more,' she laughed.

'You'll always be part of my family, Evie. Just because we're not together any more doesn't mean I've stopped caring about you.'

She wished he wouldn't look at her like that, stirring up all those feelings she'd tried so hard to stop having for the past five years.

She turned away, changing the subject. 'Have you seen all that food Frankie's made? It's enough to feed an army.'

Oliver sighed. 'I told him not to go mad. Everyone's been stuffing themselves all day, they're not going to want to do it all again. I don't know why he does it.'

'Because he loves you?' Eve found a corkscrew and started to open the bottle.

Oliver looked amused. 'You'd better not let him hear you say that. He wouldn't want anyone thinking he's a bloody poof!' He mimicked the chef's gruff Yorkshire accent.

Eve laughed, then yelped with pain as the corkscrew slipped. 'Bugger!'

'Let me see.' He reached for her hand but she pulled away.

'It's just a scrape.' She looked at where blood was already oozing out of a small, jagged cut.

'Let me see,' he insisted, taking her hand and inspecting it. 'It's bleeding quite a bit. We'd better run it under the tap.'

'I can do it.'

'For heaven's sake, let me help you.'

She watched the water running over their hands. 'Well? What's the verdict? Will I be able to play the piano after this?'

'I expect so.'

'That's good news. I couldn't play before.'

Oliver grinned. 'Maybe this'll teach you not to mess around with sharp objects.'

'Says the man who almost took his fingers off in an onion-chopping contest.'

'That just goes to show I know what I'm talking about, doesn't it?'

They were still laughing when Anna walked in.

'Sorry to interrupt,' she said, 'but everyone's wondering where you are.'

Oliver let go of her hand. 'Sorry, Eve had an accident. I had to apply some first aid.'

Anna glared at Eve. 'I'll tell them you're on your way, shall I?'

She slammed back through the doors, allowing them to swing shut behind her.

Eve turned to Oliver. 'And you still think she's fine about us?' she said.

Chapter 2

Eve was looking so good, Anna thought enviously, with her thick blonde hair and curvy body under that red dress. *She* felt a wreck. She hadn't had time to shower or wash her hair, and her old black dress showed up all the shadows under her eyes. And she was worried she might still smell of sick from where Charlie had thrown up over her just before they left the house.

She looked around the room. How did she end up here? A few years ago she would have been slumped on her mum's sofa with her feet up, working her way through a giant tin of Quality Street and watching the *EastEnders* Christmas special with her nan, nothing more taxing on her mind than what to wear to meet her friends that night and whether anyone would notice if she ate all the noisette triangles.

Now look at her. Twenty-four years old, with a three-year-old son and a crippling mortgage. Not to mention a couple of teenage stepchildren and a new group of forty-something friends who, no matter how hard she tried, she felt didn't really belong to her.

Talk about growing up fast.

She went to the bar to top up her drink and found Georgia crouched by the dishwasher, sneakily helping herself to a Bacardi Breezer.

She jumped and nearly dropped the bottle when she saw Anna.

'Don't worry, I won't tell anyone.' Anna bent down beside her. 'Actually, I wouldn't mind one of those myself.'

Georgia handed her a neon-pink bottle. She was very pretty, with her flawless skin, long shiny dark hair and her father's grey eyes fringed with thick lashes. She was dressed in a short denim skirt, black footless tights and green Che Guevara t-shirt with a shrunken black cardigan over the top. The kind of outfit that only a teenager or Kate Moss could get away with without looking random and mad.

'I didn't think grown-ups liked that kind of thing,' she said.

'I'm not feeling very grown-up tonight.' What Anna felt like doing was getting steaming drunk, telling Oliver's wretched ex-wife what she really thought of her, then heading off to the nearest club to get even drunker and possibly wake up in a skip clutching a kebab.

She popped the cap on her drink and sat down next to Georgia, side by side under the bar, contemplating the rows of bottles and glasses.

Georgia's mobile bleeped, announcing a text message. She pounced on it.

'Anything interesting?' Anna asked.

'Just my friend Stacey. She's having a party.'

'Shame you couldn't go.'

'Mum wouldn't let me. She doesn't approve of Stacey's family.' She rolled her eyes. 'She says her mum's a middle-aged chav.'

'And is she?'

'I like her, she's a real laugh. And she's not strict or anything. Stacey's allowed to do whatever she likes.'

'I can see why your mum wouldn't approve, then.' Anna sometimes thought Eve was a bit too tough with her children, but it was hardly her place to interfere. She could just imagine what the reaction would be if she started handing out advice.

Georgia abandoned her drink and went outside to call Stacey for a private update. Anna slumped against the dishwasher, sipped her pink drink and called her mum.

'How's Charlie?' she asked brightly.

'He's fine. Just like he was when you rang ten minutes ago. And ten minutes before that.'

'I can't help worrying, can I?'

'There's no need. He seems okay now. I've given him his bath and put him in his pyjamas and now he's watching TV with your nana.'

'What are they watching?'

'I don't know, a James Bond film, I think. Neither of them have got the foggiest idea what's going on, they could be watching anything.' Her mother chuckled. 'I take it you're not having a very good time?'

'Not really.' Anna's merry façade crumbled. 'Everyone's ignoring me, and I've just caught Oliver in a clinch with Eve.'

'What?'

'Well, maybe not actually a clinch, but too close for my liking, anyway.'

'And what did you say?'

'Not much. I just left them to it.'

'Anna!'

'What could I do? Start a fight?' She heard the sound of the TV playing in the background and ached with loneliness. 'I hate it here. Can I come home and watch James Bond with you instead?'

'No way. You're staying where you are, Anna Bowman. It's not like you to walk away from anything.'

'Maybe it's time I did.' Anna peeped over the bar. Oliver was playing the genial host as usual, filling everyone's glasses, laughing and joking with his friends. Eve wasn't far behind, as if she was attached to him by an invisible thread. 'Nobody would notice if I left.'

'Oliver would notice.'

'I doubt it.'

'Oh, love.' She heard her mother's sigh on the other end of the line. 'Just stay and give it another try. It's only for an hour or two. If you leave now it'll be like you're admitting defeat.'

Eve was standing behind Oliver now, her hand resting lightly on his shoulder. He didn't look as if he was fighting her off.

'I'll try,' she promised. 'But don't blame me if I end up tipping a glass of wine over someone.'

★

'There you are.' Oliver greeted her with a kiss on the cheek. 'I thought you'd run out on me.'

'I called my mum to check on Charlie.'

'And?'

'She said he was fine.'

'You see? I told you he'd be okay.' He put his arm round her. 'Come and have another drink. Everyone's been asking where you are.'

She did her best to fit in with Oliver's friends. They all tried to be nice to her, but it seemed as if every conversation ended with a joke or a story about the Good Old Days, when Oliver and Eve were still married.

'I'm sure Anna doesn't want to hear that old stuff.' Oliver cut off his friend Peter as he launched into another jolly anecdote about the time they all went camping in Italy together.

'I don't mind,' said Anna, bracing herself to hear again what a terrific laugh Eve was.

It wasn't just the stories that troubled her, but the fact that they seemed to talk in a kind of shorthand she didn't understand. They had a special language, a set of private jokes that came from a lifetime of shared history. No matter how much she tried, she couldn't be part of it.

'I'm really sorry,' Oliver said, as they queued up for food later.

'It doesn't matter,' Anna lied.

'It does matter. I don't want you to feel left out.' He looked troubled.

'You can't help it, you and Eve have a history together. I can't change that, and neither can you.'

That was what her head told her, anyway. Her heart still fretted that if Oliver kept being reminded what a great person his ex was, he might decide he wanted her back.

Of course, Fate conspired to make sure the only empty seats were on Eve's table. They'd hardly sat down before she ambushed Oliver, talking about a bill he'd promised to sort out. Anna gritted her teeth to stop herself asking why Eve couldn't pay her own damn bills. Instead, she tuned out and watched Matt messing around with his mobile across the table.

'Expecting a call?' she asked.

He looked up, his eyes just visible through his mane of dark curls. He was tall and angular, a gawky collection of arms and legs and hair.

'Just checking my bids on eBay.'

'What are you after?'

'A drum kit.'

'Excuse me?' Eve looked up. 'You're not having a drum kit.'

'Apparently not,' he shrugged. 'I've just been outbid.'

'Thank God for that. Anyway, you don't even play the drums.'

'He might if he had a drum kit,' Anna pointed out.

Eve shot her a look. 'In that case, perhaps you could keep it at your father's place?' she said. 'Maybe he could put up with the noise.'

'*Our* place might be a bit small,' Anna replied.

'More wine?' Oliver reached for the bottle.

Anna tried again, asking Matt about his university plans. Soon they were chatting about the colleges he'd applied to, and discussing the merits of various cities and campuses. All the time she was aware of Eve listening in.

'You should ask Anna for some tips,' she said. 'She's sure to be an expert. After all, it wasn't that long ago she was there herself.'

Be nice, Anna told herself, gripping her fork until her knuckles turned white. 'What course are you thinking of taking?'

'Forensic science.'

'Sounds impressive,' Oliver said.

'Do you know what it is?' Matt asked him.

'Of course. It's – um – the study of – er—'

'It's what they do on *CSI*,' Eve said helpfully.

Georgia rolled her eyes. 'How pathetic is that? You only know about it because of some lame telly programme.'

'She's right,' Oliver said, shamefaced. 'How did a pair of ignoramuses like us end up with such brainy children?'

'Speak for yourself. I'll have you know I worked hard at university – unlike some people.'

And then they were off again, tripping hand in hand down Memory Lane and laughing about all the things they got up to when they were students. Matt and Georgia joined in, groaning as they heard the usual stories about their mum's puffball skirts and their dad's Phil Oakey haircut.

They were so like a proper, happy family it made Anna's heart ache. She put down her napkin. 'I'm going to get some more food.'

Oliver caught up with her at the buffet table. 'I'm sorry,' he said. 'I did it again, didn't I?'

'I'm amazed you ever split up with her, if your life was that wonderful.'

He looked hurt. 'You know it wasn't.'

'You could have fooled me.'

They were interrupted by one of the guests nudging up alongside them to get to the chicken wings. Oliver lowered his voice. 'Okay, we were happy. Once. But that was a long time ago. Don't you see, the only reason we get on so well now is because we're not together?'

'Maybe you should tell her that.' Anna glanced back at Eve, who was watching them while picking at her salmon.

'What do you mean?'

'I mean she wants you back.'

He laughed. 'For heaven's sake! We're just friends.'

'I don't think your ex sees it like that. Why do you think she hangs around all the time? She's staying in the picture, waiting for you to get tired of me so she can be there to pick up the pieces.'

'That's not going to happen.'

'Like I said, maybe you should tell her that.' Across the room, Eve caught her eye and gave her a smile, as if she knew they were talking about her. Anna didn't smile back. 'Anyway, why shouldn't she think that? It's not as if you're actually committed to me or anything, is it?'

'I live with you. We have a son together. What more commitment could there be?'

You could marry me, she thought, but didn't dare say it. She was too scared.

'Look, Eve knows where we both stand,' Oliver said. 'We're just trying to be mature about our break-up for the sake of the kids. Or would you rather we were at each other's throats?'

Anna was tempted to say yes, but deep down she knew she didn't mean it. She'd seen enough messy, bitter divorces in her work at the community advice centre to know that it was a nightmare for the children. 'Of course not,' she mumbled.

'I love you, but I love her too. We had twenty years together, she's the mother of my children. She'll always be important to me. I know I can't expect you to understand what it's like, being so young—'

Anna's head snapped up. 'Meaning?'

'Nothing. I just said you were young, that's all.'

'So I'm not expected to understand, is that it? I'm not mature and grown-up like you and Eve.'

'That's not what I said—'

'Well, I'm sorry, but I don't think there's anything particularly mature about hanging around someone like a lovesick teenager. If anyone needs to grow up, it's your bloody ex-wife!'

She thrust her plate into Oliver's hands. He looked down at it, then back at her. 'Where are you going? Anna, don't walk away—'

But she was already heading for the door.

Her mum didn't seem surprised to find Anna shivering on her doorstep half an hour later. 'I had a feeling you'd turn up,' she said, pulling her towelling dressing gown around her. 'Have you walked all this way?'

'I couldn't find a taxi. And I left my bag at the restaurant.' As flounce-outs go, it hadn't exactly been well planned. She hadn't even remembered her coat, and it had started to snow, great fluffy flakes soaking through her dress as she slipped and slithered along Bootham nearly sick with cold.

'Come in before you die of hypothermia,' her mum said, ushering her inside.

Keith, her mother's partner, was in the sitting room, watching TV with a glass of beer in his hand. He took one look at Anna standing in the doorway, dripping and bedraggled, and put down his glass. 'I'll – um – make myself scarce, shall I?'

'No, you stay and watch the end of the film. We'll go in the kitchen.'

Her mum's kitchen was modern but warm and homely. It reflected Jackie Bowman's personality perfectly, with its brightly coloured bits and pieces, the array of plants flourishing on the windowsill, and the social-work textbooks crammed on the shelf next to Jamie Oliver and Delia.

'You're lucky you came when you did. I'd just got out of the bath,' Jackie said, tightening the cord of her lemon dressing gown. With her short fluffy blonde hair and bright, dark eyes, she reminded Anna of a chirpy little Easter chick.

She fussed around, finding her daughter a pair of jeans and a jumper to change into, and drying her hair with a warm towel. Then she busied herself putting on the kettle. Anna had never known her mother sit still for longer than five minutes. When she wasn't working part time as a teaching assistant at the local primary school, she was looking after her grandchildren, doing her elderly mother's shopping or catching up with coursework for her social studies degree. In her spare time, she was active in the local community association, firing off angry letters to the council and rallying the residents.

But then, Jackie had always worked hard. When Anna's father died, leaving his wife with three children, she'd worked double shifts at the chocolate factory and cleaned offices to make ends meet while going back to college to improve her skills. Anna admired her mum more than any other woman in the world.

Jackie put down the bright yellow teapot in the middle of the table. 'So,' she said. 'Tell me all about it.'

She sat and listened as Anna poured out her troubles. 'Let me get this straight,' she smiled. 'You're worried Oliver's ex is after him, so you walk out and leave him in her clutches?'

'It wasn't a very good move, was it?' Anna agreed glumly. Eve was probably consoling him right at that very moment.

'For what it's worth, I don't think you've got anything to

worry about,' Jackie said, adding another spoonful of sugar to her tea. 'Oliver obviously adores you and little Charlie.'

'So why won't he marry me?'

'Have you asked him?'

She huddled inside her mum's jumper, breathing in the comfortingly familiar scent of her through the soft wool. 'I'm too scared.'

Never in a million years did she imagine she would be that desperate to get married. At school, she'd always despised the girls who'd obsessed about getting serious with their boyfriends, who acted as if they didn't have any purpose in their lives except to have a ring on their finger. Anna had bigger plans than that: she was going to be a hot-shot lawyer, defending the underdog. While other girls dreamed about wedding dresses and champagne receptions, she imagined striding around the courtroom arena, winning over juries and rendering her opposing counsel speechless with her incisive legal arguments.

And then Oliver came along.

She'd first met him when she'd worked as a waitress in his restaurant during the university holidays. She'd liked him immediately, but there was never anything more to it than friendship. He was happily married, or so she thought.

But by the time she went back to work there the following summer, Oliver and Eve had split up. Although he insisted it was his idea, being away from his family was obviously destroying him. He wasn't the warm, funny man Anna knew; it was as if a light had gone off inside him.

He needed a shoulder to cry on, and she was there. Every night after work she'd stay behind to help him clear up, and they'd talk. He told her about the break-up, explained how he and Eve had grown apart, how they wanted different things out of life. He was a free spirit, she craved security. He wanted adventure, she wanted cosy domesticity. Realising how unhappy they were making each other, he'd walked away.

Anna confided in him, too, about her on-off relationship. She'd been seeing Danny Lynch, a solicitor in a law firm near her college, for over a year. But he was young and ambitious, and he'd made it clear he had his sights set firmly on a future that didn't include her. Anna also suspected he didn't go short of female company while she was at home during the holidays.

At first it was just friendship between her and Oliver, but as time went on Anna began to realise she was falling in love. She fought it like mad. She knew Oliver and Eve were having counselling, and the last thing she wanted to do was get in their way.

But in the end she couldn't help herself. She and Oliver felt like soulmates. They had the same quirky sense of humour, the same passion for life. They would talk for hours, sharing their wild dreams about going round the world in a camper van. Anna loved Oliver's gentleness, his optimistic way of looking at everything. He never judged anyone and people loved him because he made them feel good about themselves.

Not that it was easy for either of them. Her mother was concerned about the age gap at first, but once she saw how much Oliver adored her daughter, she came to terms with that.

Eve was a different story. She was furious when she found out Oliver was seeing someone else. Anna couldn't imagine why she was reacting so badly – after all, it wasn't as if she'd stolen Oliver from her. She tried to be sympathetic and understanding, but Eve didn't want to know. The separation became ugly and Anna, seeing how it tore Oliver apart, thought about ending the relationship.

Then, just to make life even more complicated, she found that she was pregnant. She was immediately thrown into confusion. She was in her last year at college, her whole life was ahead of her, and she had her career to think about. She was sure Oliver wouldn't want a baby, especially with all the hassle he was getting from Eve.

It took her ages to pluck up the courage to tell him. Like a coward, she did it on the phone from uni.

'So what do you want to do?' he'd asked.

She took a deep breath. She'd been waiting for this. 'I suppose the sensible thing would be not to go ahead.'

Silence. 'And is that what you want?'

'Like I said, it's the only sensible option.'

He didn't argue, although she wanted him to. So with a heavy heart, Anna booked an appointment at the clinic.

But while she was sitting in the waiting room, she realised she couldn't do it. She made up her mind there and then that she would have the baby and bring it up herself. Oliver didn't have to be involved if he didn't want to be, but it was her child and she was going to have it, whatever he did.

As she came out of the clinic into the sunshine, she was almost run down by Oliver's dark green MG screeching to a halt in front of her.

He got out and slammed the door. 'Have you — has it happened?'

She shook her head. 'I couldn't.'

'Thank God for that.'

'I know what you're going to say, and I'm not doing it to trap you or anything,' she went on in a rush. 'I've been thinking about it, and— What did you say?'

'Anna, I didn't just drive nearly a hundred miles to deliver a get-well card. I haven't been able to sleep since you told me.'

'So why didn't you say anything?'

'Because I didn't want to put any pressure on you. I knew I was being totally selfish, especially when you sounded so determined to do this.' He looked up at the clinic, his expression grim.

'I thought it was what you wanted.'

'Like you said, it would be the sensible option. Let's face it, having a baby is the last thing either of us should be considering right now.'

'True.'

'It's a hell of a lot to take on. It'll change everything for both of us.'

She frowned. 'Are you trying to talk me out of it? Because if you are, you're doing a damn good job.'

'No, but I need you to understand what you're doing.'

She looked at him ruefully. 'I suppose this means we'll have to cancel the round-the-world trip?'

'Oh, I don't know,' he grinned. 'You can get a cot in a camper van, can't you?'

And that was how it had been. Even when Charlie was born, they hadn't lost their sense of adventure. They hadn't quite made it round the world yet, but they hadn't settled down either. Anna knew Oliver was a free spirit, and she was careful not to try and tie him down, knowing that was where Eve had made her big mistake.

She still didn't want to tie him down, but after five years, she really wanted some status in his life. It infuriated her to see Eve still wearing her wedding ring, as if she were the permanent fixture in Oliver's life and Anna was the passing fling.

'So why don't you think he'd want to marry you?' her mother asked.

'He doesn't think he's any good at it.' Anna stared at the magnets covering the fridge door. Jokey little slogans, cute animals, all pinning a fluttering array of lists, reminders, and photos of Jackie's family – Anna, her two brothers and all the grandchildren. 'He blames himself for the break-up with Eve. Just because it went wrong first time around he thinks it might happen again.'

'He might have a point.'

'It wasn't all his fault. And now I have to pay for Eve's mistakes.'

Jackie helped herself to a shortbread biscuit from the open packet. 'Having a ring on your finger is no guarantee of lifelong happiness,' she said. 'It didn't work with him and Eve, did it? A piece of paper is never going to keep you together.'

'Is that why you've never married Keith?' It was a standing joke that he proposed at least twice a year, but Jackie always said no.

Her mother's smile faded. 'I was married once, and that's enough for me,' she said. 'I told myself when your dad died I wouldn't marry again. Anyway, Keith and I are fine as we are. And Oliver obviously feels the same.'

'I wonder if that's the only reason?' Anna said.

Jackie paused, halfway through picking up shortbread crumbs. 'What do you mean?'

'I sometimes wonder if he doesn't want to marry me because he wants to keep his options open.'

There it was. Her worst fear, out in the open.

'It makes sense, doesn't it?' she went on. 'I mean, he and Eve were great together. Everyone says so. She's a brilliant mother, a fantastic cook, and basically everything I'm not.'

'Don't put yourself down.'

'Mum, I bought our Christmas dinner from Marks and Spencer. I send Charlie to nursery school with a tuna sandwich from the petrol station. He's listened to me swearing in the car so many times he now sits in the back calling everyone dickheads.'

'I wondered where he got that word,' Jackie mused. 'I thought it was from your nana.'

'I bet Eve never swears in front of her children. I bet she's perfect.'

'Maybe she is, but Oliver doesn't want a domestic goddess, does he? He wants you.'

Anna pulled a face. 'Is that supposed to make me feel better?' She crunched a shortbread biscuit. 'Let's face it, Eve's the one for him. They might have got back together if I hadn't come along and got pregnant.'

'Or he might still be living on his own,' Jackie said.

'I know Eve would take him back in a second,' Anna said, not listening. 'Maybe he's just waiting for the right time?'

'If you feel like that, maybe you should say something.'

'What can I say? I'm frightened to talk to him about it in case I give him the chance he's looking for.'

They were interrupted by Keith. 'There's someone to see you,' he said. Oliver stood behind him in the doorway, looking sheepish. His face was ruddy with cold, and melting snowflakes glistened in his dark hair.

Jackie picked up her cup and the packet of biscuits. 'We'll catch the end of that film,' she said, hustling a bemused Keith back up the hallway.

'What are you doing here?' Anna asked, when they were alone.

'I came to find you.'

'You walked out on your own party?'

'There didn't seem much point in being there without you. I thought you might be needing these.' He handed over her coat and bag. 'Can I walk you home?'

The snow had settled quickly, laying a thick, muffling blanket over the deserted streets of the Cliffmead estate. By tomorrow morning it would be churned into grey-black slush, but for now theirs were the only footprints in the perfect, crisp whiteness as they crunched up the street.

'They should take a photo of this and turn it into a Christmas card,' Oliver said.

Anna laughed. 'I'll suggest it to my mum. She could sell it to make money for the residents' association. Christmas on Cliffmead.'

'It's different.'

'I don't think it would be quite as popular as a snowy scene of the Minster, somehow.'

'Oh, I don't know. You don't get flashing Santas on the Minster. Or reindeer.' He pointed up to the roof of one of the houses where a neon sleigh scene was casting an eerie light over the white below. 'We should do something like that next year. I bet Charlie would love a flashing reindeer on the roof.'

'I'm sure he would, but I'm not sure what the neighbours would say.'

They emerged on to Clifton Green, where the sprawl of post-war council houses gave way to rows of elegant Edwardian villas surrounding a triangle of snow-covered green.

They'd just crossed the main road when they spotted a huddled figure in the bus shelter.

'Jesus,' Oliver muttered. 'Poor sod. Imagine being out on a night like this.'

'Maybe he's just waiting for a bus.'

'On Christmas night? He'll be lucky.'

'Don't go near him.' Anna pulled him back as he started to approach the shelter. 'He might mug you or something.'

'It would be good if he did. At least he'd get to spend the night in a nice warm police cell.'

Anna stayed at a cautious distance while Oliver went over to the man and shook him awake. The figure stirred, mumbled something and went back to sleep.

'At least he's alive,' Oliver said. 'Stinks of drink, though.'

Please don't say you want to take him home, Anna prayed silently, stamping her feet as the wet cold seeped into her shoes. It wouldn't be the first time Oliver had taken pity on a passing waif or stray. She felt mean for thinking it, but she really didn't want another drunk sleeping it off in the spare room. The last one had left with her handbag and the CD player.

Oliver shrugged off his coat and laid it carefully over the man. As an afterthought, he took some notes out of his wallet and stuffed them in the coat pocket. 'There,' he said. 'That'll be a nice surprise for him when he wakes up.'

'You do realise he'll probably just spend it all on more booze?' Anna tried to sound disapproving.

'If I had to spend every night sleeping out in weather like this I'd probably want to be half cut too.' He reached for her hand, his thick leather glove wrapped around her frozen fingers as they headed across the green. 'It makes you realise how lucky we are, doesn't it?' he said.

Anna looked sidelong at him. Snowflakes were settling on his hair and shoulders and he could hardly speak he was shivering so much, but he was still smiling.

He'd just given his coat to a stranger on a freezing night. How could she bear to lose him for the sake of a ring on her finger?

'Doesn't it?' she agreed.

Chapter 3

JANUARY

'Don't you think it's time we got a divorce?'

Eve went on unpacking her shopping from the supermarket carrier bags, giving herself time to think.

'What's brought this on?' she finally managed.

'I've been thinking about it for a while.' Oliver sat at the table, his long legs stretched out in front of him. 'We can't let things drag on for ever, we should make a clean break. It's not fair on you or on Anna.'

Eve went on stacking tins of beans in the cupboard, as if her life hadn't just been turned upside down. 'Was this her idea?'

'No. She doesn't know I'm here.'

I bet she doesn't, Eve thought bitterly. She'd probably been nagging him for months, urging him to cut the ties, make everything legal.

'I don't suppose it's come as a surprise to you,' Oliver said. 'We knew it was bound to happen one day, didn't we?'

'Of course.' Except she hadn't. When Oliver first announced he was leaving and she'd found out about Anna, she'd panicked and thought she'd lost him for ever. Then, as time went on, she'd allowed herself the shred of hope that he was clinging on to their marriage because it meant as much to him as it did to her.

Now he'd dashed all her hopes. This time it was even more final than the day he walked out.

She opened the cupboard under the sink and began unpacking the household items, mentally listing them as she went. Dishwasher tablets, Mr Muscle oven cleaner, Cillit Bang. It was

28

all she could do to stop herself howling.

She'd never imagined this was what Oliver wanted to discuss. When he'd met her from the school gates after work and said he needed to talk, she'd just assumed it was some boring domestic stuff, maybe another piece of paperwork he needed her to sign. They still had a couple of joint accounts they'd never got round to splitting up.

'Can't it wait?' she'd said. 'I need to go to Sainsbury's.'

'I'll come with you.'

He'd trailed around the supermarket after her, broodingly silent. Eve knew he had something on his mind; after five years apart she could still read him like a book.

She'd started to wonder if maybe he and Anna were going through some kind of crisis, and by the time they got home, she'd composed the whole scenario in her mind. Anna and Oliver had split up, and now he was trying to work out how to ask if he could come back. And despite her New Year's resolution to forget him and get on with her life, Eve was ready to say yes.

Which was why his words were even more of a slap in the face.

She wedged a roll of bin bags behind the bleach at the back of the cupboard. 'So why are you telling me all this?' she asked. 'Surely after all these years you could just go to the solicitor's and do it?'

'You know I wouldn't do that.' Oliver frowned. 'I wanted to talk to you about it first. I didn't want you to suddenly get divorce papers out of the blue and wonder what was going on.'

As if anything could make her hurt any less than she was now, Eve thought.

'I suppose this means you're planning to get married?' She managed to get the words out without choking.

'I don't know. Probably.' He laughed feebly. 'She might not have me.'

'Oh, she'll have you all right.'

Something in her tone must have given her away, because Oliver came and squatted down beside her, his gaze level with hers. 'You are okay about this, aren't you, Evie?'

'Would it make any difference if I wasn't?'

He looked troubled. 'Well—'

'Look, forget it.' She turned away and went on stacking. 'Like you said, it had to happen one day.'

He stood up, towering over her. 'What about the kids? How do you think they'll take it?'

'You'd better ask them.' Part of her hoped they'd be distraught, but she knew they wouldn't. They'd accepted the situation a long time ago. It was only she who was stuck in the past. 'I'm sure they'll be fine,' she added.

She finished unpacking, screwed up the carrier bags and crammed them into an already overstuffed drawer. As she rammed it shut, the handle came off in her hand.

'Shit,' she muttered. 'That's all I need.'

'I'll fix it.' He took it from her and went to the box where they kept the tools. It gave her a pang that he knew exactly where to find everything.

'I suppose I'm going to have to learn to fix my own drawer handles once our divorce is official?' she joked, as she watched him screw it back in place.

'I don't see why. It won't change anything.'

'Yeah, right.'

'It won't. I'll still be here for you and the children. Nothing will ever change that.'

Eve watched him testing the drawer handle. Was he really that naïve? Didn't he understand this changed everything? It wasn't just the end of all her hopes; once Anna was Oliver's wife, she'd make damn sure there was no place in his life for her.

Instead she just smiled and said, 'We'll see.'

'I mean it. You'll always be part of my life, Eve.'

'Oh, please. You'll have me in tears in a minute.' She forced a smile. 'Now go home, before Anna thinks you've been kid-napped.'

At times like this, she wished she had a mother she could phone for sympathy and advice. But Eve knew she'd be wasting her time calling Vanessa, always assuming she could even find her; the last time she'd heard from her, just after New Year, her mother was heading off to Bali with her latest lover, a young Peruvian named Raoul.

Anyway, Eve already knew what she'd say. Vanessa had never been convinced by her marriage to Oliver in the first place. She hadn't even come to the wedding because she was so certain it wouldn't last.

'But why, darling?' she'd said. 'Marriage is so outdated, so vulgar. I'm sure I never brought you up to be so conventional.'

Exactly, Eve wanted to say. It was because of her upbringing that she longed for marriage, no matter how vulgar it might be.

Vanessa Gifford was notorious even before Eve became a fact of her life. She was a sociologist who'd written several academic books on world cultures. But that wasn't how most people knew her. Mostly, she was remembered for her explosive theories on sex and relationships. She believed in free love, which she practised enthusiastically in her commune in the Cotswolds. She was brilliant, and fearlessly outspoken; TV shows and magazines always called on her when they wanted an outrageous opinion, and Vanessa, a six-foot Nordic beauty with white-blonde hair, bare feet and flowing kaftans, didn't disappoint. She was happy to parade her latest lovers in the Sunday supplements and argue with apoplectic clergymen on discussion programmes. Back in the 1970s, she became famous for crudely propositioning the Archbishop of Canterbury on *Nationwide*.

Vanessa freely admitted her daughter was an experiment. Eve never knew her father; her mother couldn't decide whether he was a Harvard psychology professor or a Hackney barman called Jon. She couldn't see why it was so important to Eve anyway.

Eve didn't mind growing up in the commune when she was small. It was only when she was sent to boarding school that it became really excruciating. The other girls were either awestruck by her mother's exotic reputation or just plain cruel. Either way, Eve was an outcast. She longed to be like the other girls, whose mothers sent them food parcels and loving letters and sobbed when they dropped them back at school after the holidays. The only time Vanessa had ever turned up to see one of Eve's school plays, she'd swept in halfway through the first act with a muscular young African, then sat in the back row smoking a joint until the police were called.

But she could have put up with the teasing and torment. She could have tolerated her mother's communal living, and even her occasional experiments with lesbianism, because she was still her mother and she loved her.

What really hurt her was The Book.

She was fifteen when her mother published *The Motherhood Myth*, as it was called. Like most of her mother's books, Eve didn't even bother to read it, until one of the girls found an interview with Vanessa in the *Sunday Times*.

By Vanessa Gifford's standards, it was hardly shocking. There was no sex, no cranky ideas. Just the calm, measured statement that she had never loved her daughter. Maternal feelings were all in the mind, she said. There was no such thing as a mother-daughter bond. She cared no more for her own child than she did for anyone else's.

Eve had cried for two days after she read this. It was as though an atom bomb dropped into the middle of her life, blowing her whole world apart. She wouldn't eat, stayed in bed and refused to go to lessons. In the end she was sent to the sick bay and her mother was summoned.

But Vanessa was too busy promoting her book to come.

Eventually Eve pulled herself together like the sensible girl she was, and got on with her life. She and Vanessa treated each other much as they'd always done, and the book was never discussed. But there was something missing, a hole in Eve's life that she couldn't fill.

She didn't realise what it was until she went to university, and met Oliver.

She had no idea what made him notice her. Maybe, with his characteristic kindness, he realised she needed rescuing. Or maybe he was intrigued by the quiet, bookish girl who sat in the library and never spoke up in lectures. Either way, no one was more astounded than Eve when he asked her out.

His supreme self-confidence dazzled her. She'd never met

anyone who was so sure of himself, so outgoing and at ease with other people. But, at the same time, he was warm and compassionate. Being with him, Eve finally realised what had been missing from her life: someone who put her first and cared about her feelings more than their own.

It was a strange, heady sensation to love, and be loved in return.

Eve even adored Oliver's family. He often complained that his parents were boring and suburban, but to Eve they seemed utterly perfect. She loved the Sunday lunches, his father's obsession with his garden, and his mother's addiction to the *Antiques Roadshow*. It was all so wonderfully ordinary.

They married soon after leaving university, and despite her mother's dire predictions, they were blissfully happy. Eve was carried along by Oliver's dreams of owning his own restaurant. She'd never had any ambitions of her own, apart from having a normal, loving family, but Oliver's dreams were big enough for both of them and she loved sharing his goal. They lived on the breadline in a tiny flat, she taught at a local school while Oliver worked as a trainee chef in a restaurant, and they both saved like mad.

Luckily for Oliver, the owner took a shine to him and taught him all about the restaurant business. Then, when he decided to retire, he gave Oliver the chance to buy the place.

It should have been their dream come true, but Eve had just found out she was pregnant. Although Oliver wanted to buy the restaurant, she was determined they should have a proper home for their new baby first.

In the end, she won, but it was a hollow victory. He tried not to show it, but Eve could see how disappointed Oliver was. So when, three years later, the restaurant came back on the market, she took a chance and encouraged him to remortgage their home, even though by then she was pregnant with Georgia.

The early years were a real struggle. The man who'd briefly owned the place before Oliver knew nothing about the business and had allowed the restaurant to fail. Its reputation had plummeted and it had been closed down by the environmental health inspectors. It seemed as if they were taking on a nightmare.

But they refused to give up. Eve worked during the day while Oliver took care of the children at the restaurant. Then, in the evenings she'd take over. Sometimes she'd be waiting on tables and helping out in the kitchen while Georgia slept in her Moses basket behind the till, and Matt watched videos in the tiny cubby hole of an office. They were busy, exhausted and broke, but Eve had never been happier.

Then, as the years went by, things started to unravel. The restaurant was doing well and Eve wanted to relax, settle down and enjoy the fruits of their labours. But Oliver had other ideas. He wanted to move on, expand the business, maybe move to different premises. While Eve was content with what they'd achieved, he was always chasing the next dream around another corner. She couldn't understand why he wasn't satisfied with what they had. A perfect, loving family and a nice home was all she'd ever wanted, but Oliver craved adventure, excitement. He wanted to take risks, while she was scared of playing Russian roulette with her family's future.

Eve sensed that Oliver was growing restless, and she panicked. She tried to hold on to him but, like sand, the tighter she held on, the faster he seemed to slip through her fingers. In the end, she knew what was coming, even before he told her he was leaving. Just a break, he'd said, to decide what they both wanted. She already knew what she wanted, but she realised it was no use fighting the inevitable.

In some ways it was a relief. Things had got so tense between them, he'd lost sight of all the good things in their marriage. She comforted herself that once he was away it would give him a chance to realise what he was missing and come home.

But then Anna came along and changed everything.

She was chopping onions when Matt and Georgia came home. She listened to them clattering around in the hall, bickering as usual.

Matt came into the kitchen first. He dumped his guitar in the

34

corner, and without looking at her went straight to the fridge as per normal.

'Great. You've been shopping.' He sighed with satisfaction at the sight of the crammed shelves.

'We'll be eating supper in half an hour,' Eve warned, as he emerged with a plastic-wrapped cheese in one hand and a jar of Branston pickle in the other. 'I hope you'll be hungry.'

'I'm always hungry.'

'Fat pig.' Georgia came in, throwing down her schoolbag and frantically texting with her spare hand.

'Airhead.'

'Brain-dead.'

'Be quiet, you two.' Eve massaged her temples, which had begun to throb.

Matt put the food down on the table and peered at her. 'Are you all right, Mum?'

'I'm fine.' She chopped the onions into a mush, her knife moving up and down rapidly. 'Your father came round to see me earlier.'

'Oh yeah?'

'We're getting a divorce.'

Georgia went on texting. Matt stopped buttering his sandwich and looked at her.

'You're all right about that, are you?'

'Of course she's all right,' Georgia said, before Eve could reply. 'It's not like they're ever going to get back together, are they?' She pressed the 'send' button on her phone and stuffed it in her pocket. 'Anyway, this could be the closure you need,' she said to her mother.

'The what?'

'I read about it in a magazine. You need to make things final before you can move on with your life. Now you can meet someone else.' She picked up her schoolbag and hitched it over her shoulder. 'I'm going upstairs to do my chemistry.'

Matt looked at his mother and shrugged. 'She's all heart, my sister,' he said.

Chapter 4

FEBRUARY

'And then I got home and found she'd cleaned me out. Taken everything. TV, microwave – you name it, she'd had it. She even took my railway memorabilia collection, and I know for a fact she hates trains.' The man looked at Anna across the desk. 'What do you think I should do?'

'You could try talking to her. I've got some information on mediation here—'

'Not about *her*. I don't care if I never see her again. But that railway memorabilia was unique.'

Anna gathered together some information on divorce and property and handed them over to the man, who went away still grumbling about his missing rolling stock.

'Now there's someone who's got his priorities sorted out,' Elliott, the advice centre manager, said as he flicked through that morning's post.

'I didn't like to tell him she's probably got rid of the whole lot on eBay by now.'

'I don't blame her if she has.' Barbara the receptionist looked up from the Sudoku puzzle in that morning's *Daily Mail*. 'Nasty little man. Did you see his shoes? My Bernard always says you can tell a lot from a man by looking at his shoes. And he should know, he was in the army.'

'Panzer division, presumably,' Elliott muttered to Anna.

'I hardly think it's our place to judge our clients,' Neil, ever the peacemaker, put in.

'And his eyebrows met in the middle,' Barbara went on,

36

ignoring him. 'You can never trust a man whose eyebrows meet. That's a fact.'

Anna smiled. 'So let's get this straight. According to your theories, we can't trust anyone under twenty-five or foreign, anyone who has ginger hair, body odour, more than three children, an IQ of less than a hundred and fifty, defective eyebrows or scruffy shoes.'

'You forgot the squint,' Elliott pointed out.

'Visual impairment, please,' Neil winced.

'Sounds like most of our clients.'

'You said it,' Barbara sniffed.

Sometimes Anna wondered why Barbara worked in a community advice centre. It was like Bluebeard becoming a marriage guidance counsellor. She made no secret of the fact that she despised everyone who came through the doors. To her, they were all either asylum seekers or criminals – or worse still, Labour voters. Anna was convinced it was only a matter of time before she put on gloves to hand over the leaflets.

Neil, the other advisor, couldn't have been more different. He was in his thirties, quietly spoken, earnest and bespectacled. A vegan who rode a battered old bike, Neil lived in fear of being politically incorrect or accidentally wearing leather shoes. But at least his heart was in the right place, unlike Barbara, who didn't have one.

'Here's one for you.' Elliott handed Anna an envelope. 'Looks like a Valentine's card. Does Oliver know you have a secret admirer?'

'Hardly.' She ripped it open. 'It's an invitation to a debt-management workshop. Very romantic, I'm sure.'

'Oh, I don't know. Individual Voluntary Arrangements can be quite a turn-on to some people.'

'Personally, I think Valentine's Day is nothing more than another chance for big business to exploit the hapless consumer,' Neil said.

'You old romantic,' Anna teased him. 'I suppose that's what you told your girlfriend when you didn't get her a card?'

'I prefer the term "partner" if you don't mind. And Ruth feels the same as me. It's all an act of rampant commercialism.'

'If you ask me, you're taking your life in your hands, not buying her anything,' Elliott said. 'Especially with her being pregnant and her hormones all over the place. She's probably planning to kill you even as we speak.'

'I doubt that. Ruth's a Buddhist, like me.' Neil tugged nervously at his sparse goatee.

'Oh yes? And how can you be a Buddhist when you're white?' Barbara demanded.

As Neil wearily launched into yet another explanation of world religions, Elliott turned to Anna.

'So have you and Oliver got anything special planned for Valentine's night? Or am I too young and innocent to hear the sordid details?' He lifted his eyebrows suggestively.

'We *were* planning to go out to dinner.'

'Sounds ominous. What happened?'

'His ex, of course.'

With her usual impeccable timing, Eve had called the previous night to announce that her boiler had broken. And, of course, Oliver was the only person in the world who could fix it.

'Can't you do it another time?' Anna had pleaded.

'They haven't had a shower in two days.'

'Tell her to call a plumber. That's what everyone else does.'

'It'd be easier if I just went round there. I'll only be half an hour.'

'So you're spending Valentine's night with your ex.'

'I'm spending it with her hot-water system. It's hardly romantic.'

'She only has to say the word and you come running.'

'That's not true.'

'Really? What about the so-called gas leak a couple of weeks ago, or the time she rang in the middle of the night because she thought she heard burglars? She's a big girl, Oliver. She's not your responsibility any more.'

'No, but Matt and Georgia are still my kids.'

'They won't fall apart if you fix their boiler tomorrow.'

He thought for a moment. 'You're right,' he said.

'I am?' Anna replied, dazed.

'I'll call her and tell her she'll have to wait until tomorrow.'

'She won't like that.'

'She'll have to deal with it.'

Anna experienced a brief flare of triumph before the guilt flooded in. 'You'd better go,' she sighed.

'But you just said—'

'I know. But I also know we're both going to feel terrible about it if you don't go.'

He kissed her. 'You're wonderful, do you know that?'

'No, I'm not,' she grumbled. 'I'm an idiot, and so are you.'

'That's probably why we're so well suited.' He planted another kiss on the top of her head. 'I'll drop in straight from work. I'll be back as soon as I can.'

'Unless Eve wants you to paint her landing, or get a spider out of the bath.'

'Behave,' Oliver grinned. He grabbed his leather jacket from the hook. 'I'll see you later, okay?'

'One nil to Eve, then,' Elliott said when she told him.

'As usual. Anyway, how about you? Have you got a treat planned for a special lady?'

'Two, actually. I'm taking Becky and Jessica out for a burger, then to the pictures.'

'What are you going to see?'

'No idea. Something very girly with princesses in it, if Jessica gets her way. Something with Johnny Depp if Becky does.'

'Sounds like fun.'

'You think?' Elliott pulled a face. 'You could always come with us if Oliver blows you out.'

'He wouldn't dare.'

He finished sorting the post and tucked his letters under his arm. 'I'm going to make a few calls. I'll be in my office if anyone needs me.'

He was barely out of earshot when Barbara said, 'Isn't that terrible?'

'Awful,' Neil agreed.

'I mean, to be a widower so young. He can't be more than – what? Thirty-five?'

'Oh. Right. I was thinking more of the burger. I wonder if he knows how many miles of tropical rainforest are cut down every year by fast-food chains looking to expand production.'

'It must be so hard for him,' Barbara went on, ignoring him. 'How long has his wife been gone?'

'About five years, I think,' Anna said.

'And to be left with two little kiddies at that age. It's heart-breaking, it really is.' Barbara shook her head pityingly. 'I'm surprised he hasn't found someone else. Those little girls need a mother.'

Anna watched Elliott through the glass wall that separated his office from the rest of the centre. He was on the phone, gesturing with his hand the way he always did to make his point, as if the caller on the other end could see him. He reminded her of a young, absent-minded professor with his Clark Kent glasses and light curly brown hair that looked as if it had been cut with a lawnmower. Anna hadn't known him when his wife was alive, and he rarely talked about her. But he doted on his two young daughters.

'Maybe he's never found anyone to take her place,' she said.

He looked up, saw her watching him and pulled a questioning face. Anna waved back, embarrassed at being caught staring.

'Oh no, look who it is.' Barbara nodded towards the door. 'I wonder what he wants this time?'

Anna switched on her professional smile to greet the man who'd just walked in. Roy Munge was one of their best custom-ers, always coming in to complain about someone, or to make sure his consumer rights weren't being violated in some way. Barbara reckoned it was because he had no life.

Today he was complaining about a pair of trousers that turned out to have a faulty zip. As Anna tried patiently to explain why he couldn't sue the charity shop he'd bought them from, the door opened and a delivery man staggered in under the weight of a huge bouquet.

'Now are they for me or for you, do you think?' Barbara asked archly.

'They could be for me,' Neil pointed out. 'It's sexist to assume only women receive flowers.'

'Oh yes? And who'd be sending you flowers? Not your Buddhist girlfriend, you've just said she doesn't believe in it.'

'Partner,' Neil muttered, and went back to stacking the rack with leaflets on local gay support groups. Barbara refused to do it in case she caught AIDS.

Barbara glanced at the delivery note and handed them over to Anna. 'Someone loves you,' she commented.

'They do, don't they?' Anna could feel herself blushing as she read the card. How had Oliver dictated that to the florist with a straight face?

'He should have sent a potted plant,' Neil said. 'It's so much better for the environment.'

'And some of those roses look a bit wilted to me,' Roy Munge joined in. 'You could probably get your money back if you tried.'

Since Oliver wasn't due home until later and her mum was looking after Charlie for the evening, Anna arranged to go for a run after work with her friends Rachel and Meg.

Rachel was already limbering up on the river path beside Museum Gardens, watched by a few ducks and various men in the houseboats moored alongside. It was five o'clock and beginning to grow dark. The yellow lights along the path twinkled on the still, black water.

Anna shivered in her tracksuit top. 'No sign of Meg yet?'

'You know what she's like, always late.' Rachel did an elegant stretch, her foot balanced on the back of a bench. She was tall and toned, her dark hair pulled back in a swinging pony tail. 'Let's give her another five minutes, you know she can never drag herself away from those demanding brats – ah, here she comes now.' She nodded to where Meg was puffing down the path towards them. 'We were just about to give up on you.'

'Sorry I'm late,' she panted. 'Philippa needed me to check her spellings, and I had to pick Corey up from a play date. Then that cow from the PTA rang just as I was leaving. She wants me to bake a cake for the coffee morning on Friday.'

'Bitch. I hope you said no?' Rachel said. Meg looked shame-faced. 'God, you're such a doormat.'

'You don't know what she's like,' Meg wailed, struggling to capture her curly red hair in a rubber band. She was the opposite to Rachel in every way, small and plump with a round, harassed face. 'That woman could talk the Virgin Mary into becoming a Scientologist.'

'I still reckon you're a mug.' Rachel glanced at her watch. 'Shall we go? I'm meeting Mark for a drink later.'

'On Valentine's Day?' Anna and Meg looked at each other. 'Does this mean you and he are—'

'No, it bloody doesn't! Not as far as I'm concerned, anyway. I'm quite happy being single, thanks very much.'

Rachel was a recruitment consultant, a successful divorcee in her thirties, with a designer wardrobe, a sporty BMW and a converted wharf flat on the most desirable stretch of the river Ouse, right in the trendy heart of the city. She and her husband, Mark, had split up shortly after their four-year-old son was born. Anna and Meg had the feeling he wanted to get back with her, but Rachel was having none of it.

They'd all met at playgroup when Charlie was a year old and Anna was still feeling shell-shocked by motherhood, wondering how she'd ended up in a draughty church hall with a load of toddlers when she should have been downing tequila shots in the Student Union bar, and had found herself next to Rachel in the Singalong Circle.

Rachel wasn't like the other mums, in their jeans and fleeces and no make-up. She wore a tailored Hobbs suit and kept inter-rupting the songs to take calls from Japan on her mobile.

All the other mothers eyed her teeny Prada handbag with resentment and shunned her, but Rachel didn't seem to notice, let alone care. Halfway through an action-filled rendition of 'The Wheels on the Bus', she'd turned to Anna and drawled, 'Stuff this. I don't know about you but I could murder a Martini.'

In the car park later they'd met Meg. Inside, she'd seemed like one of the most frighteningly competent of the mums, bringing in home-made biscuits, making tea, and enthusiastically discussing potty-training methods with the others. But outside, they'd found her weeping behind the wheel of her Vauxhall Zafira while her two small children watched her with bug-eyed dismay and her baby howled in sympathy.

'Sorry,' she'd sniffed, wiping her nose on her sleeve. 'I think my Prozac must have worn off.'

Later, over a drink – a serious drink, not the weak tea they served up at the playgroup – the three women had made friends. Now they met up regularly to run together. It kept them fit, gave them a chance to escape from their families, and it was a good excuse for a gossip.

'So what did Dave get you for Valentine's Day?' Anna asked, as they jogged over the railway bridge, their feet clanging on the metal decking. 'Not more underwear?' Comfortably upholstered, Meg had been understandably upset last year when her husband bought her a size-ten thong.

'Dave's working in Dublin. He called to wish me happy Valentine's, though,' she said, briskly cheerful. 'He asked me what I wanted as a present. I told him a vasectomy would be nice.'

'So is he going to have one?'

'I doubt it. He's too terrified of the pain.'

'He should try having a baby,' Anna said.

'He did say I could get sterilised if I really didn't want any more kids,' Meg went on.

'Big of him,' Rachel muttered. She and Anna had only met Meg's husband a couple of times, but they'd agreed he was a smug, irritating git.

Anna's phone rang and she stopped to answer it, bending double to catch her breath. It was Eve.

'Have you seen Oliver?' she demanded.

'Hello, Eve. How lovely to hear from you.' Anna pulled a face at the others. 'No, I haven't seen him since this morning. I thought he was coming round to see you.'

'So did I, but he hasn't turned up and I can't reach him on his mobile.'

'Have you tried the restaurant?'

'The line's engaged. Are you sure you don't know where he is?'

Yes, I've got him locked up so you can't get your hands on him. 'No idea. Sorry. Maybe he's changed his mind?'

'I doubt it. Oliver wouldn't let me down. I'll try his mobile again,' she said, and hung up.

'Or better still, call a plumber,' Anna muttered as she shoved her phone back into her tracksuit pocket.

'She's got a nerve,' Rachel said.

'Tell me about it.' She wasn't too troubled as she sprinted after the others. Knowing Oliver, he was probably still at the restaurant, testing recipes with Frankie, the phone off the hook so they wouldn't be disturbed. Hours could slip by when he was distracted by work.

They did a lap over Lendal Bridge, threading their way through the early evening commuters heading for the station, then back down to the crumbling medieval tower at the corner of Marygate where they'd started. Anna and Meg said goodbye to Rachel as she headed home back along the river path.

'Want a lift?' Meg said.

Her people carrier was like a mobile nursery. Every seat pocket was stuffed with spare disposable nappies, dummies and the remains of various McDonald's Happy Meals.

'I wouldn't sit there if I were you,' Meg advised, as Anna started to climb into the passenger seat. 'Jack upended a carton of Ribena earlier.'

Anna got into the back, pushing aside broken plastic toys.

'I know, it's a nightmare.' Meg caught her eye in the rear-view mirror. 'I keep telling myself I'll be more organised one day.'

Anna retrieved a piece of Duplo from under her backside. 'I'm surprised you're still sane with four kids.'

'I don't think I am.' Meg gave a slightly manic laugh. 'No wonder Dave's away so much. The only time he gets any peace and quiet is when he's staying in a hotel.'

'It's a shame you can't take a break sometimes.'

'Oh, I'm not complaining, I'd rather be at home anyway. And I know Dave would, too. He hates living out of suitcases, but he has to do it for us. He works so hard,' she sighed.

I know, all that room service and spa facilities must be soul-destroying, Anna thought, eyeing the crayon scrawl on the back of Meg's seat.

She thought again of her lovely Oliver and felt incredibly lucky to have him.

They headed up towards Clifton Green. As they approached Rosslea Street, Meg jammed on the brakes to give way to a police car turning into the narrow terrace before them.

'Ooh, look,' Meg said, as she followed it along the street, manoeuvring down the strip of road between parked cars. 'Which of your neighbours has been naughty, I wonder?'

Anna didn't reply. With a creeping feeling of dread, she knew whose house they would be stopping at.

Chapter 5

To Anna, it just looked as if Oliver was asleep. All he had was a tiny bruise on his head, as if he'd banged it on a cupboard door, the way he was always doing at home.

And yet there were all those machines. Tubes and wires, and the whooshing sound of the ventilator breaking the silence of the room. Breathing for him, the doctors had explained. That much she had managed to take in. She'd shut out everything else. It was too big, too frightening. If she let herself think about that then she might have to think about the fact that he may not make it.

She held his hand, hating that his fingers lay so cool and lifeless, not curling around hers the way they always did when she reached for him. As if he'd already gone.

That was the way the doctors were talking, preparing her for the worst. As if they'd already given up on him. It made her want to scream with rage, but the oppressive hospital atmosphere had taken away her voice.

Extensive head injuries, they said. They couldn't operate because there was too much bleeding around his brain. They needed to carry out tests to assess his chances.

The nurse came in and Anna reluctantly let go of Oliver's hand. 'I'll be back soon,' she whispered, and went out to where her mum was waiting in the corridor.

Jackie looked up sharply. 'How is he?'

'No change.' As she sat down, she noticed her mum was still wearing her fluffy mules under her jeans. She'd run straight to the hospital as soon as she'd got the call. 'Where's Meg?'

'I sent her home. She wanted to wait but I told her she ought to get back to her kids.'

'You're right.' Thank God Meg had been there to drive her to the hospital. Anna was shaking so much she could never have got there on her own.

As soon as she saw the police car pulling up outside the house, she'd known. She'd stared at the police officer's mouth moving, not taking in anything he said. It was Meg who'd dealt with it all, getting her back into the car, calling her mum, and then finding the right place to go in the hospital, while Anna was blind with panic.

'I didn't get a chance to thank her.'

'I'm sure she understands.'

She thought about Oliver leaving that morning, shrugging on his leather jacket, promising to be back as soon as he could.

To think she'd been jealous that he was going to see Eve. She wouldn't have cared if they'd been having a raging affair now, as long as he was still alive.

He *is* alive, she reminded herself. Where there's life, there's hope. Isn't that what everyone says?

She plucked at the zip of her top. Besides, Oliver couldn't die while she was still wearing her scruffy tracksuit, her hair all spiky and in need of a shower.

'I called Eve,' her mother said. 'I thought she should know.'

She couldn't even summon up a niggle of irritation. Any animosity she had was deeply buried under the weight of all her other emotions. 'You're right. She should be here.'

Then she remembered something else, and panicked. 'Who's looking after Charlie?'

'I've left him with Keith.'

'He'll be wondering where I am.' She took a big, gulping breath. 'How am I going to tell him about this?'

Jackie reached for her hand. 'We'll cross that bridge when we come to it.'

She didn't say 'if'. She knew too. They all knew Oliver wasn't going to make it, but no one wanted to say it out loud.

The doors at the end of the corridor burst open and in came Eve, followed by Georgia and Matt.

She went straight up to Anna, her coat flapping. There were smudges of mascara under her eyes, the only colour in her white face.

'How is he?'

'We don't know yet. They're doing some tests.'

'What kind of tests?'

Anna glanced at the children. Georgia was already crying, Matt was biting his lip. Trying to be a man.

She didn't need to say any more. Eve understood. She took a deep breath. 'I want to see him,' she said.

It was strange, Anna thought. The very worst moment of her life and she was sharing it with Eve. Neither of them spoke as they sat either side of his bed, holding his hands. The children were waiting outside. They'd stayed for a few minutes but Georgia had fled and Matt had followed her.

Time went by, the silence broken only by the whooshing of the ventilator.

'Your mum said he had a heart attack?' Eve said at last. Her voice sounded too loud in the quiet room.

Anna nodded. Those last few moments of Oliver's life had been running through her head like a never-ending reel of film. She imagined him speeding along the ring road in his beloved MG, singing tunelessly to one of the Smiths CDs he loved to play at top volume. Knowing Oliver, his thoughts would be all over the place. He'd be thinking about work, planning the staff rotas for the following week, wondering whether he'd be able to fix Eve's boiler and how soon he could get home, and then—

She squeezed her eyes tight shut, trying to block out the picture. What was he thinking in those last few seconds? Was it all over too quickly for him to react, or had he known what was happening? She wanted to believe that he'd been spared the pain and the panic, but she didn't know for sure.

She saw the look on Eve's face and realised she was thinking the same thing.

'He's too young to die like this,' Eve said.

'He's not going to die,' Anna insisted. 'He'll pull through this. He can fight it.'

Eve said nothing. She looked down at Oliver's sleeping face, biting her lip.

She looked so pathetic, Anna wanted to yell at her. How could she give up on him? Why wasn't she willing him to live? She felt exhausted, as if it was her own sheer effort and not the ventilator that kept him breathing.

The doctor came in a few minutes later. 'Mrs Robinson?' he said to Anna.

'I'm Mrs Robinson,' Eve said.

He looked from one to the other in confusion. 'I don't understand. I thought—'

'We're not married.' Anna stared at the floor.

The doctor turned to Eve. 'In that case, could I have a few words in private?'

Anna opened her mouth to argue, but Eve got there first. 'I think Anna should hear whatever you've got to say.'

The doctor's grave face said it all. 'It's not good news, I'm afraid. The results of the tests show that brain-stem death has already occurred.' He paused. 'I know this is difficult for you, but you might want to think about making a decision to switch off the ventilator.'

'No,' Anna said straight away. 'No way.'

Eve ignored her. 'So you're sure there's absolutely no chance he could survive this?' she asked the doctor.

He shook his head. 'The tests are conclusive.' He looked from one to the other, Eve's face pale but composed, Anna's set with furious determination. 'I'll leave you alone to discuss this. You can have me paged at any time if you need me.'

He'd barely left the room before Anna started. 'We can't switch off that machine. You read about cases like this all the time. People coming back from comas after years and years—'

'This isn't a coma,' Eve said. 'You heard what the doctor said. It's only the machine keeping him alive.'

Then let it keep him alive a bit longer, Anna wanted to yell. She wasn't ready to face a world without Oliver in it. Not unless

49

they could switch off a machine and stop her heart beating too.

'I don't want to let him go,' she whispered.

'You think I do?'

Their eyes met across the bed.

'He's already gone, Anna.'

The machine whooshed, monitors beeped, filling the silence.

'So I'll tell the doctor, shall I?' said Eve.

Half an hour later it was just the two of them. The children came in to say goodbye to their father and then went outside to wait. Anna had sent her mum home.

She and Eve sat across the bed, holding Oliver's hands. They didn't look at each other, but kept their eyes fixed on his face. Anna wondered if, like her, Eve was trying to memorise every line and feature, knowing she'd never see them again.

The nurse had unhooked the various drips and monitors, so he was just Oliver again. The same man she'd woken up beside every morning for nearly four years. She half expected him to open his eyes, smile that amazing smile of his, and jokingly ask if it was her turn to make the tea.

She tasted panic, metallic in her mouth.

'Are you ready?' the doctor asked. Eve looked at her.

'Anna?'

'I – I'm okay,' she stammered, but her heart was crashing against her ribs. Across the bed, Eve's face was a blur. All she could see was her wedding ring glinting as she laid her hand across Oliver's.

The doctor nodded to the nurse, who lowered the lights. The sound of the machine seemed to fill the room. In a moment it would stop, and then Oliver would be gone.

'Anna?' Eve's voice came from a million miles away. The room started to spin as she stumbled to her feet.

'I can't do it,' she said. 'I'm sorry.'

Outside, the bright lights of the corridor hurt her eyes. She flattened herself against the wall, forcing herself to breathe until the world slowly came back into focus.

Matt and Georgia were sitting further down the corridor. Matt had his arm wrapped awkwardly around his sobbing sister. He sat up when he saw Anna.

'Where's Mum?'

'Still in there.' Suddenly Anna felt incredibly foolish. Why had she run away? Why couldn't she stay and see it through like Eve?

Matt's voice was gruff. 'Is he – is it over?'

'Not yet.'

She sat down beside them, put her arm around Georgia and reached for Matt's hand. It seemed too large for his body, his fingers long and calloused from hours of guitar plucking.

A few minutes later the door opened and Eve came out. She looked dazed, as if she'd just woken from a heavy sleep.

'Mum!' Georgia shook Anna off to run to her mother. Matt followed. Eve seemed confused to see them there at first, then suddenly she snapped back into focus. She gathered them into her arms, hugging them fiercely.

Anna watched them, feeling very alone. She wished she hadn't sent her mother home. She needed someone to hold her.

But the only arms she wanted around her were gone for ever.

She left them holding on to each other and crept away.

Down in the reception area, she passed a man heading for the lift, weighed down with flowers. A silver helium balloon printed with the words 'Happy Valentine's Day' floated above his head. He grinned at Anna as he hit the lift button.

'It's a boy,' he said.

'Sorry?'

'My wife's just had a baby boy. On Valentine's Day.'

Outside, her mother was waiting, shivering in the February rain, smoking a cigarette. Anna hadn't seen her smoke for ten years.

'I thought you'd gone home,' she said.

'I couldn't leave you, could I?'

She stubbed out her cigarette and held out her arms. Anna fell into them.

'I couldn't do it,' she sobbed into her mother's shoulder. 'I couldn't stay.'

'Shh, love. It's okay.' Jackie rubbed her back.

'But I let him down.'

'You didn't let anyone down.'

'I did, I should have been there.' It should have been her who stayed with him, held his hand so he wouldn't be alone. She owed him that. But instead she'd run away like a coward and left Eve to say that final goodbye.

'He wouldn't have minded,' Jackie said.

'That's not the point. He needed me.' Oliver might have forgiven her, but she would never forgive herself.

The children didn't ask what it had been like, and Eve knew she would never tell them. But the pain of those final moments would stay with her like a piece of ice lodged in her heart.

The doctor had asked her if she wanted to turn off the machine, but she couldn't bring herself to do it. She'd held Oliver's hand, stroking his fingers, hoping that wherever he was, somehow he would know she was there. Within seconds the monitor flatlined, and the long, continuous beep filled the room. The doctor quickly switched off all the machines, and everything fell silent.

'Mum?' Georgia's face was anxious, looking up at her. Eve hadn't realised she'd been holding her daughter so tightly, crushing her in her arms.

'Sorry.' She let her go and looked around. 'Where's Anna?'

'She was here a minute ago. She must have left,' Matt said.

Eve felt a twinge of concern for her. 'Did she seem okay?'

'She looked a bit shaken up.'

'I'm not surprised.' She'd thought she was going to pass out earlier.

But in a way she was glad Anna had gone, and she'd been able to spend those last few minutes alone with Oliver. To have him to herself one last time. It seemed right somehow.

'Can we go home?' Georgia pleaded. 'I hate this place.'

As they were leaving, a nurse called Eve to one side.

'There's never a good time to do this,' she said, handing her a plastic bag. 'They're your husband's personal effects.'

Eve snatched her hand away. 'Anna should have them.'

'I was told to give them to you,' the nurse said.

She walked away, leaving Eve staring at the bag. Keys, watch, phone, that battered old wallet she'd bought him years ago. They looked so unfamiliar, as if they belonged to a stranger.

There was something else in the bag. A small velvet-covered box. She had a strange feeling what was going to be inside before she'd even opened it.

The ring was exquisite, white gold with a discreet diamond glittering at its heart. There could only ever be one reason a man gave a woman a ring like that.

He was going to propose to Anna. It was Valentine's Day, after all.

She had a sudden picture of the moment he'd proposed to her, at the graduation ball. Being broke, all he could afford was a cheap cubic zirconia ring from a discount jeweller's. A few years later, when the restaurant showed its first profit, he'd offered to replace it with a wonderful sapphire and diamond cluster. But she'd insisted on keeping the cheap ring. It meant more to her than the Crown jewels.

Eve looked down at Anna's ring, fresh tears pricking her eyes, imagining Oliver's excitement as he planned when to give it to her. He always did love surprises.

'What's that?' She snapped the box shut as Matt came up behind her.

'Just a few of your father's things.' She stuffed it back into the bag.

'What are you going to do with them?'

'Give them to Anna, if I can find her.'

But when they got to the car park, there was no sign of her.

Eve couldn't help feeling relieved. They'd both been through enough, without having to handle something like that as well.

Chapter 6

It should have been miserable on the day of Oliver's funeral, but after a week of heavy grey clouds the February sun perversely decided to shine on the church, sending brilliant jewel-coloured beams of light through the stained-glass windows on to the assembled mourners.

The church overflowed with Oliver's friends. Looking around, Eve was overwhelmed to realise how many lives he'd touched over the years. She didn't even recognise some of the faces.

Beside her, Matt and Georgia shuffled in their seats and stared down at their service books. Eve wished she could have made it easier for them. She would have given anything to spare them the pain they were going through.

The past week had seemed unreal. Eve felt as if she was coping, but she wasn't sure it had really sunk in. A couple of times she'd even found herself picking up the phone to call him. It had been too sudden. There was no time to get used to it, no chance to say goodbye. One minute he was there, full of life, and the next he was gone.

There was a stir as Anna and her family entered the church. She was flanked by her mother and two burly men Eve assumed were her brothers. An older man – her mother's boyfriend, Eve guessed – followed behind, with an elderly woman leaning on his arm.

Anna glanced across the aisle at her as she took her seat. She looked even more childlike in her sombre black coat, her dark eyes huge and fearful in her pale face.

At least she had her family to support her. Eve envied her that. Her own mother had done her best to be sympathetic, but told Eve she couldn't be at the funeral because she would be in the States, drawing political attention to the plight of the South American Wanga people, whose lands were being eaten up by global expansionism.

'They're disappearing in droves, darling,' Vanessa had said. 'It's absolutely appalling. If we don't act soon a unique culture will be entirely lost.'

'But what about me?' Eve said.

'You'll be fine,' Vanessa said breezily. 'It's not like you were even still married.'

'Actually, we were.'

'Only just, sweetheart. And after what he put you through, you hardly owe him your grief.'

So why do I still feel it? Eve thought, as she put down the phone. She was in a strange position. She was Oliver's widow and yet she wasn't expected to mourn him. But that didn't stop her emotions being all over the place. The other day she'd cried her eyes out over a soppy song on the radio. Then she'd gone to order Oliver's flowers and found herself in hysterical giggles over the florist's ill-fitting wig. Nothing made sense any more.

Thank God for Adam. He'd been so brilliant over the past week, organising the funeral and everything that went with it, helping her and Anna over the awkwardness of who should do what. He'd called her every day just to check how she was doing.

She studied the back of his head as he sat in front of her. He reminded her so much of Oliver it hurt. The broad shoulders, the dark hair curling over his collar. It was only when he half turned and she caught sight of his rugged profile and flattened nose that she felt the plummet of disappointment.

Finally everyone was settled and the service began. Once again, she silently thanked Adam for doing such a good job. He'd managed to get the tone of the occasion just right, with Oliver's favourite songs instead of hymns, and his friends sharing their memories. There were a few laughs and lots of tears, but as Eve dabbed her eyes she couldn't help feeling amused at what Oliver would have made of it all. He wasn't especially religious; she'd had a fight on her hands to get Matt and Georgia christened. She could imagine him standing behind the pulpit making wry faces as the vicar told everyone what a great guy he was.

And then it was her turn. She'd decided to read Christina Rossetti's poem *Remember*. She heard the vicar say her name and managed to get to the front of the church, her heels clicking on the flagstones. But when she reached the lectern and looked out over the sea of expectant faces, her stomach began to flutter.

'Remember me when I am gone away, Gone far away into the silent land; When you can no more hold me by the hand.'

Her voice quavered, remembering how she'd gripped on to him so tightly in the hospital when the doctor switched off the machine. She couldn't hold him back from that silent land, no matter how much she'd wanted to.

'Remember me when no more day by day You tell me of our future that you plann'd.'

She suddenly had a picture of the two of them, newly married, in bed in their dingy little rented flat on a freezing December day. It was the middle of the afternoon but they couldn't afford to turn on the heating so they huddled under the duvet for warmth. She lay in the circle of his arms, gazing up at the growing patch of mould on the ceiling, listening to him as he mapped out their future, telling her about the successful restaurant he would run one day, the big house they'd live in and the wonderful life they'd have together.

He sounded so sure of himself, Eve didn't doubt he would make their dreams come true. But she also knew that their life couldn't get more wonderful than it was at that moment, being in his arms, knowing he loved her more than anyone else in the world.

That was the afternoon Matt was conceived, she'd been sure.

She saw the faces looking at her and realised she'd stopped reading. How long had she been standing there, tears running down her face? It could have been seconds or hours, she had no idea.

She looked back down at the page, searching for her place, but the words were a blurred jumble. She caught sight of Georgia's anguished face, but she couldn't move. She was stranded there, her feet rooted to the spot. She couldn't even speak because her tongue had glued itself to the roof of her mouth.

There was someone at her side. She looked round and there was Anna. She reached over, took the book out of Eve's hands and began reading from where she'd left off, her voice calm and clear. Eve could only stand there, feeling foolish, as her words rang out over the silent church.

She finished reading and closed the book. She touched Eve's arm gently, and guided her down the steps and back to her seat. Not a word was spoken between them.

Eve couldn't meet anyone's eye as she sat down. She could feel everyone watching her, and she knew what they were all thinking. She'd made an utter fool of herself.

She and Anna didn't speak as they spilled out of the church or as they faced each other across Oliver's grave for the burial.

Afterwards, everyone headed back to the restaurant. Frankie the chef, still in his black suit, was carrying trays of food to the table.

'Can I help?' Eve asked.

'I've got it all sorted, thanks.' He must have realised she was at a loss because he added kindly, 'But you could fold some napkins, if you like?'

'It all looks wonderful,' Eve said, as she folded each paper triangle and arranged them in a pile.

'Do you think so?' Frankie ran his hand over his smooth, cropped head. He looked ill at ease out of his chef's whites. He was in his early forties, heavyset and attractive in an *EastEnders* hard-man kind of way.

'You've done Oliver proud.'

'Pity he's not here to see it.' His voice was gruff with emotion.

'He always did love a party.'

'He did, didn't he? I wanted to get it right for him. He was a good mate, I owe him more than I can ever repay.'

Eve felt a twinge of guilt. When Frankie first approached them about a job shortly after the restaurant had opened, she'd taken one look at his broken nose, scorpion tattoo and prison record and said no straight away. But typically, Oliver had insisted on giving him a chance.

'Let's just see what he can do,' he'd said.

And he'd been proved right. Frankie might have looked like a prizefighter and cursed enough to make Gordon Ramsay sound like a nun, but he was as fiercely loyal to Oliver as an ill-treated Rottweiler who'd been saved from doggy Death Row.

He stepped back to check the table arrangement. 'I know it's probably not the right time,' he said, 'but I just wanted you to know you don't have to worry about the restaurant. I can keep things ticking over for as long as you want.'

'Thanks.'

He moved a plate of vol-au-vents to the other end of the table, then squinted at it again. 'I don't suppose you know what's going to happen to this place now?'

'To be honest, I hadn't really thought about it.'

'No, I daresay you haven't.' He swapped the vol-au-vents with a tray of chicken wings and nodded, satisfied. 'Anyway, as long as you know I'm here to help. If there's anything you need, you only have to ask.'

'That's really kind of you, Frankie.'

'Like I said, I owe it to Oliver.'

People began to drift up to the table, looking for something to eat. Eve left Frankie organising them and headed off to find a quiet table on the other side of the room.

She looked for Matt and Georgia, but they'd gone off somewhere. Eve didn't blame them; she would have preferred to be somewhere else too.

'Not eating?' Adam stood over her.

'I don't really feel like it.'

'I'm not surprised.' He put his glass down on the table. 'Do you mind if I join you? Or would you rather be on your own?'

'No, it's fine.' She pulled out a chair. 'Have you seen Anna?'

'I don't think she's here. I saw her leaving with her family just after the service. Why?'

'I had something for her.' She still had the ring in her bag. She couldn't decide when would be the best time to give it to her. 'It can wait, I suppose.'

'I don't think she could handle all this,' Adam said.

'She seemed very calm in the church. Much better than me, anyway.'

'You did fine,' Adam reassured her.

'I made a complete idiot of myself.' Eve grimaced at the memory. 'I'd still be standing there now if Anna hadn't rescued me.'

'It all got too much for you. People understand that.'

'I wanted to get it right for Oliver,' Eve said.

'Oliver would have understood too. If he was here, he'd be telling you not to be so hard on yourself.'

'Or having a good laugh.'

'True.'

They were silent for a moment, lost in their thoughts. Then Eve said, 'Imogen didn't come, then?'

'I didn't invite her. I didn't think it was a fun way to spend a date.'

'So you're still together?'

'Don't sound so surprised about it.' His eyes twinkled.

'Sorry.'

Another silence. 'Thank you for organising all this,' Eve said. 'I don't think I could have done it myself.'

'It's no problem. I hope you didn't mind me using this place? I thought it would be appropriate somehow.'

'It's perfect. Oliver had so many happy times here. We all did.' She stared glumly into the depths of her glass.

'I wonder what will happen to it now,' Adam said.

'Frankie was just saying the same thing. He said he'd keep running it for as long as I wanted. As if it's got anything to do with me.'

Adam looked thoughtful. 'It might have. Do you know if Oliver left a will?'

'I doubt it. You know how disorganised he was. Anyway, he probably didn't expect to—' She trailed off.

59

'No, of course not. It might be best if you found out, though.'

'Me?'

'You're still his next of kin, remember?'

'Couldn't I do it some other time? It's only been a week.'

'Do you want me to have a word with his solicitor? I could find out if he left a will, at least.'

'Would you? That would be really kind.'

'It might help set your mind at rest.'

She didn't like to tell him her mind didn't need setting at rest. She didn't care what happened to Oliver's restaurant, or his money.

'I suppose this means we won't be getting any sandwiches?' Nana said, as they huddled in the back of Keith's Ford Mondeo.

Keith caught Anna's eye in the rear-view mirror. 'She'd go anywhere for a free sausage roll, your nana.'

Anna smiled wearily back, her thoughts elsewhere.

Keeping herself together for the funeral had exhausted her. There was no way she wanted to face everyone afterwards. Saying goodbye to Oliver had been hard enough without having to make small talk with his friends.

Now all she wanted to do was curl up and sleep. But she knew if she went to bed she would only end up staring at the ceiling like every other night.

They turned off the main road and entered the sprawl of wide, grass-edged streets that formed the Cliffmead estate. It was late afternoon and children streamed out of the gates of the local school, running along the verges followed by harassed-looking mums negotiating shopping and buggies. Pensioners gossiped outside the post office. A couple of builders were replacing a sign outside the chemist's shop. Anna watched it all, bewildered. It amazed her that normal life was still going on everywhere, when for her it had stopped completely.

They passed her brothers' houses, and her nan's. Her whole family lived within two streets of each other. She was the only one who'd broken away. The first to pass her A levels, the first to go to university. The first to move out of Cliffmead.

And now she felt as if she was right back where she started.

Her sister-in-law Debbie was looking after Charlie with her own two toddlers at Jackie's house. They were all cuddled up on the sofa, watching a *Balamory* DVD.

'How was it?' Anna heard her ask her brother Tony. He shrugged back, and they both looked at Anna. She'd got used to that half-pitying, half-curious look over the past few days.

'I'll put the kettle on,' her mother said, heading for the kitchen.

'Good idea.' Nana pulled off her hat. 'I'm spitting feathers. Funerals always make me parched.'

'Not for me,' Anna said. 'I'm going upstairs to pack.'

Her mother came to the kitchen door, the kettle still in her hand. 'Pack? Whatever for?'

'I'm going home.'

Jackie followed her to the foot of the stairs. 'You don't have to do that. You can stay here as long as you like.'

'I know. But I need to go back sometime.'

They'd all been so good to her, but Anna could feel herself struggling under the weight of their concern. Their kindness was beginning to feel oppressive.

She'd barely been out of the house. All she'd done for the past week was sit on the sofa in her dressing gown, watching television with Charlie and her nana while her mother made endless cups of tea. Sometimes she didn't even have time to finish one before the next appeared. She'd lost all track of time; she only knew it was night when her mother stopped making tea and told her it was time for bed.

She was grateful to them, but she felt as if she couldn't breathe sometimes. She needed to reconnect with reality, no matter how painful it was.

'Are you sure you're ready to be on your own?'

'I won't know until I try, will I?'

Her mother looked as if she might argue, then gave up. 'If that's what you want,' she sighed, 'but it seems a bit soon to me.'

'Honestly, I need to go. It's for the best.'

'If you say so. But don't forget, if it all gets too much you can come back here any time you want.'

Keith insisted on driving her home. Her courage almost failed her as they turned into her street and it was all she could do to stop herself begging him to take her back to Cliffmead.

It was the first time she and Charlie had been back to the house since the night Oliver died. Then she'd just grabbed a few things and rushed out again. Now as she put her key in the door she dreaded what she would find when she walked in.

But everything was so heartbreakingly normal. She felt if she called out Oliver's name he'd appear in the kitchen doorway, holding his arms out to greet her the way he always did.

Someone – her mum, she guessed – had been in and cleaned up. The post was stacked in a neat pile on the hall table. Anna picked up the top letter and put it down quickly when she saw Oliver's name on the electricity bill.

Once again she fought the urge to run, to get in the car and drive straight back to her mum's house, where she felt warm and safe and not so very alone.

'Where's Daddy?' Charlie asked.

Anna steeled herself. 'Don't you remember, sweetheart? We talked about this. Daddy died.'

Charlie frowned. 'He's not coming home?'

'I'm afraid not, baby.'

'Never ever?' She shook her head. Charlie considered it for a moment. 'Can I watch a DVD?' he asked.

Anna smiled. 'Good idea.'

She helped him out of his coat and sat him down on the bottom stair while she pulled off his shoes, listening to him chattering away, forcing herself to be brisk and cheerful as they discussed what they could have for tea.

Once she'd found his favourite Barney DVD and put it on, she set about unpacking their things and sorting out something to eat.

She walked around the house cautiously, bracing herself before

62

she opened each door. Everywhere she looked there seemed to be another memory to face, another stab of pain and loneliness. Taking her bags into her bedroom and seeing the bed she and Oliver had shared, she was worried that his clothes might still be strewn over the chair where he always left them, but her mother had got there first and tidied them away. But when she opened her wardrobe, there they were. Anna put out a hand to touch them, then snatched it back and slammed the door.

The kitchen was another challenge. As she heated up a can of soup, she kept her eyes averted from the open shelves, where Oliver's rows of spices and herbs and various other exotic ingredients were lined up. She'd often nagged him about the clutter. Now she wished she hadn't wasted so much time. If only she'd known how little of it they would have, she would have made the most of every minute.

The phone rang, making her jump.

It was her mother. 'Just checking everything's all right?'

'Mum, I've only been out of your sight for ten minutes.'

'I know, but we're all worried about you.' She could imagine her family all sitting round the phone, counting the minutes until they could call.

'There's no need, I'm fine.' No need to tell her she'd been cracking up about thirty seconds ago, on the verge of tears over a jar of pesto she'd found in the fridge with Oliver's scrawly handwriting on the label.

'Are you sure?'

'Well, no, it's a bit scary. But I've got to learn to stand on my own two feet.'

'It's not going to be easy,' Jackie warned.

'*You* did it.'

'That's how I know how hard it is.'

'Yes, but you coped, didn't you?'

'Well—'

'You did. You were brilliant. And if you can manage on your own with three kids, I reckon I can cope with just me and Charlie.'

'I never said you couldn't cope,' Jackie said. 'As long as you know you can come round or call me any time you like. There's no shame in asking for help.'

After a few more minutes of reassuring her mother she wasn't going to go into meltdown, the call ended. Anna didn't know why Jackie was so worried about her. She'd got through it when Anna's father died, leaving her with three children under ten. Anna could still remember how great she was, helping them all through their grief. She was determined to be just as strong for Charlie.

She gave him his tea – she couldn't face anything herself – and they cuddled up on the sofa watching DVDs until long after his bedtime. She had no idea what they were watching, but the bright colours and happy music filled her head and kept the dark thoughts at bay.

Everywhere she looked, she saw Oliver. His laughing face gazed down at her from the photographs on the mantelpiece. His cookery books and those crime novels he loved were crammed on the shelves. Every time she looked at them she wanted to howl with rage and pain, but she couldn't bear to take them down and hide them away either. It would feel like a betrayal.

Charlie finally dropped off to sleep, his dark head resting on her chest. Anna disentangled her numb arm from around him and carried him upstairs.

'Bath?' he mumbled sleepily.

'Not tonight.' She'd had every intention of keeping to his routine, to try to make life as normal as she could for his sake. She'd just about managed it when she had her mum to help. But now just pushing herself through every little task felt like an enormous battle.

She hesitated outside her bedroom door. She was tempted to put Charlie to sleep in her bed so she wouldn't feel so alone. But in the end she took him into his blue bedroom, with its star-patterned curtains and model aeroplanes hanging over the bed.

'Night night.' His hair tickled her face as she kissed his soft cheek.

'I want to say goodnight to Daddy.'

She felt a stab of pain. 'Daddy's gone, sweetheart.'

64

'Will he be home later?'

Dear God, would she have to go through this every time? 'No, baby.'

'I remember,' he yawned. Then he turned over and went to sleep, his chubby hand protectively clutching his toy monkey.

She went back downstairs, opened a bottle of wine and watched TV until midnight. Then she switched channels and watched snatches of ancient comedy repeats until she finally drifted off to sleep on the sofa. She woke up at two a.m. to the sound of Mr Humphries being very camp about a pair of trousers on *Are You Being Served?* Sitting up and massaging her stiff neck, she reached for the wine and realised the bottle was empty. She couldn't put it off any longer, she had to go to bed.

It didn't feel too strange, being in bed on her own. When Oliver was working late at the restaurant, she was often already asleep when he came home. She kept to her own side of the bed out of habit, but as she reached over to switch off the bedside lamp, she caught the smell of his aftershave lingering on his pillow. Anna held the pillow to her stomach, her body curved around it, breathing in the faint scent of him as she lay there longing for sleep.

Chapter 7

MARCH

Mum was going out to walk the dog again. Georgia had a nervy feeling in the pit of her stomach as she watched Eve clip on Benson's lead.

'Where are you going?' she asked.

'I don't know. Depends where we end up.'

'Shall I come with you?'

Her mother gave her a strange, amused look. 'Since when have you ever wanted to walk the dog?' Then, before Georgia could reply, she added, 'Anyway, don't you have homework to do?'

'I could do it later.'

'Oh no, you don't, young lady. Homework comes first. Besides, I'd like some time on my own. I need to clear my head.'

Georgia thought she'd done a bit too much head clearing in the two weeks since Dad's funeral. Poor Benson was nearly exhausted from the new exercise regime. He'd even started to whimper whenever anyone took his lead off its hook.

She followed her mother to the door. 'How long will you be?'

'I'm not sure.'

'What's for supper?'

'That's a good point.' She stopped, distracted. 'I forgot to take anything out of the freezer. I'll have to bring back a takeaway.'

'Again? I'm sick of takeaways.'

'You used to love them.'

'That was before we started having them every day.'

'Then maybe you should cook,' her mother snapped. 'You know how the oven works, don't you?'

Georgia flinched. 'No need to bite my head off.'

'I'm sorry, I've got a headache. I'll feel better when I've had a walk.'

I doubt it, Georgia thought as the front door closed. Her mum had been walking for days now and she still hadn't got any better.

Meanwhile, the house was falling apart and she didn't seem to notice. When she wasn't out, she was in a daze. There was no nagging, no 'to do' list stuck to the fridge. The washing basket overflowed and no one bothered to sort out the recycling. Georgia longed for the comfort of seeing those cans and bottles neatly separated, or hearing her mother yell at her not to throw away the newspapers.

She'd been late home twice in the past week, both times on a school night, and her mum hadn't said a word. She was beginning to wonder if she even cared.

She stomped upstairs to retrieve her PE kit from the washing basket, sniffing back tears. She missed her dad, but she missed her mum even more.

She hauled her dirty clothes down to the kitchen and opened the washing machine. A load of damp, musty-smelling stuff fell out. How long had that been there? Georgia piled it back in with her own things, then frowned at the various knobs and dials, wondering which one to push.

She was still studying them when Matt came in. 'Do you know how this thing works?' she called over her shoulder.

'No idea. Where's Mum?'

'Out, as usual. And before you ask, there's nothing for dinner,' she added, as he opened the fridge.

Infuriatingly, he didn't seem to care. Georgia watched him go to the larder and help himself to a bowl of cereal.

'Don't you think Mum's acting a bit weird?' she said.

'In what way?'

'In every way. Look around, Matt. Even you must have noticed this place is a mess.'

He gazed around. 'It looks okay to me.'

Georgia watched him shovelling cereal into his mouth. Of

course he wouldn't care if he lived in a pigsty; he *was* a pig.

She twiddled a few knobs experimentally and the washing machine gushed into life. 'It's not just the housework. She's doing all this strange stuff. I hear her walking about all night. And she's started smoking again.' She'd tried to hide it, but Georgia had found a cigarette butt on the patio. 'You don't think she's losing it, do you?'

'She's hardly going to be running around the house singing, is she?'

'No, but—' She couldn't tell Matt how afraid she was. He'd only laugh at her. 'What about us?'

'What about us?'

'She's not helping us, is she? She should be taking care of us, not the other way round.' Now Dad was gone, she needed to know she could rely on her mum to keep her safe, make life sane and normal. At the moment it felt as if she was walking on quicksand. 'I don't know why she's so upset. He wasn't even her husband any more, but he was our dad.'

Matt stared at her, his spoon halfway to his mouth. 'You really are a selfish little bitch, aren't you?'

'It's all right for you, you're going to university soon,' Georgia fired back. 'I'll be the one stuck here looking after her.' How the hell was she going to cope then?

'If I had to be looked after by you I think I'd shoot myself.' Matt finished his cereal and threw the bowl into the sink.

'Stuff you.' Georgia picked up her bag and slung it over her shoulder.

'Where are you going?'

'Out. Seeing as I'm such a selfish bitch, *you* can look after Mum when she comes back.' If she comes back, she thought. That was something else that haunted her, the fear that one day her mum might go out on one of her walks and just keep walking.

'Suit yourself.' As she left, he called after her, 'I hope you remembered to put washing powder in that machine. Otherwise you'll have to do the whole lot again.'

★

She went next door to call for her friend Stacey. The back door was open as usual, and her mum was in the kitchen, frying egg and chips.

'Stacey's upstairs doing her homework.' She caught Georgia's longing gaze at the frying pan. 'Do you want some?'

'Oh no, I couldn't—'

'Go on, there's plenty. I made some for Stacey's sister but she's just called to say she's working late. Grab a plate.'

'Are you sure? That's really kind of you.'

'Don't get too excited, it's only a fry-up.'

It was still more than she was likely to get at home. Georgia fetched a plate from the cupboard.

'I saw your mum go out with the dog again. How's she getting on?'

'She's all right,' Georgia squirmed in her seat.

'I keep meaning to come round and offer my condolences, but I wouldn't really know what to say.'

No one ever knew what to say. That was the trouble. Most of her friends tried to pretend it hadn't happened, which suited her fine. She hated it when people stared and felt sorry for her.

'What about you? How are you coping?'

She was saved from answering by Stacey coming into the kitchen. Every time she saw her, Georgia wondered why they were ever friends. Stacey was a serious spoff, from her ill-fitting chainstore jeans and scraped-back mousey hair to the glasses that kept slipping to the end of her nose. She was also kind, wise, good at keeping secrets and the closest thing to a best friend Georgia had.

'Here she is. My little angel.' Her mother ruffled her hair affectionately. 'I've been telling her to get contact lenses. What do you think, Georgie?'

'I told you, I don't want them.'

'But you know what they say? Boys don't make passes at girls who wear glasses.'

'Exactly.' Stacey pushed her spectacles further up her nose. 'I've got more important things to worry about than boys.'

'You never heard me say that when I was your age.'

69

'Yes, and look what happened. You ended up with Dad.'

'True!' Her mum laughed. Georgia watched them, smiling. It was such a relief to be somewhere normal and fun, where there wasn't a mist of misery hanging over everyone.

'So what do you want to do tonight?' Georgia asked, when they'd finished their tea and watched *Hollyoaks*.

'I've got English coursework to do.'

'Can't it wait?'

'Not really. I need to get it done by the end of the week and I don't want to rush it.' Stacey picked up the remote control and flicked off the TV.

Georgia felt guilty. Stacey went to the local comp and worked far harder than she did at her private school.

'We could just go down to Jackson's and buy some sweets, then you could get on with your work while I watch TV,' she suggested, desperate not to go home.

When they got there, a group of teenage boys were messing about outside the shop, lolling on bikes and pretending to push each other into the road. Stacey slowed down when she saw them.

'Oh, bloody hell,' she muttered. 'That's all we need.'

'Do you know them?'

'They go to my school. When they bother to turn up, anyway. That one in the white hoodie is Andy Taylor, he's the worst.' She took Georgia's arm. 'Take no notice of them. Just walk past, okay?'

They tried, but the boys saw them and wheeled their bikes into a barricade, blocking their way.

'All right, Stace?' Andy called out to her. 'Who's your friend?'

'None of your business.' Stacey tried to move past him but he reversed his bike across her path. She sighed loudly. 'Do you have to be such a moron?'

'Do you have to be such a nerd?' Andy drained his Coke can and tossed it into the gutter, then turned to Georgia. 'What's your name?'

'Georgia.'

'Ooh, Georgia.' He mimicked her accent. 'You're dead posh, you are.'

His mates fell about laughing. Georgia looked around at them blankly. 'What's so funny?'

'What's so funny?' Andy mimicked again.

'You see? I told you they were idiots. Come on.' Stacey pulled at her arm.

They spent ages choosing sweets and Georgia bought a copy of *Heat* magazine, but when they came out the boys were still waiting. They nudged each other and laughed when they saw them.

'Andy fancies you,' one of them called out, and was shoved off his bike.

'Take no notice, they'll soon get bored,' Stacey whispered as the boys followed them up the street. But Georgia was quite enjoying the attention. Going to an all-girls school she never met any boys, apart from the wimpy ones who came to their yearly disco.

She couldn't resist sneaking glances back at them. 'You shouldn't encourage them,' Stacey grumbled.

'I'm not.' But a moment later Andy pedalled up alongside her. Steering his bike with one hand he pulled a packet of cigarettes out of his pocket with the other and offered it to her.

She shook her head. 'No thanks, I don't smoke.'

'Why? Too scared?' he jeered.

'No, too intelligent. I don't see the point in paying a fortune to the tobacco companies for something that will kill me.'

'All right, love, I don't need a lecture. Anyway, who said I spent anything?'

'You stole them?'

'No, it was my birthday and the nice shopkeeper gave them to me.' As he stuck a cigarette between his lips, Georgia noticed the crude tattoo on the back of his hand. He saw her looking and showed it off to her. 'Like it? My brother did it for me. He learned how to do it in Young Offenders.'

'You're lucky you didn't get blood poisoning.'

'I didn't know you cared.'

'I don't.'

'Liar.' He lit his cigarette one-handed and took a long drag, blowing smoke into the air above her head. 'I got a present for you.' He reached into his pocket and pulled out a Mars bar.

'I expect it's nicked,' Stacey said.

'You're only jealous 'cos I didn't get you one.' He winked at Georgia. 'See you,' he said, and then he was off, his gang following. Georgia stared after him, the chocolate bar still in her hand.

'Moron,' Stacey muttered.

'He wasn't bad.'

Stacey stared at her, appalled. 'Don't tell me you fancied him?'

Georgia shrugged.

She wished she hadn't said anything as, all the way home, Stacey gave her a lecture on the trouble Andy had been in, from fighting with teachers to smoking dope and stealing from the other kids. 'And he was suspended for starting a fire in the chemistry lab.'

'I didn't say I was going to marry him, did I?'

'Just as well,' Stacey replied. 'Your mum would go insane if you went anywhere near him.'

Georgia thought about her mother, so preoccupied with her own problems. 'She probably wouldn't even notice,' she said wistfully.

The churchyard was coming to life after the long winter. Yellow and purple crocuses dotted the grass and frothy white blossom was bursting out on the trees lining the path.

It was all wrong, Eve thought as she let Benson out of the car. It couldn't be right that everywhere she looked the world seemed to be springing up with new life when Oliver wasn't there to see it.

Benson trotted ahead of her, straight through the church gates, following the path that led around to the rear of the church. They'd been here so many times over the past few days he knew exactly where to go.

Maybe it wasn't right for her to come here every day, but nothing felt right at the moment. Her whole life seemed to be falling apart and it was all Eve could do to hang on to the shattered pieces. She tried to stay strong for the children, but inside she could feel herself losing it. Just getting through the day took a massive act of will, from forcing herself out of bed in the morning to finding some clothes to put on. She had taken to wearing the same pair of jeans and sweater just because she didn't have it in her to find anything else.

Normal life seemed to bruise her. She could just about get through the day if she didn't have to think or speak to anyone. But as soon as someone asked her to function, even if it was only Georgia asking what was for supper, she could feel the pressure building up inside her head. Then she'd fly into a rage and lash out, or burst into tears.

She hated herself when she saw the hurt and confusion on her children's faces. They'd lost their father; she should be helping them through their grief, not adding to their misery.

That was why she came here – to be alone and release some of the emotional pressure, so at least she could try to appear normal for the kids.

So she was not at all pleased when she turned the corner of the church and saw Anna bending beside Oliver's grave, rearranging the flowers beside his makeshift wooden headstone.

Then she turned her head, and Eve realised it wasn't Anna at all.

'Hello?' she called out.

The girl swung round, dropping the posy she'd been holding.

'I – I'm sorry,' she stammered. 'I didn't mean to intrude.'

As she got closer, Eve realised why she'd mistaken her for Anna. They were both young, dark-haired and doe-eyed. Except, unlike Anna's spiky crop, the girl's hair was long and drawn back in a plait.

'It's okay.' Eve smiled at her. 'I was just surprised to see some-one else here, that's all.' She glanced at the flowers at the girl's feet. 'Aren't you going to pick them up?'

The girl reached down stiffly. Eve noticed the bandage around her knee under her skirt.

'I'm sorry, you must think I'm a bit strange, putting flowers on your husband's grave,' she said. 'I'm Laura Morris. I used to work at Oliver's restaurant.'

'Ah.'

'I couldn't get to the funeral, so I thought I'd bring these now.' She brushed the earth off the flowers.

'That's very thoughtful of you.'

'It was the least I could do. Oliver was a nice man.' She looked up at Eve. 'I was really sorry when I found out he'd died.'

Eve didn't reply. She never knew what to say when people told her they were sorry.

'I know what it's like to lose someone you love,' Laura went on. 'My dad died five years ago. He's buried here too.'

'You must have been very young?'

'I was fifteen.'

'The same age as my daughter,' Eve said.

'Georgia, isn't it? Oliver used to talk about her a lot. And your son, Matt. He was so proud of them.'

Eve turned away abruptly, pretending to look for Benson, who'd wandered off to look for rabbits among the gravestones.

'I'm sorry,' Laura said. 'I didn't mean to upset you. I'd better go.'

'No, it's fine, really. It's just hard to talk about him sometimes.'

'If it's any help, it does get easier,' Laura said. 'I thought my world had ended when my dad died, but you gradually get used to it. Coming here helps,' she added. 'I try to visit at least once a week. It helps me feel closer to him somehow.' She smiled. 'I even tell him my problems.'

'I talk to Oliver,' Eve said. 'Just stupid stuff, you know? Matt's university applications, Georgia's latest tantrum. I even tell him what was on telly last night.' She had felt silly doing this at first, but she found it comforting. Like talking to him on the phone. 'I probably shouldn't do it,' she said.

'I reckon you should do whatever you need to get through,' Laura said.

They sat down on the bench and chatted for a while. Laura told her she was a medical student at the university.

'Do you live at home?' Eve asked.

'God, no. My mum lives miles away, down south.'

'Really? I just assumed as your dad was buried up here—'

'We used to live around here but she moved away after he died. She couldn't bear the memories.' Laura looked down at the flowers still in her hands. 'Actually she was very ill after he died. A kind of breakdown, the doctors said.'

'I'm sorry.'

'She's getting better now.' She smiled. 'Oliver was so kind to me when she was ill. He was always asking after her, letting me drone on for hours about my problems. No matter how busy he was, he always had time to listen.'

'That sounds like Oliver.'

'He was a very special man.' Laura looked at her watch. 'God, is that the time? I should be going. My flatmate will be wondering where I am.'

As she stood up, Eve noticed her catch her breath with pain.

'What happened to your leg?' she asked.

'I had an accident.' She hobbled over to Oliver's grave and propped the posy against the wooden cross. 'It was nice meeting you, Mrs Robinson.'

'Please, call me Eve.'

'Eve.' Laura smiled. She was a very pretty girl, Eve noticed. 'Maybe we'll meet here again sometime?'

Chapter 8

Perhaps this wasn't such a good idea after all, Anna thought, as she walked into the community advice centre on Monday morning, three weeks after Oliver's funeral. Her mum had been horrified at the idea of her going back to work so soon. But the days and nights had gradually begun to blur into one, and when Anna realised she'd worn the same pair of pyjamas for four days and found herself giving Charlie Coco Pops for his tea she realised the time had come to try to pull herself together.

'You've got to go back sometime,' she told herself aloud in the bathroom mirror.

But now she wondered if this was the right time. Barbara and Neil fell silent as she entered the office. She felt like a baddie walking into a Wild West saloon.

She forced a bright smile as she hung up her coat. 'Good morning.'

'What are you doing here?' Barbara finally found her voice.

'I work here.' She waved at Elliott through the glass partition of his office, went to her desk and switched on her computer, aware of Neil and Barbara watching her every move.

'Shouldn't you be at home?' Barbara asked.

'Doing what?'

'I don't know. You must allow yourself to grieve. Isn't that what they say?' She looked at Neil, who nodded earnestly.

She'd been reading those women's magazine problem pages again. 'How exactly do I do that, Barbara?'

'Not by sitting at a desk listening to other people's problems, that's for sure.'

She's only being kind, Anna told herself. 'As you can see, I'm absolutely fine.' She did a little twirl in front of them. No need to tell them the sheer effort it had taken to step into the shower, let alone put on real clothes. As it was, she was wearing her old tracksuit, the closest thing she could find to her pyjamas. 'Now, would anyone like a cup of tea?'

She heard them discussing her as she stood in the cupboard-sized kitchen at the back of the office, waiting for the kettle to boil.

'I still think it's too soon,' Barbara hissed. 'All I know is if it was my Bernard, I wouldn't even be able to think about going back to work.'

'Maybe it hasn't hit her yet,' Neil whispered.

'Well, I'd rather she wasn't here when it does.'

Anna poured boiling water into the mugs, fighting a feeling of despair. She'd had the idea that if she could go back to work then she might start to feel normal again, and the awful aching void would begin to fade. But it didn't work like that. She could never escape from the way she felt. She dragged it with her like a heavy weight, bringing her down. She would never fit into her old, normal life again. Being touched by death had marked her out as a special case. One to be watched.

Elliott looked up and smiled when she put his tea down in front of him. 'Welcome back,' he said.

'I'm glad someone's pleased to see me.'

'I'm more pleased to see a decent cup of tea.' He picked up his Leeds United mug. 'Between Barbara's Earl Grey and Neil's cat's pee camomile I was beginning to lose hope.' He nodded towards the glass partition. 'How are they treating you?'

'Neil's trying to pretend I don't exist, and Barbara thinks I should be at home rending my garments.'

'Quite right too,' Elliott agreed. 'Do you know, if you were an Igbo tribeswoman you would have shaved your head and rubbed yourself in sand by now? And you'd only be allowed back into the tribe once you'd been beaten around the head with banana leaves by the other widows.'

'I think I could handle that,' Anna said. 'At least then I'd know what to do. At the moment I'm just at a loss. If I sit at home crying it embarrasses people, and if I go out and try to get on with life it embarrasses them even more.'

'Ah, the life of a social leper,' Elliott sighed. 'I remember it well.'

Anna looked at him sharply. In her fog of misery she'd forgotten he'd been through it too. 'Does it ever end?' she asked.

'Not as far as I know. All I can tell you is it does become more bearable eventually, although you probably won't believe that at the moment.'

She didn't. She couldn't imagine a time when she would ever wake up and not get that horrible feeling of having to drag herself through another day. That was the cruellest time, a moment after she opened her eyes and she'd forgotten what had happened. And then it would come back to her in a sickening rush, like losing him all over again.

'Don't forget, I'm here if you want to talk,' Elliott said, bringing her back to reality.

'Thanks.'

But somewhere over the past month she'd lost the knack of talking. Especially small talk. And it seemed Neil and Barbara had, too. The three of them sat in awkward silence, like patients in a dentist's waiting room. Whenever Anna glanced to her right she caught Barbara casting sidelong glances at her as if she wanted to say something but wasn't sure quite how to start.

Finally, as Anna was sifting through her emails, Barbara cracked.

'At least it was quick,' she said.

'Sorry?'

'Your Oliver didn't suffer, did he? I always think that must be worse, seeing someone you love go through a long, lingering illness.'

Worse than seeing them on life support after driving their car into a crash barrier, you mean? 'At least you'd have the chance to say goodbye,' she said.

'My cousin Julia lost her husband to cancer,' Barbara went

on. 'She said no one should ever go through it. Seeing them slip away like that. She reckons when it's her time to go, she'd rather walk in front of a lorry.'

'You're right,' Anna said. 'I really should count my blessings, shouldn't I?'

The phone rang and Barbara answered it, leaving Neil to apologise. 'She means well,' he said. 'You've got to remember it's coming from a good place.'

From her backside, more like, Anna thought.

Fortunately, they were busy for the rest of the morning, which meant Anna was spared any more of Barbara's bereavement counselling. But just before lunch she started again.

'I suppose you've got to think yourself lucky really, haven't you?'

'Oh?'

'I mean, it could be worse, couldn't it? You could be a lonely old pensioner. At least you're still young, aren't you?'

'I suppose so.' Anna's hand closed around her stapler. If Barbara told her she had her whole life ahead of her, she would definitely aim it at her head.

'Just think, in a few years' time you could meet someone else, settle down and be really happy. You have your whole life ahead of—'

'Anna?'

She jumped, dropping the stapler at the sound of Elliott's voice. 'Yes?'

'I'm going out to get a sandwich. Would you like to join me?'

'Well, no, I was planning to work through—' She caught his fixed stare and realised this was an offer she wasn't supposed to refuse. 'I suppose I could do with some fresh air,' she agreed.

'Seems to me I got to you just in time,' he said as they walked up Petergate, dodging the tourists who stood in the middle of the narrow medieval street with their cameras poised, trying to capture the best view of the Minster. 'You looked as if you were about to go for Barbara's jugular.'

'I was.'

'Oh dear, what's she been saying now?'

She told him. Elliott sighed. 'You know she—'

'Means well? So Neil kept telling me, but the last thing I need to hear is that I should be looking for a new boyfriend.'

'Actually, I'm surprised she left it so long before she said that. I was coming out of the church after Karen's funeral when one of my aunts offered to introduce me to a nice girl from her WI.'

'Really?' Anna was shocked. 'What did you say?'

'I said it was very kind of her but since I'd only buried my wife ten minutes ago I thought it might be a bit too soon.'

Petergate opened up on to the broad, sunny square where the imposing Minster stood, its ornate wedding-cake walls gleaming against the blue March sky, casting a benign shadow over the maze of streets around it.

They crossed the road, past the war memorial where the horse-and-carriages plied their trade, and headed towards Starbucks.

'Do you think we could risk a lecture on global consumerism from Neil?' Elliott asked.

'I'd risk anything for a skinny latte.'

'Do you know what I wish?' she said, as they joined the queue, waiting for a gang of Spanish girls to painstakingly count out their coins.

'For world peace? The end of poverty in Africa? Money growing on trees?'

'I wish that undertakers supplied a couple of minders after every funeral. They could walk ahead of you and stop people saying daft things or asking how you are.'

'Death makes people awkward. They don't know what to say, so either they avoid you or they put their foot in it like Barbara.'

'Or they stare at you like they're scared you're going to burst into tears in front of them.'

'And then they're disappointed when you don't.' Elliott reached the head of the queue and handed his roasted-vegetable panini to the girl behind the counter. 'Aren't you having anything?' he asked Anna.

'Just a coffee and a bottle of water. I'll get something to eat later.' Elliott looked concerned but said nothing. At least he didn't try to nag her about eating, like her mother did.

'Do you want me to have a word with Barbara?' he asked as they sat down at a window table.

'What can you say? She's Barbara. She'll always insert her foot every time she opens her mouth. It's part of her charm.'

She took a pill bottle out of her bag and tipped one into her hand.

'What are they?' Elliott asked.

'Happy pills. I went to see the doctor and he gave me some anti-depressants. He reckons I should be feeling much better in a week or so.'

She took one and washed it down with water. Elliott watched her, frowning.

'Are you sure that's a good idea?'

'Feeling better? Well, no, obviously I would have preferred to stagger around in a pit of grief being utterly suicidal, but you can't have everything, can you?' She glanced sidelong at him. 'Why do I get the feeling you don't approve?'

'It's nothing to do with me,' Elliott shrugged. 'I've just always been a bit wary of them, that's all. All they do is mask the pain.'

'So what, as long as they make it bearable?'

'They might make it bearable, but they don't make it go away. Sometimes it's healthier just to go through it and come out the other side.'

'And what if you don't come out the other side? What if the pain just takes you over and you can't function any more? What if you decide it's too bad and you don't want to go on living?'

His dark eyes were gentle behind his glasses. 'It passes,' he said. 'No matter how bad it feels, one day it stops hurting so much. Just give it time.'

'I haven't got time, have I? I've got a three-year-old son to look after. He needs me to be strong for him now, not in a year or two. I can't afford to fall apart.' Her voice shook. 'So if something will help me cope and look after him then I've got to try it. I'm sorry if you don't approve.'

'Like I said, it's nothing to do with me.'

'You're right. It isn't.' She pushed her cup away and stood up. 'I'm going back to the office.'

'But you haven't touched your coffee.'

'I don't feel like it any more.'

She couldn't face going straight back to the office. She headed in the opposite direction, taking the quiet, tree-lined path that curved around the back of the Minster, past the gates of the stonemason's yard. The children of the Minster school were out to play, their bright red jumpers catching the sunlight as they ran around.

She sat on a bench on the grassy area behind the Minster. It was one of her favourite, hidden corners of the city. Sitting there under the shady trees, across the cobbled street from the ancient St William's College and a row of houses belonging to the church – all low doors, crooked sills and mullioned windows – was like going back in time.

But she was in no mood to be charmed by the view today. She was too annoyed. Elliott had touched a nerve. She did feel like a failure, having to go to the doctor and admit she needed help. She would have preferred to be strong like her mum and get through it by gritting her teeth, but in the end she had to admit she needed help. She could feel herself unravelling, and she couldn't allow that to happen, for Charlie's sake.

Maybe pills weren't the answer, but she couldn't go on feeling pole-axed by grief for ever. If drugs stopped her feeling mad and angry and kept the black despair at bay, even for a while, then she was willing to try them.

Eventually she couldn't put it off any longer, and headed back to the office. Elliott looked up behind his glass partition as she came in, but Anna deliberately refused to catch his eye.

'Nice lunch?' Barbara asked, scenting gossip.

'Yes, thanks.'

'I thought you were having lunch with Elliott?'

'I changed my mind. Is this a message for me?' She plucked at the Post-It stuck to her computer monitor. *Call Dennis Watson*, it said. 'Who's Dennis Watson?'

82

'How should I know?' Barbara looked sulky. 'No one tells me anything in this place.'

'It turns out he's Oliver's solicitor,' Anna said. 'I didn't even know he had one.'

She and Rachel jogged along the river path, dodging dog walkers, and cyclists whizzing past them.

'Fat lot of use he was,' Rachel said. 'So Oliver didn't leave any will at all?'

'Apparently not.' She didn't know why everyone seemed so surprised. She'd never known Oliver make a shopping list, let alone a will.

'Of course, you know what this means, don't you? Eve gets everything.'

'Seems that way.'

Rachel swerved around a pair of greyhounds chasing each other on the path. 'What are you going to do about it?'

'What can I do?'

'You've got to fight it, surely?'

'Why should I? I don't really care, anyway.' The only thing she really wanted was Oliver, and no will in the world was going to bring him back.

Rachel stopped, her hands on her hips.

'Anna, she gets everything. Do you think that's what Oliver would have wanted?' A train rattled past them over Scarborough Bridge, and she shouted to make herself heard. 'You've got to see a solicitor about this. For Charlie's sake.'

'I do know something about the law, remember? I know Charlie's entitled to some of Oliver's estate even if he dies without a will.'

'Exactly. And you've got to fight for it.'

How could she explain it took all the fight she had just to get through the day?

'I might not have a very high opinion of Eve Robinson, but I don't believe she'd cheat a three-year-old child. She'll probably sell the business and divide the money.'

'And she might decide to keep it all for herself and her kids,'

Rachel said.

'She can't do that.'

'She could try. Promise me you'll see a solicitor, Anna.'

'I'll think about it. Shall we go?' She sprinted off before Rachel could nag her any more.

'I wonder why Meg didn't turn up,' Anna said, as they chugged up the steps back to Lendal Bridge.

'Probably some domestic crisis. You know Meg.'

Something about the way Rachel said it made Anna suspicious.

'She's not avoiding me, is she?'

'What? God, no, of course she isn't. Why do you say that?'

'I haven't heard from her recently.'

'She's probably been busy.'

On their way back down they passed a gang of teenagers hanging around on the other side of the bridge.

'Nice arse,' one of them sneered as they went past.

'Shame I can't say the same about your face,' Anna snapped. Then she caught sight of one of the girls skulking at the back, and stopped. 'Georgia?'

Anna hardly recognised her under all the make-up, her dark hair scraped back in a pony tail. She wore tight jeans and an ugly pink t-shirt that showed off her thin, pale arms. She must be cold. 'What are you doing here?'

'Nothing,' Georgia shrugged.

'She's doing nowt wrong,' the tallest boy cut in. 'What's it to you, anyway?'

'I wasn't talking to you.' Anna turned back to Georgia. 'Does your mum know you're here?'

'She doesn't care.' Georgia lifted her chin with a touch of defiance.

'I'm sure that's not true.'

'You don't know what she's like.'

'What are you, her bloody social worker or something?' the boy said. Anna ignored him. 'Do you want a lift home?' she asked.

Georgia shook her head.

'I'm staying here.'

'Are you sure?'

'You heard her.'

'Leave it, Andy. I want to stay with my friends,' Georgia insisted to Anna.

'Friends?' She looked at the gang of youths in their hoodies, doing their best to look menacing. Her nana could have taken them on with one hand tied behind her back.

She thought about arguing, then caught sight of Rachel waiting for her in the distance, her trainers tapping impatiently.

'Suit yourself,' she said. 'You've got my number if you need me, haven't you?'

As Anna jogged off, she glanced back and caught Georgia watching her wistfully. Then one of the boys said something and they all laughed.

'Who was that?' Rachel asked, when Anna had caught up with her. 'One of your clients?'

'Georgia.'

'Oliver's daughter? You're kidding?' Rachel looked back over her shoulder. 'What's her mother doing, letting her hang around on street corners with a bunch of yobs?'

'I don't think she knows.' Anna wondered if she should call Eve, then decided against it. She didn't want to tell tales behind Georgia's back. Besides, hadn't her mum always warned her not to judge a book by its cover? Maybe they were nice boys after all.

Chapter 9

'I still can't believe it's mine.'

Eve stood in the middle of Fossgate, gazing across the street. It was early morning and the place had a slightly hungover feeling, as if it hadn't quite roused itself after a heavy night.

'What did I tell you?' Frankie put his arm around her. 'I always knew Oliver would want you to have this place.'

'Except he didn't, did he?' If things had worked out differently, it would probably have been Anna standing here, not her.

In a way, she wished it was.

Frankie was dismissive. 'It's what he would have wanted,' he insisted. 'You of all people understood how much this place meant to him.' He pointed up at the sign over the door, the name 'Oliver's' written in beautifully scripted gold letters. 'Remember how proud he was when that went up? We sank some champagne that day, didn't we?'

'You and Oliver did. I couldn't have any because I was pregnant, remember?'

Frankie chuckled. 'I had a hangover for a week!'

'So did Oliver. He only woke up when I went into labour. All the midwives wondered why he was wearing sunglasses in the delivery room.'

'Eve?' She turned round to see Spike Mullins heading across the street towards her. He was a cool black guy in his thirties who owned the restaurant next to Oliver's, an American-style diner called the Burger Shack. He and Oliver had always kept up a friendly rivalry. 'Long time no see.'

'Hello, Spike.'

'I was hoping I'd run into you sometime. I just wanted to say how sorry I was about Oliver.' His usual broad grin was subdued. 'I know we had our ups and downs, but he was a good guy.'

'Yes, he was.'

Spike nodded back towards the restaurant. 'Any idea what you'll do with this place, now he's gone?'

'We were just talking about that.'

'Well, if you're looking to sell, you know I'd be interested?'

'I—'

'We'll let you know.' Frankie took Eve's arm and guided her firmly across the street, back into the empty restaurant.

'Fucking vulture!' he snapped, slamming the door behind them. 'Look at him, standing there in his Gucci suit. He couldn't wait, could he? Why didn't he just turn up at the funeral with a bloody contract?'

Eve followed him into the kitchen. Simon the commis chef was sautéeing onions for the day's soup while Lizzy the trainee prepped vegetables.

Frankie took the cloth off a bowl of dough he'd left to rise, and tipped it on to the work surface. Eve watched him pound and stretch it between his big hands.

'He's got a point,' she said. 'I probably will have to sell this place sooner or later.'

'You can't do that!'

'It's the law. If someone dies without leaving a will, their estate has to be divided between their next of kin.'

'So it's down to Anna,' he said bitterly.

'Actually, Anna isn't entitled to a penny, unless she makes a claim that she was financially dependent on Oliver. It's Charlie who needs his share.'

'But do you have to sell the restaurant? Can't you buy them out?'

'I can't afford to do that. Anyway, why would I want to?'

'To make sure it doesn't end up in Spike Mullins's hands.' Frankie punched the dough with his fists, making her flinch. 'He was always pestering Oliver with offers, but he always said no.

He reckoned he'd rather burn it down than see this place full of waitresses on roller skates.'

'Maybe Spike won't buy it.'

'Are you joking? You saw the look on his face. I'm surprised he's not in here now, measuring up.'

'I don't have to sell to him.'

'You'll have no say once it gets into the hands of the solicitors, they'll have to get the best price they can. And we all know who that will be.' He looked defeated. 'You wait and see. In a couple of months' time this place will be all neon lights and fries with everything.'

Eve gazed around the kitchen, the busy little heart of the restaurant, with its gleaming steel surfaces and shelves crammed with pans and baking trays. The air was scented with onions, tomatoes and basil.

It was quiet now, but in a few hours it would burst into steamy, clattering, sizzling life as they all ran around, fired up with adrenalin, shouting and falling over each other as they rushed to get the food out.

Oliver had loved that buzz so much. He enjoyed being on the other side of the doors, charming the customers, but he liked the passion of the kitchen even more.

She doubted if there was much passion going on next door. It was probably just a gang of dull-eyed teenagers flipping burgers.

'What choice do I have?' she said.

'You could take this place over and run it yourself.'

Eve stared at him in amazement. 'You *are* joking?'

'Why not? Charlie's only a toddler, he doesn't need his inheritance until he's older. You could look after this place and sell it when the time comes. It'll probably be worth a bit more by then, too.'

'But I don't know the first thing about running a restaurant.'

'How can you say that? You were here when Oliver first opened this place. You helped build the business up.'

'That was a long time ago.'

'So what? You've still got the experience. I bet you could run this place as well as Oliver.'

88

'Believe me, Frankie, I can't. At the moment it's all I can do to look after myself, let alone a business.'

'But there's nothing to it. I do all the cooking and the ordering anyway. All you'd need to do is keep the customers happy.' He nodded towards the swing doors that led out to the restaurant. 'We'd make a good team. It'd be just like the old days.'

He made it sound so simple. But then Frankie could make the most complicated dish seem simple.

She thought about telling him how hard it was for her, how the smallest task seemed like a mountain to climb. How could she even think about running a restaurant when she couldn't manage to make herself a cup of tea in the morning?

'I wouldn't be able to cope,' she said.

Frankie was silent for a moment as he shaped the bread dough into rounds and put them on a baking tray. 'I know it seems tough, but maybe this is just what you need,' he said at last. 'It could be a purpose for you, give you something to think about.'

'I have enough to think about, thanks.'

'I mean something else. Apart from Oliver.'

Eve stared at him. Did he honestly think working in Oliver's restaurant day after day would help her forget him?

'I couldn't do it,' she said.

Frankie sighed. 'It's up to you,' he said heavily. 'But you do know we'll all lose our jobs if you decide to sell up?'

'That's not fair!' Eve protested.

'Maybe, but it's the truth.'

She caught Simon and Lizzy watching her, their faces reproachful.

Oh, Oliver, why did you do this to me? she thought.

Eve sat in her car outside the little terraced house. She hadn't been there since the day Anna moved in with Oliver. That first night, in a moment of utter insanity, Eve had parked her car across the street and sat staring up at the lighted windows for hours, until she'd finally come to her senses and driven home.

There was no driving away this time. She got out of the car and knocked on Anna's door. No reply.

'She won't be home from work yet.' A woman stuck her head out from next door. 'She has to pick up her little boy from her mum's. I don't suppose she'll be too long, if you want to wait.'

'I'll leave her a note.'

Eve was scrabbling in her bag for a pen when Anna's battered Volkswagen came round the corner. 'Looks like she's home early,' the neighbour said. 'That's lucky, isn't it?'

'Isn't it?' Eve watched her unstrapping Charlie from the back seat with a gathering feeling of dread.

Anna came up to the front door, juggling Charlie and a couple of Tesco's carrier bags in her arms. She looked surprisingly to-gether, dressed for work in black trousers and a denim jacket, until Eve spotted she was only wearing one earring.

She stopped when she saw Eve. 'Hello,' she said warily.

Eve took a deep breath. 'Can we talk?'

Anna glanced at her neighbour, who was listening. 'You'd better come in.'

The house was just as she'd imagined it would be, cluttered but cosy. A real little love nest.

'I'll put the TV on for Charlie.' Anna went into the sitting room, picking her way through the toys that littered the floor. Eve stood in the doorway, her eyes fixed on the photos crammed on to the mantelpiece. Happy snaps of Oliver and his new family.

'You don't mind if I get on with his tea?' Without waiting for an answer, Anna headed for the kitchen. It was a narrow galley tacked on to the end of the house, opening out into a little dining room with French doors leading to the postage-stamp garden. The room was untidy, with damp washing draped over the radi-ators, dishes in the sink and coffee rings on the table.

Eve recognised all the signs of a defeated woman, trying and failing to make it through the day. She found it quite heartening that despite Anna's suspiciously bright-eyed appearance, she was struggling too. At least she wasn't the only one.

Anna noticed her looking around. 'Sorry,' she said defensively. 'I wasn't expecting visitors.'

'My place is just the same.' Eve moved a pile of ironing off one of the dining chairs and sat down. 'Some days it's all I can do to get out of bed, let alone get out the hoover.'

Anna's brows rose. She opened her mouth to say something, then closed it again and went back to arranging fish fingers on the grill pan. She moved sluggishly, as if everything was an effort. Eve wondered if she was sleeping as badly as she was.

'I was wondering when you'd turn up,' Anna said.

'You know why I'm here?'

'Oliver's will?'

'Or lack of it.'

Anna smiled briefly. 'So what's going on?'

Eve hesitated, choosing her words carefully. 'I think we would agree that the situation isn't what Oliver would have wanted,' she began. 'We need to sort out his estate and make sure it's divided up properly.'

Relief flickered in Anna's eyes. 'I'm glad you think so.'

'I've come up with an idea that I think will work for all of us. I wanted to discuss it with you.'

Anna sat down across the table from her. 'Go on,' she said.

'I thought I could take over the restaurant and run it myself.' There, she'd said it. There was no going back now. 'I think we'll make more money if we look at the business as a long-term prospect,' she rushed on, mindlessly tidying up crumbs with her finger, unable to meet Anna's eye. 'If we sell it now we'll probably end up with a few thousand each, but if we keep it on, we could have a steady income. And we can still sell in a few years' time.'

She'd practised the speech several times in the car. But even as she said it, she could feel her confidence crumbling. She didn't really believe it. And neither did Anna, judging from her ominous silence.

'Well?' she said, when she'd finished her speech. 'What do you think?'

'I think those fish fingers are burning.'

Eve watched her flipping them over. It was impossible to guess what was going on behind those expressionless brown eyes.

She stuck the pan back under the grill and sat back down. 'Why?' she said.

'Sorry?'

'Why do you want to run Oliver's?'

Eve opened and closed her mouth. 'I don't really know,' she admitted. 'I just feel it's something I should do.'

'For Oliver?'

'Not just for him. If we sell the restaurant Spike Mullins will buy it and everyone will lose their jobs. I don't want that to happen. They were loyal to Oliver and I can't let them down now.'

'And what exactly do you know about running a restaurant?' Anna asked.

She was expecting this. 'I helped Oliver start up the business. I've done the books and worked in the kitchen. I've seen how he runs the place.'

'I've seen a few episodes of *Casualty*, but that doesn't mean I could perform open heart surgery. What do you know about VAT? Or stock ordering?'

'Well—'

'How about hiring and firing staff?'

Eve stiffened. 'I could learn.'

'And while you're learning, the business could be going down the pan.'

'Thanks for being so positive,' Eve muttered.

'I'm just being realistic.' Anna traced a coffee ring with her finger. 'I'm sorry. I don't mean to sound harsh, but I've got Charlie to think about. I have to do what's best for him.'

Eve looked around the little house, with its shabby, junk-shop furniture. It hadn't occurred to her before, but Anna was probably struggling to pay the mortgage on her own. 'Look, if money's a problem, I'm sure we could arrange with the solicitors for you to get some kind of pay-out in the meantime—'

She saw Anna's nostrils flare and knew she'd said the wrong thing.

'I don't need any charity handouts,' she snapped.

'I didn't mean that. I just thought if you were finding it hard to cope—'

'I think you'd better go,' Anna cut her off.

'But we still have to discuss this—'

'We'll discuss it through our lawyers. Now if you'll excuse me, I have to get my son's tea.'

'But—' Eve started to argue, but Anna was already at the cooker, her back to her. 'Fine,' she said, gathering up her bag. 'I had hoped we could discuss this like adults, but that's obviously beyond you.' Anna still didn't react.

Eve stared in frustration at her back. 'I'll see you in court,' she said.

Chapter 10

'What do you mean, she's not available?' Anna stared at the girl behind the reception desk.

'I'm sorry, but Miss Metcalfe has been called away to see another client. She sends her apologies,' she added, as if that would make up for Anna trailing halfway across town in her lunch hour. 'If you'd like to make another appointment—'

'No, I would not.' It had taken enough effort to keep this one. 'I've come to see a solicitor and I'm not leaving here until I do.'

The receptionist looked panicky. 'But everyone's at lunch.'

'Then I'll wait until someone turns up.' She plonked herself down on one of the easy chairs in the waiting area and picked up a copy of *Time* magazine. Out of the corner of her eye she saw the girl pick up the phone. Anna heard snatches of her whispered conversation and guessed it was about her when she heard the words '... a bit mad, actually'.

She flicked open the magazine and stared unseeingly at a headline about the latest oil crisis. It was the first she'd heard about it. But then, the country could have been on the verge of nuclear war for the past four weeks and she wouldn't have known anything. When she slumped in front of the TV every night, she never knew whether she was watching Jeremy Paxman or *Blue Peter*.

She was still trying to make sense of the article when a man walked into the reception area five minutes later. 'What's the problem?' she heard him say. She looked up to see the receptionist pointing her pen accusingly towards her.

The man turned round and Anna felt a lurch of instant recognition.

'Lynch?'

'Anna? Bloody hell!'

He hadn't changed at all. He was still the Danny Lynch who'd almost broken her heart back in college, with his dark blond hair and tall, lean body.

Not to mention a smile that could scorch a woman's underwear at fifty paces.

'Anna Bowman.' He shook his head in disbelief. 'You're the last person I expected to see.'

'You too. I thought you'd be living it up in London by now.' Even when they were together he'd always made it clear he was destined for bigger and better things.

'I was. It's a long story.' He looked her up and down. Anna was suddenly conscious of her lack of make-up and the scruffy coat thrown over her jeans. 'When was the last time we met?'

'About four years ago.' There was a brief, awkward moment as they both remembered the last time they'd seen each other, when Anna had broken the news that she was leaving college because she was pregnant.

He was probably looking at her now and thinking what a lucky escape he'd had.

'So what can I do for you?'

'Would you believe, I need a solicitor?'

He grinned. 'Sorry, stupid question. Why don't you come into my office?'

'You've got an appointment in ten minutes,' the receptionist, who'd been listening in avidly, reminded him.

'I'm sure you can charm them into waiting, can't you, Sonia?' He gave her one of his killer smiles.

'Another of your conquests?' Anna asked as she followed him down the corridor.

'Let's just say I'm working on it.'

She glanced back over her shoulder. Sonia the receptionist was still watching them. 'I don't think you'll have to work too hard.'

'You're probably right. Actually, I'm trying to decide if it's worth the trouble. It might be fun while it lasts, but it could end up being a bit messy.' He opened the door and stood aside to let her in. 'I had a bit of a thing with one of the secretaries in my last place, and I swear she spat in my coffee for a year afterwards.'

'Nice to see you're still treating women with the same respect.'

'You know what they say. A leopard can't change its spots.'

And predators don't come much more lethal than you, Anna thought, as she watched him leaning back in his leather executive chair. Thank God she'd been wise enough not to take their relationship too seriously.

'So how's life treating you?' he asked. 'Not too good presumably, or you wouldn't be needing a lawyer.' He looked her over with lazy appraisal. 'Are you still with that old guy you dumped me for – what was his name?'

'Oliver.' Just saying it brought a treacherous lump to her throat.

'Oliver.' He nodded, remembering. 'What happened to him? I suppose he must be in some nice cosy retirement home by now?'

'He's dead,' Anna said flatly.

There was a short, stunned silence. 'Oh God, I'm so sorry.' Lynch looked appalled. 'When did that happen?'

'A month ago. That's why I'm here. I—'

The phone rang. Lynch ignored it. 'Go on,' he said.

Anna tried, but the clamouring phone distracted her. 'You'd better answer it.'

He snatched it up. 'Yes?' He listened for a moment. 'I thought I told you to keep them talking ... What do you mean, they can't wait?' He muttered an impatient expletive. 'Look, give them a coffee and tell them I'll be there when I'm ready.' He put the phone down. 'You were saying?'

'I'd better go.' Anna stood up.

'Don't.'

'But you've got people waiting.'

'Screw them. Sit down and tell me what all this is about.'

'No, really. It's complicated and I don't want to make you late.'

'But I want to help.' He thought for a moment. 'Let me take you to lunch.'

'I don't eat lunch.' She hardly ate anything these days.

'Don't be difficult. Tell me where you work, and I'll pick you up in an hour.'

'There's no need, really. I can make another appointment with Miss Metcalfe.' It might be easier to talk to a stranger anyway.

'Bugger Miss Metcalfe. You're my client now.' The phone rang again, breaking the silence. 'Tell me where to find you,' he said.

Anna finally gave in and scribbled down the address. 'You can't miss it, it's right next to Bootham Bar. There's usually a dosser sitting outside.'

'Sounds delightful.' Lynch looked down at the piece of paper. 'I'll be there in an hour.'

An hour and fifteen minutes later, he still hadn't turned up. Anna was disappointed but hardly surprised. Lynch had never been one for keeping appointments, or promises. He'd probably forgotten about her, she thought. Either that or he'd decided he didn't want to spend his lunch hour listening to her sob story after all.

She was in the back office talking a client through his mortgage arrears and trying to explain why ignoring letters from the building society wouldn't actually make them go away, when Elliott stuck his head round the door. 'There's someone to see you. Says he's your lawyer.'

'Lynch?'

'He didn't give his name. But from the snappy suit and the Porsche parked outside I'm guessing he hasn't come for advice on housing benefits. Would you like me to take over here while you see him?'

Anna craned her neck and caught a glimpse of Lynch's fair head as he stood studying a poster on domestic violence. 'No, tell him to wait. It'll do him good.'

She didn't expect him to still be there when she finally finished with her client twenty minutes later. But there he was, lounging in her chair, chatting away to Barbara like they were old friends.

'Sorry to keep you,' she said.

'No problem. Barbara's been entertaining me, haven't you, Babs?'

'I don't know about that.' Barbara giggled and knocked over a pen-tidy in her confusion.

'I wasn't sure you'd still be here,' Anna said.

'I promised to take you to lunch, and here I am.' He held up a brown paper bag. 'I brought sandwiches.'

'I told you I don't eat lunch. Besides, I've already taken my break. I came to see you, remember?'

'So? I'm sure your boss will let you have half an hour off, if you ask him nicely.'

'We can hold the fort,' Barbara offered.

'Babs, you're an angel,' Lynch said.

She'd certainly had some kind of celestial transformation, Anna thought. Normally she got very tight-lipped when anyone asked her to cover.

'Half an hour,' she said firmly. 'I'll just clear it with Elliott.'

'What kind of a place is that?' Lynch wanted to know, as they stepped into spring sunshine. The grassy banks of the city walls were bright with daffodils.

'It's a community advice centre,' Anna told him. 'We tell people their rights, fill in forms for them, that kind of thing.'

Lynch looked perplexed. 'And you do that for free?'

'Of course.' Anna laughed at his bemused expression. 'Not everyone can afford a hot-shot lawyer like you, you know.'

'Obviously not.' He stepped over the tramp slouched under the old city gateway. 'So what's in it for you?'

'We get to help people.' She rooted in her pocket and dropped a pound coin into the man's paper cup.

'And that's it?'

'Well, there is the company BMW and the free private health insurance ... I'm joking,' she said, seeing his face change. 'Actually, we barely get paid. We have to rely on local funding, and sometimes there isn't enough cash to go round.'

'Why do you do it?'

'I like helping people,' she shrugged. 'That's why I wanted to become a lawyer in the first place.'

'Really? I only wanted to make money.'

Anna looked him up and down. 'It certainly looks like you've done that.'

'I'm not doing too badly.'

They sat on a bench in bustling St Helen's Square, facing the Georgian Mansion House with its elegant red and white façade. On the other side of the square, the usual queue of tourists waiting to get into Betty's famous tearoom snaked their way past the art deco windows.

'Are you sure you wouldn't rather go somewhere else?' Lynch asked, pulling his overcoat around him. 'There's a nice-looking pub over there.'

'I'm fine, thanks.'

'I'm glad someone is.' He sunk his chin into his collar.

'Southern softie,' Anna teased him. 'The sun's shining.'

'I don't know about that, but I'm bloody cold.' He handed her a sandwich. 'Cheese and pickle, your favourite. See? I remembered.'

'Thanks.' Actually, she couldn't stand pickle, but Lynch looked so pleased with himself she didn't have the heart to tell him. It didn't matter, anyway. She only ate out of habit these days.

She nibbled the crust off her sandwich. 'What brought you to York?'

'Work. I was head-hunted by this firm when I was in London.'

'Sounds very impressive.'

'I'm very good.'

'And so modest with it.'

'I thought I'd stand a better chance of securing a partnership up here than I would in London. Big fish in a little pond and all that.'

'What kind of work do you do?'

'A bit of everything. Personal injury, mostly.'

'You're an ambulance chaser?'

'Don't knock it. At least I'm chasing them in my Porsche.'

They watched a busker setting up on the corner of Coney Street, carefully unpacking his violin and spreading out his cloth around his feet.

'Why do you need a solicitor?' Lynch asked.

She told him about Oliver not leaving a will, and her last meeting with Eve. She tried to stay calm, but she could feel rage building up inside her at the memory. She could still see Eve sitting at the table, looking down her nose at Anna's home, offering her handouts as if she was some kind of charity case. It was obvious how much she was enjoying her new-found power.

Lynch listened carefully. 'I can see her point,' he said when she'd finished. 'Keeping the restaurant running could be a good investment in the long term.'

'Not when she's finished with it.' Anna pulled a piece of crust off her sandwich and threw it to the pigeons gathering around her feet. 'She doesn't know the first thing about running a business. She couldn't even change a light bulb without running to Oliver for help. I'm worried she'll run the place into the ground and then Charlie will end up with nothing.'

'And that's the only thing bothering you?' Lynch asked.

Anna was instantly defensive. 'I don't know what you mean.'

'It must be difficult, seeing her end up with everything when you've been living with the guy for four years. Are you sure you're not just doing this to spite her?'

'Maybe you should ask her why she's doing it,' Anna fired back. 'It's got nothing to do with long-term investments. That restaurant is the only thing she's got left of Oliver, and she doesn't want to let it go. Just like she never wanted to let go of him when he was alive.'

'And you don't mind about letting him go?'

'Of course I mind! But that restaurant is just bricks, it isn't Oliver. Hanging on to it won't bring him back.' She stared straight ahead of her, daring the tears to come. 'I have to think about the future, and what's best for our son. We can't live on memories.'

'Of course not.' He regarded her thoughtfully. 'I must say, you seem to be handling it really well. You're so – together.'

You wouldn't say that if you could see inside my head, she thought.

'That'll be the medication,' she said. It had certainly stopped her wanting to cry, but it had stopped her wanting to laugh, too.

Lynch smiled uncertainly. Anna was about to tell him she was serious, then thought better of it.

'Are you going to eat that, or feed it all to the pigeons?' he pointed at her sandwich, which she was mindlessly shredding.

'I'm not really hungry.'

Lynch tutted. 'When was the last time you ate?'

'This morning.' Almost. A cup of coffee and a cigarette practically counted as food these days. 'What do you think?'

'I think the pigeons have had more than enough.' He helped himself to the untouched half of her sandwich, and took a bite. 'I can certainly see you've got a problem,' he said. 'Do you want me to look into it for you?'

Anna hesitated. 'Are you very expensive?'

'Very.' He smiled. 'But I offer reduced rates for old friends.'

'In that case, yes please.' She hadn't been too sure at first, but now she realised how much she needed someone like him on her side.

As he walked her back to the office, he said, 'The first thing to do is talk to Oliver's solicitor, see what all this is about. Then I'll set up a meeting with his accountant, try to put some kind of value on the business. That way we can see what your share of the estate might be worth.'

'I'll give you all the details I have.'

'But I have to warn you, you should try to settle this as quickly as possible. Much as I love a good fight, a legal battle could drag on for ever and erode away Oliver's estate. Are you sure you can't reach some kind of compromise?'

Anna thought about Eve's smug face. 'I doubt it.'

'I'd think about it very carefully, if I were you,' Lynch advised, 'otherwise you might both find yourselves with nothing.'

Chapter 11

'What did you think?'

It was mid-afternoon, and Eve and Matt were driving home after visiting a university campus. The day's drizzle had given way to heavy rain that rattled against the windscreen like handfuls of gravel.

Matt gazed at the rivulets of water running down the window. 'S'all right, I suppose.'

'The accommodation seemed nice, didn't it?' She made a supreme effort to sound enthusiastic. 'And it's in a good location, not far from the city centre. Close to the station, too. You wouldn't have too far to bring your dirty washing home every weekend!'

'Hmm.'

She glanced at his expressionless face. 'You could show a bit more interest. I thought you wanted to go there?'

'I might not get in.'

'Of course you will. They've already made you a great offer and your teachers reckon you'll easily get those grades.'

'I'm not sure it's what I want any more.'

'Ah.' Silence followed, broken only by the heavy patter of rain and the rhythmic squeak of the windscreen wipers.

Maybe she was expecting too much of Matt. He'd just lost his father. If Oliver's death had hit her hard, what would it have done to his son?

She focused on the back of the dark green van in front of her, just visible through the bleary windscreen.

'I suppose it's all too much to think about at the moment,' she said. 'If you want to put off your place for a year, I'm sure they'll understand—'

'Will you drop me off at Steve's?' he interrupted her. 'We've got the Battle of the Bands coming up, we need to rehearse.'

'Shouldn't we talk about college?'

'Later, okay?'

She suppressed a sigh. 'Okay.'

He didn't say another word to her until they reached his friend's house twenty minutes later.

At least he was getting out at last, she thought as she watched him ambling up to the front door, his shoulders hunched against the rain. She was beginning to worry that he spent so much time locked in his room.

Poor Matt. She'd assumed he was coping because he was so easy-going; not like his sister who could turn a broken nail into a full Greek tragedy. She never knew what was going on in her son's head, but he was obviously a lot more troubled than he let on.

She'd meant to go straight home, but Georgia was still at school and she couldn't face going back to an empty house, so she called in at Oliver's. Frankie had asked her to go in and sign some cheques, but she'd been avoiding it for a couple of days.

Lizzy was on her own in the kitchen, stacking the dishwasher after the lunchtime service.

'Where is everyone?' Eve asked.

'Simon's gone home and Frankie's out there –' she nodded towards the back door '– talking to someone.'

Eve peered through the window into the yard, where Frankie was having an animated conversation with two men in black leather coats.

'Who are they?'

'Don't know,' Lizzy shrugged, 'but they've been out there in the rain for half an hour.'

Two minutes later Frankie returned, shaking water off his hat and muttering under his breath.

He broke into a smile when he saw Eve. 'Hello there. This is a nice surprise.'

'You asked me to come in. To sign some cheques?'

'Oh, right. Yes, of course. I've got the invoices in the office.'

'The office' was little more than a cubby hole, a former store-room leading from the office. There was barely room for two of them inside.

'Who were those men?' Eve asked, as Frankie squeezed his way in behind the desk.

'Suppliers.'

'What did they want?'

'Money, what else?' He unlocked the desk drawer and took out the cheque book and a stack of papers.

'They didn't look very friendly.'

'They're okay. I just had to explain that things were taking a bit longer now there's no one around to pay the bills on time.' He sorted through the papers until he found what he was looking for. 'Here we go. I've already written out the cheques, so all you have to do is put your name on them.'

He edged out from behind the desk so Eve could sit down.

'It would be a lot easier if you could just pay them yourself,' she said, taking out a pen.

'Oh no, I couldn't do that. Oliver always dealt with the money side, not me.'

'Oliver isn't here, is he? And it just holds everything up if you have to wait for me. Why don't I get on to the bank and have you made an authorised signatory?'

'Are you sure?' Frankie lowered his voice so Lizzy wouldn't hear. 'I thought with my record—'

'That was a long time ago. Anyway, you know I trust you completely.'

'Thanks. That means a lot to me.' He stood over her as she wrote out the cheques. 'I suppose this means you've decided not to run the place, then?'

Eve stifled a sigh. She'd been dreading this. 'I don't think I can, Frankie.'

'You could do it with your eyes closed, and you know it.' He paused. 'I bet Oliver would have wanted you to try.'

'Anna doesn't.' She still felt bruised from their encounter the previous week.

Frankie gave a dismissive snort. 'What's it got to do with her, anyway?'

'That depends on how good a lawyer she's got.'

'Oliver wouldn't have wanted to see you two fighting. He knew he could trust you to look after this place, and see Anna right too.'

'Try telling *her* that.' She'd done her best to convince her, now she didn't have enough fight left to argue. If Anna was determined to sell up, then so be it. Perhaps it was for the best after all.

'I reckon this place could be good therapy for you,' Frankie said. 'It might help take your mind off what's happened. Give you a purpose in life, like?'

'I've already got a purpose in life. Looking after my family.' And she was making a bad enough job of that, without taking on the extra responsibility of the business too.

'Promise me you'll think about it again, at least?' Frankie begged.

Eve was about to argue, then gave up. 'I'll think about it all you like,' she said, 'but I still won't change my mind.'

'We'll see.' Frankie beamed. 'In the meantime, while you're thinking about it, maybe you'd like to look through this morning's post?'

Eve took the pile of letters reluctantly. 'More bills?'

'Probably. Anyway, I've got a lemon meringue pie to make, so I'll leave you to it. Have fun, won't you?'

She didn't exactly have fun, but sorting through the post did keep her occupied for a few minutes. Until she opened the last letter.

She went back to the kitchen, where Frankie was whisking up meringue in the industrial-sized mixer.

She waved the letter at him to get his attention. 'Do you know anything about this?' she shouted over the drone of the mixer.

He switched it off. 'About what?'

She handed him the letter and he read through it. 'Looks like just another bill to me,' he said, handing it back to her.

'It's from a loan company. Why would Oliver borrow money from people like this?'

Frankie checked the consistency of his meringue and gave the mixer another blast. 'Maybe he needed the cash to keep this place going?'

'But I thought business was okay?' That was the impression Oliver had always given her.

'There's only one way to find out. Check the books.'

'Oh no, I couldn't do that.' She shrank away from the idea.

'It's the only way you're going to find out what's going on.'

She didn't want to find out. If there was a problem, she didn't want to know about it. All she wanted to do was run away.

Frankie must have read the reluctance on her face. 'Even if you go ahead and sell this place, you're still going to need to know what it's worth,' he said.

'I suppose so.' She looked down at the bill in her hand. 'Are you sure Oliver didn't mention anything to you about this?'

'Finance was his department. He didn't tell me how to cook, and I didn't tell him how to run the business.'

'Adam's here,' Lizzy interrupted them, looking through the window. A moment later she added, 'All right if I take a five-minute break, chef?'

'Gone to put her lippy on,' Frankie commented wryly as she scuttled off to the loo. 'Got a bit of a crush on him, I reckon. Her and half the waitresses.'

'Who, Adam?'

Eve watched through the window as Adam unloaded boxes from the back of his battered old transit van. Now she looked at him, she supposed he was attractive in a healthy, outdoorsy kind of way.

'I blame Lady Chatterley,' Frankie said. 'They've all got fantasies about being ravished among the radishes.'

'Or bonked in the broccoli.'

'And God knows what in the fennel.'

They were still laughing when Adam shouldered his way in

through the back door, his arms full of boxes. He looked from one to the other, bemused. 'Have I missed something?'

'We were just talking about the effect you have on women,' Eve said.

Adam blushed deeply. 'Here's your delivery,' he mumbled, putting the boxes down on the floor. 'The salad onions weren't quite ready so I'll drop them in on Thursday, if that's okay?'

'Let's see what you've got.'

While Frankie rummaged through the produce, Adam said to Eve, 'I didn't expect to see you here.'

'You'll be seeing a lot more of her from now on,' Frankie said, before she could reply. 'She's thinking of running the place. Are you sure these are fresh?' He held up a bunch of carrots.

'I picked them myself three hours ago.' He turned back to Eve. 'Is this true?'

'Nothing's been decided yet.'

Lizzy came hurtling back into the kitchen, her hair newly fluffed under her white cap. She screeched to a halt when she saw Adam, then casually sauntered back to her station, but Adam was too preoccupied to notice. 'Are you sure that's a good idea?' he asked Eve.

'Don't you think I can do it?'

'I didn't say that. I'm just wondering why you'd want to.'

'She's doing it for Oliver,' Frankie butted in. 'It's what he would have wanted.'

'Ah.' Adam nodded, as if that explained everything. 'For Oliver. I see.'

Eve followed him out to the van. 'Take no notice of Frankie. I still haven't made up my mind to do it.'

'He sounded pretty convinced.' He threw open the van doors and began stacking the empty boxes inside.

'He's just worried they're all going to lose their jobs. And he's got some daft idea about me carrying on Oliver's dream,' she smiled.

Adam regarded her seriously. 'And is that what you want to do?'

'I know being here helps take my mind off everything else,

107

and I suppose I do feel closer to him.' Adam said nothing. 'Why do I get the impression you don't approve?'

'It's nothing to do with me. I just hope you know what you're doing.'

Eve watched him drive away, feeling troubled. She thought Adam of all people would understand.

She went back inside, where Frankie was still unpacking the vegetables.

'What's he been saying to you?' he demanded.

'Not much.' That was what really bothered her. She hadn't realised how much his approval meant to her.

'You don't want to take any notice of him,' Frankie said. 'If you ask me, he's just miffed. I expect he was hoping to get his hands on some of Oliver's money once this place was sold.'

Eve was shocked. 'Adam wouldn't make a claim.'

'Don't you believe it,' Frankie said grimly. 'That business of his can't make a fortune. I daresay he wouldn't say no to a bit of extra cash.'

Frankie's words still haunted her when she visited Oliver's grave on the way home. Surely he couldn't be right about Adam, could he? It was all so confusing. The more she found out, the more out of her depth she felt. She'd come to the churchyard hoping for some inspiration. But it seemed for once Oliver wasn't offering his support. She'd never felt so alone.

The rain had settled to a steady drizzle as she crouched beside his grave under her umbrella, mindlessly removing the fading flowers. Talk to me, she pleaded silently. Tell me what I should do.

'Hi. Remember me?' She turned round. There was Laura, huddled in a long black coat, her dark hair dripping with rain.

'Hello there.' Eve dredged up a smile. 'You're very wet.'

'I've been here a while. I had a lot of thinking to do.'

You and me both, she thought. 'Did it help?'

'Not really.'

'I'm sorry about that.'

Eve turned back to rearranging Oliver's flowers and waited for her to leave, but Laura stood over her, watching her. In the end she gave up and headed back to her car. Laura fell into step beside her.

'My flatmate's moved out,' she said. 'I'll have to find someone else to share or I'll lose the flat. I can't afford the rent on my own.'

'Ah.'

'I don't suppose you've got any work going at the restaurant? I could really use the extra cash at the moment. It would buy me some time to find another flatmate.'

'Well, I don't really—'

'Please?' Laura begged. 'I've got loads of experience, and I don't mind what shifts I work. It would mean so much to me.'

'I'm not really involved with the hiring and firing.'

'But you could give me a job, couldn't you? You own the place.'

Eve saw the desperate look in her big dark eyes. 'Come and see me tomorrow,' she sighed. 'I'm sure we can sort something out.'

They reached her car. 'Can I give you a lift?' Eve offered.

'I've got my bike.' Laura hitched her bag on to her shoulder. 'Thanks again for giving me a job. I knew you'd help me out.'

Eve watched her running up the street through the rain to where she'd left her bicycle chained to the railings.

She'd just hired her first member of staff. It looked as if she was running Oliver's whether she liked it or not.

Georgia was checking her mobile-phone messages when Eve got home later.

'Matt rang,' she said, not looking up. 'He says he'll sleep over at Steve's, if that's all right with you.'

'I suppose it'll have to be.' She wondered if he was trying to avoid their little chat about his future.

She put the carrier bag containing the restaurant books on the kitchen table. Georgia looked up from her phone.

'What's that?'

'The accounts from your dad's restaurant.'

'Why have you got them?'

'I thought I'd take a look at them.'

'You?'

'Anything wrong with that?'

Georgia shook her head, amused. 'I just didn't think you'd understand them.'

'Thanks for the vote of confidence.' Eve went to the freezer and peered inside. 'What would you like for supper? Or shall we get a takeaway?'

'I'm going out.'

'Where are you going?'

'I'm meeting some friends.'

'Anyone I know?'

Georgia sent her a withering look. 'I doubt it.' Her phone bleeped, announcing a text message. She read it quickly. 'Got to go. Bye.'

'What time will you—' But she was already gone. Eve sat down in the empty kitchen and looked around her. Even Benson couldn't be bothered to take any notice of her, snoozing in his basket by the back door.

She was losing her grip on her family, and it frightened her. Georgia was mixing with a new group of friends she knew nothing about, staying out late and getting up to heaven knows what. And Matt seemed to be on a totally different planet these days.

She'd been living on her own for years, but she'd never felt this lonely. Before, she'd always had Oliver at the end of the phone, ready to offer support. Now her safety net had gone. She had to face it all by herself, and it was all too scary.

She started to make supper for herself, then gave up and shoved a slice of bread into the toaster instead. What was the point of going to all that trouble? Especially when she wasn't remotely hungry.

Settling herself down at the table, Eve got out the accounts. She flicked through them, her chin in her hands, staring at the rows of figures until they jumbled in front of her eyes.

Georgia was right, they meant nothing to her.

She stuffed them back in the bag, despairing. There was no way she could do this. She knew nothing about the restaurant business. She'd only end up groping around in the dark, making all kinds of mistakes and ruining everything.

Her toast popped up and she threw it in the bin, her appetite gone, just as the phone rang.

It was Jan. 'How are you?'

'You don't really want to know.'

'Oh dear, that bad?'

'Let's just say it hasn't been a very good day.'

'I know what you need.'

'Several Valium, a large gin and a lie-down?'

Jan laughed. 'I was thinking more of a night out. We've hardly seen you since Oliver died.'

'Yes, well, it has rather curtailed my non-stop party lifestyle.' Eve scuffed at a small brown stain on the carpet and discovered it was a cigarette burn. How the hell had that got there?

'Why don't you come round for dinner?'

'When? Now?'

'If you like, although it's only sausage and Alphabetti Spaghetti for me and the kids,' she laughed. 'No, I was thinking about next week — say, Friday?'

'It's very sweet of you, but I'm not exactly great company at the moment.'

'No one's expecting you to be the life and soul of the party, Eve. We know what you've been through. Come on, it'll do you good.' She had her best primary school teacher's voice on, as if she was persuading a reluctant pupil to try broccoli.

'I suppose it would give me an excuse to wash my hair and iron some clothes.' Eve examined the split ends on a lank lock of hair. She'd let herself go in a spectacular fashion recently.

'Exactly. Get your glad rags on and come and see us.'

Eve put the phone down, knowing she had no intention of going. But she also knew Jan wouldn't shut up until she'd agreed to come, and she couldn't face her yakking on for hours.

Anyway, it was over a week away. Plenty of time to dream up an excuse.

Chapter 12

'Nana's dead,' Charlie greeted Anna cheerfully when she arrived to pick him up from her mother's on Friday afternoon.

'What?'

'She isn't dead, sweetheart. I told you, she's just poorly.' Her mother appeared from the kitchen, wiping her hands on a tea towel.

'Sorry, he's got a bit of an obsession with people dying at the moment,' Anna said.

'Hardly surprising, I suppose.' Jackie ruffled his hair.

'What's wrong with Nana?'

'She's got a chest infection. She called me last night, said she couldn't breathe. Keith went over and picked her up. She's upstairs now.'

'Shall I go up and see her?'

'I think she's asleep at the moment. The doctor's been out and given her a prescription for antibiotics. Which reminds me, I must get to Boots to pick them up before they close.'

'I could go,' Anna offered.

'Would you? That would be great. I wouldn't ask but I've got to finish the community newsletter.'

'Is Nana going to die like Daddy?' Charlie asked, as she parked the car in Bootham Row ten minutes later.

'I don't think so, sweetheart.'

'Are you going to die?'

'Not for a long time.'

'When I'm eight?'

'Even older than that. Not until you're all grown up.'

He considered it for a moment. 'Why didn't Daddy wait until I was grown up?'

Good question. 'People can't help when they die, Charlie. They don't know when it's going to happen.'

In Boots, she handed the prescription to the chemist and was browsing through the vitamin-pill display when Charlie suddenly called out, 'Look! Corey!'

She turned round. There was Meg, looking even more harassed than usual, waiting at the pharmacy counter. She was keeping the baby's buggy steady with one hand while two of her children strained on the other like a brace of boisterous Labradors.

'Meg?'

She looked round furtively, like a shoplifter who'd just been collared by a store detective. 'Oh, Anna. Hi.'

'Long time no see.'

'Yes, it is, isn't it? I'd better take a bottle of Calpol, too,' she said to the man behind the counter. 'I can't remember if we've run out or not.'

'Who's sick this time?'

'Philippa's got another ear infection.'

'Nasty.' Anna watched her dig in her bag for her purse, pulled sideways by her children. 'You haven't been out with us for a run in a while.'

'Yes, well, I've been up to my eyes in it. You know what the school holidays are like. Being stuck at home with four kids doesn't leave a lot of free time.'

'You should get Dave to look after them, give you a break.'

'Maybe.' The pharmacist returned with Meg's prescription and she snatched the white paper bag out of his hand. 'Anyway, I'd better get going. Philippa will be screaming the house down.'

'We must meet up soon,' Anna said.

'Yes, that would be great.' She manhandled the buggy in a hurried arc, narrowly missing an old woman's ankles.

'I'll give you a call—' Anna started to say, but Meg was already halfway across the shop, the buggy dragged along by her children like a husky sled.

Anna stared after her. Was she being paranoid, or was Meg desperate to get away? Usually she was only too happy to chat, but this time she couldn't escape fast enough.

She searched her mind, trying to think what she might have done to upset her. Surely she wasn't avoiding her because of Oliver? Anna was aware that some people, mostly neighbours she didn't know well, who now crossed the street rather than have to speak to her, but she'd never have imagined Meg would be one of them.

She took the prescription back to her mum's, went up to see her nana, then packed Charlie into the car and headed for home.

She didn't recognise the silver Porsche parked outside her house at first, until she saw Lynch getting out of it.

'I've been trying to call you,' he said. He looked like an off-duty male model in faded jeans, a black cashmere sweater and well-cut soft leather jacket. 'We need to talk.'

'I didn't realise you did house calls? I hope you don't charge extra,' she joked feebly. But something in his expression made her wary.

'What I have to say can't wait,' he said.

Anna stared at the papers spread out on the kitchen table in front of her. 'So let me get this straight. You're telling me the business isn't actually worth anything?'

'With all the loans on it, it's worth less than nothing.'

'But how can that be? Oliver always said they were doing well.'

'Maybe they were. But these loan repayments would have taken up most of what they made. Looking at these figures, I reckon he probably had to take out more loans just to stay afloat.'

Anna picked up a piece of paper, scanned the jumble of figures and put it down again. Lynch had spent the last half-hour going over it all in painstaking detail, but even he couldn't explain why it had happened. It made no sense to her. Apparently Oliver had taken out several big loans against the business.

'How did the bank let him get into this mess? Surely they

shouldn't have lent him so much money if they knew he couldn't pay it back?'

'Not all the loans came from the bank. Some of the later ones came from other companies.'

Anna looked up sharply. 'What kind of companies?'

'Mostly legit. But obviously, the interest rates reflect the amount of risk involved.'

'I know all about that.' She'd dealt with enough desperate clients at the advice centre, people who'd been refused loans by the bank and had turned to a loan company. They were seduced by the advertising, by the comforting promise to 'consolidate' their outstanding debts, no awkward questions asked. Then, five years later, they realised they still owed much more than they'd borrowed in the first place, with no chance of ever paying it back.

But never in a million years had she imagined Oliver would ever be that gullible. She reached for the brandy Lynch had insisted on pouring her before they started. At the time she'd thought he was over-reacting, but now she needed it.

'Why didn't he tell me?' she said.

'He probably didn't want to worry you.'

'I'm worried now!'

'I'm sure he was, too.'

The thought sobered her. Poor Oliver, what kind of stress must he have been under, knowing his business was teetering on the brink of collapse? And yet he never gave any sign he was in trouble.

Was that what killed him? She could imagine his heart giving out under the strain of all those money worries, all those secrets.

'Why didn't I realise?' she whispered.

'It wasn't your fault,' Lynch said.

'It's my fault he couldn't confide in me. We loved each other, we were supposed to share everything.'

'He probably felt ashamed.'

'All the more reason why he should have been able to turn to me.' And yet he couldn't. What did that say about her, about their relationship?

Lynch tried to put his hand over hers but she drew it away. She didn't deserve any comfort.

'So Eve probably wouldn't be able to sell anyway?' she said, changing the subject.

'She wouldn't get much for it,' Lynch agreed.

'What about the building? That must be worth something, surely?'

'It might if he owned it, but it's leasehold, unfortunately. According to the paperwork, Oliver recently took out another large loan to pay for the new lease. I've got it here somewhere ...'

Anna watched him sifting through the papers. 'It's okay, you don't have to show me. I believe you.' After what she'd just heard, she was ready to believe anything.

Lynch looked across the table at her. He'd been very business-like and matter-of-fact as he went through all the figures. Now his blue-green eyes were full of sympathy. 'I'm sorry, Anna. I hate to be the bearer of bad news.'

'It's not your fault. I'm glad you told me.' She took a deep breath. 'Look, it's not the end of the world. So there's nothing for Charlie to inherit – so what? We'll be all right, as long as I can keep a roof over our heads—' She trailed off, seeing Lynch's face. 'What?'

'There's something I still haven't told you.'

Warning prickles went up her spine. 'Whatever it is, it can't be worse than what I already know.'

He said nothing. Reaching into his briefcase, he drew out a sheet of paper. Anna recognised yet another loan-company logo on the headed notepaper. 'When Oliver took out the loans, he had to put something up as security. In case the loan couldn't be paid off.'

Anna nodded. 'I know that. I deal with people in debt every day, remember?'

'Obviously he couldn't take any more loans out against the business because that was already so in debt.'

'So what did he use as security?' It dawned on her before she'd finished the sentence. 'Oh no,' she whispered. 'He couldn't. Not this house. Not without my consent.'

'Was it in both your names?'

She shook her head. 'Oliver bought it before I moved in with him. We'd always meant to put my name on the deeds, but we never got round to it.'

She took a gulp of her brandy, hardly noticing as it burned a fiery trail down her throat. 'He wouldn't do it,' she said, 'he'd never risk our home.'

'Maybe he didn't feel he *was* risking it,' Lynch reasoned. 'He probably reckoned he could turn a corner, pay off the loans and you'd never be in danger.'

Yes, that sounded like Oliver. Always expecting the best, leaving everyone else to deal with the grim realities of life.

She was suddenly filled with bitterness and anger towards him. She wanted to rage and scream and howl at him for his blind selfishness and arrogance. Why hadn't he talked to her, warned her? Why the hell had he left her like this?

Lynch seemed to read her thoughts. 'He never expected to die, Anna.'

She glanced at Charlie, sitting on the floor constructing a tower out of Lego bricks. She couldn't let herself cry in front of him. She had to be strong for his sake.

She braced herself. 'So what you're saying is the business is worth nothing, and if we do by some miracle manage to find someone idiot enough to buy it, the money we make won't be enough to repay the outstanding loans, so I'll probably lose my home?'

Lynch winced. 'That's pretty much it, I'm afraid. I'm so sorry.'

But she didn't want his sympathy. Much as she felt like sobbing in a heap, she was determined to stay practical.

'So what would you advise?'

'You'd have to talk to an accountant about that. But the way I see it, your only real chance is to keep the restaurant going. At least if there's money coming in you can meet the loan repayments and keep a roof over your head. And if business is as good as you say, you might even be able to pay them off.'

He didn't sound too hopeful, Anna noticed. He was probably

just being kind because he didn't want her to break down in front of him.

Charlie came over, his wobbly Lego tower in one hand, a chocolate Hobnob in the other. Anna took a moment to admire his handiwork, her mind racing as she tried to work out what her next move should be.

'Of course, a lot depends on his ex,' Lynch went on, discreetly brushing Charlie's biscuit crumbs from his jeans. 'It's lucky for you she wants to keep the restaurant going. You're really going to need her on your side.'

'She doesn't stand to make anything either if she sells the business,' Anna pointed out.

'Maybe not, but she won't end up having her house repossessed.' He put the papers back in his briefcase and snapped it shut. 'If I were you, I'd start being very nice to Eve Robinson because, right now, she's all that stands between you and total financial meltdown.'

Chapter 13

APRIL

It was Monday morning, the first day after the Easter holidays, and Eve was going back to school.

It was Matt's idea. 'Don't you think it's time you did something?' he'd suggested gently, when he came home to find Eve huddled in her dressing gown, watching *Deal or No Deal* on TV. 'All this sitting around doing nothing isn't good for you.'

Eve was nonplussed. 'I am doing something,' she said. 'I'm—' She stopped. She wasn't really sure how she filled her days, but they still slipped by somehow. Was it really six weeks since Oliver died?

Going back to work had seemed like a good idea when she'd called the headteacher. It had still seemed like a good idea last night, when she forced herself to iron something to wear.

It was only in the early hours of the morning that she woke up in a complete panic, thinking she couldn't do it. She lay staring at the ceiling, thinking of every nightmare scenario. What if she'd forgotten all their names? What if she'd forgotten how to teach? She had a mental picture of herself standing in the middle of the classroom, her mouth opening and closing like a stranded fish while a bunch of Year Ones ran amok around her.

She looked at the bedside clock. The red letters glowed: four twenty-four. She could either lie here for another three hours, thinking herself into madness, or she could get up and do something.

She decided to make a cake.

Why she had the sudden urge to bake, she didn't know. Up

until then beans on toast had been about as much as she could manage, but standing in the moonlit kitchen, weighing out flour, sugar and butter was surprisingly calming.

Benson watched her from his basket by the door. Even he could tell there was something not quite right with the picture of a woman in her pyjamas, beating eggs at nearly five in the morning.

Georgia was just as taken aback when she stumbled sleepily into the kitchen two hours later to find Eve perfecting the peaks in her buttercream icing with the flat side of a knife.

She eyed the knife warily. 'What are you doing?'

'Icing this cake. What does it look like?' Eve stood back to admire her handiwork. 'Do you think I should stick some walnuts on it, or leave it as it is?'

Georgia said nothing, but when Eve went upstairs to get dressed she heard her complaining to her brother, 'We've got no bread in the house and she's making a bloody cake. I told you she was mad.'

In her bedroom, Eve stood in her underwear, staring at her carefully arranged clothes hanging up on the wardrobe door. She'd worn the beige wool trousers and cream t-shirt many times for work but they didn't look like hers any more. They belonged to another Eve, another life.

'Now, are you sure you're all right about this?' Matt checked as they got into the car.

'For God's sake,' Georgia muttered. 'She's only going to teach a bunch of kids, not perform brain surgery!'

'You don't have to go if you don't feel up to it,' Matt said again to Eve, ignoring his sister.

'*We* still have to go to school,' Georgia grumbled. She flung her schoolbag on to the back seat and clambered in after it.

'Of course I feel up to it.' Eve's bright smile was stretched across her face. 'I've had a lovely rest and now I'm ready to face the world again.'

'About time too,' came the voice from the back seat.

'You don't have to worry about me,' Eve said. 'I'm absolutely fine.'

Matt looked at her, his grey eyes pitying under his shaggy fringe. 'So why are you wearing odd shoes?' he asked.

She managed to get through the morning quite well. The children were sweet and touchingly pleased to see her, the rest of the staff were kind, and after floundering a bit with the register first thing, Eve slowly began to feel as if she was back in control.

Matt was right, she decided, as she helped a group of children through their guided reading. She should have done this a long time ago.

She was feeling very pleased with herself by the time they filed into the school hall for lunch. The place was filled with the usual school-dinner smells – overcooked cabbage and gravy.

'Why does it always smell like that, even when it's fish and chips on the menu?' one of the other teachers whispered as they ushered the children to their tables.

Whatever was on the menu Eve couldn't face it, so she sat with a group of packed-lunch children. She was bent double, her knees under her chin on the munchkin-sized chair.

She had no idea how or why it happened. One minute she was opening a packet of Wotsits for a five-year-old, the next everything had fallen apart.

There was a small boy sitting at the other end of the table. His name was Gregory, and he'd started last term after his family moved to the area. He was six years old, and already it seemed like all the odds were stacked against him. He was little and painfully skinny in his too-big school sweatshirt, with white-blond hair, translucent skin and pale blue eyes behind wire-rimmed glasses. A major spoff, as Georgia would have called him.

All the other children at the table ignored him, chattering among themselves, but Gregory didn't seem to mind. Eve watched him as he slowly unpacked his lunchbox, carefully unwrapping each treasure and arranging them in a row in front of him – sandwiches, chocolate biscuits, an apple and a carton of Ribena. Then he sat back and looked at them, his gaze moving slowly along the line, assessing every item.

He caught Eve watching him, and grinned at her. It was the most heartbreakingly brave and lovely smile she'd ever seen.

'Please, Miss,' the girl next to Eve piped up. 'Gregory's a spastic.'

'He's not a spastic, he's special,' another little girl said. 'Isn't that right, Miss?'

'Look at him,' the first girl said, her lip curling. 'Why's he doing that? He can't be right in the head, can he, Miss? You're not right in the head, Gregory.'

'Jade, stop it,' her friend warned. 'Miss is crying.'

Seven solemn little faces turned to look at her, a grown woman sitting with her knees under her chin and tears pouring down her face.

The headteacher was very good about it. She arranged supply cover for that afternoon and suggested Eve should go home and rest.

'Maybe it's still a bit too soon?' she said kindly. 'You might not be ready just yet.'

'I don't know if I'll ever be ready,' Eve said.

'That's for you to decide. Your job will be waiting for you if you want to come back.'

But as she walked out of the school gates Eve knew she wouldn't be going back. Teaching was all she'd ever wanted to do, but now she felt as if she'd forgotten how. Just as she'd forgotten how to feel normal.

She stopped at the church on the way home. She hadn't even reached Oliver's grave when she got a call on her mobile.

'Eve? It's Laura.'

She looked around the deserted churchyard, half expecting her to pop up from behind a headstone. Was she ever going to be able to come here without Laura appearing in one way or another?

'I'm at the restaurant. We thought you should know, the health inspector's turned up.'

'Why? Has someone made a complaint?'

'Apparently it's a random inspection. Could you come over?'

'Can't Frankie deal with it?'

'It's his day off. I've tried calling him but his mobile's switched off.'

I wish mine was, Eve thought. 'So tell Simon to sort it out.'

'He said I should call you.'

Why? Eve wanted to shout. Why can't you all understand, it's nothing to do with me. 'Can't you get him to come another time?'

'I don't think so.' Laura lowered her voice. 'It's a her, and she's a bit scary, to be honest.'

Eve sighed. 'All right, I'll come. If I have to,' she added heavily.

Laura was right, the health inspector was scary. Large, and solidly built with a spotless white coat, sensible shoes and a no-nonsense haircut.

She bore down on Eve, her clipboard like a shield. 'Are you the owner of this establishment?'

'No. I mean, yes, I suppose so. My husband's dead,' she blurted out.

'Ah.' The woman made a mark on her clipboard. Eve wondered if she was ticking the 'Husband is dead' box, or the 'Owner is not all there' one. It didn't matter, they were both true anyway.

'Our chef is away today,' Eve explained. 'Would it be possible for you to come back when he's here?'

The inspector bristled. 'Do you understand the term "random inspection", Mrs Robinson?'

'Yes, of course.'

'Then you'll know it would rather defeat the object to make another appointment, wouldn't it?'

She allowed herself a little sneer as she put another cross on her clipboard. Eve fought the urge to grab the pen and stick it up her nose.

This was hopeless, she was going to make a complete mess of everything. The restaurant would probably be closed down by the end of the day and everyone would be out of a job, but it was their own fault for trying to put her in charge.

I don't want to do this, she wailed silently.

Then, out of the blue, she remembered a story Oliver had once told her about a run-in with a particularly brutal Nazi of a health inspector, who'd made him turn the kitchen virtually upside down and inside out, looking for non-existent problems.

'Didn't you want to kill him?' Eve had asked.

Oliver shook his head. 'I wouldn't give him the satisfaction. No, I was utterly charming. That really pisses them off.'

'Mrs Robinson?'

She came back to the present to find the health inspector frowning at her, her bushy monobrow crinking like a caterpillar across her face.

'Can I inspect your drains?' she said.

Eve smiled. 'How about a nice cup of tea first?'

Chapter 14

'I just don't know how we ended up like this,' the woman sobbed.

Anna pulled a tissue from the box and handed it to her. They were in the back room of the advice centre, the quiet area they kept for dealing with confidential situations. In front of them on the coffee table an array of bills were spread out, all stamped with the words 'final demand'.

'We were fine while my husband was working.' The woman stopped to blow her nose. 'But then when he had the accident and lost his job, it all started to get on top of us. As fast as we try to pay off the credit-card bills, the interest mounts up again and we're back to square one. And we're falling behind with the mortgage.' She crumpled her tissue into a soggy ball. 'I dread the post coming every morning. I can't even answer the door in case it's the bailiffs. I've got three kids, I don't want to end up on the streets.'

'It won't come to that.' Anna handed her another tissue. 'But you mustn't ignore the situation and hope it'll go away.'

As she painstakingly began totting up the family's finances to work out a repayment plan, Anna was uncomfortably aware she wasn't taking her own advice.

She knew she should see Eve, explain about her house being under threat, but she couldn't bring herself to do it. Her pride wouldn't let her admit she needed anyone's help, least of all Eve's.

And part of her was afraid that if Eve realised she had the upper hand, she might decide to use it against her. Anna couldn't blame her if she did. There was no love lost between them, after all. Why should she do anything to help her?

She knew she was only putting off the inevitable, but the idea of seeing the look of triumph on Eve's face as she realised she held all the cards, made her feel physically ill.

As if he could read her mind, later that day she got a call from Lynch.

'Have you talked to her yet?'

'Not exactly.'

'What does that mean?'

'It means I haven't.'

'Anna!'

'It's not that easy,' she protested.

'I know it isn't, but you've got to start building some bridges with her.' He paused. 'Tell you what. Why don't you go to see her today and then I'll take you out to dinner tonight as a reward?'

'I don't want—'

'I'll pick you up at eight. You can tell me all about it then,' he said, and rang off.

'Manipulative swine,' Anna muttered. She tried to call him back but the receptionist told her he'd had to leave the office urgently and wouldn't be back all day.

Resigned to her fate, Anna went to see Elliott in his office. It was lunchtime and he was playing solitaire on his computer.

'Is this what you do with yourself all day?' she said.

'Absolutely not.' He looked outraged. 'Sometimes I play Minesweeper.' He picked up his sandwich and took a bite. 'What can I do for you?'

'I wondered if I could take a couple of hours off this afternoon?'

'Out of the question. As you can see, we're rushed off our feet.' He nodded towards the main office, where Barbara was buffing the leaves of her rubber plant.

Elliott took another bite of his sandwich. 'Oh, go on, then. Abandon me if you must. But if Barbara gets one of her urges and tries to ravish me over the photocopier I'll hold you personally responsible.'

Anna grinned. 'You should be safe enough. Neil will be back from his natural childbirth class any minute. I'm sure you can keep her at bay until then.'

'I wouldn't bet on it. Look at the way she's caressing that J–cloth. That woman has needs, I can tell.' Elliott sat back in his chair. 'That reminds me. Tell me again why Neil has to go poncing about with cushions and birthing pools and whale music? Is he the one having the baby?'

'You sound just like Barbara.'

'In this case, she might have a point. He'll be asking for maternity leave next.'

'I think it's crossed his mind, actually.'

'As long as he doesn't start going on about his piles and stretch-marks.'

As she turned to go, Elliott asked, 'What's so urgent you have to drag yourself away from this place?'

'I've got some business to sort out. About the restaurant.'

'Shouldn't your solicitor be dealing with that?'

'I only wish he could,' Anna sighed.

It was the start of the main tourist season and all the bars and cafes were doing a roaring trade, so Anna was surprised to find Oliver's almost deserted, apart from an elderly couple at a corner table.

A dark-haired girl was leaning on the till flicking through *Heat* magazine. She dropped it as soon as she saw Anna.

'Hello,' she said. 'You're Anna, aren't you? I'm Laura.'

'Hi. Is Eve around?'

'She's in the back.'

'Can you tell her I'm here? I'd like a word.'

Laura chewed her lip. 'She's a bit busy at the moment.'

'All the same, I'd like to see her.'

'Now really might not be the best time—'

At that moment Eve hurried out from the kitchen, looking harassed. Her face fell when she saw Anna. 'What do you want?'

'I need to have a word with you.'

Eve glanced over her shoulder. 'Now's not a good time.'

'So I've been told.' She looked past her towards the swing doors. 'Why? What's going on?'

'If you must know –' she lowered her voice '– we've got the health inspector in.'

'Health inspector! Bloody hell.'

'Shh!' Eve glanced at the elderly couple. 'It's just a random check. They like to surprise people sometimes.'

'They haven't found anything, have they?'

'Of course not. I don't think so, anyway. Look, I've got to go back.' She nodded at an empty table. 'Get Laura to bring you a coffee, I'll be out in a minute.'

Anna tried to tell herself it was none of her business as she sat down at a corner table. Laura brought her a cappuccino and Anna was surprised that she'd brought one for herself too.

'Aren't you supposed to be working?' she asked.

'We're not busy. I thought I'd take my break.' Anna felt slightly uncomfortable as the girl sat down opposite her, but Laura seemed intent on chatting.

'I worked here before, while Oliver was here,' she said. 'Maybe he mentioned me?'

'Sorry, no.' Anna glanced past Laura's shoulder at the kitchen doors, wondering what was going on beyond them.

'No, I don't suppose he would.' Laura turned her cup around in the saucer. 'I mean, what reason would he have to talk about me?' The corner of her mouth lifted in a smile. 'You were a waitress here too, weren't you? When you and he met?'

'That's right.'

'And then you fell in love.' She lifted her cup to her lips and stared at Anna over the rim. 'Do you miss him?'

Anna blinked at her. What kind of question was that?

Laura seemed to guess what she was thinking. 'That was a daft thing to say. Of course you miss him. Who wouldn't miss someone like Oliver?'

She went on, reminiscing about Oliver and what fun it had been working at the restaurant when he was around, but Anna was hardly listening.

In the end she couldn't stand it any longer.

'I'm sorry,' she interrupted Laura, putting down her cup. 'I've got to find out what's happening in the kitchen.'

'I'm sure Eve's handling it,' Laura said.

I'm not, Anna thought. She couldn't trust Eve to handle anything.

The health inspector stood in the middle of the kitchen, brandishing her clipboard.

'There's a general lack of cleanliness in here,' she announced. 'The floors need to be cleaned, the splashbacks and ceiling need a thorough wiping down, and as for your freezer ...'

Anna cringed as she went through her list. It was obvious the woman was a bully, but why wasn't Eve standing up to her, instead of dancing like a worm on the end of a fishing line?

'And there's a broken tile on your floor that could be a health hazard,' the woman droned on.

'Where?'

The word popped out before Anna had a chance to think about it.

They all turned to look towards the doorway where she stood. The inspector stared at her as if she was something unpleasant she'd found behind the sink.

'I beg your pardon?'

'Where's the broken tile? I don't see it.'

'It's there.' The inspector pointed with the toe of her brogue.

'I'd hardly call that broken. It's just a crack.'

The inspector drew in a deep breath, her nostrils flaring. 'If I say it's broken, then it's broken.'

'But—' Anna opened her mouth to argue, then caught Eve's warning look and shut up.

'As I was saying,' the woman carried on. 'I've also noticed a split door seal on your fridge and –' she lowered her voice dramatically '– I've spotted evidence of low-level mouse activity behind your cupboards. Is something funny?' She whipped round to face Anna, who was stifling a giggle behind her hand.

'Sorry, but I was just wondering what other level of mouse activity there might be. Unless we've got flying mice?'

The inspector thrust her imposing bulk towards Anna, her eyes narrowing into slits. 'Who *are* you, exactly?'

'She's no one,' Eve said.

Anna shot her a furious look. 'I'm Anna Bowman,' she said. 'My partner owned this place.'

'Really?' The inspector glanced at Eve. 'But I thought—'

Eve shook her head. 'It's complicated.'

The woman turned back to Anna. 'I wonder, Ms Bowman, would you find it so funny if I were to close it down?'

Anna stared right back at her, refusing to be intimidated. 'You can hardly close us down over a couple of low-level mice and a cracked tile.'

'Then I'd better take another look around; see what else I can find.'

Anna had a feeling she'd gone too far as she watched the woman painstakingly taking swabs of every work surface. Eve followed her. She didn't look at Anna, but she could feel the waves of hostility coming off her.

After an hour, the inspector had come up with an impressive list of faulty thermostats in the fridge, greasy residue on the roasting pans and a lack of soap in the staff toilets. As she handed Eve the list she said, 'You have seven days to put all these right. I'll return for a re-inspection in a week, by which time I expect to find this place spotless.'

'Oh, it will be,' Eve promised.

She showed her out, leaving Anna with Simon and Lizzy. They both stared at her reproachfully.

'Don't look at me like that,' she said. 'She deserved it.'

'Next time you want to pick a fight with a health inspector, do you think you could do it somewhere else?' Simon said.

Eve slammed back through the swing doors, eyes blazing. 'Thanks a lot!' she said. 'I've just had to sweet-talk her into letting us stay open, thanks to you and your big mouth.'

'She was a bitch. And a bully.'

'I know that, but she could have closed us down. Why didn't you just stay out of it?'

'Why didn't *you* stand up to her?'

'Like you, you mean? That really worked, didn't it?' She opened the cupboard and started pulling out mops and brooms. 'Now, thanks to you, we've got to scrub this place from top to bottom.'

'That's going to take years!' Lizzy complained.

'Then we'd better make a start, hadn't we?'

Eve thrust a broom at Anna. 'What's that for?'

'Take a wild guess.'

'But I've got to get back to work.'

'Then you'd better call and let them know you're going to be a bit late. You got us into this mess, you can help get us out.'

Anna took the broom reluctantly. 'Where's Frankie? He should be dealing with this.'

'He's taken the day off.'

'Terrific. So he's having a lovely day out while we're getting an earful from Miss Whiplash. He shouldn't be skiving off just when we're getting busy.'

'We're not that busy,' Eve mumbled, sweeping furiously.

'That's another thing. How come this place is dead when they're turning them away everywhere else?'

'I don't know, do I? I expect it will pick up this evening.'

'How do you know that? Do you have many bookings?'

'Not many.'

'How many is not many?'

'None.'

'No bookings?' Anna stopped sweeping. 'But that's impossible.' She tried to control the panic in her voice. It was happening already. The restaurant was falling apart. She was going to lose everything. 'Even the lowest dive in town has bookings. What have you been doing to this place?'

She jumped as Eve dropped her broom with a clatter.

'Right, that's it,' she said. 'I don't have to listen to this.'

'Where are you going?'

'Home. You're right, I'm hopeless at running this place so why should I even try?'

Anna watched in dismay as she pulled on her coat. 'But you can't just walk out!'

'Give me one good reason why not.'

Anna swallowed hard. 'Is there somewhere we could talk?' she said.

They went into the yard. Eve sat on the step while Anna perched on a dustbin and told her the whole story.

'I don't understand,' Eve said when she'd finished. 'Why would Oliver do something like that?'

She'd been trying to work that out herself. 'He was desperate for the money, I suppose.'

'But to take out all those loans? The business wasn't in that much trouble.'

'We can't really ask him now, can we?' She picked paint off the windowsill with her fingernail. 'Look, I'm not going to beg,' she said. 'If you want to sell up or do whatever you want with this place, it's up to you. Charlie and I will survive whatever happens.'

'There's hardly any point in selling, if what you say is true. Neither of us would make anything out of it. And you'd end up homeless.'

'It would give you a chance to get even, I suppose.'

She knew she'd said the wrong thing when she saw the look of shock and revulsion on Eve's face.

'Do you really think I'd put a three-year-old child out on the streets for *revenge*? What kind of a person do you think I am?'

'I'm sorry,' Anna said, 'I'm not thinking straight at the moment.'

Some of Eve's anger faded away. 'I'm not surprised. This must have been a hell of a shock for you.'

'These haven't exactly been the best few weeks of my life.'

'I know what you mean.'

They were both silent for a moment.

'So what are you going to do?' Anna steeled herself to ask the question.

'I suppose we're going to have to keep this place on. Although as everyone keeps reminding me, I don't have the first idea about running a business.'

Anna blushed guiltily. 'We could run it together.'

Eve looked up at her. 'Are you serious?'

'Why not? Obviously I couldn't give up my job because I need the money, so I couldn't be here all the time. But I'm sure we could sort something out.'

'Why would you want to help? Don't you trust me?'

'I've got a lot at stake. I wouldn't trust anyone with my future, least of all—'

'Least of all me?' Eve finished for her. She took out a packet of cigarettes and lit one up. It was the first time Anna had ever seen her smoke.

'It wouldn't work,' she said.

'How do you know?'

'You really need to ask me that? Think about what happened with that health inspector earlier. Do you honestly believe we could work together?'

'It doesn't have to be like that.'

'No, but it would be. We'd be arguing the whole time.' She blew a smoke ring towards the sky. 'No, if we do this, we'll do it my way. Agreed?'

'Do I have any choice?' Anna said.

Whether it was the stress of her meeting with Eve she didn't know, but an hour later Anna flipped out in the middle of Sainsbury's.

She wasn't sure how it happened. One minute she was racing down the Canned Foods aisle, throwing tins of Mr Men pasta shapes into her trolley, the next she was standing in Condiments weeping silently over a jar of Branston pickle.

She knew it must have had something to do with the family she'd bumped into in Wines and Spirits – a young couple and their toddler son, pushing their trolley around without a care in the world. The man kept the little boy entertained by pulling faces at him, while his wife deliberated over which bottle of wine they should have with their takeaway that night.

It was so ordinary, so cosily domestic, Anna wanted to rush up and tell them to treasure every minute because they never knew when it might be snatched away from them. Only the thought of being manhandled out of the store by a couple of burly security men had stopped her.

Then she'd looked from their laden trolley to her own and realised how empty it was, with just a few cans, a loaf of bread and some apples rolling around in its depths. But she couldn't bring herself to swap it for a basket because that would be like admitting to the world how utterly alone she was.

A huge wave of anger boiled up inside her. She wanted to smash the jar of pickle to the ground in sheer rage at Oliver for leaving her in such a mess.

Voices rose from the next aisle, a fierce debate over Coco Pops versus Crunchy Nut Clusters.

'You chose last time,' a petulant voice accused.

'So? I'm the eldest.'

'Dad, tell her!'

'I'm telling both of you.' Anna pricked up her ears at the sound of Elliott's weary voice. 'For heaven's sake, get both of them and let's get out of here before I lose the will to live.'

A moment later Elliott and his trolley rounded the corner. He was still in his work suit, but his tie was off and hanging out of his jacket pocket. Two pretty, dark-haired girls trailed after him, one around eight, the other a few years older. They were both wearing red school jumpers, their hair fastened in untidy plaits.

He stopped when he saw her. 'Anna?'

'Hi.' She tried to sound casual, hoping he wouldn't notice her red-rimmed eyes. 'Fancy seeing you here.'

'Yes, well, I like to come here to pick up women, but unfortunately these two keep scaring them off.' He ruffled the younger girl's head. 'This is Jessica, and this is Becky, my eldest. Girls, this is Anna from my office.'

The girls regarded her with solemn brown eyes just like their father's.

'Did you get your business sorted out?' Elliott asked.

'In a way.'

They stood for a moment in silence, surveying the rows of mint sauce and pickled onions.

'Why don't you girls go and choose some sweets?' Elliott said finally.

'You said we weren't allowed,' Jessica reminded him. '*You* said only on weekends.'

'Just for this week I've changed my mind. Now get lost before I change it back again.'

Jessica scurried off, but Becky stood her ground. 'How much?' she said.

'Fifty pence.'

'Each?'

'Between you.' She folded her arms across her chest. Elliott sighed. 'Okay, a pound.'

'Each?'

'Becky!'

'She drives a hard bargain,' Anna said, as they watched her run after her sister.

'If you thought that was bad, you should see her in Top Shop.' He looked at the jar in Anna's hand. 'Is it rude to ask why you're crying over a jar of Branston?'

'It was Oliver's favourite.'

'Ah,' Elliott said, as if she wasn't being mad at all. 'May I?' He took the jar out of her hand and put it back on the shelf.

'I don't know what's wrong with me. I feel so pathetic,' Anna said.

'Don't be too hard on yourself. It took me six months before I ventured to the supermarket on my own. I'd probably still be living on Pot Noodles if it hadn't been for the girls.'

'Everything seems a bit pointless when you're on your own.'

'Tell me about it.' He looked cautiously at her. 'I'm guessing the happy pills aren't making you too happy any more?'

'They're great,' Anna said defensively. 'I've just had a stressful day.'

The girls came running back before he could reply. As they were heading for the checkout Elliott said, 'Why don't you come round for supper tonight? I can't promise it'll be cordon bleu, but it's better than eating alone. Bring Charlie along, too. I'd love to meet him.'

'That's really nice of you, but I've already got plans. I'm going out to dinner with my friend Lynch.'

'Your solicitor?'

'Actually, he's an ex-boyfriend too.'

'I thought you seemed on very good terms.' He looked thoughtful for a moment. 'Oh well, I doubt if my shepherd's pie could compete with a night on the town.'

'I'd still like to try it sometime.'

He smiled. 'Just say the word.'

Chapter 15

Anna stared at herself in the bathroom mirror, trying to focus on her reflection. The doctor had said alcohol and anti-depressants didn't mix, and by God he was right. She felt as if she was on the deck of a ship, lurching on a rough ocean. It was only her fingers clinging to the marble counter that stopped her slipping to the floor.

She was drunk. Very, very drunk. And she was about to do something very, very stupid.

The terrible, reckless feeling tingled up through her feet to her head. It was like standing on a clifftop, getting ready to jump. She knew it would end badly but she was going to do it anyway.

She'd met Lynch for dinner a couple of hours earlier, in one of the newest bars in York. It was achingly hip, noisy and crowded.

'Are you sure this is okay?' Lynch mouthed over the thumping drum and bass. 'We can go somewhere else, if you like?'

Anna shook her head. This was exactly what she needed. There was no need to make small talk, and the loud music filled her head, crowding out the black thoughts that kept trying to force their way in.

They found a booth where the noise wasn't quite so deafening, and settled down to eat. She wasn't hungry, so she nibbled on a bowl of nachos while Lynch ate a steak.

And she drank. One vodka tonic after another, tipping down her throat so fast she could hardly feel them.

'Are you sure that's a good idea?' Lynch laughed uneasily.

'No,' she said, pushing her empty glass across the table for a refill. 'But I'm doing it anyway.'

They talked. Lynch was exactly what she needed, making her laugh with his outrageous stories and gossip.

He was very attractive, too. He looked like he'd just stepped out of the pages of *GQ*, tall, blond and lean in a black Prada suit, with those striking blue-green eyes she remembered so well.

Was it okay to develop a crush on him she wondered, as she watched him at the bar laughing and joking with a curvy redhead as they waited to be served.

'Did you get her phone number?' she asked, when he returned with their drinks.

He looked shocked. 'Bloody hell, what kind of low-life do you think I am, taking another woman's number while I'm out with you?' Then, when she went on staring at him, he added, 'Okay, but only because she forced it on me. And I didn't give her mine.'

'I wouldn't care if you did.'

'You mean you're not even a teeny bit jealous?'

'Why should I be?' She glanced across to the bar, where the redhead was watching them resentfully. 'Anyway, it looks like your friend's jealous enough for both of us.'

'She's probably wondering what I'm doing with someone like you.'

'Thanks a lot!' Although she knew they made an odd couple, him so well groomed, her in a cotton skirt, and an old denim jacket. 'You're lucky I didn't come out in my pyjamas.'

'That's okay. I go for personality anyway.'

'So how come most of your exes look like supermodels?'

'Just luck, I suppose.'

'I must have been the exception to the rule.'

He smiled at her, his blue-green eyes crinkling. 'You had some redeeming qualities, as I recall.'

She gulped her drink. Oh God, he was flirting with her. Was this really what she wanted?

'Do you have a girlfriend at the moment?'

'Why? Are you interested?'

'Oh, please. I wouldn't go there again.'

He looked hurt. 'Why not?'

'Let's see ...' She pretended to think about it. 'You never call when you say you will, you disappear for weeks on end without telling anyone – oh, and you sleep with other women.'

'But I am very good in bed,' he pointed out.

'As I'm sure many, many women will testify.'

'Including you.'

She laughed. The combination of heat, noise and alcohol was making her head spin. 'I wasn't the only one with redeeming qualities,' she said.

Now she was flirting with him. Suddenly, unexpectedly, a vision of Oliver's face came into her mind. She pushed it away again.

'Shall we have another drink?' she said.

Much later, they stumbled out into the night. When the cool air hit her, she leaned against Lynch, trying to stay upright as she squinted at the cars passing over Ouse Bridge.

'I think I might be a teeny bit drunk,' she confided in a loud whisper.

'You don't say.' Lynch laughed. 'Come on, I'll pour you into a taxi.'

The thought of going home to an empty house filled her with panic.

'Is that it?' she said, disappointed.

'What else did you have in mind?'

'We could go back to your place?'

They stared at each other for a moment. They both knew exactly what she meant.

'Are you sure?' Lynch said. 'What about your little boy?'

'He's staying over at my mum's. I don't have anyone to go home to.' She gulped, tears filling her eyes.

Lynch put his arm round her, pulling her close. 'We'll walk back to mine,' he said. 'The fresh air will do you good.'

Lynch lived in a trendy wharf conversion just along the river. It was typically him – modern, minimalist and tasteful, with low leather sofas, arty chrome lamps and absolutely clutter-free. One glass wall gave a fantastic view over the river and the rooftops of the city to the Minster beyond.

To Anna, it looked more like a smart boutique hotel than a home. Somewhere suitably anonymous for an illicit liaison.

Panic assailed her. 'Can I use your loo?' she said.

The bathroom was just like the rest of the flat, flawlessly modern with creamy marble and subtle spotlights. Anna sat on the loo, her head in her hands, trying to stop the room spinning.

I should leave, she told herself, but she knew deep down she didn't want to. She could feel herself falling, but she couldn't put out her hands to stop.

She splashed her face with cold water and joined Lynch, who had made coffee, dark espresso in tiny chrome cups.

'No more drink?' she said, disappointed.

'I think you've had enough, don't you?'

She collapsed into one of the low sofas. Lynch sat opposite. Anna stared at him. This wasn't quite how she'd imagined the evening panning out. She should have been fighting him off by now.

Instead, they sipped their coffee and talked about work. Or rather, Lynch talked. Anna watched him, her eyes moving from the tantalising triangle of tanned skin at his throat, to the golden stubble on his chin, to his sensuous mouth. She fought the urge to kiss him into silence.

He was so unbelievably sexy, and she could feel herself sobering up. Soon it would be too late and the moment, and her courage, would be lost.

Finally she blurted out, 'Aren't you even going to try to seduce me?'

Lynch stopped talking. 'Do you want me to?'

'I'm here, aren't I? And I have to say, I'm very disappointed. I thought we'd be halfway to the bedroom by now.'

His mouth curved. 'You always did play hard to get.'

'I'm serious.'

He leaned back, his long legs stretched out in front of him. 'What's all this about?'

'Isn't that obvious?'

'It's obvious you came here to get laid. I just wondered why.'
He regarded her consideringly. 'I'm guessing it's all about revenge?'

'I don't know what you mean.'

'Think about it. You've just found out Oliver's let you down.
You feel angry, disappointed, confused. You're wondering if
you really knew the man you've spent the last few years loving.
You're scared and hurt, and you want to get even.'

He was right. The realisation crashed in on her, and she started
to cry.

Lynch came over and sat next to her, holding her close. He
smelled of shampoo and clean, expensive aftershave. It felt so
good to be in a man's arms again. Anna buried her face in the
smooth fabric of his shirt.

'I'm sick of being alone,' she sobbed.

He put his fingers under her chin, tipping her face up to look
at him. The next moment he was kissing her, his mouth warm
and soft and infinitely tender.

'Let me take you to bed,' he whispered.

There was no tenderness, no lingering foreplay, no slow and
sexy unpeeling of each other's clothes. Lynch tried to be gentle
with her, but Anna took control, pressing herself into the hard,
lean length of his body, her mouth open hungrily to his explor-
ing tongue. It felt like a whistle going off inside her head, letting
off the head of steam that had built inside her. She knew her
intensity shocked him, but it excited him too.

Right now she didn't want the kind of gentle love-making
she'd had with Oliver. All she wanted was the sensation of someone else's body against hers, to blank out all the pain and anger
and loneliness.

It wasn't until the following morning that the hideous guilt
overwhelmed her. It crashed over her a second after she opened
her eyes and found herself with a churning, sick stomach and a
pounding head amid a tangle of white sheets.

She lay paralysed for a moment, waiting for the wave of nausea
to subside and hoping that if she lay very still then all this might
go away too. But when she opened her eyes again she was still

blindingly hungover, and Lynch was still sleeping beside her, his skin tanned against the snowy sheets, his head resting on one muscled arm.

She stared up at the ceiling as the room began to spin. Oh God, what kind of a woman was she, jumping into bed with another man? She couldn't just blame the alcohol, much as she wanted to. She'd known exactly what she was doing. And she'd wanted it to happen. She'd had her chance to back out and leave, but she'd stayed. Not just because she was lonely, but because she wanted to punish Oliver for what he'd done to her.

Now all her feelings of rage and revenge disappeared, replaced by utter remorse. She felt as if she'd cheated on him. How could she say she loved him when she'd jumped into bed with the first man who came along?

She was a bad, bad person.

She screwed up her eyes and tried to focus on her watch. A few minutes after five. She crawled out of bed, careful not to wake Lynch, and gathered her clothes from where they lay scattered all over the polished wooden floor, reeling with humiliation as she remembered how she'd shed them the previous night. She dressed as quickly and quietly as she could, then crept out of the apartment. She felt like a coward, sneaking out without saying goodbye. But she couldn't face Lynch. She didn't know if she could face anyone ever again.

What the hell must Lynch think of her, she wondered as she hurried over Ouse Bridge, deserted in the early morning. All evening she'd been telling him how heartbroken she was. Then a couple of glasses of vodka later, and she was throwing off her underwear and dragging him off to bed.

She couldn't even accuse him of leading her on. He'd been willing enough, but it was all her idea. She was sick with humiliation and had to stop halfway up Coney Street because she thought she was actually going to throw up.

Home didn't offer her any sanctuary. The walls seemed to close in on her, and every smiling photo of Oliver and Charlie seemed to look down at her in silent reproach.

She made herself a cup of black coffee and downed a couple

of paracetamol, then headed for the shower. She scrubbed every inch of her skin, but she couldn't rub away the grubby feeling inside herself. Even the paracetamol didn't work; the pounding pain inside her head was like a punishment, an inescapable reminder of what she'd done.

Her mother rang just before eight. 'What happened to you last night?' she said.

'What?' Anna looked furtively around, certain that her mother's all-seeing eye had somehow detected her guilt and shame from all the way across Clifton Green. 'What do you mean?'

'You said you'd call when you got in last night.'

'Did I? Sorry. I was – um – a bit tired.'

'I was worried about you. I was going to come round but Keith said you were a big girl and I shouldn't keep checking up on you.' She paused. 'You are all right, aren't you? You sound a bit strange.'

'I'm okay. How's Charlie?'

'Oh, he's very happy as usual. He's eating his cereal and watching Lorraine Kelly with Nana. Anna?'

Anna, who'd been absent-mindedly picking the polish off her toenails and torturing herself with flashbacks of the previous night, came back to life. 'Yes?'

'You are all right, aren't you?'

'I'm fine, honestly. I've just got a bit of a headache, that's all.'

'Poor love. Do you want me to come over?'

'No! Honestly, I'll be okay.' The last thing she wanted was her mother fussing over her.

'You're sure you're not – depressed, or anything?'

'What makes you say that?'

'I don't know. I just got a strange feeling last night.' Her mother laughed shakily. 'I know you're going to think I'm daft, but I was worried you might do something, you know, stupid.'

If you only knew, Anna thought.

Anna finally crawled into work just after nine, still wretchedly hungover.

'Good night, was it?' Elliott asked wryly.

'What's that supposed to mean?'

He backed off, holding up his hands. 'Easy, tiger, I wasn't accusing you of anything. I just wondered if you'd enjoyed yourself, that's all.'

'Sorry.' She sank her head in her hands.

Barbara came in from taking a package to the post office. She took one look at Anna's green-tinged face and was unusually sympathetic.

'You poor dear,' she said. 'I'll make you a cup of tea, shall I?'

Anna heard her whispering to Elliott in the tea cupboard as she waited for the kettle to boil. 'She's been putting such a brave face on, I knew it would all catch up with her sooner or later. Just look at her. The poor girl's so overcome with grief she can hardly lift her head off the desk.'

'I think that's called a hangover, Barbara,' Elliott said, amused.

There was a shocked silence. Then Barbara hissed, 'Oh no, don't tell me she's taken to drink?'

'Not exactly. She went out on the lash last night.'

'Oh, did she?' Barbara's voice was frosty, all trace of sympathy gone.

A moment later she returned and crashed Anna's mug down on the desk.

'You've forgotten the sugar,' Anna said.

'Did I? Oh dear.'

Barbara didn't speak to her for the next half an hour, until she found an article in the *Daily Mail* about the dangers of binge drinking in young women.

'It says here that by the time she was twenty-five her liver was like a kipper,' she quoted. She glanced across at Anna, who was trying to scroll through her emails. 'You want to be careful that doesn't happen to you.'

'I had a couple of vodkas, Barbara. That doesn't make me Oliver Reed.'

'You should try milk thistle,' Neil put in. 'That's very good for repairing liver damage.'

'There's nothing wrong with my liver!'

'You'd be better off with a big fried egg and bacon sandwich,' Elliott said.

'Oh, please.' Anna's stomach churned.

'It's a foolproof hangover cure. I'll get you one.'

'No, really, I'm feeling much better—'

'Back in a minute.'

He returned five minutes later. Anna winced as he slapped a grease-stained bag down in front of her.

'There you go,' he said.

Anna held her breath so the smell wouldn't make her sick. 'Are you trying to kill me?'

'Stop being a wimp and get it down you. It'll work miracles. And don't even think about throwing it away,' he added, as she gingerly picked up the bag. 'Because I'll know, okay?'

He went back to his office, leaving her to stare queasily at the sandwich.

'You'd better eat it,' Neil advised. 'It'll only be worse when it's cold.'

'Kill or cure,' Barbara added cheerfully.

Actually, once she'd got over the first few nauseating bites, she found it wasn't too bad after all. By the time she was halfway through it, she began to feel almost human again.

And then the phone rang.

Barbara answered it.

'Hello?' Anna saw her face turn pink. 'I'm sorry, I think you must want to speak to my colleague.' She handed the phone over to her. 'A friend of yours,' she said tautly.

'Oops,' Lynch laughed. 'I think I may have just made an obscene suggestion to your receptionist.'

'Oh God.' Anna glanced at Barbara, who'd gone very tight-lipped.

'So what happened to you this morning?'

She turned away so Barbara wouldn't hear her. 'I had to go home.'

'Without saying goodbye?'

'Sorry. I – um – remembered something.'

'Pity. I was looking forward to a repeat performance.'

Anna felt the colour rush into her face. 'I was going to call you,' she said lamely.

'No you weren't.'

'Sorry?'

'That's typical of a girl. You take what you want and then you never call. I feel so used.'

It took a moment for her to realise he was joking. 'I really don't know what happened to me last night,' she said.

'Do you want me to draw you a diagram?'

She looked at Barbara, who was listening in. 'Look, we can't talk about this now. I'll call you back in five minutes, okay?'

'So you say,' Lynch said, mock hurt. 'I don't suppose I'll ever hear from you again.'

She hung up. 'I'm just going out for some paracetamol.'

Barbara ignored her. She looked as if she was going to explode with disapproval.

Anna rang Lynch back from her mobile outside the art gallery.

'Sorry about that, where was I?'

'You were just about to tell me last night was a huge mistake and should never have happened.'

'How did you know?'

'Just a hunch. Maybe it had something to do with the way you slunk off this morning.'

'I didn't slink—' she stopped. Slinking was exactly what she'd done. 'Like I said, I wasn't myself last night. I was angry, confused—'

'Drunk?' Lynch added helpfully.

'That too.'

There was an awkward pause. 'So you'd like us to forget it ever happened?'

'If we can.'

'That could be difficult,' Lynch said.

'Why?'

'I think I might be pregnant.'

'Lynch! This isn't funny.'

'Oh, come on. Why can't we have a laugh about it? Why do you have to get so stressed out?'

'Because ...' She thought for a moment. 'Because I love Oliver.'

'Oliver's dead,' Lynch said gently.

'I know, but it still feels wrong.' She paused, realising how unkind she must sound. 'I'm sorry,' she said. 'I don't want you to think I was using you—'

'Anna!' She could hear the laughter in his voice. 'This is me you're talking to. Danny Lynch. Mr Commitment-Phobic, remember? Look, last night was great, but it doesn't mean we're engaged or anything. If you don't want to take it any further, that's fine by me.'

'Thanks.'

'As a matter of fact, the reason I was ringing was to let you know I'm not going to be around for a week or two. I'm off to the States on business.'

'Sounds like fun.'

'I hope so. Maybe we could catch up when I get back?'

'That would be nice.'

'And you never know, it might give you time to miss me.'

Chapter 16

Eve stood in Jan's kitchen, clutching a bottle of Pinot Grigio in one hand and a banana and honey cheesecake in the other, and fighting the urge to run.

Just supper, she'd said. Eve had exhausted all her excuses, and Jan didn't believe them anyway. When she'd made one last effort to lie her way out of going by claiming her car had broken down, Jan had sent Peter round to pick her up.

Maybe it wouldn't be too bad, Eve told herself. But when she'd arrived and heard the sound of laughter and voices coming from the living room, her heart sank to her sandals.

'You didn't tell me it was a dinner party!'

'Didn't I? Sorry. It doesn't matter, does it? It's nothing formal.'

Jan handed her a glass of wine. 'That cheesecake looks fabulous, by the way. Thanks so much for making it.'

'It was no trouble.' No need to tell her she'd made it at three a.m. She was keeping some weird hours these days.

Jan took the cake from her and put it in the fridge. 'Cheer up, it won't be that bad,' she said bracingly. 'Adam's coming,' she added, as if that would make up for everything.

'I'm not even dressed for a dinner party.' Her pink linen dress had gone past Stylishly Rumpled to the Been Living at the Bottom of the Washing Basket for the Past Six Months stage. 'You look fine,' Jan said. 'Anyway, I haven't invited any single men, if that's what you're worried about. I wouldn't be *that* insensitive!'

No, Eve thought as they sat around the table half an hour later.

No single men. Just a load of couples, which was almost worse.

It wasn't Jan's fault, she was only trying to be nice. But Eve had the feeling everyone would have had a much better time if she'd been allowed to stay at home and watch *Midsomer Murders*.

She would have liked to talk to Adam, but he'd turned up with Imogen. Eve watched them at the other end of the table, laughing together over a shared joke, and felt the sharp sting of jealousy. Even Adam was paired up now.

But she was happy for him too. He was such a nice guy, he deserved to find someone special.

She made a big effort to join in with the general dinner-party conversation. She talked to the man on her left, a chartered surveyor called Edward, but after about five minutes they'd exhausted almost everything she knew about the world of surveying.

'And what do you do?' Edward asked.

'I—' What could she say? Grieve, mostly. Visit my husband's grave, cry in front of the TV and stay up all night baking.

'Eve runs a restaurant,' Jan cut in from across the table.

'Really?' Interest sparked in his eyes. 'That sounds fascinating.'

Doesn't it? Eve thought, throwing Jan a puzzled look. 'I wouldn't say I actually run it—'

'She owns it,' Jan interrupted again. 'And she's a fabulous cook, too. She made that delicious cheesecake you're eating.'

'Really?' said a woman across the table. She was called Sue and she was a secretary at Jan's school. 'You must give me the recipe. Tell me, how do you get ideas for the menu?'

Suddenly everyone seemed to want to talk to her. Eve was used to people ignoring her once they found out she was just a dull old nobody. Or worse still, a dull old nobody with a recently dead husband. But suddenly, in a flash, she'd become a restaurateur, a person with glamour and status.

'To be honest, I don't know much about the restaurant business,' she admitted. 'I only ended up with it because my husband's just died.'

'I thought Jan said you were divorced?' Sue said.

'Not quite.' Eve looked at her across the table. Sue had obviously been getting stuck into the wine in a big way.

149

'So he left it to you instead of his girlfriend?' Sue persisted.

Eve pleated her napkin between her fingers, aware that everyone had gone quiet. 'He died without a will.'

'And you ended up with it all?' Sue snorted. 'I bet that was one in the eye for the other woman.'

Eve caught Adam watching her intently from the other end of the table. 'It's not quite like that,' she said.

Sue refilled her glass. 'Well, you must be an incredibly forgiving woman to want to take his business on, after what he did to you. If it was me, I'd sell up, take the cash and say bugger the lot of you.'

'That's not what Oliver would have wanted.'

'Why would you care what he wanted?'

'Well, I do,' Eve said quietly.

Everyone was suddenly staring fixedly at their cheesecake.

'More fool you, then.'

The room fell silent as everyone's spoon stopped clinking. Eve put hers down. 'You think so? Let me tell you something. It doesn't matter a damn how long Oliver and I had been apart, or who he was living with. He was the father of my children, we shared half our lives together. You can't just sign away those feelings with a set of divorce papers. Or bury them in the ground with a coffin.' Her voice shook. 'You don't know me, and you didn't know my husband. So don't you dare presume to tell me how I should think or feel now he's dead.'

She stopped, staring at the circle of shocked faces. The only one who wasn't looking at her was Adam.

'Coffee, anyone?' Jan said.

'I went too far, didn't I?' Eve said to Adam as he and Imogen gave her a lift home later.

'It was a bit of a conversation stopper,' Adam agreed, his eyes fixed on the road ahead.

'Well, I thought it was brilliant,' Imogen said. 'That woman deserved to be put in her place. Big-mouthed bitch.'

'All the same, I'll have to call Jan in the morning and apologise. Although to look on the bright side, I suppose this is the last time

I'll be invited to any dinner parties.'

'You didn't enjoy it, then?'

'I haven't had that much fun since I had my wisdom teeth out.'

Imogen laughed. Eve caught Adam's eye in the rear-view mirror. His face was grim.

'Are you okay, Adam?' she asked.

'Probably his wretched crops,' Imogen said. 'He worries about those vegetables like they're his own children. I must be the only woman in the world to be jealous of a carrot!'

Adam smiled, but there was no warmth in it. Eve knew him well enough to realise when there was something on his mind.

She found out what it was when he dropped her off at home.

Eve thanked them for the lift and got out of the car. Adam caught her up before she'd reached her front door.

'Can I talk to you?' he asked.

'Sure, what is it?' She sighed. 'Look, if it's about me running the restaurant, I've talked to Anna about it, and she—'

'It's not about that. I just wondered how business was doing.'

'Fine,' Eve lied. No need to tell him how disastrous takings had been lately.

'Are you sure?'

Something about the way he looked at her made her wary.

'Why do you ask?'

He paused for a moment. 'I wasn't going to mention it, but a couple of your cheques have bounced recently. It's no problem,' he said quickly. 'I just wanted to say that if you're having money troubles I'm sure we could come to some arrangement.'

'There's no need,' Eve said, flustered. 'We've got a bit behind with the accounts lately, what with me only just taking over. If you'd like to call in to the restaurant in a couple of days, I'll have your money ready for you. In cash.'

'Like I said, it's no problem. I'm not desperate for it.'

'All the same, I want to get it sorted out.'

'Fine, I'll call round. As long as you're sure everything's okay? You would tell me if there was a problem, wouldn't you?'

Loyalty to Oliver stopped her blurting out the truth. She didn't want anyone, least of all his family, to think badly of him.

'There's no problem,' she said.

'If you say so.'

She wished she could confide in Adam, but she'd made up her mind not to tell anyone about the mess they were in. She owed it to Oliver to protect him.

She watched them drive off together. She imagined them laughing and joking about the party the way she and Oliver always did. He always said the best thing about a dinner party was the post-mortem, when they could have a good old bitch.

But they hadn't been to a dinner party together for five years, so why did she miss it so much now?

The same reason she suddenly missed the sound of his key in the door, and his warm, reassuring presence in her bed. Because she would never, ever know them again. That door had been closed in a far more final way than his leaving had ever done.

With a sigh, she rifled in her bag for her key and let herself into the empty house.

Chapter 17

MAY

Three months after Oliver's funeral, Anna and Eve finally met to choose a headstone for his grave.

It was six weeks since they'd last spoken to each other. In that time, Anna had tried to do as Eve wanted and left her to run the restaurant alone, but it hadn't been easy. Especially as she kept hearing rumours about how badly it was doing. She'd bumped into Lizzy, who'd let slip that on some nights the restaurant was virtually empty.

And then there'd been a bad review in the local paper. Reading it, she'd hardly recognised Oliver's restaurant, and the writer commented on the fall in standards since his last review.

Anna couldn't understand it. How had it all gone so wrong? There was only one answer to that, she decided. Eve was letting Frankie and the rest of the staff get away with murder.

She'd given her a chance to prove herself. Perhaps it was time for her to step in and take some action?

But all that was far from her mind when she arrived at Eve's house on a rainy morning in late May.

Eve seemed distracted when she answered the door. 'Sorry about the mess,' she gestured to her floury apron. 'I was trying out a new cake recipe.'

'It smells really good,' Anna followed the warm fragrance of cinnamon, apples and spices into the big farmhouse-style kitchen. 'What is it?'

'Brandy and apple cake. I've just taken it out of the oven. You can have some when it's cooled down. Take a seat. I'll make some coffee.'

As she took off her apron, Anna noticed she was wearing a man's flannel shirt over her jeans. It must have been one of Oliver's, left behind when he moved out. She felt a brief stab of resentment. Why was Eve wearing it?

For the same reason, Anna told herself, that she wore his old Ramones t-shirt to bed and sang along to his Smiths CDs in the car even though she couldn't stand them when he was alive.

'You can take a look at these while you're waiting.' Eve dumped a heap of brochures in front of her.

Anna shrank back in her seat when she saw the pink granite headstone on the front cover.

'I know, it's a grim job,' Eve said. 'But we've put it off long enough. The sooner we get it done, the better.'

While Eve busied herself brewing the coffee, Anna gingerly picked up the top brochure and steeled herself to flick through it. At first she could only look at the photos with her eyes half closed. But then she came to a page that made her open them wide.

'Who the hell would want something like *that*?' she said aloud.

Eve smiled over her shoulder. 'I'm guessing you've found the seven-foot stone angel. It is a bit kitsch, isn't it?'

'Kitsch? It's horrendous.' Anna stared at the photograph. Apart from being huge, the angel had a mullet hairstyle and huge, out-stretched hands like a goalie waiting to save a penalty.

'If you think that's bad, wait until you get to the pearly gates.'

Anna turned over the page. 'Oh my God! I see what you mean.'

'I suppose it's one way to show you care.'

'There must be a better one.'

Eve put a mug down in front of her. 'I suppose we'd better get on with it,' she said.

'I was thinking of something very plain,' she said.

'I agree,' Eve said. 'Black or white?'

'Definitely white.'

'With engraved lettering.'

Anna looked down at the brochure. 'What kind of wording were you thinking about?'

She'd thought about this long and hard. She was already on the defensive, ready to walk out if Eve suggested putting on her name and not Anna's.

'I've been thinking about that,' Eve said. 'I reckon it might be best if we just put something simple. How about "Oliver Robinson, beloved father of Matthew, Georgia and Charles"?'

'Charlie,' Anna said. 'No one calls him Charles.'

'And maybe we could have a quote he liked?' Eve suggested. 'I thought perhaps something from one of his favourite songs?'

'It would have to be the Smiths.'

'Who else?'

They looked at each other, surprised that they were so in agreement. Anna had come expecting an argument.

'Or we could just say sod it and get the stone angel,' Eve said.

Anna laughed. 'The stupid thing is, he'd probably love it.'

'You're right, he would.'

Eve moved the brochures to one side. 'Now that's out of the way, would you like to try some of that cake?'

It was a slightly surreal experience, sitting in Eve's kitchen eating cake. Anna didn't think she was hungry, but it was so delicious she found herself agreeing to an extra slice.

'This is amazing,' she said. 'And I hate food at the moment.'

'I wish I did,' Eve groaned. 'I've put on half a stone since Oliver died.'

Anna crammed another forkful into her mouth. 'I suppose working in the restaurant can't help. Who's looking after it today?'

'I've left Frankie on his own. I'll go in later. We're not that busy.'

'So I've heard,' Anna said quietly.

'I'm sorry ...?'

She took a deep breath. This was the chance she'd been waiting for. 'I've heard the restaurant isn't doing too well.'

'Who told you that?'

'I read the review.'

'Oh, that.' Eve was dismissive. 'They just caught us on an off day.'

So how come no one wants to eat there any more, Anna thought. 'Have you come up with any ideas to get the customers back?'

Eve pushed her plate away. 'I've been busy finding my feet,' she said. 'I haven't had much time for long-term planning yet. But I'm going to start putting a few specials on the menu, maybe doing some promotions—'

'I reckon you're going to have to do more than tinker with the menu if you want to improve trade.'

Eve looked at her coldly. 'What did you have in mind?'

'I think we should give the place a makeover, a brand-new start. Change the décor, the mood—'

'No,' Eve said firmly. 'No way. We're not making those kind of changes.'

'Why not?'

'Because the place is fine as it is.'

'So why don't we have any customers?'

'It's just a temporary blip. Frankie says when the summer comes—'

'I've got news for you, Eve. The summer's already here. It's May Bank Holiday this weekend, the city's bursting with tourists. Yet none of them are coming through our doors. Why is that?'

'I told you, it's a blip.'

'It's more than a blip.' Anna was exasperated. Why couldn't Eve see that? 'You must admit the place is looking a bit tired. The cosy French bistro thing might have gone down well with the punters when it first opened, but it's old hat now. The customers want something new, different.'

'Like Burger Shack, you mean?' Eve said. 'Maybe we should get Frankie on a pair of roller skates, frying up some onion rings?'

'I'd put on a pair myself if I thought it would improve trade.'

'We don't need to make big changes,' Eve insisted stubbornly. 'This is the way Oliver wanted it.'

'Oliver wouldn't have wanted to stand still. You know what he was like, always coming up with new ideas.'

'He liked the place the way it is. And so do I.'

Anna stared at Eve's face across the table. She looked so sure of herself, so totally unwilling to listen to anyone else's point of view. She could feel herself getting angry again. She'd promised herself she wouldn't, but she couldn't help it.

'Oliver liked looking forward,' she said. 'It's only you who wants to keep looking back.'

'What's that supposed to mean?'

'I mean you want to keep it as some kind of shrine to him. You've never wanted anything to change. That's why he left you, because you wanted to stand still.'

'He left me because you took him away!'

'And you couldn't get over that, could you? You've never got over that.' She knew she was saying too much, but her anger had taken on a life of its own. 'That's why you insisted on hanging around, because you couldn't accept it was over.'

Eve stood up. 'I think you'd better leave now.'

'I'm going.' Anna picked up her bag. 'There's no point in me trying to talk to you, because you'll never listen.'

As she headed for the door she caught sight of the memorial brochures stacked on the dresser.

'I don't know why we're even bothering with a headstone,' she said. 'That whole restaurant is Oliver's memorial!'

Eve threw the dishes into the sink, still fuming. How dare Anna preach to her like that? She was talking out of her backside, anyway. Eve didn't want to keep the restaurant as a memorial to Oliver, but she certainly didn't see any reason to make rash changes that might only lead them further into disaster either. She had no confidence in her own judgement, so she had to rely on Oliver's.

Tension knotted her shoulders, snaking up her neck and gripping her skull like a clawed hand. She finished the washing-up and went upstairs to get some paracetamol out of her bedside drawer.

She was putting the packet back when she spotted the small velvet box tucked at the back of the drawer.

Anna's engagement ring.

She took it out and stared at it. She'd almost forgotten it was there. She'd meant to give it to Anna after Oliver died, but somehow it never seemed to be the right time. And as the weeks went by, the moment slipped by completely.

She tossed it back into the drawer and slammed it shut. There was no way she was giving it to her now. Not after the things she'd said.

She was still seething when Adam arrived at the restaurant with his order that afternoon.

She watched him unloading the van. 'Can I ask you a question?'

'Is it fruit or vegetable-related?'

'Not really.' She hesitated. 'Do you think I'm keeping this place as a shrine to Oliver?'

He vaulted down from the back of the van. 'What's brought this on?'

'Just something Anna said. She thinks we ought to make some big changes to this place, but she says I won't because I'm trying to hold on to Oliver's memory. Do you think that's true?'

She waited for him to laugh, or tell her Anna was talking rubbish, but he considered it. 'This place obviously has very happy memories for you,' he said. 'I suppose it's possible you'd have trouble letting go of them.'

'So you reckon she's right?'

'I reckon you've got to make up your mind whether you're going to let your past get in the way of your future.'

'Sometimes I don't feel I have any future,' Eve said. 'Sometimes I feel as though my whole life is stuck in the past.'

'Like I said, that's up to you.' He pulled the van doors closed and looked around. 'Is Frankie about? I wondered if he wanted to place another order before I go.'

'Frankie's at the cash and carry. But I can do the order, if you like.'

He looked unsure. 'Doesn't Frankie deal with all the stock?'

'Do you want this order or don't you?'

He shrugged. 'You're the boss.'

They went through the order and dealt with all the paperwork in the office. As he was leaving, Eve said, 'So you think we should give this place a makeover, then?'

He regarded her for a long time. 'A new start doesn't hurt anyone,' he said.

Frankie was more forthright in his opinion.

'She's talking out of her backside,' he declared, stirring risotto rice around the big pan. A delicious smell of frying butter, olive oil, garlic and onions rose into the air. 'What does she know about running a restaurant anyway? She waits on a couple of tables and suddenly she's Gordon bloody Ramsay.' He pointed his finger at Eve. 'You're the boss of this place, not her. And I reckon you're doing a grand job.'

'Then how come we've got no customers?'

'I told you, they'll come. All businesses have their ups and downs.'

Eve smiled. She always felt better after talking to Frankie. He made her feel she wasn't totally useless, no matter how dire everything seemed.

'She might have a point, though,' she said. 'Maybe this place could do with a new image?'

'It's good food that brings customers in, not pink walls and moody lighting. Pass me that stock, would you?'

It's not bringing in any customers at the moment, is it, she thought, handing him the jug.

'Are you sure this stock is okay? It looks like it's been made up out of a packet.'

'It has.'

'Since when have we been using readymade stock?'

'Since this place ran out of money.' He grabbed the jug from her. The pan hissed as he sloshed the liquid into the rice mixture. 'We have to save cash somewhere.'

'Surely it's false economy to cut corners with our ingredients?'

she said. 'Once the quality of the food goes down—'

'Who said it's going down?' Frankie turned on her, wooden spoon in hand. 'Did I say it was going down? Did I?'

'Well, no, but—'

'Do you honestly think I'd stake Oliver's reputation just to save a few quid?'

'I—' Eve glanced at Lizzy. She had her head down, rinsing lettuce at the sink. 'Of course not,' she said. 'I'm sorry.'

Frankie's shoulders relaxed. 'No, it's me who should apologise,' he said. 'I've been getting a bit wound up lately. I don't like making economies any more than you do, but what choice do I have?'

'You're right.'

'Look, it'll be okay,' he reassured her. 'Business will pick up again, and then everything will be fine. In the meantime, no one will notice if we use a few tins and packets.'

Eve thought about the terrible review in the local paper, but said nothing. She was too shaken by Frankie's outburst to argue with him.

'There's something else you should know,' Frankie said.

She looked up at him. 'Not more bad news?'

He nodded. 'Simon's handed his notice in. He's going to work at The Burger Shack.'

'No!'

''Fraid so. Spike Mullins has offered him more money and more time off than he gets here. And all the fries he can eat, probably.'

'I can't believe it.'

'Oh, I can. That Mullins is a sneaky bastard. He can't buy you out so he nicks your staff instead. And Simon had the makings of a decent chef, too.'

Eve glanced at Lizzy, who still had her head down. She wondered how much she'd known about Simon's plans to defect next door.

'What are we going to do?' she asked.

'I'll have to cope on my own until we find someone else.' He pushed his cap to the back of his head. 'Lizzy can help, but she's still at college two days a week.' He caught Eve's worried expression and patted her shoulder. 'I'll sort it out. The kitchen's my problem, remember?'

For once Eve was thankful that hardly anyone turned up for lunch so Frankie and Lizzy were able to muddle through.

That afternoon she sat down in the empty restaurant to go over the books. She'd started to make sense of them over the weeks, but the figures still frightened her.

No matter how much she looked at them, they still had barely enough coming in to pay the bills, especially with the huge loan repayments. It seemed as though no sooner had she paid one than another arrived. Every week she had to juggle the numbers just to be able to pay the staff's wages. She was terrified that the time would come when she wouldn't be able to make the figures balance.

She thought about Anna, and anger rose inside her. If she thought it was so easy, she should try running the place!

'Problems?' Laura put a cup of coffee down in front of her.

'Just a bit.' Eve smiled ruefully.

'Anything I can help with?'

'Not unless you know a good chef? Simon's just quit.'

Laura sat down opposite her. 'As a matter of fact, I do know someone,' she said.

'Oh yes?'

'How about you?'

'Me?' Eve laughed.

'You're a brilliant cook. That apricot tart you brought in last week was heaven.'

'There's a difference between making a pie and cooking for a restaurant full of people.' As Frankie would no doubt point out to her. He hadn't been too impressed when all the staff had raved about her tart, and even less when Lizzy suggested they should put it on the menu. He'd sulked for hours, until Eve decided she'd be better off keeping her ideas – and her cooking – to herself.

'All the same, I bet you could do it.'

'I have enough trouble running this side of things.' Although she had to admit, she'd started to enjoy coming to work, she still felt as if she was muddling through most of the time, but at least it gave her a reason to get up in the morning.

Laura went off to empty the dishwasher, and Eve turned her attention back to her paperwork. They would have to do something about Simon, that was for sure. Although with the takings down, she wasn't certain they could afford to replace him.

Unless there was another way of looking at the problem. She picked up a menu and looked at it. Lists of dishes, many of which never seemed to get ordered. Yet they spent a lot of time in the kitchen preparing them, just in case, and then ended up throwing quite a few of them away.

Surely if they reduced the menu, it would save time and money? They could put all their efforts into producing a few things well and changing the menu frequently, instead of over-stretching themselves. It would save on stock, too.

She was still trying to work out how she would sell the idea to Frankie when her mobile rang.

'Hello?'

'Mrs Robinson?' She didn't recognise the voice on the other end of the phone. 'It's Heathwood School. We were just wondering if you knew where Matthew is today?'

She glanced at her watch. 'Sitting his biology A-level paper, isn't he?'

There was a pause on the other end of the line. 'That's just it,' the voice said. 'He isn't.'

Chapter 18

He was upstairs playing his guitar when she came home from work.

Eve put her head around the door. 'How was your day?' she shouted over the electric twang.

'Not bad.'

'How did the exam go?'

'Okay, I s'pose.' He strummed a few more notes.

'Biology, wasn't it?'

'S'right.'

'So you think you did okay?'

'Sorry?'

'Your exam. You think you did okay?'

'S'pose.'

She crossed the room and pulled the plug out of the wall, plunging the room into silence.

'That's funny, because your school called me at work, wanting to know why you hadn't turned up.' He froze, his fingers still poised over the strings, head bent. 'Is there something you want to tell me, Matthew?'

He went on strumming soundlessly. 'I didn't see the point. I've decided not to go to uni.'

She took a deep breath. Stay calm, she told herself. 'Right. I see. And when were you going to tell me this?' He didn't reply. 'Look, I can understand you wanting to put it off, after everything that's happened. But surely, even if you decide to defer your place, you've still got to sit the exams?'

'You don't get it, do you? I'm not going to university. Ever. Full stop.'

His back was turned to her, shoulders hunched in his black Linkin Park t-shirt.

'So what are you planning to do?'

'Get a job.'

'And what kind of job do you expect to get with no qualifications?'

'I'll find something.'

'I thought you wanted to be a forensic scientist? You don't find something like that down at the job centre.'

'Then I'll do something else. Give it a rest, will you?' He threw his guitar on the bed and headed for the door, but Eve stepped in his path.

'I can't believe I'm hearing this. Not from you.' She had to look up to meet his eye as he towered over her. 'You were always so ambitious, so determined to do something with your life, and now you're saying you want to waste it.'

'It's my life.' Matt eyed her warily from under his wild mop of hair. 'Can I go now?'

'Not yet. We need to sort this out.' She folded her arms across her chest. 'So what do you plan to do with your life, Matt? Go on the road? Become a rock star? Because I'm telling you, not everyone can be Keith Richards.'

'Keith who?' he said sullenly.

Eve stared at him. Where had her lovely, amiable son gone? And when did this surly idiot turn up to take his place?

'Matt, are you in some kind of trouble? You're not mixed up with drugs, or anything?'

'Mum! Jesus, what do you think I am?'

'At the moment I don't know.'

'Look, don't worry about it, okay?'

'How can I not worry? I don't know what's happening with my children. There's Georgia, going off with those friends of hers I've never met, doing all kinds of things I dread to think about, and now you've said you want to throw away your future and join a band!'

164

'I never said that. *You* did.'

'What, then? Work in Burger King? Because that's where you'll end up.' She sat down on the bed and buried her face in her hands. Where was Oliver when she needed him? Her family was falling apart and he'd buggered off and left her. 'I don't think I can deal with all this on my own.'

She felt Matt's hand on her shoulder. 'Why do you think I can't go to uni?'

She fumbled up her sleeve for a tissue. 'What do you mean?'

He sat down next to her. 'I don't want to leave you on your own. I'm worried about you.'

'About me?'

'I don't know how you'll cope. You said yourself, Georgia's being a pain, and you've got loads of stress with the business and everything. You need me around, Mum. You might fall apart otherwise.'

'I'm not going to fall apart!'

'You haven't seen yourself lately.'

She stared at her son and realised the truth. She'd been acting like a crazy woman, wallowing in her grief when she should have been strong for her children. All this time, when she thought they hadn't noticed, they'd been worried sick about her, terrified she was going to crack up.

And here was Matt, struggling to be the man of the house, to look after her and Georgia as well as coping with his own grief and the pressure of his exams. It was amazing he hadn't fallen apart under the strain.

She felt proud, guilty, grateful and ashamed all at the same time.

'You're a wonderful boy, do you know that?' she said, wiping away her tears.

'Mum!'

'You are. But there's no way I'm going to let you sacrifice your future for my sake. I couldn't live with myself if I did that.'

'It's what Dad would have wanted. He would have wanted me to take care of you and Georgia.'

'He would have wanted you to make something of your life,'

she said. 'He was as proud as I am that you were going to university. If you really want to do something for him and for me, you should go.'

'But—'

'Listen, I'll be fine. I can take care of myself. I *can*,' she insisted, as Matt looked doubtful. 'Besides, it's not as if you're going into outer space, is it? I expect you'll still be home every weekend with your dirty washing. You can still keep an eye on us.'

Matt smiled uncertainly. He still didn't seem convinced. 'What about Georgia?'

'She'll be fine too. She's just going through a funny phase at the moment, that's all.'

Walking out of school was easy. Georgia kept expecting someone would see her heading for the gates and stop her, maybe call her mum. But no one did. They hadn't even noticed when she'd changed into her jeans in the girls' toilets at lunchtime.

Andy Taylor and his mates were lolling around outside the gates, smoking. There was another girl with them, someone Georgia hadn't seen before. Blonde, in a pink anorak, puffing on a Silk Cut, she regarded Georgia with hard, assessing eyes.

'All right?' Georgia braced herself as Andy kissed her, his tongue invading her mouth. He tasted of beer and stale tobacco.

He let her go and passed her his cigarette. Georgia took a defiant puff and nearly gagged as the smoke hit her lungs.

The other girl looked away, sneering. 'Are we going to hang around here all day?' she demanded. 'I want some chips.'

'Who's that?' Georgia asked as they waited outside the KFC.

'Her name's Kayleigh. She's Murphy's sister. She's all right,' one of the boys shrugged.

Georgia watched her through the window, feeding Andy a chicken drumstick. She didn't seem all right to her.

'Where are we going?' she asked Andy as they headed along Blossom Street.

'Dunno. Hang around the shops, probably.'

'Why don't we ever do anything else?'

'You could always go back to school if you don't like it.'

Kayleigh raised a blade-thin eyebrow at her.

Georgia was tempted. She'd never imagined it, but at that moment doing double geography with the rest of her class seemed a lot more exciting than hanging around with Andy and his mates.

But at least Andy was interested in her, which was more than she could say about anyone else.

They ended up in Woolworths on Coney Street. As Andy and his friends filled their pockets with Pick 'n' Mix, Georgia surreptitiously checked her phone. Surely someone must have missed her by now?

'Expecting a call?' Andy slipped a hazelnut cluster into her hand.

'Just making sure it's switched off,' she lied, stuffing it back into her bag. 'I thought the school might ring my mum or something.'

'My school doesn't bother any more.' Andy grinned. 'They're just glad when I don't show up.'

Georgia watched them browsing through the computer games, trying to decide which to nick. Kayleigh hung close to him, reading over his shoulder.

'Can we go?' she said.

'I'm busy,' Andy snapped back.

Georgia caught the triumphant little smirk on Kayleigh's face. On impulse, she snatched the computer game from his hand, stuffed it in her schoolbag and made for the door.

It was an odd, thrilling feeling, when the alarm bells started ringing. She'd barely got through the doors before a woman in uniform descended on her.

'Just a minute, love.' She laid her hand on Georgia's shoulder. 'Can I take a look in your bag?'

Georgia glanced up the street. At the first sign of trouble Andy and his mates had scattered. Now they'd regrouped and were watching her from a safe distance outside the jeweller's on the corner.

She handed her bag over to the woman. Now the thrill had subsided she suddenly felt very lost and frightened.

'I'm really sorry, I – I didn't mean to do it,' she stammered.

'I think you'd better come inside,' the woman said wearily.

Andy and the others were still loitering outside when she emerged half an hour later.

'What happened?' He yanked her into the nearest doorway. 'Did they call the police? You didn't mention my name, did you?'

She shook her head. Her eyes swam with hot tears. 'They just gave me a warning and told me not to come back.'

'What? They didn't even threaten to prosecute, or 'owt?'

'No.' Georgia pulled her wrist from his grasp and fumbled for the tissue the nice security woman had given her.

She could hardly believe it herself, she was still numb with shock that she'd been catapulted out so fast. They'd all been so kind to her. They were angry at first, but when they found out her dad had just died they were really sympathetic and understanding. The assistant manager had said she didn't look like the kind of girl to get mixed up in trouble, and if she promised to go back to school they'd forget all about it. They wouldn't even ring her mum, even though Georgia had insisted on giving them the number.

Andy grinned with grudging admiration. 'Nice one. You've got some bloody nerve, d'you know that? You're fucking lucky they didn't phone the police.'

Am I? Georgia thought. Even the sour look on Kayleigh's face couldn't make up for how frustrated she felt.

Chapter 19

JUNE

'I see what you mean about this place. Bit of a dive, isn't it?'

The builder stuck his pencil behind his ear and cast an expert eye around the restaurant.

'It's not that bad,' Anna said.

'I thought you said it all had to go?'

'I know, but ...' That didn't stop her feeling a stab of disloyalty. Oliver had loved this place, patchy paintwork and all. 'It's got a lot of character.'

'So does the Leaning Tower of Pisa, but I wouldn't want to go for a meal there.' He eyed her narrowly. 'Are you saying you don't want it done now?'

She hesitated. Oh God, she was turning into Eve, hanging on to her memories.

'Yes, do it,' she said.

Anna followed him around as he inspected corners and took measurements, her eye moving from her watch to the door and back again. She kept telling herself she had every right to be here, but that didn't stop her feeling like an intruder – she'd let herself in with Oliver's old keys and tapped in the burglar-alarm code.

'Are you going to be long?' she blurted out.

'In a rush, are you?'

'You could say that.'

It was Eve's fault. She wouldn't have had to skulk around behind everyone's backs if she'd been reasonable. Now Anna felt she had to take drastic measures to stop the business going down the pan.

Finally, after another agonising fifteen minutes, the builder snapped his tape measure back and stuffed it in his pocket. 'All done,' he said. 'I'll get some figures together and let you have an estimate in the next few days, if that's all right?'

'Fine,' Anna hustled him towards the door. 'But could you send it to me at home?'

The builder frowned. 'Are you sure this is your place?'

'No, it isn't.'

They turned, and saw Frankie standing in the kitchen doorway, his arms folded menacingly across his bulky chest.

The builder looked from one to the other. 'What's going on?'

'You tell me,' Frankie said.

They both stared at Anna, who fought the urge to panic.

She faced Frankie. 'I'm getting an estimate done for some work on this place.'

'Does Eve know about this?'

'We've talked about it.'

'Would someone mind telling me what's going on?' the builder said.

Frankie held Anna's gaze. 'I'm sorry, mate, I reckon someone's been wasting your time. There's no work to be done on this place without the owner's permission.'

The builder looked blankly at Anna. 'I thought *you* were the owner?'

'I—'

'She isn't,' Frankie said bluntly.

Anna burned with rage and humiliation as the builder packed up and left, muttering about 'time wasters'. When he'd gone, she turned on Frankie.

'You had no right to send him away like that.'

'You had no right to bring him here in the first place. This is Eve's restaurant.'

'No, it isn't.'

'It is in the eyes of the law. And you −' he jabbed a fat finger at her '− are trespassing.'

'So call the police.'

'I'd rather throw you out myself.'

He was so close she could feel the sour warmth of his breath. 'I'd like to see you try,' she said.

For a split second she thought he was going to grab her, but he backed off.

'You're not worth going back to jail for,' he said. 'You've got what you deserve, anyway.'

'Which is?'

'Absolutely nothing.' His thin lips curled into a sneer. 'Christ, that must have hurt, didn't it? All those years wasted, chasing after him, and in the end his wife got it all.'

'If that's what you want to think,' Anna said.

'Oh, I don't think, love. I know. I know exactly what you're like. I watched you when Oliver was alive, swanning around like you owned the place. Jumped-up little tart.' His voice was sing-song with mockery. 'And now look at you. Back in the gutter where you belong.'

'At least I've got you for company.'

'Bitch!'

She saw the sparks of anger in his tiny eyes and flinched, thinking she'd gone too far.

'Hello? Frankie?' Eve's voice called out from the kitchen.

'In here.' Frankie stepped back, just as she walked through the swing doors.

Her smile disappeared when she saw Anna. 'What are you doing here?'

Frankie turned to Anna. 'Well? Are you going to tell her, or shall I?'

'I—'

'I caught her skulking around with a builder this morning,' he said, without waiting for a reply. 'Making plans to get this place redone behind your back.'

'Is this true?' Eve stared at her.

'I was going to talk to you again once I'd got some figures together,' Anna defended herself.

'I told you, we're not making any changes.'

'We have to do something.'

171

'We?' Frankie said. 'I don't think it's your decision.'

'It's not yours either, in case you hadn't noticed,' Anna snapped back. 'So why don't you keep your nose out of it and concentrate on what you're paid to do? Because from what I can tell you're not making a very good job of it.'

Frankie opened his mouth to speak, but Eve stepped between them.

'I think you'd better leave,' she said.

Anna looked from one to the other, totally frustrated.

'All right, I'll go,' she said. 'But I'm going to speak to my lawyer. I want to save this place even if you two don't!'

She called Lynch from her mobile on the way back to her office.

'I'm sorry, Mr Lynch is still away,' his PA told her in a resigned voice.

'But it's been two months! When is he due back?'

'We're expecting him later this month. Can I get someone else to deal with your query?'

Anna left her number and hung up. And to think she'd been worried about meeting Lynch again after their one-night stand. Little did she know he was going to disappear off the face of the earth.

There was a visitor for her when she got back to the office. Anna's heart leaped into her mouth when she saw the tall, dark-haired man standing in the waiting area. She was just about to call out Oliver's name when he turned round and she realised it was his cousin Adam.

Cruel disappointment assailed her.

He was in his work clothes, jeans and a dark green t-shirt, and looked ill at ease, flicking through a leaflet on housing benefits.

'This is a surprise,' Anna greeted him. He was the last person she'd expected to see. He was a nice man, and he'd always been close to Oliver, but he hadn't had much to do with them as a couple since they got together. Anna got the impression he didn't really approve. 'What can I do for you?'

'I want to talk to you about Eve.' He was as blunt and direct as ever. He certainly didn't have any of Oliver's smooth charm.

'You'd better come into the back room. We can talk privately in there.'

They faced each other in the bland, brightly lit office. 'I suppose Eve sent you?' Anna said.

'She doesn't know I'm here.'

'So this isn't about the builder?'

He frowned. 'What builder?'

'It doesn't matter. What did you want to talk about?'

He shifted uncomfortably on the tiny vinyl-covered sofa, his long legs stretched out in front of him. 'I want you to give her a break,' he said.

'Sorry?'

'She's doing her best. She's working all hours at the restaurant, trying to make a go of it.' He stared down at his work-roughened hands, his thumbs circling around each other. 'Life hasn't been easy for her lately. She's had to cope with taking over the business, looking after the kids—'

'She's not the only one who's had a tough time,' Anna reminded him.

He raised his eyes to meet hers. His were warm and grey, and so like Oliver's it broke her heart. 'I'm sorry,' he said gruffly. 'I realise you've been through a lot too. But you're different. Eve isn't as strong as you.'

Anna forced herself to bite back a stinging reply. Just because she wouldn't allow herself to fall apart, that didn't make her strong.

'She's scared,' Adam went on. 'She relied on Oliver so much. Now she's on her own she doesn't know what to do without him.'

'She didn't lose Oliver. I did.'

'You both did. Whether anyone liked it or not, Eve was still in love with him.' He stared over her shoulder for a moment at a benefit-fraud poster while he searched for the right words. 'I'm just trying to explain why she finds it so hard to let go, why she's not ready to make any changes to the restaurant. She can't trust her own judgement, and she's terrified of getting it wrong, but if you just give her time I'm sure she'll sort it out.'

'But we don't have time,' Anna said, exasperated. 'If the business goes under, I lose everything!'

He leaned forward, his gaze suddenly sharp. 'What do you mean?'

Anna regarded him warily, wondering if she should tell him about the loans Oliver had taken out, the chance that she could lose her house.

'It doesn't matter,' she said.

He pursed his mouth in frustration. 'Why do I get the feeling there's something you and Eve aren't telling me?'

'There's nothing to tell. The restaurant is going through a few money troubles at the moment, that's all.'

'How bad?'

'Pretty bad.' That much she felt she could give away.

'I guessed things weren't going too well.' He ran his hand through his springy dark hair. 'Why didn't Eve tell me?'

'You'll have to ask her that.' She glanced through the glass-panelled door to the reception area, which had started to get busy. 'Now if you'll excuse me, I ought to get back to work.'

'Yes, of course. I'm sorry.' He sprang to his feet. 'Thank you for sparing the time to see me.'

She followed him outside. As he unlocked the door, he turned back to her and said, 'You won't tell Eve we've had this talk, will you? I wouldn't want her to think I was sticking my nose in where it wasn't wanted.'

'I doubt if Eve and I will be talking any time soon.' Not after their stand-off this morning.

As she watched Adam drive away, she wondered what had brought him all the way across town to plead Eve's case. She had a feeling it had more to do with his feelings for her than any family loyalty.

Chapter 20

'Why not?' Andy demanded. His face was twisted, his lower lip jutting, like a spoilt kid.

Georgia looked up at the sky. It was yellow-grey, promising a big storm. The air felt warm and damp against her skin.

'I'm not ready,' she said.

'You've been saying that for weeks!' Andy whined. 'What's the matter with you? Don't you fancy me or something?'

'Yeah.'

'So why won't you do it?'

They were in the kids' playground at the park, on the swings. On the other side of the playground, Andy's friends were messing around on the roundabout, trying to spin each other off. Kayleigh was with them as usual, laughing louder than anyone else.

'You have done it before, haven't you?' Andy said suddenly. 'I mean, you're not a virgin or anything?'

'No way.' Georgia turned circles on her swing, letting the chain get tighter and tighter, twisting around itself. Her dad used to do that when he took her to the park. He'd wind it all the way to the top and then let it go so she spun round and round.

'It's Father's Day tomorrow,' she said out loud.

'So? I don't even know where my old man is. And yours is—' he stopped. He wasn't exactly sensitive, but even he knew when to shut up. 'So are we going to do it or not?' He changed the subject.

Georgia sighed. 'If you want.'

'When?'

'Soon.'

'This Saturday? Liam's having a party, we could sleep over.'

Georgia nodded over towards the roundabout. 'Will she be there?'

Andy glanced over his shoulder at Kayleigh without interest. 'I s'pose. Why? You jealous?'

'No!'

'Good, 'cos she's not my type.'

'And I am?'

He grinned at her. 'I'm still here, aren't I?'

Big drops of rain began to fall from the sky, splashing into the dust at their feet. Across the playground, Andy's friends were already running for cover.

He slid off the swing and went to follow them. 'You coming?'

'In a minute.'

'But it's pissing down.'

'I like it.'

He shook his head. 'You're mad, you.' He started to walk away, then turned back. 'So are we fixed for Saturday night?'

'I suppose.'

'Sweet.'

She watched him follow the others to the shelter. They were all running, but he swaggered arrogantly, defying the rain.

She didn't want to sleep with him. She certainly didn't want him to be her first. But Kayleigh was waiting to step into her shoes, and she didn't want that either.

She let the swing go, twisting round and round until the park was a blur. Somehow it wasn't so much fun without her dad there.

'I'm going to a party next Saturday night, all right?'

Georgia stood with her arms folded across her chest, bracing herself for the usual barrage of questions. But her mum just said, 'That's nice, darling,' and went on tapping numbers into her calculator.

Georgia fought the urge to snatch it out of her hand and fling it against the wall.

'I might stay over for the night.'

That got her attention. Her mother stopped and looked at her over the top of her glasses.

'Whose party is it?'

'Just a friend. No one you know.'

'And are their parents okay about you staying over?'

'Dunno. Haven't asked them.' Georgia inspected her fingernails and waited for her mother to explode.

'As long as you let me have the address and phone number,' she said, and went back to the pile of papers in front of her.

Georgia stared at her in disbelief. 'You're letting me go?'

'I thought that's what you wanted?'

'I—' Of course it's not what I want, she felt like shouting. I want you to ask me a million questions until I get fed up and scream at you. I want you to get enraged and tell me I can't go. Most of all I just want you to notice me.

'Fine,' she snapped. 'I'm going.'

'Now are you sure you're going to be all right?'

Anna sighed. 'I've told you a hundred times, I'll be fine. You go and enjoy yourselves.'

'Fat chance of that, with your nana,' Keith grumbled, putting another case in the car.

'I heard that.' Nana hobbled out, clutching a box of teabags to her chest.

'They do have tea in Whitby, you know,' Keith said.

'They might not have my special sort.' She handed him the box. 'The other groceries are in the kitchen. And my bags are in the hall.'

Keith rolled his eyes at Anna and went back inside, while Nana eased herself into the back seat of his Mondeo.

'You could always come with us, you know,' Jackie said.

'I don't think there's room for me with all the stuff you're taking.'

'Of course there is. There's always room for you and Charlie. It would do you both good.'

Anna looked at Charlie, who was digging up her mother's

pansies with a stick he'd found. 'So you can keep an eye on me, you mean? It's okay, I can manage on my own for two weeks. I haven't cracked up yet, have I?'

'I suppose not. Are you still taking those tablets?'

'Yes.' Anna was instantly on the defensive.

'I thought they were only meant to be for a short time? It's been more than three months now.'

'The doctor seems to think I need them.'

'The doctor probably hands out a repeat prescription without even thinking about it.'

'They help me cope, okay? Or would you rather I just went mad?'

'I'd rather you stopped running away from your feelings.'

What was so great about letting herself go? Anna wondered. Why couldn't they feel proud of her for soldiering on, instead of wanting her to be a soggy, suicidal grief heap?

'I'm just worried you might be starting to rely on them,' her mother said.

'Fine. If that's the way you feel about it—' Anna fished in her bag and drew out the bottle of pills. 'Here, you take them. Throw them in the sea, if you like.'

'Anna—' Jackie tried to hand them back.

'I mean it. You're right, I don't need them.'

'Don't be silly. You can't just give them up like that. You'll make yourself ill.'

'I don't want them,' Anna insisted feebly, but she didn't resist as her mother stuffed them back into her bag. She didn't want to admit to the panic she'd felt for the few moments they'd been out of her hands.

Jackie held out her arms. 'Come here, you. Don't let's fall out, I won't see you for two weeks.' She hugged her tightly. 'You know I only go on at you because I worry so much.'

'I would never have guessed.'

Keith came out of the house, staggering under the weight of various bags and boxes. 'Kitchen sink coming through,' he shouted. 'Blimey, Alice, how much stuff are you taking?'

'You need a lot of things at my age,' Nana said. 'My days

of going off to the coast with just a couple of bikinis are long gone.'

Keith shuddered. 'Dear God, what a picture.'

Anna stood at her mother's gate and waved them off. 'Where are they going?' Charlie asked, as Keith's car disappeared round the corner.

'They're going on holiday. To the seaside.'

She knew she'd said the wrong thing as soon as Charlie's lip started to wobble. 'I want to go to the seaside!'

Anna suddenly felt very selfish. Her mother had offered to take him, but she'd wanted him to stay with her. 'I'll take you,' she promised.

'When?'

'Soon. We'll go to Scarborough for the day and you can ride a donkey on the beach. How about that?'

Charlie nodded, pacified, but as they got into the car to go home it was Anna who suddenly felt anxious. Her mother had only been gone two minutes and already she had a sinking feeling of dread and panic, wondering how she was going to cope.

She thought about the magic pills in her bag, and felt slightly calmer. Was her mum right? Was she relying on them too much? Maybe she was, but she couldn't trust herself to do without them and her mum at the same time.

The rest of Saturday passed quickly. Anna was pleased with herself as she buzzed through her chores, going round the supermarket, cleaning the house and paying bills. In the evening, she played with Charlie and they watched a DVD before going to bed.

But the next day was a different story. The storm that had cracked the sky so spectacularly the previous day had settled into grey, depressing rain. Sunday was a difficult day anyway, with so many hours to fill. She usually ended up going to visit her mother just to get out of the house. Now she felt as if her lifeline had been cut, leaving her adrift.

And just to make it even worse, it was Father's Day. At least Charlie wasn't aware of it, but Anna couldn't pass a shop without seeing a reminder.

She lasted until lunchtime, then called Rachel. Luckily, she jumped at Anna's suggestion that they should take the kids to the local indoor play area to work off some energy.

'Great idea,' she said. 'Josh is climbing the walls here, and there are only so many times I can re-enact *Star Wars* without wanting to shoot myself.'

'Why don't we call Meg and invite her along?'

There was an awkward pause. 'I think she might be busy.'

Anna knew an excuse when she heard one. 'Rach, what's going on?'

'I don't know what you mean.'

'I'm not stupid. I haven't seen her for months. She never comes out for a run with us any more, and the last time she saw me she couldn't get away fast enough. Doesn't she want us to be friends, or something?'

'Of course she does.'

'Then why is she avoiding me?'

'I don't know.' She could sense Rachel squirming on the other end of the phone.

'Fine. If you won't tell me I'll just have to ask her myself.'

'No! Don't do that. It might be better if you just left her alone for a while, okay?'

'So she *is* avoiding me?'

'No. I mean – well, yes, sort of. But it's got nothing to do with you.'

'Of course it hasn't,' Anna said sarcastically.

'Anna, listen—'

But Anna had put the phone down. She'd heard enough.

Chapter 21

'Thanks a lot,' were Anna's first words when Meg opened the door.

'What?'

'I can understand other people blanking me, but not you. I thought you were my friend?'

'Anna—'

'Have I grown two heads? Is that why you don't want to be seen with me?'

'No.'

'Do you think bereavement is catching? You don't want to come near me in case someone you love dies, is that it?'

'No, of course not. I—'

'Then tell me, what's your problem?'

Meg stared at her for a moment. 'Dave's left me,' she said, and burst into tears.

Ten minutes later they were sitting side by side on the sofa, nursing cups of tea while Meg told her the whole sorry story.

'He left nearly two months ago, but I was expecting it. Things have been bad for months.' Her voice was flat, as if she'd cried all her emotion out a long time ago. 'Apparently it's been going on for ages, him and this regional sales manager. I should have known, shouldn't I? All the signs were there. The gym membership, the new clothes, all those weekend courses with his mobile switched off. How could I have been so stupid?'

'You mustn't blame yourself,' Anna said.

'Why not? He says it's my fault. I didn't put enough effort into our marriage.'

'Only because you were too busy looking after all his kids!'

'That's just it. He said I put the children before him. I got too mumsy and boring for him, apparently. All I ever talked about was the kids' spelling tests and the latest outbreak of nits.'

From somewhere upstairs came the thump of running footsteps and the sound of a child wailing in protest. Usually Meg would have been on her feet, distracting them with finger painting or some other fun activity, but now she looked as if she didn't care if they tarred, feathered and set fire to each other.

She sat in the middle of a chaos of toys, dressed in a baggy sweater and jeans. The merry sparkle had gone out of her eyes, and her usually rosy cheeks were pale. Also she'd lost weight.

'Bastard,' Anna said.

'He's right, though, isn't he? I mean, look at me. Who'd ever fancy me?' She pushed her tangled curls back off her face. 'No wonder he left me for a younger, sexier model.'

'Now you listen to me,' Anna said. 'Don't you dare blame yourself for any of this. As far as I can see the only thing you ever did wrong was trusting the slimeball.'

Meg managed a trembling smile before her face dissolved again. 'I'm really sorry, Anna. The last thing you want to hear is me feeling sorry for myself. You've been through much worse than me.'

'Is that why you've been avoiding me?'

Meg sniffed back tears. 'You had enough misery of your own, you didn't need mine too.'

'But that's what friends are for, isn't it? Sharing troubles?'

'Yes, but mine are so trivial compared to all the awful stuff you're going through.'

'I thought I must have done something wrong,' Anna said. 'I thought you didn't want to be my friend any more because of what happened to Oliver.'

'Oh Christ, you didn't?' Meg started to cry again. She fumbled up her sleeve for a tissue, then gave up and blew her nose on the edge of her jumper. 'I'm so sorry, Anna. I really wanted to be there for you, but I didn't think I could manage it. I even picked up the phone to call you a few times but I chickened out. I knew I'd end up blurting it all out about Dave, and I didn't want you to think I was being selfish and pathetic.'

'You're not selfish or pathetic.'

'I am. I just feel sorry for myself the whole time. I can't think straight, and I'm snappy and vile with the kids. I think I must be the world's worst mother at the moment.'

'Come on, you can't be worse than me and Rachel!' Anna joked feebly.

'Sometimes I just feel like walking out and leaving them. They'd be better off without me.'

'Don't say that.' Anna shivered. Four months ago, just after Oliver died, she'd stood on the river path staring into the inky-black waters of the Ouse and thought exactly the same thing. Life just seemed too big and too difficult to face without him.

Meg realised what she'd said. 'Oh God, I'm so sorry. See what I mean? This is why I wanted to stay away from you. I'm so disgustingly full of self-pity, when you've been through much, much worse—'

Anna reached for her hand. 'Maybe I'm the one person you should have talked to. I know what it's like to lose someone.'

'This is different, isn't it? Oliver didn't walk out on you.'

'It still hurts.'

They drank their tea and Meg cried some more and told Anna over and over again what a useless person she was. The more she talked, the more Anna wanted to thump Dave. He'd taken away every last shred of Meg's self-esteem and left her with nothing.

Finally, when Meg had cried all her tears out again, Anna decided it was time to take action.

'Rachel and I are taking the kids to the Play Zone this after-noon. Why don't we take your lot with us? It'll give you some time to catch up on your sleep.'

'Or the housework,' Meg said, looking around her.

'Definitely sleep. Housework can wait,' Anna said firmly. 'Then next weekend, we'll find babysitters and all meet up and go out. Just the three of us. We deserve a good laugh and a gossip, I reckon.'

Georgia walked past the condom display in Boots five times, trying to look sidelong at them without anyone noticing.

Why were there so *many*? What did they all mean? Surely they all did the same thing – or did they?

She really wished she'd listened in sex ed, instead of laughing at Cassie Evans when she flicked one out of the biology-lab window. She did a quick right turn past the paracetamol, then doubled back on herself and pretended to be looking at the cough medicines.

What if she bought the wrong kind? She'd die of shame if Andy laughed at her. Maybe he would come prepared, she thought. Or then again, maybe he wouldn't. He seemed like the kind of boy to take risks.

She'd already been cruising the aisles for half an hour; it was a miracle she didn't have a conga line of store detectives following her by now. She looked at her watch. Twenty minutes to closing time – it was now or never. She headed purposefully towards the condom counter, hand outstretched, blindly grabbed the first packet she could reach, and darted away again.

Right. Mission accomplished. Now she actually had them in her hand, all she had to do was pay for them, and— Oh God, no! It couldn't be.

Emma Standish was on the pharmacy till. Officially the biggest mouth in the school, if not the entire world, she was standing at the counter in her pale blue overall, ringing up a packet of Rennies for a middle-aged customer. Georgia shuddered. There was absolutely no way she could go up to her and pay.

She forced herself to stay calm. Look for another till. Except everywhere she looked, suddenly she seemed to see people she knew. Girls from her school, friends of her mother's, her English teacher – everyone in the whole world had come to Boots shopping on that Sunday afternoon.

There was nothing else for it. With another quick look round to make sure no one was watching, she feigned a coughing fit, slipped the packet into her bag and hurried out of the shop.

This time there were no alarm bells and no security people stopping her at the door.

All those weeks hanging around with Andy and his mates had obviously improved her technique, she decided.

On the way back from Play Zone, Anna stopped off at Smiths to buy Charlie some sweets and herself a magazine.

It was her reward to herself for two hours in kiddie hell. She and Rachel and about a million other desperate parents had crammed together at one end of the play barn while their children, and Meg's, ran and climbed and shrieked on the multi-storey play equipment, throwing themselves down slides and headlong into ball pools. As a result, Charlie was mercifully exhausted and she had the beginnings of a migraine.

It took Charlie about three seconds to choose a packet of Smarties and her a moment longer to pick out a gossipy celeb magazine. Something nice and undemanding that would go very well with a glass of wine and help her pass the evening.

Now all she needed was a way to pass the other thirteen evenings before her mum came home.

At least she had her girlie lunch with Rachel and Meg to look forward to. She was glad she'd sorted things out with her friend, and even happier that it hadn't been her fault.

'Look! Georgie!'

Charlie pointed excitedly towards the checkout line with his Smarties.

Georgia turned round at the sound of her name. Her face paled when she saw them.

'Oh, hello.' She was holding the same magazine as Anna was about to buy.

'Glad to see we've got the same fine taste in literature,' Anna said.

'What? Oh, yeah.'

Anna frowned at her. 'Are you okay?'

'I'm fine.'

As Georgia moved forward to the next checkout, something slipped from between the pages of her magazine.

They both dived for it at the same time, but Anna got there first. She'd already picked it up before she realised it was a Father's Day card.

'Dunno how that got there,' Georgia mumbled, red-faced.

'Must have got mixed up with the magazine, I suppose.'

'Probably. S'not mine, anyway. Obviously.'

Georgia hurried to the checkout with her magazine, leaving Anna holding the card.

'Obviously.' Anna looked at the card. 'To a Very Special Dad' was written in curly gold lettering against a background of a tasteful watercolour lake. Very different to the funny, mocking cards Georgia and Matt used to send.

But it wasn't the card that disturbed her. It was what she'd spied in Georgia's bag as she reached for the card. Did Eve know what her daughter was doing, she wondered. Anna wasn't sure she should be the one to tell her. She probably wouldn't be thanked for it.

Or maybe she already knew, in which case she definitely wouldn't appreciate Anna butting in. As far as Eve was concerned, Anna had stuck her nose in where it wasn't wanted a bit too much lately.

She decided it was probably better if she said nothing. After all, it wasn't really her business.

And at least Georgia was being careful.

Chapter 22

'Have you heard?' Barbara greeted her when she walked in on Monday morning. 'Ruth's had the baby. A little boy, seven pounds-two.'

'When did this happen?' Anna asked.

'Saturday. Neil called me yesterday to let me know.' She looked smug. 'And I was right about the pain relief. Apparently she sank her teeth into Neil's hand and wouldn't let go until he got her an epidural. She almost had his thumb off before the anaesthetist arrived. Natural childbirth, my eye!'

They were still discussing it when Elliott walked in ten minutes later. 'Please don't tell me I'm going to have to listen to you two swapping grisly birth stories all morning,' he pleaded.

Anna turned to him. 'Did you know about this?'

He nodded. 'Neil called me yesterday.'

'He didn't call me,' Anna said.

'He probably didn't feel he should. Under the circumstances,' Barbara said.

'What circumstances?'

'You know – after your Sad Loss.' Barbara mouthed the words the way she always did. 'I expect he was trying to be sensitive.'

'Why do people keep trying to protect me?' Anna protested, when Barbara had gone to put the kettle on. First it was Meg shielding her from bad news, then Neil shielding her from good. 'Can't they see I just want to feel normal again?'

'I don't treat you like that, do I?'

'No, but you're different. You're—'

'One of the walking wounded too?' he finished for her.

She smiled wryly. 'Something like that.'

He was quiet for a moment as he went through the post. Then he said, 'Do you fancy coming to a party on Saturday night?'

'I'm not sure I'm ready to feel that normal.'

'Before you get too excited I should warn you it's hardly going to be a night of drunken debauchery. Jessica's having a birthday sleepover. My mother was coming over to help me organise it but she's slipped a disc and can't make it. And frankly, the thought of all those eight-year-olds loose in the house doesn't exactly fill me with confidence. You'd be doing me a big favour.'

'My mum's away, but I suppose I could try to find a babysitter for Charlie.'

'Bring him along. The more the merrier.'

'In that case, I'd love to come.'

'Great. Don't forget your toothbrush, will you, because I'll expect you to stay the night.'

Unfortunately, Barbara just happened to emerge from the kitchen at that moment. She almost dropped the mugs she was carrying as she hurried back to her desk, her eyes averted.

Elliott and Anna smiled at each other. 'Do you think I should set her straight?' she whispered.

'Not just yet,' Elliott grinned. 'We can enjoy the peace and quiet while she works out how she missed that bit of office gossip!'

Georgia slumped in the bathroom, the walls reeling around her. She wished the room would stop spinning long enough for her to reach the door. Every time she tried, she needed to throw up again. She couldn't remember how much she'd had to drink – still not enough to want to be alone with Andy, that was for sure.

She kept very still and tried to focus on the row of toiletries on the shelf above the washbasin. From beyond the door came the sound of thumping music, shouting and laughter.

She wanted to go home, and she wanted her mum.

Someone thumped on the bathroom door.

'Georgia? You in there?' Andy called.

'Just a minute.' She crawled across the room and managed to pull the bolt to let him in.

'Bloody hell,' he laughed. 'You're in a right state.'

'I don't feel well,' she moaned.

'I'm not surprised. You're off your fucking head.' He took her by the arm and hauled her to her feet. 'Come with me.'

'Where are we going?'

'To make you feel better.'

Next thing she knew, they were in a bedroom.

'I think I'm going to be sick again,' Georgia mumbled.

'You'll be okay. Just lie down on the bed.'

It felt so good to close her eyes and let the room stop spinning. She drifted away, letting the peace and darkness take her over.

A second later she was awake again, all her senses on full alert. Andy was fumbling with her top.

She pulled away sharply, panic sobering her. 'What are you doing?'

'What do you think?'

She tried to sit up but he pushed her down again, pinning her to the bed.

'Relax,' he whispered. 'Just enjoy it, okay?'

The front door of Elliott's modern town house was festooned with pink and silver balloons.

'Very camp,' Anna said, when Elliott opened the door.

He looked down at his jeans and black t-shirt. 'You think so? I wondered if I'd used too much hair gel.'

'I meant the balloons.'

'Oh, right.'

He crouched down to greet Charlie, who clung shyly to his mother's leg. 'You must be Charlie. I can't tell you what a relief it is to have another man in the house. At least now I can have a sensible conversation.'

She followed him into the house. 'I wouldn't rely on it, unless you're a world expert on *Thomas the Tank Engine*.'

'As a matter of fact, I am.'

'Why doesn't that surprise me?' She gazed up at the ceiling. 'They seem very quiet.'

'You should have been here ten minutes ago when they were coming to blows over the dance mat. I feel like I'm in the Barbie version of *The Lord of the Flies*.'

'What are they doing now?'

'God knows. Some sort of ritual sacrifice, I think. Or putting on make-up. Either way, I'm staying well out of it. Would you like a glass of wine?'

'Please.'

He led the way through the sitting room, hung with pink glittery banners and more balloons, into the small, modern kitchen.

'Looks like you've got it all pretty well under control,' Anna remarked.

'All except the food. I was hoping you'd give me a hand with that.' He threw open the larder door. 'It's all here, it just needs setting out.'

Anna gazed at all the cakes and biscuits piled up in the cupboard. 'Wow, it's all so—'

'Pink,' Charlie finished for her, eyes wide.

'Blame my sister. She did a big shop at Tesco for me. And she made the cake.' He pointed to another frosted baby-pink creation, scattered with Love Hearts and glittery candles.

'All those E-numbers,' Anna said wonderingly.

'I know,' Elliott groaned. 'They'll be bouncing around like Duracell bunnies.'

'At least I match.' Unsure what to wear for an eight-year-old's party, she'd opted for a pink t-shirt and white jeans.

'My daughter will be impressed,' Elliott said.

The party turned out to be great fun. Jessica and her friends were, despite Elliott's dire warnings, very sweet. Her sister, Becky, three years older, was utterly dismissive but still joined in. They were even lovely to Charlie, adopting him as a little mascot, laughing at his antics and dancing around him as if he was a human handbag.

Later, when Charlie had finally gone to bed after far too much cake, Anna helped calm down the girls by giving them manicures and putting their hair in French plaits while they watched a chick flick. Elliott beat a tactful retreat to the kitchen to wash up, leaving them all to it.

Finally, at about midnight, they all went to sleep in Jessica's room. Anna and Elliott flopped on the sofa, amid the debris of banners, balloons, glittery wrapping paper, and other girlie clutter.

'Are you sure it's okay for me to stay?' Anna asked. 'They might be more comfortable if they spread out to the spare room.'

'Apparently being squashed in like sardines is all part of the fun,' Elliott told her. 'When Becky had her sleepover it looked like the field hospital at Scutari.' He tut-tutted. 'Don't you know *anything*?'

'I know how to do the Macarena. Which apparently you don't.'

He looked hurt. 'I tried.'

'You looked like you were having some kind of seizure.'

'Actually, I was very impressed by your skills. I never had you down as a dance-floor diva.'

'I have all kinds of talents you know nothing about.'

'Really?' He raised his eyebrow. 'Such as?'

'Such as ...' She thought for a moment. 'I can sing all the words to "La Bamba". And I can suck my own toes.'

'At the same time?'

'No.'

'Pity. That might have been worth watching.' He refilled her wine glass and handed it to her. 'Thanks for coming to my rescue, by the way. I couldn't have got through it without you.'

'Thanks for inviting me.'

'You don't have to be polite. I'm sure you've got better things to do than spend the evening with a load of hyperactive eight-year-old girls.'

'It's better than spending it on my own.'

'Weekends are the worst, aren't they?' Elliott said sympathetically.

'It's different during the week because I've got work to look forward to – I know,' she laughed, as Elliott's eyebrows shot up, 'I never thought I'd say it but I actually miss Barbara's witty banter. On the weekend, though, time just seems to crawl by. There's nothing to do except sit and brood.'

'You know what Barbara would say to that, don't you?'

'"Get yourself a nice hobby." She's already suggested I join her macramé class, but I don't think it would help somehow.'

He looked at her thoughtfully. 'I thought you had your friend Lynch to keep you company these days?'

'I haven't seen him for a while.'

'I'm sorry.'

'I'm not. It got a bit awkward, to tell the truth.'

'I can guess why,' Elliott said.

She blushed. She'd forgotten the whole office knew about their encounter. 'It was a stupid thing to do. I don't even know why it happened.'

'Because you were lonely.'

'Maybe, but I still feel guilty.'

'Why? It's not a crime to want to feel loved.'

'You sound as if you've been there yourself.'

He was quiet for a long time, then he said, 'Her name was Amanda. She was a friend of Karen's. She helped me after Karen died, looking after the girls, keeping me company, that sort of thing. Trying to keep me sane. Then one night it just happened.' He stared into the depths of his glass. 'I knew it was a mistake, and I felt so ashamed of myself, as if I'd betrayed Karen's memory. She'd only been gone a month, but I just needed someone.'

'What happened?'

'It ended pretty badly. I realised I was only with Amanda because I was afraid of being alone. But our friendship ended with it, that's what I regret most of all.'

'I know what you mean.' She missed Lynch being around to make her laugh and forget her troubles. 'So have you been out with anyone else since?'

Elliott laughed. 'Anna, it's been five years. I know you might think I'm dull, but I'm not a monk!'

Actually, he was quite attractive. Not obviously gorgeous like Lynch, but in the kind of way that crept up on you. Those warm, melting chocolate eyes, that thick curly hair that you want to run your hands through ...

Oh no, she thought, it's happening again. Another adolescent crush.

She put down her glass. 'I think I'll go to bed.'

'Are you sure you don't want to finish the bottle?' Elliott asked.

'No thanks.' She was tempted, but she didn't want to lose her inhibitions again. Or another friend.

Her mobile rang, right on cue. Anna jumped to answer it.

'Anna?' Georgia's voice trembled on the other end of the line. 'Where are you?'

'I'm at a friend's. Where are you?'

'Outside your house.' She heard the sound of a police siren somewhere in the background. 'Can you come home, please? I need you.'

Chapter 23

Anna left Charlie at Elliott's and raced straight home.

Georgia was on her doorstep, her knees tucked under her chin. Her thin, bare arms were pale in the moonlight. Even in the darkness, Anna could see she'd been crying.

As soon as she saw Anna, Georgia jumped to her feet and ran to her. Anna staggered back as the girl fell full force into her arms. She reeked of alcohol and cigarettes.

'Let's go inside.' Still holding on to Georgia with one arm, Anna fumbled in her pocket for her key. She helped her into the house, guided her into the sitting room and switched on the light.

Georgia, who was dressed in drainpipes and a skimpy black vest top, sat shivering on the sofa. There were livid bruises on the insides of her arms.

Anna sat down beside her, her arm around the girl's trembling shoulders.

'Can you tell me what's wrong?' she asked gently.

'It – it's Andy.'

'The boy I saw you with that time?' Georgia nodded. Her dark hair fell across her face, sticking to her wet cheeks. 'What happened? What did he do to you?' Panic ran through her. 'Has he hurt you?'

Georgia started to cry again. Anna stroked the hair off her face and tried to stop herself fearing the worst.

She reached for the phone. 'I'm calling your mum.'

'No!' Georgia looked up, her eyes swimming with tears. 'I don't want her to know.'

'But—'

'Why do you think I came here? You were the only one I could think of. The only one I could trust.'

They faced each other for a moment, then Anna reluctantly put the phone down. 'You'd better tell me everything,' she said.

Slowly, haltingly, it all came out. How this Andy creep had put pressure on her to sleep with him, but she was scared.

'I knew it would happen at this party or he'd dump me, so I tried to get myself drunk. But it didn't work.' She took a big, shuddering breath, trying to calm herself. 'I nearly passed out. Andy found me and took me into the bedroom. I thought he was being nice, but it turned out he wanted to – you know.'

Anna could feel the bones of Georgia's shoulders working underneath her skin. She was so small, so fragile.

'He pinned me down to the bed, he was trying to take my top off. I panicked, and then—'

'Then what?' Anna's fingers tightened on Georgia's bare arm.

'I – I threw up on him.' Georgia was sobbing again, her face buried in her hands.

Anna hadn't realised she'd stopped breathing until it all came out in a whoosh of relief. 'You did what?'

'I was sick. Really, really sick. All over the bed – and him. It was terrible,' she cried.

She was so mortified she could hardly speak, but it was all Anna could do to stop herself smiling. 'And then what happened?'

'He got really angry. He was wearing new trainers and they cost a fortune. He said I was stupid and frigid.' She hung her head so Anna couldn't see her face. 'Then, as I was leaving, I saw him kissing Kayleigh. And he said she wasn't even his type!'

'Sounds like Kayleigh's not too fussy either.'

'She's a slag,' Georgia said vehemently.

She broke into fresh sobs. Anna pulled her close. 'I know it won't seem like it at the moment, but I reckon you've had a lucky escape.'

'But I liked him. He was the only one who ever noticed me. He treated me like I was something special.'

You must have been very special if he could snog someone

195

else after five minutes, Anna thought, but she didn't say anything. She could still remember how devastated she was when Aaron Barker wrote insulting graffiti about her on the boys' toilet wall, ten minutes after dumping her.

Georgia pulled away, wiping her nose with the back of her hand. 'Can I stay here tonight?'

'Won't your mum wonder where you are?'

'She thinks I'm staying over at the party. She wouldn't care, anyway.'

'That's not true.'

'You don't know what she's like. She's changed since Dad died. The only thing she ever thinks about is that restaurant.'

'She's bound to be working hard at the moment—'

'You don't get it, do you? She's *obsessed*. It's the only thing she cares about. That and visiting Dad's grave.' Her face hardened. 'She thinks we don't know, but we're not stupid. She cares more about him than she does about us.'

Anna put Georgia to bed, then went back to Elliott's to pick up Charlie.

Elliott was waiting up for her. 'Everything all right?' he asked.

'Just a teenage trauma, thank God.' She suppressed a shudder. It could have been so much worse than a broken heart and hurt pride.

Elliott frowned. 'Shouldn't her mother be dealing with all that?'

'You're telling me.' If she hadn't promised Georgia, she would have had a few things to say to Eve Robinson.

Georgia was pale, subdued and hungover the following morning. She sat at the kitchen table in a pair of Anna's borrowed pyjamas, clutching a glass of orange juice as if her life depended on it.

'I'm really sorry about last night.' She pushed away the plate of toast Anna put in front of her. 'Did I wreck your evening?'

Anna poured herself a coffee and thought of Elliott. 'Actually, you probably did me a favour.'

'Was it really boring?'

'Compared to your evening, it probably was.'

A blush of embarrassment stained her white face. 'Oh God, I was such a freak. I can't believe I was actually sick on Andy Taylor.'

'Sounds like no less than he deserved.' Anna took the untouched plate of toast and threw it in the bin.

'Promise you won't tell Mum?' Georgia said.

Anna let the bin lid drop and turned to face her. 'She's your mother. She'd want to know. I'd want to know if I was her.'

'You're different,' Georgia said. 'I told you, she doesn't care about us.' She turned her anxious grey eyes to Anna. 'Please don't tell her, will you?'

'I promised I wouldn't, didn't I?' But she was beginning to wish she hadn't. She itched to pick up the phone right now and tell Eve just how much her wallowing in grief was hurting her children. 'Get dressed and I'll give you a lift home.'

Georgia shook her head. 'If Mum sees your car she might start asking questions.'

'I thought you said she didn't care?'

'She doesn't.'

Half an hour later she watched Georgia head off down the road, still in last night's party clothes. Apart from a hangover and a bit of dented pride, she seemed none the worse for the previous night's ordeal.

She was a teenage drama queen, there was no doubt about that, but all this Andy business had obviously been a big cry for attention. She couldn't believe Eve had ignored it for so long.

She closed the door, checked Charlie was happily watching the Sunday morning kids' shows on TV, then went upstairs for a quick shower. She'd just put her dressing gown on when there was a knock on the door. Thinking it was Georgia, she ran down to answer it.

Lynch took off his sunglasses and looked her up and down, his gaze falling for a moment on the neckline of her dressing gown. In his crumpled linen chinos and white t-shirt, he looked tanned and sexy in a dishevelled, morning-after-the-night-before kind of way.

'Hi. Remember me?'

'Vaguely. Didn't you used to be my lawyer?'

'I seem to remember I was a lot more than that the last time we met.'

She pulled the edges of her dressing gown together. 'I thought we'd agreed not to talk about that?'

'That doesn't stop me thinking about it.' He glanced past her into the hall. 'Is that coffee I can smell?'

'I tried to call you last night but there was no reply,' he said as he followed her into the kitchen. 'Where were you?'

'I could ask you the same question. You've been gone for months.'

He smiled. 'You've been counting the days? That's so sweet.'

'Don't flatter yourself. Surely you haven't been on business all this time?'

'It took a lot longer than I thought in New York. Then, because I'd been working so hard, I treated myself to some time off and flew down to Miami to catch up with some old friends.'

'That explains the tan.' She put the coffee down in front of him and flicked on the answer machine. There were three messages, two from Lynch and one from her mother, telling her the weather in Whitby was terrible and Nana's sciatica was playing her up again.

Lynch looked amused. 'Don't you lead an exciting life?'

'Not as exciting as yours, obviously. But I have my moments.'

He pulled out a chair and sat down. 'So who's this mystery man you were with last night?'

'None of your business. I don't ask who you've been with while you were sunning yourself in the States. Although I daresay there must have been several,' she added.

'Jealous?' he taunted.

'Why should I be?'

'I had hoped maybe absence might have made your heart grow fonder?'

'Lynch! The only reason I missed you was because I needed a lawyer.'

He frowned. 'Problems?'

She thought about her latest bust-up with Eve. 'Let's just say the situation has changed.'

'Why don't we have dinner on Tuesday? We can catch up then.'

She hesitated. 'Couldn't I just come and see you at your office?'

'What's wrong? Not sure you can trust yourself?'

'Not sure I can trust *you*, more like.'

'As I recall, it wasn't me who made the first move that night.' He saw Anna's warning look. 'Okay, I get the message, I won't ever mention it again. So how about dinner?'

She considered it. 'If I can find a babysitter.'

'Great. The table's booked for eight.'

'How did you know I'd say yes?'

He grinned, supremely confident. 'How could you say no to me?'

'Arrogant swine.' She couldn't help smiling. She'd missed him more than she liked to admit.

'So who was he?' he asked as he left.

'Who?'

'Your mystery man. The one you were with last night.'

'If you must know, it was my boss, Elliott.'

He looked relieved. 'That's okay, then. For a moment there, I thought I had a serious rival, but I guess you're safe enough with Mr Prozac. He wouldn't make a move on you in a million years.'

Chapter 24

The following Saturday, Anna met up for her girlie lunch with Rachel and Meg at Oliver's.

'Clever move, getting us to eat here,' Rachel commented as they sat down. 'You get to spend time with us and make money at the same time.'

'I'm not sure how much money we're making.' Anna looked around the near-empty restaurant. The only other customers were a solitary businessman shovelling down pasta with one hand and toying with his PDA with the other, and a glum-looking middle-aged couple.

'Business still isn't too good?' Meg said.

'I have no idea. Eve never tells me anything.'

She'd almost given up trying to get information out of her. She'd called in at the restaurant once or twice, but somehow Eve was always too busy to see her. She'd even offered to help out a few times, but was turned down.

'Anyway, forget about work. We're here to talk about you,' she said to Meg. 'You're looking great, by the way.'

It was certainly an improvement on the last time Anna had seen her. She'd washed her hair, put on some make-up and, even though she was still wearing jeans, at least she'd changed that awful sweater for a decent t-shirt.

'I had to do something. I was frightening the children.' Meg ran her hand through her curls.

'Shall we order before we start bitching about your ex?' Rachel said, as Laura came over with the menus.

'Sorry, the sea bass is off,' she said. 'So is the salmon. The fishmonger hasn't supplied this week.'

'You're kidding.' Anna put her menu down. 'How did that happen?'

'You'll have to ask Eve. All I know is there's no fish on the menu.'

'You see what I mean?' Anna said, when they'd finally all decided on pasta. 'This place is going to the dogs. No wonder we haven't got any customers.'

'Can't you talk to Eve?' Meg said.

'I might as well talk to that brick wall. The only person she listens to is Frankie. As far as she's concerned, he can do no wrong.'

And between them, they were ruining Oliver's reputation. That was what really hurt.

'Excuse me,' Meg interrupted. 'Sorry to sound like a selfish cow, but when are we going to stop talking about work and start bitching about my ex? It's just that my babysitter's only booked until teatime, and I want to get a nice therapeutic slagging session in before then.'

Of course they were happy to oblige. As the wine flowed, they got stuck in to Dave and His Many Faults. At first Meg held back, but gradually she began to admit that perhaps he did have some bad points after all. By the time their food arrived, she'd finally realised what an uncaring, selfish pig she'd married. It was all they could do to stop her breaking into a rousing chorus of 'I Will Survive'.

Then they moved on to Dave's new fancy woman. 'I can see her now,' Rachel said, twirling spaghetti around her fork. 'All big tits and teabag tan. I bet she's dead tacky.'

'Actually, I met her at a Christmas party and she seems very nice.' Meg gulped her wine, forgetting that she was supposed to be well rid of him. 'Really attractive, with a fabulous designer wardrobe.'

'A label freak,' Rachel said dismissively. 'I bet she looks like a footballer's wife.'

'No, she's really stylish and understated. She's clever, too.'

'What's she doing with a drip like Dave, then?' Rachel said. Anna laughed, Meg didn't.

'She's got a PhD in marketing. And she lives in a wonderful loft apartment, with stainless-steel appliances and white sofas and everything.'

Anna and Rachel looked at each other worriedly. 'Meg—'

But there was no stopping her. 'And she does Pilates in her spare time, so she's really bendy and she probably knows all kinds of unusual sexual positions. My idea of adventurous sex was taking my nightie off.' A tear rolled down her cheek. 'Oh God, no wonder he left me. I would probably have run off with her too, if I'd had the chance.'

'Now you listen to me.' Rachel waved her glass in front of Meg's face. 'She might have all that going for her now, but give it six months and wait until the novelty wears off. She'll be schlepping around in her dressing gown and telling him she's too tired just like the rest of us.'

'Or wait until he starts leaving his dirty socks scattered on her designer bedroom floor, expecting her to pick them up,' Anna chimed in.

'Or he moans because his dinner isn't on the table,' Rachel added.

'Better still, why don't you send the kids over to stay at their place? I bet her white sofas won't be quite so pristine when they've been let loose on them for an hour.'

'Great idea,' Rachel agreed. 'It's about time she found out what she's taking on, don't you think?'

While Rachel and Meg enthusiastically planned the rapid end of Dave and his new woman's honeymoon, Anna couldn't help noticing an argument going on between Laura and the glum couple at the corner table.

She tried to ignore it, but in the end she couldn't help herself.

'It's no good, I've got to find out what's wrong,' she said, putting down her napkin.

'Stay out of it, Anna,' Rachel warned, but she was already halfway to their table.

'Excuse me, is there a problem?' she asked politely.

The man glared at her. 'Are you the manager?'

'No, but—'

'Then what's it got to do with you?'

'They won't pay for their meal,' Laura explained.

'Why not?'

'I'll tell you why not.' Angry spittle flew from the man's lips. 'First, there was hardly anything on the menu we wanted to eat. Then when we did finally find something, we had to wait ages for it. And when it did arrive, it was cold. Now do you think that's acceptable?'

If he hadn't been so rude about it, Anna might have been more sympathetic. But there was something about his pugnacious little face that made her hackles rise.

She eyed the empty plates. 'You've eaten it all, so it can't have been that bad.'

'What should we have done? Sent it back and waited another two hours? Of course we ate it!'

Anna clenched her hands into fists at her sides to control her temper. 'In which case, you'll have to pay for your meal.'

'I don't think so, young lady.' The man drew himself upright. Opposite him, his wife pleated her napkin between her fingers and said nothing. 'The food and service have been utterly appalling. My wife and I will certainly never be coming back here again.'

'That's your choice,' Anna said, 'But you're still going to have to pay for your meal.'

'And who's going to make me?'

'The police, if necessary.'

'Now you listen here—'

'Is there a problem?'

There was Eve, standing behind them, looking harassed. Anna had been so caught up in her argument with the customer, she hadn't noticed Laura sneak off to the kitchen to fetch her.

'Nothing I can't handle,' she muttered.

Eve ignored her. 'Can I help?' she asked the man.

'I was just explaining that it's customary to pay one's bill after eating a meal in a restaurant,' Anna interrupted.

'And I was just explaining that it's customary for a restaurant to provide food that isn't completely inedible.'

'You didn't seem to have any trouble eating it,' Anna said.

Eve held up her hand. 'Will you let me handle this?' She turned to the man. 'I'm so sorry you didn't enjoy your meal, sir,' she said in a resigned voice. 'Of course, if it's failed to meet your expectations we wouldn't dream of asking you to pay.'

Anna's mouth fell open. 'But—'

'I should damn well think not,' the man blustered. 'And what about her threatening to call the police?'

'I regret that, as I'm sure my colleague does too.' She glanced at Anna. 'And we'd like to give you a bottle of wine to take home with you, as a token of our apology.'

Anna fumed quietly as Eve fussed over the couple, helping them into their coats.

As he left, the man thrust his face close to hers and sneered, 'You should take a leaf out of your boss's book. At least she knows how to treat a customer.'

Doesn't she just, Anna thought.

She barely waited until the door had closed on Mr and Mrs Obnoxious before she turned on Eve. 'Why didn't you just pay for their taxi, while you were at it?'

'He had a genuine complaint,' Eve said calmly, picking up their empty plates.

'Genuine, my eye! You do realise he's going to run straight off and tell all his friends where they can get a free meal, don't you?'

'He might also tell them what a great place this is.'

'Yeah, right. I bet they'll be queuing out of the door to get their free food. Not to mention a nice bottle of wine to take home as a reward for fleecing us. We can't afford to give away meals like that, or hadn't you noticed?'

'Oh, I'd noticed, all right.' Eve massaged her temples. 'I'm the one who has to balance the books, remember?'

Anna stifled a sigh. Eve's exhausted martyr act was getting a bit too much for her. 'Only because you won't let anyone else help.'

'I don't need your help. I can manage by myself.'

Is that why you've got no staff, no money and no customers? Anna wanted to shout. 'Why do you have to keep shutting me out? What are you trying to prove?'

The businessman was watching them avidly; Rachel was shaking her head and Meg had hidden behind her hands.

'I'm not trying to prove anything, I'm just trying to run a business.'

'And you think you're the only one good enough to do it, do you? You reckon if you run this place it will show everyone how much you cared about Oliver.'

'That's not true!'

'Let's face it, Eve, that's the only reason you want to do this. You want to prove to everyone that you're the one he trusted, the one he wanted to take over. Well, I'm sorry, but you're not going to push me out of Oliver's life by pushing me out of the restaurant.'

Anger flared in Eve's eyes. 'And what would you do? Turn this place into a pizza parlour so you could make more money? That's all you're interested in, isn't it? You don't really care what this place meant to him, as long as it keeps paying your bills!'

Anna heard Rachel's sharp intake of breath behind her. Stung, she snapped back, 'It's a pity you don't worry about your kids as much as you do about keeping Oliver's memory alive. Then maybe I wouldn't have your daughter turning up at midnight on my doorstep because she doesn't want to go home!'

She clamped her mouth shut, knowing she'd said too much.

Eve went very still. 'What? When was this?'

'It doesn't matter.'

Anna moved to turn away, but Eve grabbed her. 'If you know something, you've got to tell me.'

Anna met her gaze. Eve's eyes were no longer angry, they were full of fear.

'Talk to Georgia,' she said quietly.

Eve froze for a moment. Then she began ripping off her apron.

'Where are you going?' Anna asked.

'Home.'

'But what about this place?'

'You want to help? *You* do it.' Eve stuffed her apron into Anna's hands. 'I'm going to see my daughter.'

Chapter 25

Georgia applied the last of the peroxide to her hair and wrapped it carefully in a plastic cap, trying to catch the drips that ran down her neck. She covered the whole lot in a towel and checked her watch. Not long now and she'd be a stunning blonde, just like the girl on the packet.

Across the landing, Matt was playing his guitar again. Georgia went into her bedroom and turned on the Red Hot Chili Peppers full volume. Up went Matt's guitar amp in response, whining through the house. The pictures trembled on the walls and Benson fled downstairs to the kitchen.

Georgia stomped across the landing and hammered on his door. 'Do you mind? I'm trying to listen to some decent music.'

'Piss off,' came the muffled reply.

'Piss off yourself.' She turned round, and jumped when she saw her mother standing at the foot of the stairs.

'Will you tell him?' She pointed at Matt's door. 'He's driving me mad. He can't even play that thing.'

She went into her own room and turned off her music. A second later her mother appeared in her doorway.

'What's going on, Georgia?' she asked.

'It's not me, it's him. He started it. I'll be glad when he goes to university and takes his stupid guitar with him—'

She caught the look on her mum's face and instantly knew she was in trouble.

'I've been talking to Anna.'

Oh shit. Georgia's mind raced. 'What did she tell you?'

'I'd rather hear it from you.'

There was no getting away from it. All this time Georgia thought she'd wanted her mum to find out. But now she was sitting on the end of her bed, watching and waiting, suddenly Georgia realised she didn't want to talk about it after all.

She took the CD from the player and put it back into its case. 'It's nothing,' she mumbled. 'I just had a bit of trouble with a boy, that's all.'

'What kind of trouble?' Georgia said nothing. 'You might as well tell me,' her mother said, folding her arms, 'I'm not moving from here until you do.'

It was an awkward conversation. Georgia sat squashed up against the head of her bed, as far away from her mother as she could get, her body hunched, knees drawn up under her chin. She hugged a pillow for protection, her face buried in it so she wouldn't have to look at her mother's face.

She'd barely got as far as saying Andy's name when the barrage of questions started.

'You had a boyfriend? How long for? Where did you meet him?'

Georgia stifled a sigh. This was going to take for ever. 'He was just someone Stacey knew from school.'

'Oh well, why doesn't that surprise me.' Her mother rolled her eyes. 'I might have known that family would be involved.'

'You've got it wrong. Stacey tried to stop me going out with him. She warned me he was trouble.'

'Trouble? What kind of trouble?'

Georgia told her about Andy, being careful to leave out all the bits about her skipping school, stealing condoms and briefly taking up smoking. She wasn't sure her mum could handle it.

It was just as well she did. 'Georgia, what were you thinking? What made you get involved with a low-life like that?'

Because I wanted you to notice me, she wanted to scream, but it all seemed childish and pointless now. To tell the truth, she felt a bit ashamed. Looking back on it, she couldn't remember what she'd ever seen in Andy Taylor. He wasn't clever, he wasn't even remotely good-looking. And he tasted like an ashtray when he kissed her.

Kayleigh was welcome to him.

'What's this about you turning up at Anna's house?' her mother asked.

Georgia stared down at the chipped polish on her toes. 'It was that night I went to the party. Something went wrong, and I didn't have anywhere to go, so I went round to her place. She promised she wouldn't tell.'

'What went wrong?' Georgia was stubbornly silent, still staring at her toes. She wondered what it would feel like to have a proper pedicure in a beauty salon. 'What went wrong, Georgia? You'd better tell me now, because whatever it is, it can't be any worse than what I'm imagining.'

She told her. Her mother hardly seemed to be listening. Her face was rigid, like a mask.

'It's okay, nothing happened,' Georgia assured her quickly. Still her mother's expression didn't change.

'Oh God.' Her voice was very faint, as if it was coming from a long way away.

At first Georgia thought she was angry, until she looked up and she saw the tears running down her face.

'Why didn't you tell me?' she said. 'Why did you go to Anna?'

'I – I didn't think you cared,' she stammered.

Her mother flinched, as if she'd slapped her. 'How can you say that? I love you, you know that.'

'It didn't feel like it. You were never here. You spent all your time at the restaurant. It was like you didn't want to be with us.'

Her mother stared at her for a moment. Then her face crumpled.

'Don't cry. Please don't cry,' Georgia begged. She put down the pillow and crawled down the bed to her. 'I'm sorry.'

'It's me who should be sorry. I've let you both down so much.'

'You haven't, really. You—' She felt the icy trickle running down the back of her neck and suddenly remembered. 'Quick, what's the time?'

Her mother wiped away her tears and looked blearily at her watch. 'Twenty past. Why?'

'Oh shit!' She sprang off the bed and ran to the bathroom slamming the door behind her. With shaking hands she peeled off the towel, to reveal—

'No!' Her wail of despair rang through the house.

There was a soft tap on the door. 'Is everything all right in there?' her mother asked.

'No. No, it bloody well isn't!'

'Can I help?'

'No.' No one could help. She might as well die.

'At least let me come in and take a look?'

Georgia hesitated. 'You can look,' she said. 'Just don't say anything, okay?'

She heard her mother's sigh. 'I won't say a word.'

She unbolted the door but before her mother could slide inside, Matt flung it open.

'Jesus!' He laughed. 'You're a ginger!'

'Sod off!' Georgia slammed the door in his face. 'I hate you! I hate everybody.' Most of all she hated the fucking girl on the packet, with her swingy, shiny blonde hair.

Her mother lifted the plastic and examined a lock of hair. 'It's not too bad,' she said.

'It's orange!' Georgia wailed.

'That's only because you haven't left it on long enough. Another fifteen minutes and it'll be fine.'

Georgia looked at her uncertainly. 'Are you sure?'

'Trust me, I'm an expert.' Her mum pointed to her own honey-blonde hair. 'Do you think God gave me this colour?'

She tucked Georgia's sticky orange hair back inside the plastic cap. 'Would you like me to help you?' she said.

'Don't you have to go back to work?'

Her mother smiled, her face still blotchy from tears. 'I think they can do without me for once.'

★

209

Later, Eve went out to do some work in the garden. It was a warm afternoon, and perspiration trickled down the inside of her t-shirt as she knelt in the flowerbed, wrenching out weeds.

She was attacking an awkward patch of dandelions when she heard the gate click. She glanced over her shoulder to see Anna walking up the path towards her.

'I thought you might need these.' She dropped the restaurant keys on to the grass beside her.

'Thanks.'

'It didn't go too well, in case you were wondering,' Anna said. 'I had a row with Frankie. And I broke the microwave.'

She said nothing. She waited for Anna to leave but she stood there, blocking out the light.

'How's Georgia?' she asked.

'She's fine.'

'Getting over Andy, then?'

'I think he's already history.'

The weeds made a satisfying tearing sound as she ripped them out of the soil. She wished she could have got hold of that Andy creature by the hair and given him the same treatment.

'Teenage hearts are pretty resilient, aren't they?' Anna said. 'If only they stayed that way.' She hesitated. 'Look, I hope you're not pissed off with me,' she said. 'It wasn't my idea to keep this whole thing a secret. I wanted to tell you, but Georgia made me promise.'

Eve looked over her shoulder at her. It suddenly dawned on her why Anna was hanging around. 'You think I'm angry with *you*?'

Anna stirred up the gravel on the path with the toe of her trainer. 'I should have told you what happened.'

Eve stood up and brushed the soil off her hands. 'I'm just glad she had someone to turn to. At least you were there for her, which is more than I was.'

Anna frowned at her. 'You mustn't blame yourself.'

'Why not? Who else can I blame?' All her anger and self-hatred came bubbling up. 'My daughter had a boyfriend I didn't even know about. She put herself in danger and I didn't have a clue. What kind of mother am I if I didn't notice something like that?'

'Teenage girls are good at hiding things when they want to.'

That's just it, Eve thought. She wasn't hiding anything. She wanted me to find out, to notice her. But I let her down.

'I bet you hid things from your mother,' Anna said.

'I didn't have to. My mother never listened to me anyway.'

And she was no better. She'd always sworn that when she had children it would be so different. She would put them first, before everything else in the world.

She sat down on the low garden wall. 'I should never have taken on the restaurant,' she said.

'You did what you thought was best.'

'It wasn't, though, was it? You were right. I had no idea what I was doing. I still don't.' She ran her hand through her hair, pushing it back off her face. 'I thought if I just carried on working hard it would all come out right in the end. But it hasn't.'

It was sheer selfishness that had driven her to it. Wanting to prove something to the world, wanting to lose herself in something, to ease her grief and loneliness.

But she'd forgotten the people who needed her most.

She stared down at the rims of dirt under her fingernails. 'I didn't want to let anyone down,' she said. 'There were so many people relying on me. I didn't want you to lose your house, or the staff to lose their jobs.'

'Or Oliver to lose his dream?' Anna said.

'Maybe,' Eve agreed. 'But I've let down the people who were most important. My children.'

'You mustn't think that.'

'I have! Matt nearly didn't go to university because he didn't think I could cope. And now Georgia's got herself in all kinds of trouble just to get noticed, and I haven't even managed to save the restaurant.' She buried her face in her hands. 'I've really made a mess of everything.'

And she didn't care. She was just so tired, she didn't want to think about any of it any more.

'Maybe you just need a break,' Anna said. 'Why don't you take a holiday, just you and the kids?'

'How can I?'

'Simple. Just pack your bags and get on a plane.'

She smiled wearily. 'It's a nice idea, but I couldn't. Who'd run Oliver's?'

'I will.'

'You?'

'I've worked there before, I think I could keep an eye on the place for a week or two.' She grinned. 'Don't worry, I won't turn it into a pizza parlour while your back's turned!'

'Right now, I don't think I'd care,' she said frankly. 'But are you sure? What about your job?'

'I'm sure they'll let me have a couple of weeks off.'

Eve hesitated. It was such a tempting idea. A couple of weeks away with the kids might be just what she needed to recharge her batteries and get her life back on track.

'You're exhausted,' Anna said. 'If you don't do something soon, you'll end up collapsing, and what good would you be to anyone then?'

True, Eve thought. But there was one thing that bothered her. 'What about Frankie? I don't think he'd like the idea.'

Anna smiled. 'He'll just have to lump it, won't he? Don't worry, I can handle him.'

That's what I'm afraid of, Eve thought. She didn't want to come back and find they had no chef as well as no customers.

Chapter 26

JULY

'Who's that man talking to Frankie?'

Laura glanced over Anna's shoulder out of the restaurant window. 'No idea. Never seen him before.'

'I think I have.' Anna pressed closer to the glass to get a better look.

She'd only ever seen photographs before, but she still recognised him.

Frankie caught her gawping and quickly ushered the man into the alley that ran down the side of the restaurant. As he turned, Anna caught a glimpse of his profile, and knew for sure who it was.

But what would Frankie be doing with Les Willis, one of the biggest crooks in York?

Not that he really was a crook. Everything in Les Willis's empire was strictly legit. It was the way he did business that was shady.

Anna often had to deal with people at the advice centre who'd fallen foul of the Willis mob. Tenants who couldn't pay the rent on their grotty bedsits; people who'd taken out loans without understanding the massive repayments they'd face for the rest of their lives.

She turned away from the window. Whatever Frankie's business was with Willis, she was very glad it wasn't hers.

'Mummy?' Charlie came towards her, brandishing a set of Barney playing cards. 'Can we play now?'

'Sorry, sweetheart, I can't. Mummy has to do the boring old staff rotas.'

'I could play with him, if you like,' Laura said. 'It's an hour until we open, I've got nothing else to do.'

'Are you sure? That would be great.' Anna ruffled his head. 'Poor kid's so bored.'

She realised it was a mistake bringing Charlie in to work with her, but there was a bug going round the nursery school so they'd sent all the kids home. And her mum had gone on a weekend course for college. She'd offered to cancel, but Anna knew how much she'd been looking forward to it.

'I don't mind. I love kids.' Laura settled down cross-legged on the floor with Charlie and began to deal out the cards. 'And Charlie's so sweet. He's just how I imagined he'd be.' She turned one of her cards face up, then waited for Charlie to do the same. 'Oliver used to talk about him all the time. His little boy. He looks so like him, doesn't he?'

'Yes, he does.' Anna felt a niggle of uneasiness as she watched them together. She was beginning to wonder if Laura had had a bit of a crush on Oliver. She never seemed to miss an opportunity to talk about him.

She soon forgot her worries as she sat down at the bar and tried to go through the staff rotas, keeping one eye on Charlie and Laura. There was a lot more to running the restaurant than she'd bargained for. She was beginning to admire Eve just for keeping it going.

Not to mention dealing with Frankie. As Eve had predicted, he didn't like the idea of Anna working in the restaurant and, although they tried to stay at least civil in front of the rest of the staff, Frankie never missed a chance to undermine her or make her look bad.

The phone rang. It was Lynch. 'Just checking you're still okay for tonight?'

'Oh God, we're supposed to be going out, aren't we?' She raked her hair with her hand. 'I'm not sure I can make it. My mum's away and I might not be able to get a babysitter at such short notice.'

'Better start trying then, hadn't you?' Lynch said. 'The table's booked for eight.'

'But I'm not sure—'

214

'I'll pick you up at quarter to, okay?' he said, and put the phone down.

'Was that your boyfriend?' Laura asked.

'Hmm?'

'Your boyfriend. Lynch, isn't it?'

'He's just a friend,' Anna said absently, picking up the rotas again.

'Really? I thought it was serious between you.'

Anna frowned at her. What did Laura know about it anyway? 'We've only been out twice. And we won't be going out tonight if I can't find a babysitter.'

'I'll do it, I'm not working tonight.'

'Don't you already have plans? I thought you students had wild social lives.'

'Not really. I've got an assignment to do, and my flatmate's got her boyfriend coming round, so I wouldn't mind some peace and quiet.'

Anna smiled wryly. 'Fat chance of that with Charlie around!'

'I don't mind. I like spending time with him.' Laura tickled Charlie, making him giggle.

'That's very kind of you,' Anna said, 'but Charlie can be a bit cranky with new people. I'll give my neighbour's daughter a call, see if she can do it.'

'Suit yourself,' Laura said. She buried her face in Charlie's neck and blew a raspberry that made him roar with laughter.

Anna watched them. Laura was so good with him, she didn't know why the idea of leaving them alone together made her uneasy.

She couldn't find anyone to look after Charlie. She tried to call Lynch but his mobile was switched off and his PA said he'd gone to Harrogate to meet a client. She promised to get hold of him and pass on Anna's message that she wouldn't be able to make their date that night.

So she was surprised when the doorbell rang as she and Charlie were in the middle of a riotous game of starships and aliens in the back garden after his tea. There was Lynch, standing on her doorstep, looking cool and male-model casual in jeans and white t-shirt.

'I can see you've made a special effort,' he commented dryly, looking from her grass-stained jeans to her hot, sweaty face topped off with an alien's helmet fashioned out of tin foil and a bent coat hanger. 'You've done something, haven't you? Let me guess. Is it your hair?'

'Very funny.' She took off the helmet, disentangling the hook from her ear. 'What are you doing here? Didn't you get my message?'

'What message?'

'The one I asked your secretary to give you. About us having to cancel tonight.'

'I take it you couldn't find a babysitter?'

'Not at such short notice. Sorry you've had a wasted journey.'

'Who says it's wasted? Have you eaten?'

'No, but—'

'Neither have I. So why don't we stay in and get a takeaway? It might be nice to have a cosy evening in, just the two of us.'

'Don't you mean three?' she said, just as Charlie came running up the passage from the kitchen, wielding a plastic light sabre and yelling for his alien prisoner to come back and surrender.

When he saw Lynch he stopped in his tracks, his head going back as his wide-eyed gaze travelled right up to Lynch's face.

'This is Mummy's friend,' Anna introduced them. 'Lynch, this is Charlie.'

'Pleased to meet you.' Lynch held out his hand. Charlie looked at it, then back up at his face.

'How old are you?' he asked.

'Have a guess.'

Charlie assessed him with utter concentration. 'Six?'

'Near enough.'

'Do you go to school?'

'Not in a while.'

'Why don't you go back and play in the garden?' Anna said.

'You're my prisoner.'

'I'll be out in a minute.'

'Now.' Charlie pointed the light sabre at her.

'Tell you what, why don't I come and be your prisoner?' Lynch said. Charlie and Anna both stared at him.

216

'I wouldn't advise it,' she said.

'Why not? It'll be fun.' Lynch grinned down at Charlie. 'What do you think?'

Charlie looked him up and down like a buyer at a slave market.

'To the space ship,' he commanded.

'Don't say I didn't warn you,' Anna called after them, as Lynch was frog-marched down the hall with a light sabre at his back.

It felt strange, having another man in Oliver's house. Strange – and wrong somehow. She stood at the French windows and watched Lynch with Charlie in the garden. He was trying hard, but he wasn't exactly throwing himself into the game.

If it was Oliver, he would have been rolling around on the grass by now, doing his Oscar-winning impression of a mortally wounded monster, not caring that they both ended up covered in dirt.

She pushed the thought from her mind. It wasn't fair to compare Lynch to Oliver. Oliver was Charlie's father, it was only natural for him to rough and tumble with his son. The only roughing and tumbling Lynch ever did was with grown women.

She'd opened a bottle of wine when Lynch came in a few minutes later, brushing grass from his jeans. 'Lively little chap, isn't he?' he said.

'I did warn you.'

'You didn't warn me he was going to try to perform an alien autopsy on me.'

'You didn't like that? I think that's the really fun part.' She handed him a glass of wine. 'Here, this will steady your nerves.'

'Thanks. I didn't realise kids were such hard work.'

'You've only been here five minutes. Wait until he gets to know you and then he'll really get going.'

'I can hardly wait.'

They sat outside on the patio with their wine, enjoying the last of the evening sun while they looked through the menu for the local Thai takeaway.

'How do you feel about stir-fried prawns?'

'Only if we can have chicken and coconut too.'

'Done.'

She went into the house to phone through their takeaway order.

When she came back, Charlie had climbed on to the chair next to Lynch and was chattering away to him.

'Why have you got a drawing on your arm?' Charlie asked.

'It's a tattoo.' He pulled up his sleeve to show off his tanned forearm.

'What does it say?'

'It's the Chinese symbol for prosperity. Or it could be an order for special fried rice, I have no idea. It was a very dodgy tattoo parlour.'

Charlie regarded him seriously. 'My daddy's dead,' he said.

'I know.'

'He's in heaven now, with David Beckham.'

'Really? That must be news to Posh.'

'Why don't you go inside and find a story to read at bedtime?' Anna suggested. 'Sorry about that,' she said to Lynch as Charlie wandered off. 'He has some strange ideas about death. I think he gets them from my nana.'

'He's very – entertaining,' Lynch said.

'Exhausting, more like.'

'I have to say, it's a lot more peaceful when he isn't around.'

Anna watched him, lounging back in his seat, graceful as a cat, his beautiful face turned up to catch the last rays of the sun, and quelled the irritation she felt. She couldn't blame Lynch, he just wasn't used to kids.

'I'll get him ready for bed before the food arrives,' she said.

When she got back downstairs, she was dismayed to find Lynch had pulled the curtains on the last of the evening sun. Candles were lit on the table, and there was a definite mood of seduction in the air.

Anna recognised it immediately and her heart sank. She'd been here before, and she didn't want to go down that road again, but it looked as if Lynch had other ideas as he handed her a glass of wine.

'I've opened another bottle,' he said. 'I thought we might as well make a night of it.'

Luckily, she had Charlie around to stop her getting any ideas. He'd adopted Lynch as his new best friend, and kept sneaking downstairs during their meal with various toys and treasures to show him.

At first Lynch played along, but by the time their meal was over and they were relaxing on the sofa in the sitting room, Anna could tell his patience was wearing thin.

She finally managed to coax Charlie into bed half an hour later.

'Alone at last,' Lynch said when she came downstairs again. 'You were a long time.'

'I had to read him a bedtime story. He likes his routine.' She curled up in the armchair a safe distance away from where Lynch lounged on the sofa. 'I'm sorry he spilt wine on your trousers.'

'No problem. They're only Dolce and Gabbana.' It was hard to tell if he was joking or not.

Anna tucked her feet beneath her, her arms folded across her chest, as if she could protect herself from the waves of sexual heat radiating across the room.

'There's something I wanted to ask you,' he said.

'If it's a proposition, you know what the answer is going to be.'

He smiled. 'How do you fancy coming to Barcelona with me?'

She nearly dropped her glass. 'When?'

'I've got to go there next Friday for work. I thought we could make a weekend of it. Do some shopping, hit a few bars – what do you think?'

'It sounds wonderful.' Then, to test him, she added, 'Charlie will love it. He's never been on a plane before.'

His smile disappeared. 'I wasn't actually thinking of taking Charlie.'

'I know you weren't,' she said, 'I just wanted to see your face. But I can't go anywhere without him.'

'Couldn't you get someone to look after him?'

'He's a little boy, not a parcel. I can't just dump him in left luggage whenever I want to go somewhere.'

'So that's a no, then?'

'I'm afraid so.'

'Pity. We could have had fun.'

'Yes,' she said, deliberately misunderstanding him. 'I would have enjoyed some sightseeing.'

'The sights from my hotel room are especially spectacular.'

'Lynch!'

'What? Come on, Anna, you know you can't resist me for ever. We're practically in a relationship, for heaven's sake.'

'We've been out three times. And this time we stayed in, so it hardly counts.'

'So? With my track record that makes us practically engaged.'

He made her laugh, which lowered her defences. Before she knew what was happening, he'd put down his drink and was sliding along the sofa towards her, like a leopard moving in for the kill. Anna felt her insides liquefy with treacherous lust, and then—

'I've wet the bed.' Charlie stood in the doorway, rubbing his eyes with one hand, trailing his toy monkey from the other.

She got up from the armchair. 'Oh dear, have you? Come on, let's get you sorted out.'

'It never ends, does it?' Lynch said under his breath.

'That's what being a parent is all about.' She didn't know whether to feel relief or regret. 'Look, I'm going to be a while, so you might as well go.'

'I could wait.'

'I don't think that would be a good idea.'

He looked as if he might argue, then put down his glass. 'I'll call you, okay?'

'Has the man gone?' Charlie asked when she'd washed him, changed him into fresh pyjamas and put him in her bed. He looked so little, lying there against the pillows.

'Yes, he's gone.'

Charlie stuck his lip out. 'Can he sleep over one day?'

'We'll see.' She tucked the quilt in around him.

'He can sleep in here. It's very big.'

Anna smiled and kissed him on the forehead. 'It's a nice idea, but somehow I don't think it's big enough for all three of us, sweetheart.'

Chapter 27

Eve battled through customs, struggling under the weight of Matt and Georgia's duty free.

'I wouldn't mind, but I didn't even get a bottle of perfume for myself,' she grumbled as she clanked through the 'Nothing to Declare' channel.

'I wish you'd let me buy the cigarettes,' Matt muttered.

'No way. I'm not encouraging an unhealthy habit,' Eve said, guiltily aware that she'd indulged in more than the odd Marlboro Light since Oliver died.

'But I could have made a fortune selling them at school!'

'Me too,' Georgia said. Eve glared at her.

Their week in Italy had done them all so much good. They'd relaxed in the Mediterranean sunshine, swum in the sea, eaten pasta till it came out of their ears and generally forgotten all their troubles.

But once home, reality hit them like the steady grey drizzle that fell as they stood in the queue waiting for a taxi.

'Back to boring old England,' Matt sighed.

'I wish you'd brought the car,' Georgia grumbled.

'And run up a fortune in the long-stay car park? We can get a cab into Leeds and then catch the train.'

Although her economy drive didn't seem such a bright idea with rain dripping down her neck. Especially as she was still wearing her holiday flip-flops.

'Yeah – us and the rest of the world. Have you seen the size of this queue?'

'And we're right at the back of it,' Matt added.

Eve turned on them. 'Will you two please stop moaning? I'm beginning to wish I'd never got off the plane.'

'Me too,' Matt said.

'Can I give you a lift?'

Suddenly there was Adam's van pulling up beside them in the queue, like a knight in shining armour. Eve didn't think she'd ever been so pleased to see anyone in her life.

'What are you doing here?' she asked.

'I remembered you'd said when your flight was coming in, and I wasn't doing anything, so I thought I'd drive down and give you a lift back to York. You don't mind, do you?'

'Mind?' Eve looked at the children, who were already piling their cases into the back of the van. 'You're a lifesaver.'

'Besides, there was someone who couldn't wait to see you.' He nodded towards the passenger seat, where Benson was frantically scratching at the window in his desperation to give them all a good licking.

'It was good of you to look after him. I hope he's behaved himself?' Eve said.

'Well, he did have a serious go at Imogen's Prada handbag, which she wasn't too impressed about.'

'Oh God, I'll have to replace it.' Eve winced at the expense. It would probably have been cheaper to send Benson to Champneys for a week.

'Don't worry, I already did.' He turned to Matt and Georgia. 'Sorry, kids, you're going to have to travel in economy.'

'Yuk, it smells of potatoes in here,' Georgia grumbled as they piled into the back of the van.

'Did you have a good holiday?' he asked, when they were heading back along the motorway.

'It was bliss,' Eve smiled. 'Just what we all needed. How's the restaurant?'

Adam laughed. 'How did I know that would be the first thing you asked about?'

'I just wanted to know if we were still in business.'

'As far as I know.'

Eve watched him sideways as he negotiated a roundabout.

222

'That's a very evasive answer,' she said. 'Is there something you're not telling me?'

'Eve, you've got nothing to worry about. The last time I looked, Oliver's was still open.'

'Thank heavens for that.' She'd had her doubts about letting Anna help out. Frankie certainly hadn't liked the idea, but she'd been at the end of her tether and needed some time with the children. 'I hope she and Frankie have got on,' she mused. 'Who knows, maybe they'll be best friends by the time I get back.'

'You never know,' Adam agreed.

They joined the steady crawl of traffic towards York. 'So what's happening in your world?' Eve asked.

'Not much. The asparagus has finished for the year, but the pumpkins are doing pretty well. We finished setting them last week, and we've already got some strong vines growing. Oh, and Britney's just about ready to give birth.'

'Britney?' Georgia said from the back.

'His goat.' Eve smiled. 'Don't you ever think about anything but that farm?'

He frowned. 'What else did you want to know about?'

'How's Imogen?'

'She's fine.'

'You two have been together for ages. It must be serious.'

'You think?'

She got the message from his non-committal response. When it came to his private life, Adam clammed up tighter than an oyster shell.

Half an hour later they were back at home.

'Thanks again for meeting us,' Eve said, as he helped unload their bags from the van. 'Are you sure you don't want to come in for a coffee?'

'No thanks, I'd better get going. A new vegetarian restaurant's opened in Swinegate and I've arranged to go in and see them.'

'Another customer for you and another rival for us,' Eve grimaced. 'I'll see you tomorrow, anyway. When you bring our delivery?' she prompted, as he looked blank.

'Oh, yes. Right.' He planted a quick kiss on her cheek. 'I'll see you soon.'

The following day at the restaurant, she found out why he'd seemed so distracted.

'I told him not to bother coming any more,' Frankie said as he put on his chef's whites.

'Why not?'

'I've found someone who can get us the same stuff a lot cheaper.' He looked up from buttoning his jacket, and caught Eve's expression. 'I thought you'd be pleased. You keep saying we need to save money.'

'I know, but—' This was Adam they were talking about. 'I wish you'd talked to me first.'

'Why?'

'It's a bit embarrassing, isn't it? He's Oliver's cousin, after all, and he's been so good to us.'

'We've been good to him, too,' Frankie said. 'He doesn't run a charity, you know. It's our orders that have kept him in business all these years. He's done very well out of this place, I reckon.'

Eve chewed her lip. 'All the same, I don't think Oliver would have liked it.'

'Oliver wouldn't have liked anyone taking advantage of you, either.'

Eve laughed. 'Adam's not taking advantage of me!'

'You'd be surprised,' Frankie said. 'If you ask me, he's been overcharging us for years. I'm only trying to protect you, Eve.'

She bristled. 'That's very kind of you, Frankie, but I can look after myself.'

Frankie looked hurt. 'I'm sorry if you think I've overstepped the mark,' he said. 'I was only doing what I thought was right for the business. I didn't realise I had to discuss it with you first, I thought we'd built up some trust.'

'We have.' Eve backed down. The last thing she needed was Frankie in a sulk. 'You're right, we should try to cut costs where we can.' If only it didn't have to be Adam. 'But I'll go and talk to him. I owe him that, at least.'

★

224

After lunchtime service was over, she went out to Adam's farm, about five miles to the north of the city. She drove through the white gates bearing the sign 'Robinson's Organic Produce' and followed the narrow track between flat fields and poly tunnels. It was a blazing-hot July day, and the sun shimmered in a heat haze over the fields.

The road led to a small cluster of buildings in the middle of the fields. There was Adam's cottage, surrounded by outbuildings that included his pride and joy, the farm shop.

As usual, the shop was busy with customers. Kate, one of the assistants, was stacking carrots in the display outside.

'If you're looking for Adam, he's ploughing a new field for potatoes,' she said, waving her hand in the direction Eve had just come.

'Thanks.' With her t-shirt already sticking to her in the heat, Eve trekked off back down the path.

She heard the rumble of the engine and saw him in the distance. He was at the wheel of the tractor, ploughing furrows ready for planting. The brown field was ribbed like thick corduroy, and there was a smell of newly churned earth in the air.

She stood at the gate, watching him. Finally he noticed her and skirted down the edge of the field, bringing the tractor to a halt in front of her.

'I didn't want to interrupt your work.' Eve shaded her eyes with her hand to look up at him. He was wearing cut-off denims and he'd taken off his shirt in the heat. Perspiration gleamed on his bronze skin, and his dark hair curled damply around his neck.

'I'd pretty much finished anyway.' He jumped down from the cab. 'What can I do for you?'

'I spoke to Frankie this morning.'

'Ah.' He reached into the cab and took out a bottle of water.

'Why didn't you tell me what had happened?'

'It's no big deal.'

He drank from the bottle. Eve watched his throat moving. 'Frankie had no right to do it without talking to me first.'

'Like I said, it's no big deal.' He offered her the bottle. She shook her head. 'I took on another contract last week, so it's not as if I've lost anything.'

His back-muscles rippled under his skin as he leaned over to put the bottle back into the tractor cab.

'Are you sure? I was really worried.'

'Don't be. In fact, I'm more worried about you.'

'Me?'

'I heard about your money problems.'

Eve opened her mouth to deny it, then closed it again. 'I suppose Frankie told you?'

He shook his head. 'I spoke to Anna.'

She was immediately on her guard. 'What did she tell you?'

'Not a lot, but enough to make me concerned. Why didn't you tell me you were having difficulties?'

'It's not your problem.'

'That doesn't stop me worrying about you.'

He picked up his shirt from the tractor cab and pocketed the keys. 'Come with me. I need to check on Britney.'

'How is the mother-to-be?' she asked as they walked back down the track towards the outbuildings.

'A bit fed-up, I think. I've put her in a pen by herself to keep her away from the others.'

The barn was warm, dark and pungent-smelling. Britney the goat lay on a bed of straw, looking sorry for herself. She struggled to get up when she saw Adam, but her spindly legs wouldn't support her distended belly.

'You're right, she is fed-up,' Eve said. 'The last few days are always the worst.'

'If only she could knit a few booties to pass the time.' Adam let himself into the pen and crouched down to scratch between her ears. 'Won't be too long now, girl.'

Britney looked up at him, her pale eyes full of trust. Eve knew exactly what the animal was thinking. She'd been just the same before Matt was born, bored and apprehensive at the same time.

'If only she knew what was going to happen to her, she'd make the most of the peace and quiet,' she said.

As they stood watching her, Adam suddenly said, 'I want to

help you.'

Eve turned to him. It was hard to read his expression in the shadowy barn. 'In what way?'

'Let me give you some money. Just to pay off your bills and make sure you're okay,' he added quickly, as she opened her mouth to refuse. 'You could even call it a loan, if it makes you feel better?'

She nearly laughed. It was a loan that had got them into this mess. 'You're very kind, but I don't want your money.'

'Why not?'

'Like I said, it isn't your problem.'

'Oliver was my cousin. I owe it to him to look after his family. And besides—' He stopped.

'Yes?'

Suddenly the atmosphere in the barn seemed too close and stifling.

'It's what he would have wanted,' Adam said.

The sunlight seemed almost blinding as they went outside. Eve took a gulp of fresh air.

'I'm sorry,' she said, 'but I can't let you do it. It's too much to ask.'

'I can afford it.'

Could he? She didn't even want to tell him how much money they owed. He'd be too shocked.

'Anyway, I owe everything to Oliver. He should have had this place. I only took over the family business because he didn't want it.'

'Yes, but you were the one who made it a success. You worked damn hard and it wouldn't be right to take your money.'

'But I *want* to give it to you.'

She looked up into his kind, rugged face. 'I need to sort this out by myself,' she said.

'Why?'

'Because I want to prove I can do it.'

'For Oliver?'

'And for myself.'

He regarded her for a long time. 'I'm not going to be able to change your mind, am I?' She shook her head. 'As long as you remember, the offer's there if you need it.'

She reached for his hand. 'You're a good friend, Adam.'

His fingers closed around hers briefly and for a second he looked as if he was about to say something, then changed his mind. 'I'll walk you to your car.'

As they headed back to the yard he said, 'If you won't take my money, at least will you have dinner with me tomorrow?'

'Why?'

'Do I need a reason?'

'I suppose not.' She smiled. 'Okay, then. On one condition.'

'What's that?'

'We don't talk about Oliver, or the restaurant.'

His grey eyes lit up. 'Definitely not.'

Chapter 28

Anna headed slowly down Fossgate on Friday morning, pausing to look in the windows of the various secondhand bookshops. She wasn't especially interested in the tattered copies of *The Railway Chronicle* on display, but she was in no hurry to get to Oliver's, either. She had something to say to Eve, and she knew she wasn't going to like it.

Luckily, it was just Eve and Laura in the kitchen. Eve was prepping vegetables for the lunchtime service. She was wearing oversized chef's whites, her cap propped on the back of her honey-blonde head. Laura was perched on a stool, sipping coffee and watching her work.

Eve looked up and smiled when she saw Anna. She seemed a lot more relaxed since she'd come home from her holiday.

'I didn't expect to see you,' she said. 'I thought you'd be sick of this place by now.'

'I wanted to talk to you.' Anna glanced at Laura. 'In private.'

Laura slid off the stool. 'I've got some napkins to fold anyway.'

Anna waited until she'd disappeared through the swing doors. 'What do you think of her?' she asked.

'She seems like a nice girl.'

'You don't find her a bit – creepy?'

'I think she's just lonely. But she's a hard worker, and very good with the customers.' Eve frowned. 'Is that why you've come? To discuss Laura?'

Anna shook her head. 'It's Frankie I wanted to talk about.' She glanced out of the window to the back yard, expecting to see him taking his first ciggie break of the day. 'Where is he?'

'He called to say he was going to be a bit late. He had to see a supplier.' Eve looked up from her chopping. 'What about him?'

Anna turned away from the window. 'Has Frankie ever mentioned a man called Les Willis to you?'

Eve thought for a moment. 'Doesn't ring a bell. Why, who is he?'

'A local crook.' She took a deep breath. 'I've seen Frankie talking to him.'

'And you assume he must be mixed up in something criminal, is that it?'

'Well—'

'Why do you have to jump to conclusions?' Eve started chopping with dangerous speed. 'Just because Frankie's been in jail doesn't mean everything he does has to be dodgy.'

'I didn't say that—'

'He did the crime, then he did the time. It's over. Haven't you ever heard of someone paying their debt to society?'

'It's his debt to Les Willis I'm worried about,' Anna said.

'What are you talking about?'

Here it comes, Anna thought. 'Did you know your friend Frankie had a gambling problem?'

Eve put her knife down. 'Who told you that?'

'I did some digging after I saw Frankie talking to Les. I had a word with my brothers, they spoke to their friends. Apparently Frankie's quite well known on the local poker circuit.'

'So?'

'Well, he's been losing pretty badly to the wrong people lately. Including Les Willis. I'm guessing that's why he turned up here, looking for his money.'

Eve picked up the knife again and went on with her work. She kept her head down so Anna couldn't see her expression. 'So he's got into some trouble. I still don't see what that's got to do with me.'

Anna stared at her. Was she being naïve, or just playing dumb because she didn't want to face up to the truth?

'Have you checked the books lately?'

Eve looked up sharply, her eyes flaring with outrage. 'Of course I've checked them. What else do you think I do all day?'

'So have I,' Anna said. 'And I've noticed quite a few of the cheques have been written by Frankie.'

'I told him he could use the cheque book to pay suppliers when I wasn't here. It's more convenient.'

I bet it is, Anna thought. 'Have you checked if the payments tally with the invoices?'

Eve flushed dark pink. 'I don't need to. I trust Frankie.'

'Maybe you shouldn't trust him quite so much.'

'Look, I don't care what kind of trouble you think Frankie's in, I know he wouldn't do anything to let me down. He's my friend.'

'Even though he's ripping you off?'

'You don't know that.'

'I can take a wild guess.'

Eve was still brooding when she met Adam for dinner that night. Just as she'd begun to think that she and Anna had reached some kind of understanding, this had happened.

Anna had no right to criticise Frankie. He'd been a good friend to her, and to Oliver. Just because he didn't like Anna, there was no reason for her to try to blacken his name.

Adam was in the middle of cooking when she got to the cottage.

'Sorry about the change of plan.' He greeted her at the door, a tea towel tucked into his jeans. 'I did book a table, but the vet called this morning. He reckons Britney could start giving birth at any time. I don't really want to leave her.'

'It's no problem.' She followed him into the kitchen. It was a typical farmhouse style, but functional and masculine with it. A scruffy waxed jacket hung from the hook, there was a line of muddy boots by the back door, and the pine dresser was piled high with paperwork. 'Will you have to keep checking up on her?'

'I've thought of that.' He nodded to a baby monitor propped up by the sink.

Eve laughed. 'You're taking this expectant-father thing really seriously, aren't you?'

'I'm not taking any chances.'

She stepped carefully over a box of salad greens. 'Dinner smells lovely. What is it?'

'Chilli con carne. My speciality dish. Actually, it's the only thing I can cook apart from beans on toast and steak.'

He took a spoon out of the drawer and dipped it into the big pot bubbling away on the stove, then held it out to Eve. 'What do you think?'

She tasted it. 'Very nice.'

'Are you sure? It's not too hot for you?'

'It's perfect.'

'I wouldn't say that. Oliver was the master chef in the family.'

'Is there anything I can do?' Eve offered.

'You could make a salad.' He pointed to the box of vegetables in the corner. 'Sorry, I'm a really crap host. We should be relaxing with a bottle of wine now while I regale you with my witty conversation.'

'I'd rather make myself useful.' Eve selected a lettuce from the box and started to tear the leaves into a colander.

They worked side by side in companionable silence. Adam cooked the rice while she prepared the salad.

He turned round and caught her smiling. 'What?'

'I was just thinking, it's a long time since I cooked with a man. Apart from Frankie, and he doesn't count.' She rinsed the lettuce under the tap. 'Oliver and I always cooked together when we were married. I used to really enjoy it. It's not quite the same, cooking on your own.' She noticed he'd gone very quiet. 'Sorry, I'm rambling.'

He grabbed his coat from the hook. 'I'm just going out to check on Britney before we eat.'

'I can't hear anything on the monitor.'

'All the same, I want to make sure she's all right.'

While he was away, she laid the table with Adam's endearingly mismatched crockery, and found a bottle of wine in the fridge.

She was lighting a couple of candles when he came back.

'How is she?'

'Labour's started, but she seems okay. It shouldn't be too long now.' He looked at the table. 'Candles?'

'I thought it would be nice.' She stopped, the lit match still in her hand. 'Sorry, were you saving them?'

'Only for a power cut.'

They settled down to eat. 'Do you cook for Imogen like this?' Eve asked.

'Imogen doesn't allow me in the kitchen. She says I'm like a bull in a china shop.'

'You're not that bad.'

'Not with you.'

'We must make a good team'

An awkward silence fell, broken only by the sound of Nina Simone on the CD player and the crackling of the baby monitor. Eve noticed Adam had gone quiet again, and wondered if she'd said the wrong thing.

She had her own thoughts to deal with. No matter how much she tried to stop herself, she couldn't help thinking about what Anna had said.

She tried to hide her turmoil, chatting to Adam, but when he put her coffee down in front of her he said, 'Okay, you might as well tell me what's wrong.'

'What do you mean?'

'You've been sitting there like a ticking time bomb for the past half an hour. If you don't come out with it soon you'll explode and that could be very nasty.'

Eve smiled. 'You know me too well.'

'So what's the problem?'

'It's Frankie.' She told him about Anna's accusations. 'Of course I know it's all rumours and lies,' she said, 'but it's still upsetting. It's Frankie I feel really sorry for. Why can't everyone just leave him alone?'

'How do you know it's all lies?'

'Not you, too?' Eve suddenly felt very weary. She was getting tired of everyone ganging up on Frankie. 'What have you heard?'

'Pretty much the same as Anna. That he's got a gambling problem and owes cash to the wrong kind of people.'

'So why didn't you tell me?'

'Would you have believed me?'

'Probably not.' She picked up her coffee cup. 'I can believe he owes a few people money. But so what? He'd never abuse Oliver's trust.'

'No, but he might abuse yours.'

'Meaning?'

'You've been relying on him a lot since Oliver died. He could have taken advantage of that. If his debts are that bad, he'd have to be a saint to resist that kind of temptation. And we all know Frankie's no saint.'

'So you think he's been helping himself out of the bank account? Well, for your information I checked the books today. All the cheques he's written tally up with suppliers' invoices.'

She'd gone through them all painstakingly that afternoon, hating herself for doing it.

'There are other ways of making money on the side,' Adam said.

'Such as?'

'Such as getting a friendly supplier to send in an invoice for higher than the price agreed, then splitting the extra profit with him. Or selling off stock.' He stirred his coffee. 'I wondered if that was why he got rid of me. Because he knew I wouldn't play ball.'

Eve was shocked. 'He did it to cut costs.'

'And is your new supplier that much cheaper?'

Come to think of it, he wasn't. Eve had been quite surprised when the bills had started to arrive.

But surely Frankie wouldn't do that to her?

She remembered those early days at the restaurant, when he'd first come to work for Oliver. He'd worked slavishly hard, always the first to arrive and the last to leave. He'd even turned up on the nights when he wasn't paid, just to lend a hand.

Then she remembered him at Oliver's funeral, promising to look after her and the business. She couldn't have coped these last few months without him.

234

She shook her head. 'There's no way Frankie would do anything like that. Oliver trusted him a hundred per cent and so do I.'

'Oliver's judgement hasn't exactly been reliable, has it?'

Eve looked at him sharply over the rim of her cup. 'If you're talking about his financial problems—'

'I was talking about you.'

Before she had a chance to reply, an unearthly sound filled the kitchen. Eve jumped, splashing hot coffee over the table. 'What the hell was that?'

'Sounds like Britney's in trouble.' Adam was already on his feet and heading for the door.

She followed him, stumbling across the darkened yard to the shed, trying to keep up with his long strides.

Inside the lamplit shed, Britney was standing in a corner of her pen, wide-eyed with terror. She was making a long, low keening sound.

'Something's not right,' Adam said. 'She should be well on the way by now.'

'Shall I call the vet?'

'I don't know if there's time for that. We could have lost the kid by the time he gets here.' He rolled up his shirt sleeves. 'I'm going to have to check her.'

Eve stared at him in the shadowy half-light. 'You mean you're going to—' She looked from his bare, muscular forearms to the goat and back.

'Unless you want to do it?'

'No!' She stepped back, colliding with the railing.

'Then I'm going to need disinfectant. And a bucket. They're in the utility room.'

'Shall I bring hot water and towels, too?'

'Why?'

'I don't know. Isn't that what people do when someone gives birth?'

'You tell me. I've never done it before.'

She rushed off to fetch the things from the house. When she returned, Adam had stripped off to the waist and was kneeling in the straw, trying to calm an agitated Britney.

'From what I can tell, the kid's got one leg pushed back,' he said. 'I'm going to see if I can ease it into position. You'll have to hold on to her, try to reassure her.'

Eve looked at Britney. She stared apprehensively back. 'How the hell do I reassure a goat?'

'I'm sure you'll think of something.'

The next few minutes were very tense. Eve knelt on the straw beside Britney, her arm around her neck, scratching the coarse hair between her ears and trying to keep her calm. She didn't dare look at what Adam was doing at the other end, but his face was shiny with sweat in the dim lamplight. The air was so hot and so still she could hardly breathe.

Finally he sat back on the straw. 'Done it,' he said, going to the disinfectant bucket and picking up a cloth 'A few more pushes and she should be able to get it out herself.'

Sure enough, a couple of minutes later Britney's baby slipped and slithered into the world.

'It's a boy,' Adam said.

Britney immediately took charge, licking and cleaning her baby while they sat on a straw bale, watching.

'It's like a miracle, isn't it?' Eve whispered.

'It's a miracle I didn't pass out.'

She grinned at him. 'You were brilliant.'

'So were you.'

'Me? I didn't do anything.'

'I couldn't have done it without you.' Their eyes met, and Eve felt her insides quiver.

She got to her feet. 'I suppose we'd better clean up.' She looked down at herself. 'Ugh! I'll never get a taxi home like this.'

'I'll lend you something.'

When she came out of the shower, Adam had laid out some clean clothes for her on the bed. Unfortunately, they were his.

'Look at me!' She came downstairs, nearly tripping over the flapping legs of his jeans. 'Haven't you got any of Imogen's clothes I could borrow?'

He turned to look at her. He'd showered and changed into jeans and a black t-shirt. 'Imogen doesn't leave her stuff here.

Anyway, I think you look very – cute.'

'Hmm.' Eve rolled up the sleeves of his oversized flannel shirt. 'Have you been out to check on Britney?'

'Mother and baby are doing well.' He reached into the fridge and took out a bottle of champagne. 'I thought we could crack this open to celebrate the new arrival?'

Eve glanced at her watch. 'I should be getting back—'

'Please? I don't really want to celebrate alone.'

She hesitated for a moment, then said, 'Why not? It's not every day you help a goat give birth, is it?'

'Thank God.' He popped the cork on the bottle. 'I don't think I could go through that every day.'

He poured them each a glass. 'To Britney,' she said, raising hers. 'And – um –'

'Gordon,' Adam said.

'Gordon? Gordon the goat?'

'Why not?'

She shrugged. 'Gordon the goat it is, then.' She looked sideways at him. 'Have you been crying?'

'No.'

'You have!'

'Look, it's been an emotional couple of hours, okay?'

She smiled. 'And there was me thinking you were some tough man of the soil.'

'Oh no,' he said. 'I'm not tough at all.'

She looked into his eyes and suddenly she found she couldn't breathe. The next moment they were kissing.

His mouth was soft, warm and gentle, and for a second she gave in, allowing herself to get lost in his kiss. A second later her senses reasserted themselves. She thought of Imogen and pulled away.

'I'm sorry,' she stammered.

'Me too. It must have been the champagne.'

They couldn't look at each other. Eve put down her glass. 'I'd – better call a cab,' she mumbled, pulling out her mobile phone.

They made embarrassed small talk until her taxi arrived. It

was a huge relief to hear it crunching across the gravel yard ten minutes later.

'Thanks for an interesting evening,' Eve said as he saw her to the door.

'Look, Eve, about what happened—'

'Forget it.' She held her hands up, not wanting to hear any more. 'It was a heat of the moment thing, that's all. Hardly worth worrying about.'

'You're right,' he said. But he still looked troubled.

As the taxi drove away, she turned back to look at him. He stood in the doorway watching her go, a long dark silhouette against the bright doorway.

Forget it, she'd said. Except she didn't think she could.

Chapter 29

Eve kept telling herself she shouldn't believe the rumours. She knew Frankie too well for that. He'd been a good, loyal friend. Besides, Oliver knew him better than anyone and *he'd* trusted him, and that was good enough for her.

And yet she couldn't quell the little niggling voice of doubt that kept whispering in her ear, driving her mad as she sat in the office trying to focus on the paperwork. She trusted Frankie, but she trusted Adam too. He wouldn't lie to her either, and he certainly wasn't the type to go around spreading gossip.

She felt a stir of emotion. She hadn't seen or spoken to Adam for a week, the longest they'd been without contact, and was surprised at how much she missed him. She hadn't realised he was such an important part of her life. She thought about calling him to ask how Britney was doing, but she was too embarrassed. That kiss had opened up a gulf between them.

Picking up a sheaf of bills, she tried to concentrate. She tapped the figures into her calculator, then cleared the screen and tapped them in again in a different order, but no matter how many combinations she tried, she couldn't make them add up. There was no getting away from the fact that they had more money going out than they had coming in.

She stared at the calendar on the wall in despair. They'd already had to find a new fish supplier after they couldn't pay the last one. The quality was suffering, which meant fewer customers were coming back. They were caught in a downward spiral, with only one thing waiting at the end of it. Closure.

And still the idea that Frankie was cheating haunted her, like a constant itch in the back of her mind.

Eve put down the calculator and pushed back her chair. She couldn't stand it any more. She would have to find out the truth for herself.

Feeling nervous as she went to the freezer, she told herself she had every right to check on the stock levels, but she was still apprehensive. The stores were Frankie's domain, and he guarded them jealously.

The sight of the near-empty freezer shelves took her by surprise. Surely there should be more than that? They'd had a delivery only three days ago.

'What are you doing?'

She swung round. Frankie stood in the doorway, watching her.

Eve felt like a naughty kid caught with her hand in the sweetie jar. 'I – er –'

'Are you looking for something in particular? Maybe I could help you find it.' He was smiling, but his eyes were hard.

She took a deep breath. 'I was just wondering what had happened to all the meat that was delivered.'

'I sold it.'

'What?'

'To a bloke in a pub. A market trader. He took the whole lot off my hands for fifty quid, which I immediately gambled away on the horses.'

He grinned, and Eve felt weak with relief. 'You're joking!'

'Of course I'm joking.' He nodded towards the freezer shelves. 'I used it.'

'All of it?'

'This is a restaurant, Eve. People come in and we're supposed to feed them. That's the general idea, anyway.'

'I didn't realise we'd been that busy.'

'You'd be surprised how quickly it goes. Oh, but I did sell some chicken to Alfredo down the road. His supplier let him down and he was desperate. I put the money straight in the petty-cash box. You can check it if you like.'

'I don't need to do that.'

'Are you sure?'

The way he looked at her made her feel uncomfortable. 'I'm sure,' she said firmly.

As she brushed past him and headed for the door, he said, 'You shouldn't listen to gossip, you know.'

She stopped. 'What do you mean?'

'You don't have to pretend, I can see it in your face. You're checking up on me.'

'I'm not.'

'You've heard rumours about me, and now you think I'm out to fleece you.' He closed the freezer door and turned to face her. 'So who was it? That bitch Anna, I suppose?'

Eve opened her mouth to deny it but her blushing face gave her away. 'She didn't say anything. She just mentioned she'd seen you talking to – someone.'

'And that someone wouldn't happen to be Les Willis, would it?' Frankie's jaw tightened. 'I thought so. I saw her spying.' He let out a long breath. 'Yes, I did meet him. To give him back the money I owed. Every penny. And before you ask, it was all out of my own pocket.'

'I never said it wasn't.'

'No, but you thought it. Same as everyone else thinks. I know what people say about me, Eve. Once a villain, always a villain, but I thought you knew me better than that.'

He looked so hurt, Eve felt ashamed. 'You're right. I'm sorry, Frankie.'

'I'm not blaming you. Like I say, I know what they all whisper about me. The only one who didn't think like that was Oliver. He gave me a chance when no one else would. Do you honestly believe I'd repay him by cheating his widow?'

'Frankie—'

He held up his hand to stop her. 'I'm going outside. I need some fresh air.'

He looked so forlorn sitting out there on the stone steps, his big shoulders drooping, Eve knew she must have really hurt him. Why did she ever listen to Adam and Anna? She should have trusted Oliver's judgement. Frankie was right; he was the only one who really understood.

It was a Tuesday towards the end of July, just over five months since Oliver's death, when Anna went into meltdown.

The day started like any other. She went into the office to find Neil proudly showing off the latest photos of his new baby son.

'Ah, very nice. He's the spitting image of his dad, isn't he, poor little devil,' Barbara added in a whisper as she handed the photos to Anna. 'Have you seen those ears? If that child doesn't get bullied at school it'll be a miracle. Are you all right? You're looking a bit peaky.'

'Just a headache, that's all.'

'And here comes another one.' Barbara nodded towards the door, where Roy Munge had just walked in clutching a Netto carrier bag bulging ominously with paperwork

He plonked himself down opposite Anna. 'I've come about my gas bill.'

Fifteen minutes later, he was still explaining his tale of woe. While he was talking, Anna's attention wandered to the photo of Neil and his new baby propped up on his computer monitor. Neil's absurdly doting grin pierced her heart with a dart of pain.

She thought about the photos of Oliver with Charlie when he was a baby. That same adoring smile, as if he couldn't quite believe his luck that he'd been given something so tiny and so precious.

'And they definitely promised me a discount if I switched,' Roy Munge droned on. 'Even more if I moved my electricity too ...'

Then she thought about all the other photos Neil and Ruth would have in their family album in years to come, documenting their son's life. His first steps, his first day at school, his graduation. She'd have those photos too, but there would always be someone missing.

'I don't know how they can say I owe them all that money when they haven't even read my meter in over a year. I mean, that can't be right, can it?'

She thought about Charlie. He'd have to go through all that growing up without his dad. What if he forgot him? She wished she'd taken more photos when she'd had the chance, instead of imagining that Oliver would always be there, smiling for the camera ...

'This is the second time it's happened,' Roy Munge said. 'They promised me it would be simple. No problem, they said. I should have known.'

A feeling of despair welled up inside Anna. She looked around. Everything seemed so familiar and normal: Barbara was at the photocopier, Neil was on the phone, Elliott was in his office, head bent over some paperwork. She felt as if she was stuck in a glass box that was slowly filling up with water, and no one could see she was drowning.

'I wish I'd never signed the direct–debit form. They can just help themselves to my money from my bank account whenever they— Miss? Are you all right?'

She put her hand up to her face and was appalled to find it was wet with tears. When she opened her mouth to speak all that came out was a great, agonised sob.

Roy Munge clutched his carrier bag in dismay. 'It's only a gas bill. No need to get so upset about it.' He looked around in panic. 'Hello? Can someone help here?'

Barbara bustled over. 'It's all right, she's grieving.' She stuffed a tissue into Anna's hand and patted her shoulder. 'She'll be right as rain in a minute.'

But she wasn't. Anna had never understood what the word breakdown really meant until she found herself sobbing and shaking uncontrollably, fighting for breath. It was as if all the fragile threads that held her life together had snapped at the same moment, plunging her into freefall. She heard someone wailing from far away, then realised with horror that it was her.

Neil and Barbara did their best. Barbara rushed off to put the kettle on, while Neil tried to force Bach's Rescue Remedy down her throat. Then, suddenly, came Elliott's voice, like a blessed oasis of calm.

'What's going on?'

'She's having a turn.' Barbara had rushed back from the kitchen in case she missed anything. 'She can't talk. She's gone hysterical.'

'It's when she stops screaming you want to worry,' Roy Munge said helpfully. 'I heard about that on Radio 4. Some woman saw her dog being run over and didn't speak for ten years.'

'Anna?' Elliott gripped her shoulders. His face was level with hers, his brown eyes seemed like the only kind, sane thing in her frightening world. She tried to speak but the words wouldn't come out.

'Told you,' Roy Munge said with satisfaction. 'If she's gone catatonic you're in trouble.'

Elliott lifted her to her feet, his arm around her shoulders. 'I'll take her upstairs,' he said. 'Neil, clear the committee room.'

'But it's Over-Sixties Yoga.'

'I don't care. Tell them to go and meditate somewhere else. This is an emergency.'

He helped her up the stairs to the small room at the top of the building, past all the disgruntled pensioners in their leotards. Anna leaned against him, not resisting.

Elliott sat her down on one of the small, hard sofas. 'Now you just rest. I'll be back in a minute.'

By the time he returned, Anna was feeling weak, washed out and thoroughly ashamed of herself, but at least she'd managed to stop herself crying.

'I've brought you a cup of tea. Barbara insisted.' He put it down in front of her. 'How are you feeling now?'

'Like a fool.' She dabbed at her eyes with a soggy tissue. 'What must everyone think of me?'

'We think you're going through a rough time.'

'But it's been months! Why should it all happen now?'

'I don't know. I don't think there's a timetable for this kind of thing, you just get through it however you can.'

'That's the point. I don't seem to be getting through it at all.' Now that her hysteria had subsided, she just felt angry with herself. She'd let herself down. 'The last thing I wanted to do was fall apart like this.'

'I don't think you get much choice in the matter.'

When she'd finished her tea she felt ready to go back to work, but Elliott insisted on taking her home. Anna didn't argue; she wasn't sure how she would cope with Barbara giving her odd looks all afternoon.

But when they parked outside the house, she felt a surge of apprehension. She couldn't bring herself to get out of the car.

'Shall I come in with you?' Elliott asked gently.

She shook her head. 'I'll be fine.'

'Are you sure? You will call me if you need anything, won't you?'

She forced herself out of the car and stood on the doorstep, waiting for him to leave. She made a big show of searching in her bag for her key until his car had turned the corner and driven out of sight. Then she ran.

She ended up in Homestead Park, on a bench in the rain. The sudden downpour had chased most people away so she was completely alone, sitting under a chestnut tree, barely noticing as the water dripped from the leaves, soaking through her thin jacket.

Anna wasn't sure how long she'd been sitting there when she saw the small blonde figure hurrying towards her under an oversized pink umbrella. She should have been surprised, but somehow she knew her mother would find her eventually.

Turning away and gazing across the empty playing field, she said, 'How did you know where I was?'

'Mother's instinct.' Jackie sat down on the bench next to her, showering them both in drips from her umbrella. 'Actually, your friend Elliott called. He said you'd had a bit of a wobble.'

Anna smiled weakly at the understatement. 'I made a complete fool of myself.'

'About bloody time, too. I was wondering when it was going to happen. You couldn't go on being tough for ever.' Her voice was severe but her eyes were full of pity. 'You might have got all this over with a lot sooner if you hadn't insisted on taking those wretched pills and telling yourself you were fine.'

'I *was* fine.' So fine she'd stopped taking the tablets a week before, ignoring the doctor's advice to wean herself off them gradually.

'No, Anna, you were *grieving*. Or you should have been, but you wouldn't let it happen.' She put her arm around her, pulling her under the shelter of her umbrella. 'Everyone needs to go through this, love. You need to deal with the pain, not try to cover it up or push it aside. It's no use telling yourself you're okay, that life goes on. All that heartache has to go somewhere.'

Anna buried her head in her mum's shoulder, breathing in the familiar washing-powder smell of her, as comforting now as it was when she was little. 'I wanted to be like you.'

'Me?'

'You were so strong when Dad died. I never saw you cry or complain. You just got on with it.'

'Oh, love.' Her voice was clogged with emotion. 'You don't know anything about it. Why do you think I hated those pills of yours so much? I know the kind of damage they can do.'

Anna pulled away from her. 'You took pills?'

'The doctor said it would help get me through, but it didn't. Oh, I'd put a brave face on for you and the boys. I had to, I didn't want to let you down. But as soon as you'd gone to bed everything would just collapse in on me. I'd sit up all night, listening to the radio, crying my eyes out, counting out those tablets and wondering how many it would take to end it all.'

'Mum!'

'The only thing that stopped me was knowing how bloody selfish I'd be. You kids had already lost your dad, I couldn't take the easy way out and leave you. But it hurt so much.'

'Oh, Mum.' Anna was crying again, unable to believe what she was hearing. All this time she'd been telling herself she had to cope like her mother, and now she found out her mum hadn't coped at all. It was a relief that she wasn't an utter failure, but at the same time she felt incredibly sad.

'I thought I was doing the right thing, pretending to be strong for you,' Jackie said. 'Now I reckon I should have let you kids see how I was feeling. Then maybe you wouldn't feel like you had to be Superwoman.'

'I don't really feel much like Superwoman at the moment.' Anna wiped the mascara from under her eyes. 'Do you still miss Dad?'

'Of course I do. Time takes away a lot of the pain, but it's still there. Sometimes I can forget all about it, then other times something will happen – I'll hear a song on the radio or his birthday will come around – and it will catch me out. But you get used to it. After a while you can remember the happy times and smile instead of feeling sad.'

They walked back home through the rain, sheltering under Jackie's umbrella. 'Are you sure you don't want me to come in with you?' she offered. 'I'd rather have a cup of tea with you than listen to your nana shouting at the telly. I can't believe anyone can get so riled about *Countdown*.'

Anna smiled. 'You'd better get back before she throws something at the set.'

'Don't even joke about it.' Jackie rolled her eyes. 'She'd do anything to wipe that smile off Carol Vorderman's face.' She hugged her daughter. 'Just try and take it one step at a time, okay? And call me if you need anything.'

Anna watched her mother disappear up the street, her trainers splashing through the puddles. She felt exhausted, as if she'd hauled herself up what she thought was a mountain, to find she'd only conquered a foothill and had an even more towering peak ahead of her.

She pulled her key out of her pocket. This time she managed to put it into the lock and let herself in.

One step at a time, she told herself.

Her mum offered to give Charlie his tea, so she decided to fill the hours before he came home by sorting through Oliver's things. She'd dithered about it for months, wondering what she should do with them. It hurt her to see them every day. The pain caught her unawares, every time she opened the wardrobe.

She got as far as pulling all his clothes out before it hit her. She sat on the bed, staring at his shirts piled up next to her, paralysed with guilt. How could she even think about getting rid of them? It would be like finally admitting he was never coming back.

The doorbell rang.

She had a feeling it might be Elliott, come to check up on her.

She was surprised to see Lynch on her doorstep.

'You look terrible,' were his first words.

'You don't look so hot yourself.' Except he did. He looked gorgeous as usual.

With her scruffy jeans, tear-ravaged face and smudged make-up, they looked like the inhabitants of two separate universes.

'I rang your office,' he said, following her into the house. 'They told me you'd come home early. Anything wrong?'

'I took the afternoon off to clear out Oliver's things,' she lied.

'Good idea. You don't want all those memories hanging around, do you?'

Don't I? she thought.

'How was Barcelona?' She changed the subject.

'Great, but it would have been better if you'd been there.'

'I'm sure you found plenty to keep you entertained.'

Something about the way he smiled made her think he hadn't been lonely for long. She waited for the sharp pang of jealousy, but it never came.

Grief had done that to her. It had blunted all her senses, thrown a muffling blanket over her emotions so she couldn't feel anything too strongly any more.

She made coffee and they chatted about nothing for a while. 'Where's Charlie?' Lynch finally remembered to ask.

'My mum's taking care of him for an extra couple of hours.'

He brightened up. 'In that case, why don't we go for a drink?'

'Sorry, I'm not really in the mood.'

He frowned at her. 'Are you sure you're okay?'

She wondered why she couldn't tell him about her break-down. He was supposed to be her friend, after all. Maybe even her boyfriend.

But he wasn't that kind of friend, she realised. Lynch was strictly a good-time guy, lovely to spend time with but not the sort she'd call up at three in the morning when she was on the edge of despair.

'I'm fine. Just a bit stressed about sorting out Oliver's stuff.'

She waited for him to offer to help. He didn't.

'In that case, maybe I'd better leave you to it.' He stood up. 'Maybe we could meet up for dinner later in the week?'

She opened her mouth to say yes, but what came out was, 'I don't think there's much point, do you?'

He looked taken aback. 'Sorry?'

'Maybe it's best if we don't see each other for a while.'

He smiled, as if he couldn't quite believe what he was hearing. 'Are you dumping me?'

'We were never really an item, were we? Let's face it, Lynch, we don't fit into each other's lives.'

'Is this about me going to Barcelona?'

She smiled sadly. 'It's about me not being able to go with you. I can't share your life, and I don't think you'd want to share mine.'

He thought for a moment. 'So that's it, then?'

'I think so, don't you?'

There was no reason why she couldn't have carried on going out with him, Anna thought as she headed back upstairs, but deep down she knew it wouldn't work.

It made her sad that Lynch wasn't the man for her. Everything about him was so right. He was sexy and successful – and he made her laugh.

But he wasn't the man she wanted.

Oliver's clothes lay reproachfully on the bed. Anna picked them up and began putting them back into the wardrobe, lovingly smoothing the creases out of his favourite shirts.

And to think she'd accused Eve of not wanting to move on.

Chapter 30

'I see. Well, thank you very much for your help.'

Eve put the phone down, feeling dazed. Beyond the door of the cubby-hole office, she could hear the clatter and clash of pans and the sound of Frankie's voice shouting orders at Lizzy. The evening service was in full swing.

She picked up the cheque book and stared at it. It must have been fate that made her come in here to pay a few bills during a quiet moment. Now she wished she'd never done it.

'Eve?' Frankie stood in the doorway. 'Customer on table six wants to see the manager.'

'I'm coming.'

'Everything all right?' he asked, as she brushed past him out of the office.

'I'm fine.'

'Sure? You seem a bit off tonight.'

'I said I'm fine.' She met his gaze. 'Why wouldn't I be?'

'No reason.'

At the end of the evening, when Lizzy and the rest of the staff had gone home, Eve took her time cashing up then went to find Frankie.

He was alone in the kitchen, humming to himself as he wiped over the work surfaces. She watched him for a moment. 'I thought that was Lizzy's job?' she said.

'I like to know it's done properly. Conscientious, that's me.'

Is that what you call it? Eve thought. 'Can I have a word?'

'If it's about that messed-up order earlier—'

'It's not about the order. It's about you.'

He didn't look up from his cleaning. 'Oh dear. What have I done?'

Eve felt a flutter of nerves. 'There's eight hundred pounds missing from the bank account. I wondered if you knew anything about it?'

His hand slowed, then sped up again. 'Oh yeah. I had to pay for the boiler to be repaired while you were away. I was going to mention it, but it slipped my mind.'

She dearly wanted to believe him, for everything to go back to normal, but she couldn't. Not this time. 'Why did you take the stub out of the cheque book?'

'I didn't want you to find out. I knew you'd worry about paying out all that money, so I thought it would be easier to deal with it and make the problem go away and you wouldn't have to know anything about it.'

'You did it for my sake?'

'If you like.'

She stared at his broad back, still bent over the work surfaces as he reached into every corner with the cloth. 'I called the bank. They said the cheque had been made out to cash.'

'So? You think this guy puts everything through the books? It was a cash-in-hand job, no questions asked. We got a better price that way.'

Eve was silent. Frankie straightened up and turned to face her. 'You don't believe me, do you? You think I took that money. I mean, it has to be me, doesn't it? I'm the one with the criminal record. Anything goes missing, blame the ex-con—'

'Frankie, don't. The emotional blackmail won't work this time.' She was too weary even to listen. 'You used that money to pay off your gambling debt, didn't you?'

'No!'

'Please, Frankie. For once in your life be honest with me.'

His eyes darted, searching the air for another lie. Then he gave up. 'I was desperate, okay? You don't know what these people are like, they would have killed me.'

'Why didn't you tell me?'

'What would you have done? Handed over the money?' He shook his head. 'It was easier just to take it and then pay it back. And I would have paid it back,' he insisted.

'But you just took it. You knew how much trouble we were in, and you stole it anyway.'

'I told you, it was just a loan.' He looked defensive. 'Oliver would have understood.'

She could feel her anger rising. 'You really think Oliver would have turned a blind eye to you robbing his business?'

There was a long pause. Frankie put down the cloth and folded his arms across his chest.

'You don't get it, do you?' he said pityingly. 'Oliver didn't have to turn a blind eye. He knew all about it. He tried to help me.'

'I don't understand. How—' Then the truth dawned on her. 'Those loans he took out – they were for *you*?'

'He knew I had a problem. I couldn't help it. Gambling's an illness with me.' Frankie was playing the victim again, his voice wheedling. 'I owed a lot of money, I'd lost my home. I told Oliver about it, and – he offered to help. It was his idea.'

'I believe you,' Eve said. That was just the kind of thing Oliver would do, try to help a friend, no matter what the cost to himself. 'So why didn't you pay him back?'

'I was trying to.'

'When you weren't gambling even more away?'

'It wasn't my fault. You don't know what it's like, being caught up in an addiction like that. It takes you over, it—'

'Spare me!' Eve cut him off. 'I've got no sympathy for you. You *used* Oliver. You let his business go under to save your own skin, and you did nothing about it.' That was what made her most angry, that Frankie had let Oliver struggle for so long. 'You do realise it was probably the stress of all this that killed him?'

'Don't you think I know that?' Frankie shouted back at her, his voice echoing around the kitchen. 'Don't you think that haunts me every day? Oliver was my best friend.'

'And look how you repaid him.'

'I don't have to listen to this.' He threw off his chef's jacket and headed for the door.

Eve pulled out her mobile phone. 'I'm calling the police.'

'You wouldn't!'

'Give me one good reason why not.'

'Oliver wouldn't like it.'

'Oliver isn't here, is he?'

She started to dial the number. Frankie watched her with narrowed eyes.

'Don't,' he said.

'Sorry, Frankie, you've given your last order in this kitchen.'

She turned away from him. The next thing she knew, the phone was snatched out of her hands.

'Give me that back.'

'Make me.' Frankie stood close to her, the heat of his breath fanning her face. Eve stood her ground, refusing to be intimidated.

'Give it back to me now,' she demanded.

'What are you going to tell them? That I've been stealing from the business? I've got witnesses to say you told me I could use the company cheque book.'

'Not to help yourself to cash!'

'I'll just tell them you knew all about it. You'll never be able to prove you didn't.'

She made a grab for the phone, but he swung away out of her reach and hurled it at the wall, smashing it.

Silence stretched between them, punctuated only by the slow, steady tick of the kitchen clock and Eve's ragged breathing. It began to dawn on her that tackling a violent ex-con in an empty restaurant after closing time wasn't exactly a good move.

But a second later he was smiling again, just like the old Frankie.

'Let's be reasonable about this, shall we? Look, I'm sorry I took that money. You're right, I should have told you. But I *will* pay it back, I promise. You can take it out of my wages if you like.'

His sheer nerve made her gasp. 'Do you really think I'd let you go on working here after this?'

253

'Why not? We make a great team. And let's face it, you couldn't run this place without me. Jesus, you can barely run it with me!' he laughed.

'You didn't say that when you were begging me to take over.'

'Yes, well, I needed the money, didn't I?'

Realisation hit her like a slap in the face. 'That's why you wanted me to take over here. If I'd sold up you would have lost your own personal cashpoint.'

'And there was you, thinking we were all doing it for Oliver.' He made a mocking face. 'As a matter of fact, I *was* doing it for him. I knew what this place meant to him. I couldn't let you make a mess of it.'

'Not until you'd squeezed every last drop of cash you could out of it.'

'Think what you like, love. It doesn't bother me.'

There was a crash from beyond the swing doors. Frankie looked round, distracted for a second – long enough for her to grab a heavy omelette pan and bring it down on the back of his head.

'Hello?' Anna called out from the restaurant. 'Did you know you'd left this door unlocked? Anyone could have – bloody hell!' She came through the swing doors and nearly tripped over Frankie's prone body sprawled across the kitchen floor. 'What the hell have you done?'

'I – I think I've killed him.' Eve looked at the pan in her hand then dropped it with a clatter.

She watched, numb with shock and terror, as Anna threw down her bag and knelt beside him. Her fingers probed the fat folds of his neck for a pulse.

'Well?' she said.

Anna sat back on her heels. 'Still alive, unfortunately. But you've knocked him out cold.'

'I'll call an ambulance.' Her hand was halfway to her bag before she remembered. 'Can I borrow your phone?'

'What happened to yours?'

'He smashed it.'

Anna looked at the shattered remnants. 'I think you'd better tell me what happened before you tell anyone else.'

'What if he wakes up?'

Anna prodded him with the toe of her trainer. He grunted and stirred. 'You're right,' she said. 'Give me a hand. We'll put him in the storeroom.'

'We can't do that!'

'Says the woman who thought she'd killed him a moment ago.'

'That was different. It was self-defence. If we leave him in the storeroom it could be murder.'

'If he comes round and finds us standing over him, it will definitely be murder.' Anna sighed. 'Look, he's not going to die if we lock him away for five minutes. And I don't know about you, but I really don't want to be here when he wakes up. Especially not with all those meat cleavers around. Now are you going to help me move him, or not?'

It took several minutes of heaving, straining effort to haul Frankie's dead weight into the storeroom, then Eve had to go back in to retrieve the keys from his trouser pocket. She kept expecting his lifeless hand to suddenly flash out and grip her round the throat.

She turned the key in the lock, and she and Anna slumped against the door, exhausted.

'I don't know about you,' Anna said, 'but I could do with a brandy.'

They made a bizarre picture, the pair of them sitting on the kitchen floor, a bottle of brandy between them. Eve was shaking so much she could barely lift the glass to her lips.

'I take it you found out he was fleecing you?' Anna said.

'Not just me. Oliver too. That was why he took out the loans, to pay off Frankie's gambling debts.'

'Typical Oliver.' Anna's mouth twisted. 'He always was too generous for his own good.'

'I suppose Frankie gave him a sob story and he fell for it.'

'He could never resist a hopeless case.'

'Or a friend.'

'Some friend.'

'I know.' Now she knew the truth, Eve felt incredibly foolish. She couldn't believe she'd let herself get taken in by Frankie for so long. 'Why didn't I see what he was really like?'

'Maybe you didn't want to,' Anna said. 'You needed someone to help you, and he was there. When you're alone and vulnerable, sometimes you cling to the wrong people.'

Eve turned her head to look at her. 'You sound as if you're speaking from experience?'

'I've made a couple of bad decisions lately.' Her face said she didn't want to talk about it.

'He was right about one thing, though. I can't run this place.'

'You haven't made such a bad job of it so far.'

'Have you seen the books lately?'

'That isn't all your fault. You've been up against it financially, finding the money for those loan repayments. And now you know he's been helping himself to your profits.' She jerked her head in the direction of the storeroom door. 'Maybe once he's out of the picture you'll be able to cope better.'

'Once he's out of the picture we won't have a chef.'

'So get another one. Or you could do it?'

'Me?'

'Why not? You're a great cook.'

She shook her head. 'I'm nothing special.'

'Oliver was always raving about how great you are. Usually after I'd managed to burn another one of my microwave specials.' She grimaced. 'It got quite annoying, actually.'

'I bet it did.' Eve sipped her brandy. She could feel it working its warming magic, calming her down.

'So why don't you take over here? You'd make a better job of it than fat Frankie.'

'I couldn't cook *and* manage this place. It would be too much.'

'I could manage it.'

'You?'

'I did it before, while you were away. I know you think I'm a bit lacking in customer skills—'

'A bit?' Eve laughed.

'But I reckon we should try. You never know, we might make a good team.'

'Us? A team?'

'Why not? Looks like that's how we've ended up, whether we like it or not.'

They both jumped at the loud groan from the other side of the storeroom door.

'Sounds like Sleeping Beauty's waking up,' Anna remarked.

'Maybe we should call that ambulance now?'

'Do we have to? Couldn't we just stick him in the freezer and forget about him?'

'I'm already facing an assault charge, I don't want to make it any worse.'

'You think he'll press charges?'

'Don't you?'

'Not if he's got any sense he won't,' Anna replied.

Chapter 31

AUGUST

Matt was already up and dressed when Eve got up the following morning, even though it was supposed to be his day off from the music shop where he worked part time.

'It's not lunchtime already, is it?' she joked. Then she saw the brown envelope on the kitchen table. Matt was sitting in front of it, his chin in his hands, staring at it as if he thought it might explode. 'Oh God. Your A-level results.'

She sat down opposite him. 'Well? What did you get?'

'I don't know. I haven't looked.'

They both looked at the envelope. 'Don't you think you should open it?' Eve said.

Matt pushed it across the table towards her. 'You do it.'

She reached for it, then pulled her hand back. 'I can't. I'm too nervous.'

'How do you think I feel?'

They were still discussing who should open it when Georgia stumbled sleepily into the room ten minutes later.

'Oh, for heaven's sake!' She snatched up the letter and ripped it open before either of them could stop her. She scanned its contents for a second, then dropped it on the table.

'Two Bs and a C,' she said in a bored voice. 'Do we have any Frosties left?'

Eve and Matt sat in frozen silence for a moment. The next minute they were whooping with joy, hugging each other and dancing round the kitchen like maniacs. Benson hid under the table, Georgia watched them with disgust.

'It's only a couple of exams,' she said dismissively. 'He hasn't, like, won the Nobel prize or anything.'

After nearly bursting with pride and excitement all morning and calling everyone she knew, by lunchtime Eve decided to ring Adam. Since that fateful night when they'd kissed, she'd been staying out of his way, and she sensed he was doing the same.

But he'd want to know about Matt, she told herself as she dialled his number with shaking fingers.

As soon as she heard his deep voice on the other end of the line she started to blush.

'Sorry to call you out of the blue like this, but I thought you might want to know Matt's passed his A levels,' she said in a rush.

'That's fantastic news. I was wondering how he'd got on when I heard the results were out. Tell him congratulations.'

'I will.' On impulse, she said, 'Why don't you come round tonight? Then you could tell him yourself.'

'Well—'

'We could all go out for a meal ... or I could cook?'

He paused a fraction too long. 'Sorry, I've got other plans for tonight.'

'Ah.'

'Maybe we could do it some other time? I could take you all out to lunch.'

She knew a brush-off when she heard it. 'That would be nice.'

She searched around, trying to think of a way to fill the awkward silence. She knew she should put the phone down but she couldn't bring herself to do it. 'So – er – are you doing anything exciting tonight?'

Another pause. 'Actually, I've got a celebration of my own.'

'Don't tell me – Britney's expecting again?'

He laughed. 'Nothing quite so momentous. Imogen and I are engaged.'

Her stomach went into freefall. She sat down on the stairs. 'Engaged? You're getting married?'

'I think that's the general idea.'

'When?'

'We haven't got that far yet. That's why we're seeing Imogen's

259

parents for dinner tonight.'

'Meeting the future in-laws? That'll be interesting.'

'Maybe they'll hate me and won't let me marry their daughter.'

'They'll love you.' How could they not?

She licked her lips, which had suddenly turned as dry as paper. If she tried to smile, they would crack.

'We're thinking of having an engagement party sometime in the next few weeks,' Adam said. 'I hope you and the kids can come.'

'Terrific,' she said automatically, her mind already racing for excuses.

There didn't seem much more to say after that. They made polite conversation about work for a minute or two, but all Eve could think about was how much she wanted to get off the phone.

Adam must have felt the same. 'I'd better go,' he said. 'Tell Matt I'm really pleased for him, won't you?'

'I will.' She hesitated. 'And Adam?'

'Yes?'

'I'm really pleased for you, too.'

So why did it feel as though her words were choking her?

Anna wondered if she was still suffering from the after-effects of coming off her medication when she saw Lynch on her doorstep on Saturday morning, carrying what appeared to be an inflatable dolphin under his arm.

'What do you think?' he said.

'It doesn't go with the Dolce and Gabbana shades.'

He grinned. 'How do you and Charlie fancy a day at the seaside?'

'Yes! Yes!' Charlie bounced up and down with excitement, tugging at her t-shirt.

'Why?' Anna asked.

'It's a lovely day. I just fancied catching some rays.'

'The only thing you'll catch in Scarborough is pneumonia.' She frowned. 'No, seriously. Why?'

'Anna!' He looked exasperated. 'Do you want to go or not?'

She looked down at Charlie, running circles of joy round her. 'Do I have a choice?'

This was bizarre, she thought as they headed off towards the coast. It had started badly when they'd had to take her car because three of them wouldn't fit in Lynch's Porsche. Lynch didn't look right somehow, folded up in the front seat of her battered Volkswagen, still wrestling with the inflatable dolphin.

As they left the city and headed towards the North York Moors, she could take it no more.

'Have you had a blow to the head or something?' she asked.

He laughed. 'No. Why?'

'I thought you might have amnesia. Because I definitely remember we agreed not to see each other again.'

'You said it, I didn't. Anyway, I've been thinking a lot about what you said about us not fitting into each other's lives.'

'And?'

'And I'd like to try.'

She glanced at Charlie in the rear-view mirror. 'I don't know if that would work.'

'Neither do I, until we give it a chance. Please?' He pecked her with the inflatable dolphin's nose. 'For Flipper's sake?'

Charlie laughed. 'See?' Lynch said. 'We're bonding already.'

Anna couldn't help smiling as she swatted the dolphin away, but deep down she still felt uneasy.

It was a warm, sunny day when they left York but by the time they'd crossed the moors to the coast, grey clouds had blotted out the sunshine, leaving dense, clammy heat.

Lynch's mood was fairly stormy too, by the time Anna had negotiated the town centre and found a parking space.

'Not exactly Club Med, is it?' he commented, as they headed past rows of gaudy souvenir shops and greasy-smelling junk-food cafes.

Despite the greying skies the beach was packed with families, mothers with lobster tans, overweight fathers in football shirts, and hordes of whining children all sweating in the sultry weather.

They finally found a spot, where Lynch tried to put up a couple of deckchairs while she changed Charlie into his turtle-patterned swimming trunks and t-shirt and applied sunscreen to his bare limbs, more in hope than expectation.

'For heaven's sake!' Lynch gave up with the deckchairs and let them collapse on the sand. 'I'm going for a swim.'

'Are you sure?' Anna eyed the flat, pewter-coloured water. 'It doesn't look too inviting.'

'It'll be okay once we get in.'

'We?' She shook her head. 'No way. I'm not going in.'

'Coward.' He unzipped his jeans.

'I haven't brought a costume, anyway.'

'So go in as you are.'

As he pulled his t-shirt over his head, Anna averted her eyes from his toned torso.

She wasn't the only one looking. All over the beach, women were sitting up and paying attention, while men collectively sucked in their beer bellies.

'Can I swim?' Charlie pleaded.

'Now look what you've done.' Anna took off her flip-flops and brushed sand from her cut-off denims. 'We'll paddle,' she said firmly.

They stood hand in hand on the water's edge with the cold water lapping between their toes. Lynch strode fearlessly into the water and plunged in, his tanned body making a perfect arc into the waves. A second later he surfaced, whipping wet hair out of his eyes.

'What's it like?' Anna called to him.

'F-f-f-fine.'

'Then how come you've gone blue?'

'Come in and find out for yourself if you don't believe me.'

'No, thanks.'

'*I* will.' Before she could stop him, Charlie had broken free of her hand and was wading into the sea.

'Charlie!' Anna went in a few more steps, gasping as the cold water splashed her knees.

'See?' Lynch caught Charlie, sweeping him into his arms. 'Even a child can do it.'

'Maybe I've just got more sense.' She saw Lynch whisper something in Charlie's ear, making him giggle. 'What are you doing? What did you say to him?' She backed away. 'Don't even think about it—'

Too late. Lynch grabbed her playfully around the middle. Anna struggled, lost her balance and pitched face first into the freezing water.

She came up a second later, screaming with rage.

'What the – you do realise these are my only clothes, don't you?' But Lynch and Charlie just fell about laughing.

'Imbeciles!' She staggered out of the water. 'Complete and utter—'

'Anna, please. Not in front of the child,' Lynch admonished primly.

'Anna!'

They looked round. Two young girls were plodding across the sand towards them. Anna recognised them straight away.

'Friends of yours?' Lynch asked.

'Jessica and Becky. Elliott's daughters.' She wrung water out of the hem of her t-shirt. 'Hi, girls. Where's your dad?'

'He's coming with all the stuff.' Becky looked Anna up and down. 'Why are you all wet?'

'I've been swimming.'

'With all your clothes on? Cool.'

'More like freezing.' She looked up the beach and saw Elliott coming over the horizon, laden down with beach bags. And he wasn't alone.

'You never told me there was a Mrs Prozac,' Lynch muttered.

'There isn't.'

The woman was a typical yummy-mummy type, immaculate in white jeans and t-shirt, her silky blonde hair tumbling around her shoulders. She and Elliott were deep in conversation, oblivious to the rest of the world.

'Very nice,' Lynch commented. 'I guess your friend Elliott must have something going for him after all.'

Anna suddenly wanted to run away, but she could only stand there, her dripping hair plastered around her face, as they approached.

She tried to look casual. 'Fancy seeing you here.'

'You know how it is. We wanted some sea and sand, and Barbados is just so over-rated.' He turned to the woman next to him. 'Justine, this is Anna, a colleague from work. Anna, this is my friend Justine.'

Justine gave her a quick once-over, assessing and dismissing her in one glance. 'Your mascara's running,' she pointed out kindly.

'Thanks.' Anna wiped it away with her finger. 'And this is—'

'Danny Lynch,' he interrupted her. He and Justine were already on full eye lock, ogling each other shamelessly. Anna wasn't surprised. Lynch looked like a Calvin Klein underwear model in his black trunks, his wet hair slicked back off his face and showing off his fabulous cheekbones.

She just stood there in a dripping puddle, stinking of seaweed.

'Been swimming?' Elliott asked.

'Not by choice. These two threw me in.'

'You should get dried off before you catch pneumonia.'

'I would if someone hadn't left the towels in the car.' She glared at Lynch.

'We've got one you could borrow.'

They found a spot further up the beach and Elliott got to work setting up windbreaks and arranging deckchairs.

'You certainly came prepared.' Lynch watched him, amused. 'You weren't a Boy Scout by any chance?'

Elliott ignored him and wrapped towels around Charlie and Anna. Anna sat in the deckchair he offered, her teeth chattering.

'Maybe you should get those wet clothes off,' Lynch suggested.

'Maybe you should put some clothes on,' Anna hissed back.

'Spoilsport.' He pulled on his faded jeans over his damp trunks. It was like a striptease in reverse. Anna wondered if it was just for her benefit until she saw Justine watching him from behind her magazine.

She felt sorry for Elliott, who looked decidedly overdressed in his overlong man shorts and polo shirt. She was sure there was a decent body under those sensible clothes, if only he chose to show it off.

'Maybe you need a hot drink,' Elliott said. 'There's a cafe up the road. I'll get you one.'

'I'll get it.' Lynch lazily unfolded himself from the deckchair.

'I'll come with you,' Justine offered.

'Can we get an ice-cream?' the girls chimed.

'I'll bring you one back,' Justine said, a bit too quickly.

'Don't they make a lovely couple?' Elliott remarked, as they watched them heading off down the beach.

'Gorgeous,' Anna agreed. They looked as though they'd stepped out of a brochure for an exclusive Caribbean resort, all gilded hair and lithe limbs.

'Sorry if we gatecrashed your date,' she said.

'Don't be.' Elliott turned his gaze to the water's edge, where the girls had taken Charlie to collect shells in a bucket. 'It wasn't going anywhere.'

'You seemed to be getting on okay when we first saw you.'

'I was advising her on the best way to sort out a leaking tap.' He looked rueful. 'To be honest, I think your friend Lynch is more her type.'

'I think she might be more his, too.'

They looked at each other and laughed. 'How the hell did they end up with us?' Elliott said.

'You're not that bad!'

'Neither are you.'

They looked at each other for a moment. His eyes weren't really dark brown at all, Anna noticed. They were almost green, flecked with gold and amber.

The girls came rushing up the beach, holding out their bucket, excited about the crab they'd just caught.

'So how's life at the restaurant?' Elliott asked, when they'd admired the poor bewildered creature and the girls were heading back to liberate it at the water's edge.

'Not bad, actually.'

As she'd promised, she'd taken a leave of absence to help Eve out at the restaurant. She'd been working there for nearly a month.

'I thought it would be meat cleavers at dawn by now?'

'So did I,' she admitted. But against all the odds, somehow their arrangement seemed to be working quite well. Mainly, she suspected, because they managed to stay out of each other's way most of the time. Eve kept to the kitchen while Anna managed the front of house.

Of course there was the odd spat, but far less often than she'd imagined. Now she was in charge of the kitchen Eve had even made some changes to the menu, cutting it right down and introducing some interesting specials.

Elliott pulled a face. 'So you're not missing us, then?'

'Like mad.'

'Good, because we're missing you. Especially Roy Munge,' he added quickly. 'And Barbara. She's thinking of starting up a grief counselling group in your honour.'

Anna swept round to look at him. 'I hope you're not serious?'

'Of course I am. And she wants you to address the group's first meeting, on the subject of Medication versus Meltdown.'

She was about to protest until she noticed his tongue wedged firmly in his cheek.

'That's something I don't miss,' she said. 'Your sick sense of humour.'

Actually, that was what she missed most of all. That, and his calm, soothing way of making her feel life wasn't so bad after all. There had been a few times when she'd felt like dropping in, just to sit at his desk and listen to him talk for a couple of hours.

They stared out to sea, watching a tanker steaming across the horizon.

'Don't forget, your job's there whenever you want to come back,' Elliott said.

'Thanks. I definitely will be back.' Much as she was enjoying the challenge of working at the restaurant, she couldn't imagine herself doing it for ever. She didn't have Eve's enthusiasm for the job. It might have been a legal oversight, but she knew for sure Oliver had picked the right person to take over from him.

'They're coming!' The girls ran back up the beach, Charlie plodding behind them. Lynch and Justine were strolling along the promenade, their hands full of styrofoam cups and ice-creams, laughing and joking and apparently in no hurry to return.

'I thought you and Lynch were history?' Elliott said, as they watched them make their way down the stone steps to the beach.

'So did I. Apparently, he's decided he wants to try playing happy families.'

'That's good, isn't it? At least he's making an effort.'

'That's what bothers me. Surely if he was right for me he wouldn't have to make an effort. It would just sort of – fit.'

'Are you sure you're not just making excuses?' Elliott said.

'Probably,' Anna sighed. The truth was, she really couldn't be bothered to make room for any man in her life.

'Maybe you should just give him a chance.'

Anna smiled at him. 'You're very good at giving advice, do you know that?'

'I should be. It's my job.'

On the way home, as Charlie slept in the back seat, Lynch said, 'Well? How did I do?'

Anna laughed. 'It's not an exam!'

He looked so earnest, she remembered what Elliott had said about giving him a chance. 'You lost points for trying to drown me.'

'Mr Prozac certainly didn't seem too impressed by that!'

'Don't call him that,' Anna snapped. 'You don't even know him.'

Lynch's brows lifted. 'Is there something I should know about you two?'

'Of course not. He's just been a very good friend to me, that's all.'

'How good? Should I be jealous?'

'Should I be jealous of you and Justine?' she dodged the question.

'Hardly! She's a bit too desperate, to be honest. Although I suppose spending time with Mr Prozac would make any woman desperate.'

'I told you, don't—'

'Call him that. Yeah, sorry.' He glanced sideways at her. 'Are you sure I shouldn't be jealous?' he said.

Chapter 32

That night after she'd put Charlie to bed, Anna made another stab at sorting out Oliver's belongings.

Armed with a glass of wine, she went upstairs to the bedroom, took a deep breath and threw open the wardrobe doors.

'I can do this, I can do this,' she muttered to herself over and over as she pulled the clothes off the rail and laid them on the bed.

Who am I kidding? she wept ten minutes later, when she'd found two theatre-ticket stubs in the pocket of his chinos. It was the night they'd been to see the Queen tribute band at the Opera House and laughed until they ached because they were so terrible.

The phone rang, shattering the silence. It was Eve.

'Sorry to call so late, but I wondered if I could come round? There's something I need to talk to you about.'

Anna glanced at her watch. Nine o'clock. 'Couldn't you tell me on the phone?'

'I'd rather see you.'

She looked at the heap of clothes on the bed. 'Can we make it another time? I'm busy at the moment.'

'Sure, no problem.' She paused. 'Are you okay, Anna? You sound as if you've been crying.'

'Just watching a soppy film on TV.'

'I thought you said you were busy?'

'Got to go. I'll see you tomorrow, okay?'

She hung up before she could be asked any more questions.

Knowing Eve, she would want to talk about work. It irritated Anna that she couldn't seem to trust her own judgement on anything. No wonder Frankie had been able to dominate her for so long. Anna sometimes wished Eve had a bit more confidence in her own decisions. She wasn't in the mood to discuss whether they could afford to take on a new washer-up or increase their salmon order.

She stared at the clothes on the bed, not quite knowing what to do. Suddenly the whole task just seemed too overwhelming, and she was tempted to stuff everything into the wardrobe for another day.

At least she could sort things into piles, she decided. One lot of stuff to be thrown away, one that could go to the charity shop, and one to keep.

She went downstairs and found a handful of black bin bags under the sink, then set to work. Steeling herself, she picked up the first item. An old khaki t-shirt, stained with blue paint. Oliver had worn it when they decorated Charlie's nursery. She was still pregnant, but Oliver had been so certain it would be a boy he'd insisted on painting the room an optimistic sky blue.

She put it on the keep pile.

Next was Oliver's favourite chunky black sweater. Anna held it up to her face, breathing in the faint traces of him that lingered there. Feeling the rough wool against her skin reminded her of all the nights she'd snuggled up to him on the sofa while they watched a movie and ate popcorn.

Another one for the keep pile.

By the time she'd worked her way through the heap of belongings, the only things she'd thrown away were an old pair of Oliver's socks, and she'd even dithered over those because he'd never let her throw them away when he was alive. He'd insisted they were his 'lucky' socks.

She'd just rescued them from the bottom of the bin bag and put them on the keep pile when the doorbell rang.

It was Eve. 'I had to come round,' she said. 'You sounded upset on the phone.' She peered at her. 'Have you been crying?'

Anna opened her mouth to make an excuse, but the truth came out. 'I've been going through Oliver's things.'

'Ah.'

'I thought it was time I should, but now I don't really know what to do.'

'Would you like some help?' Eve offered.

Once again, the words that came out of her mouth weren't what she'd planned. 'Yes, please.'

They stood in the bedroom, looking at the piles of clothes laid out on the bed. 'I don't really know what to do for the best,' Anna said. 'I can't bear to see his stuff every day, but I don't want to get rid of it, either. It doesn't seem right, somehow.'

'Like admitting he's really never coming back,' Eve said.

She nodded. That was exactly how she felt. 'What do you think I should do?'

'Who says you have to do anything? Why don't you just put them away in the loft for a while? That way you're not getting rid of them, but you don't have to see them every day either. Then you can think about it again later, when it's less painful.'

'Good idea.' Why hadn't she thought of that?

She looked sideways at Eve. 'Will you help me?'

'Are you sure? I wouldn't want to intrude.'

'I'd feel better if we did it together.'

If anyone had told her a year ago she would be sitting on her bed, sorting through Oliver's clothes with his ex-wife, she would have thought they were completely mad. Yet here they were, sipping wine, swapping memories of Oliver's wardrobe disasters and almost having a good time.

'Oh God, don't tell me he still wore this?' Eve held up a baseball cap, greying with age.

'Not if I could help it.'

'He must have had it years. We bought it on holiday in Spain when Georgia was a baby.'

'Maybe it brought back happy memories for him.'

'I doubt it. We had our passports stolen and then we ate a dodgy paella and all went down with food poisoning.'

From the wistful way she stroked the fraying peak of the cap, Anna could tell it still had fond memories for her.

'Why don't you have it?' she said.

'Oh no, I couldn't.'

'Take it, please. It means more to you than it does to me.'

'Thanks.' Eve laid the cap on her lap and picked up a shoebox from the floor. 'What's in here?'

'His toy-car collection. They're all a bit battered. Most of them are in bits.'

Eve searched through the jumble of broken metal. 'It looks like he kept everything he ever owned.'

'Pretty much,' Anna sighed. 'He could never let go of anything.'

'He's not the only one.' She took out a dented miniature police car and examined it. 'I was never very good at letting go either. Look at me and Oliver.'

Anna knew she should say something. 'It's not easy when a marriage ends.'

'That's just it. I never accepted it had ended.' The axle of the police car came off in her hand and Eve tried to clip it back into place. 'I probably made a real nuisance of myself sometimes,' she said with a sad little smile.

'I wouldn't say that.'

'Wouldn't you?' Eve gave her a knowing look.

'Maybe it was difficult sometimes,' Anna admitted. 'You always seemed to be there, in the background. Sometimes I thought you were just doing it to wind me up.'

'That was part of the reason, but mainly I just didn't want to let go. I couldn't face not being married to Oliver any more.'

'Because you were scared of being alone?'

'I was scared of losing my family. Being married was all I ever wanted.'

She gave up trying to fix the car and put it back in the box. 'That probably sounds a bit stupid and old-fashioned, doesn't it? People don't care that much about getting married these days.'

Some of us don't have much choice, Anna thought, her old resentment coming back.

'I know my mother thought I was being incredibly vulgar. She'd brought me up on the idea of free love and no commitment, and all I wanted to do was shackle myself to a man for the rest of my life.'

Anna smiled. 'I thought it was every mother's dream to see her daughter walk down the aisle.'

'Not Vanessa Gifford's daughter.'

She sat back. 'Vanessa Gifford? You mean that old hippy on the telly?' She stopped herself. 'Sorry, I didn't mean—'

'It's okay. You can't say anything I haven't heard a million times before. Anyway, you're right, she *is* an old hippy.'

'I didn't realise she was your mum.' Oliver had mentioned Eve's mother was well known, but she'd never have connected her with that ghastly woman, with her wild, flowing white hair, booming voice and outrageous opinions.

Eve must have guessed what she was thinking. 'I know. Hard to believe, isn't it? You can just imagine what an embarrassment I was to her.'

She put the box of cars down on the floor. 'But that's what I wanted. I set out to be the opposite of everything she was, everything she stood for.'

'Was that why you were so keen to get married?'

'Oh no.' She shook her head. 'I wanted to get married because I wanted someone who'd love me for the rest of my life.'

She picked up the baseball cap from her lap. 'I never had that with my mother, you see. Oh, I think she tried to love me, in her own way. But somehow she never managed it. I was always coming second to her research, her career, her lovers. I was just never that important to her.' She traced the embroidered logo with her finger. 'I only wanted what everyone else had. A loving, secure family, someone who'd put me first for once.'

Anna felt tears pricking the back of her eyes. 'No wonder you found it hard to let go.'

'I refused to let myself see what was happening. Oliver and the children were all I'd ever wanted, but it wasn't enough for him. He needed to be free, I needed security. It wasn't his fault, any more than it was mine. We just wanted different things out of life, but I wouldn't admit I couldn't make him happy.'

'You did make him happy,' Anna said. 'He loved you and the children.'

'I know he did. We spent half our lives together, we shared so much, but I was never his soulmate. Not like you.' The corner of her mouth lifted in an attempt at a smile. 'That was why I was so jealous of you. I could see you had something that Oliver and I never had. I kept telling myself that he'd come back one day, but deep down I knew he wouldn't.'

She stared down at the baseball cap in her hands, then put it down on the pile.

'Don't you want it?' Anna asked.

'Like I said, you've got to learn to let go sometime, haven't you?' She smiled. 'That's why I came over. I wanted to talk to you about your share of the restaurant.'

'I didn't know I had one.'

'That's the point. I think you should.' She took a brown envelope out of her bag. 'I've been to my solicitor and had this drawn up. I'm sorry I didn't consult you first, but I thought it would save time if I went ahead and did it.'

Anna eyed it uneasily. 'What is it?'

'A contract to transfer half my shares in the restaurant to you. I can't touch the children's shares, obviously, but I'm willing to give you mine.' She held the envelope out to her. 'All you have to do is sign it and send it back. Although I expect you'll want your solicitor to look it over first—'

'I can't take it,' Anna said.

'Why not?'

'Because—' She stared at the envelope, at a loss. 'It wouldn't be right.'

'It's what Oliver would have wanted.'

Anna looked down at the envelope in her hand. She realised it wasn't just a share in the restaurant Eve was giving her.

It was a share in Oliver's life.

'Does this mean we get to turn it into a pizza parlour?' she joked, to hide the emotion welling up inside her.

'No!' Eve said firmly. 'I haven't changed my mind about that. Oliver's isn't going to change.'

'We'll see.' Anna was relieved that in spite of everything, they could still find something to argue about. It would just be too weird otherwise.

As Eve left some time later, Anna said, 'How did Matt do in his A-levels?'

She looked surprised. 'You remembered?'

'How could I forget? Oliver wrote it on the kitchen calendar in big red letters. What did he get?'

'Two Bs and a C. Enough to get him on the university course he wanted.' Her voice was choked with pride.

'That's great.' On impulse, Anna went to hug her but held herself back at the last minute. 'Oliver would have been proud,' she said.

Eve smiled. 'Yes, he would, wouldn't he?'

Chapter 33

SEPTEMBER

'You know, you really shouldn't show your cleavage over the age of forty,' Georgia said. 'I read it in a magazine.'

'Oh yes? Which magazine was that? *Teenage Fashion Fascists Weekly?*'

Eve turned sideways in front of the mirror, trying to hold her stomach and backside in at the same time. The fitted black dress was a bit tighter than the last time she'd tried it on, in spite of the industrial-strength foundation garments she was wearing underneath.

'It's a bit Liz McDonald,' Georgia said.

'Who?'

'You know, that one in *Corrie*. The one who wears short skirts and flashes her boobs, even though she's about fifty. The desperate one.'

'Okay, I get the picture.' Eve considered her reflection again. She'd already agonised for far too long over what to wear. It was supposed to be an engagement party, so she didn't want to look like a schoolteacher, but she didn't want to look as if she was trying too hard, either.

And who would you be trying too hard for? She pushed the niggling thought to the back of her mind.

'And are you sure it's a good idea to show your arms off at your age?' Georgia said.

'Why not?'

'Two words. Bingo wings.'

'Oh, stuff it. Who cares anyway.' Eve grabbed an embroidered shawl and flung it around her shoulders. 'Come on, we'll be late.'

'What am I going to eat when I get to uni?' Matt said when they were in the car.

'What do you mean?'

'You know. Food. What's the deal about cooking and stuff?'

She thought for a moment. 'You're in a hall of residence, so I expect there'll be a kitchen.'

'And the food will be there?'

'Well, you'll have to buy it yourself, obviously.'

'Really?' Matt looked uneasy, his dark brows furrowing under his mop of hair.

'Don't worry, I'm sure there'll be a supermarket nearby.'

'A supermarket?' He couldn't have looked more panic-stricken if she'd suggested he visit the local brothel. 'But how will I know what to buy?'

'Loser,' Georgia muttered darkly.

Eve sent him a sidelong glance as he sat, feet up on the dashboard. For the first time it dawned on her how completely unprepared her son was for university life. So far the only effort he'd put in was to make sure his Panic at the Disco posters were safely packed with his vast collection of CDs and his precious guitar.

'Maybe it's time we taught you a few of the basics,' she said.

He shot her a worried look. 'Basics?'

'Or you can live on Coco Pops. That's what you do anyway,' Georgia said disdainfully.

'Like *you're* a gourmet chef or something.'

Eve listened to them bickering. She felt guilty that she hadn't given enough thought to Matt going away to university. She tried to blame it on being busy, but the truth was, she didn't want to admit he was leaving. If she didn't think about it, it wasn't really happening.

Except it *was* happening, in just over a week. She resolved to put everything else aside and concentrate on helping him get ready.

Adam and Imogen's party was already in full swing when they got to the farm. They pulled up in the yard at the same time as Jan and Peter with their brood.

'Well, this is a turn-up for the books, isn't it?' she said. 'Who'd have thought Adam would ever get married?'

'Who'd have thought it?' Eve agreed. She looked at the gift in Jan's hands, trailing complex pink and silver ribbons. 'What did you get them?'

'A photo frame. It's handmade, with their names engraved on it. How about you?'

'Just a Debenhams voucher. I didn't know what else to get,' she said. 'I'm not very good at presents, and I don't know what Imogen's taste is.'

She knew Adam's, though. She was dismayed to realise how much she did know about him, from his shoe size to the way he sounded when he laughed.

Imogen greeted them at the door. She looked stunning in a sea-green dress that shimmered like a mermaid's tail, her dark hair caught up in a loose, sexy knot. It would have taken surgery to remove her radiantly happy smile.

She enthused over the gift voucher far more than was strictly necessary.

'It's just what we need.' She lowered her voice conspiratorially. 'It's really nice of everyone to buy us all these little knick-knacks, but I'm desperate for something really *practical*, you know. All Adam's stuff is falling to bits, and I really need to start replacing it.' She rolled her eyes. 'He doesn't see the point, of course, but what do you expect? He's a man.'

She tucked her arm into Eve's and walked with her over to the drinks table. 'I'm so glad you came,' she said, handing her a glass of wine. 'Although I was a bit worried about inviting you, to be honest.'

'Really?'

'I wasn't sure how you'd feel about this – I mean, us, after … you know.' She pulled a sympathetic face. 'I know you've had a hard time lately. I didn't want you to think we were being insensitive.'

'Oh no! I couldn't be more pleased for you. It's about time Adam found someone to settle down with.' Eve tried to ignore the lump that suddenly seemed to come from nowhere in her throat.

'I'm so glad you said that.' Imogen's dark eyes shone with happiness. 'I have to say, I was amazed when he proposed. It came right out of the blue. To be honest, I was beginning to think we weren't getting anywhere.' She leaned towards her confidingly. 'Between you and me, I think there was someone in his past. I don't know who she was, but she obviously hurt him quite badly.'

'Oh?'

'Didn't you know? I thought you might, since you're so close.'

'Really?' Eve's voice came out as a squeak. 'No idea, sorry. Maybe you should talk to him.'

'Oh, you know Adam. He never talks about anything like that, it's very frustrating sometimes. Talk of the devil.' She smiled over Eve's shoulder. 'We were just talking about you.'

'Oh yes?'

Suddenly he was there, looking more handsome than Eve remembered him ever looking in all the years she'd known him. Happiness suited him, she decided.

She waited for her usual peck on the cheek, but it didn't happen.

Imogen put her arm around him. 'Doesn't he look gorgeous?' she said. 'I've told him he should wear a suit more often.'

'I'm not sure it would be very practical on the farm,' he said dryly.

Eve had to look away as he bent his head to kiss Imogen. She wanted to be happy for them, but seeing them so in love just made her feel even more alone.

'Has Adam told you about our plans?' Imogen said. 'We're having one of the outbuildings converted into a coffee shop.'

Eve looked at Adam. 'You never told me?'

'It's early days. We've only just got planning permission.'

'We're hoping to have it up and running in time for Christmas,' Imogen said. 'I'm amazed he hasn't mentioned it.'

'We haven't seen much of each other lately.' Eve felt herself blushing.

'I told him he should ask you for a few tips. Why don't you show Eve what we've done so far?' Imogen suggested.

'There's not much to see,' Adam said quickly.

'She could still get an idea of what it's going to be like. Besides,' she glanced towards the door, 'I think my godfather's just walked in. I want to get to him before he gets stuck into the drink.'

Imogen excused herself and hurried off to greet the silver-haired couple who'd just arrived.

Adam turned to her. 'Shall we go?' he said.

A cool breeze stirred the trees as she picked her way across the yard after Adam, stumbling in her high heels. He didn't slow down for her.

He pushed open a heavy wooden door. 'This is it. Like I said, there isn't much to see.'

He flicked on the light, but it did nothing to dispel the gloom of the damp, cavernous space. The air was thick and musty with the smell of wood chippings.

Eve shivered and pulled her shawl tighter around her bare shoulders. 'It's a bit different to the last time we were in a barn together,' she said, and immediately wished she hadn't. She could almost feel Adam's body tense as he stood behind her in the shadows.

'Imogen wants to call it the Cowshed Cafe.' He cleared his throat. 'Not strictly accurate, since it's never been a cowshed, but she reckons it sounds more poetic.'

She listened to him explaining all about Imogen's grand plans for converting the cafe, but all the time she was aware of him standing close to her.

'She's a very determined woman, your fiancée.'

'Isn't she? She's just what I need. Someone who'll keep me looking forward rather than living in the past.'

She turned round to face him. 'So you're happy, then?'

'Why shouldn't I be?'

They stared at each other for a long time. His eyes were dark pools in the gloom.

'Aren't you happy for me?' he said softly.

Her whole body twanged with tension, so much so that when a pigeon took off from the high rafters above their heads, flapping

279

out of a gap under the eaves, she screamed and jumped straight into his waiting arms.

For a moment they froze there. She could feel the steady beat of his heart against hers. Her eyes fixed on his face, the curve of his mouth ...

The barn door rattled and they sprang apart.

'Hello?' Imogen's voice echoed around the empty space. 'I just wanted to tell you, they're all waiting for the speeches.'

'Just coming.'

Imogen turned to Eve. 'What do you think?' She gestured around the barn.

'It'll be great.'

'I think so too. I'm going to give up my job and run it after we're married. I'd like to get more involved with the farm.' She smiled adoringly up at Adam. 'He spends so much time working it's the only way I'm ever going to see him.'

As they headed for the door, Imogen turned to her and said, 'Just think. Once this place opens we'll be rivals.'

Eve looked at her hand, clasping Adam's.

I reckon we already are, she thought.

Chapter 34

'Well, this is nice, isn't it?' Eve stood at the window and looked out over the neat square of trimmed lawn below. Parents crisscrossed it, their arms bulging with pillows, duvets and bin bags full of their children's possessions.

'Bit small,' Georgia commented, her nose wrinkling. 'And it smells funny. Like old socks.'

'I like it.' Matt sprawled on the narrow bed, his arms behind his head, his worldly goods arranged around him, clothes carelessly squashed into bin liners, his CD collection carefully stacked in labelled boxes. His guitar and laptop were already unpacked and standing ready.

Eve knew he wanted her to leave, but she couldn't bring herself to say goodbye. She turned away from the window, rubbing her hands together briskly. 'I'll give you a hand to unpack this lot, shall I?'

'S'okay. I can do it when you've gone.'

Eve stared at his old familiar duvet spread out on the new bed. It looked all wrong somehow.

'Maybe we should take a look round, help you get your bearings?' she suggested, slightly desperate.

'I've got a map.'

'I think he wants us to leave,' Georgia pointed out with her usual tact.

A couple of students loped past the half-open door, laughing. Further down the corridor, someone was playing the drums. Eve caught Matt's longing expression.

'I suppose we'd better go before the traffic gets too bad,' she said wistfully. 'Are you sure you're going to be all right?'

'Mum!'

She'd promised herself she wouldn't cry, but as soon as Matt put his arms around her she started blubbing.

'I'm sorry.' She rifled up her sleeve for a tissue. 'I don't even know why I'm crying. I'm so stupid. You're going to have a lovely time.'

It was the start of a whole new adventure for Matt, but it felt like the end of another chapter for her. No more dragging him out of bed in the morning, no more nagging him about the dirty coffee cups left to grow mould in his room. The house would no longer ring to the sound of his electric guitar.

She was still sniffing back tears as they drove home.

'God, honestly!' Georgia muttered. 'He's only gone to university, not Afghanistan.'

'I know, but he seems so young to be leaving home.'

'Can I have his room? It's bigger than mine.'

'Georgia! You could wait until he's been gone five minutes.'

Georgia grumbled to herself, but Eve knew she'd miss her brother too. They bickered constantly, but they'd grown to rely on each other since their father died.

As they reached York, Georgia suddenly said, 'Will you drop me off at Ellie's house? I said I'd go round and see her.'

'I thought we could spend the evening together, get a DVD, maybe.'

Georgia pulled a face. 'I promised Ellie. We've got a project to do for history.'

'What time will you be back?'

'I'd sort of planned to stay the night.'

Eve understood why. She didn't want to be there for the first night without Matt.

Eve didn't really want to be there either, but there wasn't much she could do about it.

She dropped Georgia off at her friend's house and headed home. It was strange walking into the empty house. She quite often spent the evening alone when Matt and Georgia were out with their friends, but somehow she'd never really felt alone because she knew they'd be coming back. She even enjoyed the peace and quiet of not having to listen to Matt's music or Georgia's latest tantrum.

Now Matt was gone, and in a few years' time Georgia would go too. Her chest tightened with panic at the thought of rattling around in the house with only Benson for company.

She needed to call a friend. She was about to pick up the phone and invite Jan round when she remembered she was on a school trip, taking a group of Year Sixes on an activity holiday in the Dales.

Then she thought of Adam. Once he would have been the first person she'd call, but now he had Imogen.

She watched some dire TV for a few hours, flicking channels between reality shows, searching for something to distract her. She was so desperate she almost called her mother, until she remembered she had no idea where in the world she was.

Maybe Vanessa had the right idea, she thought. Drifting from country to country, rootless. No ties meant no chance of getting hurt.

She switched off the TV and grabbed her coat and car keys. There was one place where she knew she'd find some distraction and human company.

The restaurant had always been a comforting place, but recently it had become like a second home to her, a haven where she could forget her creeping loneliness.

She arrived just as they were closing up. Simon and Lizzy were cleaning up in the kitchen.

'You missed a good night tonight, boss,' Simon grinned. He'd taken over as head chef after Eve lured him back from The Burger Shack. It wasn't too difficult; it turned out he'd only left because he couldn't stand working with Frankie, but a few weeks of flipping burgers and making fries had driven him to the edge of madness.

Now he'd taken over in the kitchen, it meant Eve could go back to running the restaurant, although she still took more of an interest in planning the menu than Frankie had ever allowed.

It was generally a relief to everyone that Frankie had gone. For a while, Eve had been worried about the police arriving on her doorstep to arrest her for assault or – worse – Frankie creeping up on her in the dead of night to exact his own revenge. But the last she'd heard on the grapevine, he'd left town in a hurry after falling even deeper in debt to Les Willis and his gang. Eve doubted if he would ever dare to show his face in the city again.

'Have we been busy?'

'You wouldn't believe it. I reckon putting on that display at the Food and Drink Festival helped.'

'I can't take the credit for that. It was all Anna's idea.' The festival was a big event in York every September, a showcase for all the food producers and restaurants in Yorkshire. There were events all over the city, and this year Anna had managed to get them a stand in one of the big markets. They'd served champagne and canapés, and handed out flyers offering special discounts at Oliver's. Trade had been picking up slowly but steadily ever since, helped by the new menu.

'How have the new dishes been working out?' she asked.

'They've been going down a storm, especially the Thai fish-cakes, but we're going to need more banana bread and butter pudding for tomorrow.'

'I'll make some tonight.' She looked at Lizzy, energetically scrubbing a baking tray. 'In fact, why don't you leave that? I can finish off here.'

'Are you sure?'

'You've worked hard enough. You deserve an early night.'

When they'd gone, Eve pulled down the blinds and fired up the oven, then got down to work. She was kneading some bread dough when Laura came in.

'I'm off now,' she said.

'Leave the keys, I'll lock up when I've finished.'

Laura put the bunch of keys down on the work surface. 'Something smells good. What are you making?'

'Roasted red pepper focaccia. There are some onion rolls in the oven, and I've just made those blackberry scones. Take a few home with you, if you like.'

'Thanks.' Laura took a plastic bag from the roll on the wall and helped herself to a couple. 'I suppose you're missing Matt?'

Eve paused, her hands buried in the soft, springy dough. 'The house seems very quiet without him.'

'My mum was just the same. She cried for a week when I left home to go to university. Now I don't think she'd have me back.' She frowned. 'Are you sure you're going to be okay on your own? You don't want me to stay and keep you company?'

'I'll be fine.'

She watched Laura cross the yard and let herself out of the back gate. She liked her a lot, but she was beginning to wonder if Anna was right about her being a bit creepy. She always seemed to be around, either at the restaurant or at the churchyard.

But the restaurant felt a lot spookier once she was on her own. Eve hummed uneasily to herself, trying to keep the silence at bay, as she cut up bread and mashed bananas for the bread and butter pudding.

Once the pudding was in the oven and everything else was cooling, she took a break and made herself some coffee. She'd perched on a stool to drink it when she heard a sound outside.

She stiffened, listening. There were footsteps in the yard outside. At first she thought it might be someone from a neighbouring shop, but they came closer, then stopped outside the door.

Her fingers tightened around her coffee mug. She stared at the door handle as it slowly turned, like something out of a horror film.

The door opened. Eve reacted without thinking. With a scream, she flung the remains of her coffee at the shadowy figure . . .

'What the—'

'Adam!' She put her hand to her chest. Her heart was flipping around her ribcage like a stranded fish. 'What are you doing here?'

'I was passing, and I saw the light. I thought you had burglars.' He held out his arms. Coffee dripped down the front of his leather jacket.

'Here, let me help.' She grabbed a cloth from the sink. 'I'm so sorry. I didn't mean to attack you.'

'What are you doing here, anyway?'

'I couldn't sleep.'

He looked around. 'So you thought you'd come down here and bake instead?'

'It beats taking a sleeping tablet.' She stopped dabbing. 'I think I've got the worst of it off. Would you like a coffee?'

'Could I have it *in* a cup this time?'

There was something slightly surreal about the two of them sitting in the brightly lit kitchen at one in the morning, drinking coffee and eating cake.

'Did Matt get off to university okay?' Adam asked.

'He didn't even look back. It was me who had trouble saying goodbye.'

'It must seem weird without him.'

'Why do you think I'm baking cakes in the middle of the night?' She picked a blackberry out of her scone. 'What about you? It's a funny time of night to be just passing.'

'I couldn't sleep either.'

'I suppose you must have a lot on your mind, what with the coffee shop and your wedding plans and everything?'

'You could say that.'

The fluorescent tube-light buzzed, the only sound in the silent kitchen.

Eve cleared her throat. 'So – have you set a date yet?'

'No.'

'I suppose it will be after Christmas now? They say spring is always a good time to get married—'

'Do we have to talk about it?' Adam cut her off.

'Not if you don't want to.'

He sat for a while, staring into the depths of his coffee cup, before he spoke. 'That night at the party, when I asked you if you were happy for me, you never gave me an answer.'

His question caught her unawares. 'Of course I'm happy for you. Imogen's a lovely girl.'

'Yes, she is. But that wasn't what I asked.' He looked up, his gaze direct and challenging. 'Do you want me to marry her?'

'What kind of question is that?'

'An honest one. And I'd like an honest answer.'

No, she wanted to shout. How could I want you to marry someone else when I love you?

Her feelings had crept up on her, taken her unawares. All the time she'd thought of him as nothing more than a friend, and it wasn't until Imogen came along that she'd realised how much she cared for him.

Even then, she'd thought she was just jealous because she didn't want to be alone. But now she realised there was much, much more to her feelings than that. She knew he was attracted to her too. She could sense the tension in him, waiting for her to say the word.

But how could she? He'd finally found someone to love, she couldn't confuse him by admitting how she felt. It wasn't fair to put doubts in his mind.

It wasn't fair on Imogen, either. She was so happy, so in love with him. Adam deserved someone like that – someone who could love him completely, just like she'd always wanted to be loved.

She couldn't bring their future crashing down.

She met his gaze. His eyes weren't grey like Oliver's, she noticed. They were outlined with the darkest blue, almost black. Looking at him now, she wondered how she'd ever thought they were alike.

'Yes,' she said. 'I want you to marry her.'

Chapter 35

OCTOBER

Anna and Lynch were going to Rachel's birthday party, his first official outing as her boyfriend.

And as if that wasn't nerve-wracking enough, they were doing it in fancy dress. For some reason Rachel, usually the coolest woman on the planet, had decided to hold an astonishingly un-cool Hallowe'en Saints and Sinners party.

'Aren't you going to get changed?' Anna asked, as she struggled with the sparkly wings on her angel's costume.

'I *am* changed.'

She looked him up and down, taking in the casually sexy black suit and t-shirt. 'What exactly are you supposed to be?'

'A serial killer.'

'You don't look much like a serial killer to me.'

'Have you ever seen one?'

'Well, no, but—'

'So how do you know what they look like? They don't prowl around the streets with an axe, you know.'

'Good point.' She adjusted the elastic on her wings, then tried to put them on again. They still looked lopsided. 'Do you think this dress is too short?'

'Put it this way. If everyone in heaven looks like you I can't wait to get there,' he said. There was a long pause while they both realised what he'd said. 'Sorry,' he said. 'Bad joke.'

'It's okay.'

'I still think you should have gone as a nun, though. I have a thing about nuns.'

'Lynch, you have a thing about anything female with a pulse.'

He looked outraged. 'That's not fair. I'm a changed man, remember?'

Anna was still pretty sceptical about that, although she had to admit he'd certainly been trying. Ever since Scarborough he'd been the perfect devoted boyfriend, taking her and Charlie on day trips and outings every weekend, and showering Charlie with gifts.

'So how about a spot of sin before we leave?' he said, closing in for a kiss.

'The babysitter will be here in a minute—' The doorbell rang. 'Right on cue,' she grinned, pushing him off.

'I'm not late, am I?' Laura said.

'Your timing was immaculate,' Lynch muttered through gritted teeth as he preened his hair in the mirror.

'Where's Charlie?' Laura looked around. 'I've bought him a present.'

'Another one? You didn't have to do that.'

'I like buying things for him.' At that moment Charlie hurtled into the room, in his pyjamas, his hair freshly washed and sticking up in spikes. 'Hello, sweetheart. Look what I've got for you.'

Anna watched apprehensively as he ploughed his way through the plastic packaging. There was something about Laura that still made her feel uneasy. She wouldn't have asked her to babysit but her mother had a residents' association meeting.

Charlie unwrapped the *Star Wars* action figure and his face fell.

'I've got this one.'

'Charlie! Don't be rude. Say thank you to Laura.'

'It's okay,' Laura mumbled, looking upset. 'I should have checked.'

Charlie pointed at Lynch. 'My daddy bought it for me last week.'

Silence clanged down around them like a steel door. Everything seemed to stand still and none of them looked at each other.

'Anyway,' Anna recovered briskly, 'we won't be late. You've

got my mobile number, haven't you? And I've left Rachel's number by the phone, just in case my battery goes flat.'

'No problem,' Laura said. But she wasn't smiling quite so broadly any more.

'Does she strike you as a bit odd?' Anna asked when they were in the cab.

'No, why?'

'I just wondered.'

'She seems fine to me.' Lynch stared out of the window, pre-occupied. Anna could guess why.

'I expect you're a bit shocked about Charlie calling you daddy.' She tried to laugh about it. 'I wouldn't worry about it, he calls everyone that. He gets confused. He accidentally called the postman daddy last week,' she gabbled. 'That caused a few raised eyebrows.' She glanced at him. 'You didn't mind, did you?'

'Why should I? Like you said, he gets confused.'

Luckily he seemed to lose his brooding mood by the time they got to Rachel's flat. As soon as they walked in, something seemed to click inside his head and he was the Perfect Boyfriend again, charming everyone in the room.

He even managed to dazzle the usually cynical Rachel, who was looking particularly stunning in a skin-tight red dress and a pair of glittery devil horns.

'What are you supposed to be?' Anna asked.

'A horny devil, what else?' She did a twirl, showing off her perfect figure.

'You didn't tell me he was so bloody gorgeous,' Rachel hissed when Lynch had gone to get them a drink.

'I did.'

'No, you said he was good-looking. You didn't say he was Brad fucking Pitt.' She shook her head, stunned. 'No wonder you've been keeping him to yourself. So how's it going with you two?'

'Pretty well.'

'You seem surprised?'

'I am.'

Rachel frowned at her. 'You're not still feeling guilty about Oliver?'

She shook her head. No matter how much she loved Oliver, she had to accept that he was gone. Now she faced the choice of being lonely for the rest of her life or finding someone to share it with. She'd never imagined that person would be Lynch, though. Life could be very strange sometimes.

'Are you happy?'

'I think so.'

'Then enjoy it.'

'I am.' That was the problem. 'I keep expecting it all to go wrong.'

'What makes you think it will?'

'It almost did earlier on.' She told Rachel about Charlie's slip of the tongue.

Rachel winced. 'Ooh, dear. I'm guessing Lynch wasn't exactly over the moon?'

Anna shook her head. 'Playing happy families at the weekends is one thing, but I don't think he's ready to be called daddy just yet.'

She was worried that Charlie's chance remark might have scared him off completely.

Sure enough, an hour later she was chatting to Gandhi and a couple of vampires when Lynch edged his way to her side and said, 'Something's come up at work. I've got to go.'

'Now?' Anna looked at her watch. 'But it's ten o'clock on a Saturday night.'

'One of my clients has got himself arrested. I need to get down to the station and sort it out.'

'How long will you be?'

'Depends how busy it is. On a Saturday night, it could take hours.'

'Do you want me to come with you?'

He smiled. 'Thanks, but there's no need. You might as well stay here and enjoy yourself.' He leaned forward and planted a very chaste kiss on her forehead. 'I'll ring you later, okay?'

'When?' Anna called after him, but he was already gone.

He was probably telling the truth, she thought as she poured herself another drink. Lynch did sometimes get called out at odd hours to sort out clients' problems. But what if it was just an excuse to get away from her?

No, she told herself. He wouldn't make excuses like that. He'd be upfront with her, tell her straight he didn't want to be with her any more.

She left the party early and headed home, her coat over her costume and her wings stuffed in her bag.

Laura was on the sofa, watching TV. Charlie was asleep, cuddled up next to her.

'You're early. Had a good evening?'

'It was okay. Why is Charlie still up?'

'He had a bad dream, so I let him sit with me for a while.' Laura sat up and looked around. 'Where's Lynch?'

'He had to go to work. I'll take Charlie up to bed.'

'I can take him—'

'I'll do it.' She gathered him into her arms.

When she got back downstairs, there was a bottle of wine open on the coffee table. Laura had poured them each a glass.

'You looked as if you needed a drink.' She handed her a glass. 'You and Lynch haven't had a row, have you?'

'Why should we?' Anna watched Laura curl up on the sofa, feeling slightly irritated. She'd been looking forward to having some time to think.

'I just wondered. He seemed in a funny mood when he left.'

'He was fine.' Anna put down her glass. 'Look, do you mind if we call it a night? I'm a bit tired.'

'Is it serious between you?' Laura asked suddenly.

Anna stared at her, taken aback. 'I'm sorry?'

'You and Lynch? Is it serious?'

'I don't think that's any of your business.'

'Because if it is, I don't think you should feel guilty about it,' Laura went on, as if she hadn't heard her. 'Oliver wouldn't have minded. He would have wanted you to be happy.'

She had a strange little smile on her face. 'It might even have been a relief,' she said. 'Because then he wouldn't have to worry about you any more.'

She leaned forward and topped up her glass. 'He did worry about you, you know. That was why he didn't want to—' She broke off.

'Didn't want to what?'

'It doesn't matter.' Laura put down her glass and groped for her bag. 'Look, I'd better go.'

'Not until you tell me what's going on.'

'I can't,' she said. 'I've already said too much.'

She tried to blunder past, but Anna held her by her shoulders.

'Let me go,' said Laura, her eyes fixed on the carpet. 'I don't want to talk about it.'

'Well, I do. You can't just talk in riddles and then walk away.' Anna held her at arm's length. Laura trembled like a rag doll in her grip.

'It's not fair,' she mumbled. 'I shouldn't have to do this. He always promised me I wouldn't have to be the one to tell you.'

'Tell me what?' Anna suddenly felt very frightened.

Laura raised her head slowly. Her eyes, swimming with tears, were fixed on Anna's face.

'That we were in love,' she said.

Chapter 36

Anna's hands dropped to her sides. 'You're lying.'

'I'm sorry, Anna. Believe me, I didn't want you to find out like this.' Laura's words came out in a rush. 'Oliver said he was going to tell you. He promised. But then—'

'You're lying.' They were the only words her brain could register.

'Why would I lie?' Laura sat down on the sofa. 'Maybe we should talk about this?'

'I don't want to talk to you.'

'Then maybe you should listen.' Laura was quiet for a moment, as if she didn't know where to begin. 'He didn't want to hurt you. Neither of us did. It was tearing him apart.'

Anna closed her eyes. She wanted Laura to disappear, for this to have been some horrible dream, but when she opened them again, she was still there. Still talking.

'We were just friends to start with. I was going through a really bad time. My mum was ill, and I was worried sick.' She recited the facts in a small, flat voice. 'I never really had anyone to talk to except Oliver. He was a real friend. He understood.' Her eyes had a glazed, dreamy look. 'After work, when everyone else had gone home, we'd open a bottle of wine and talk. I felt like I could tell him anything.'

Anna felt sick. She could almost picture the corner table where they would have sat, Laura pouring out her troubles, Oliver listening, his head tilted thoughtfully, those grey eyes gazing deep into her soul. Maybe reaching out and holding her hand, telling her he understood . . .

'I helped him, too. He had so many problems, he couldn't talk to anyone.'

'He could talk to me.'

Laura's look was almost sympathetic. 'Anna, you *were* the problem.'

She pulled a loose strand of hair from behind her ear and examined it idly. 'He realised he'd made a mistake with you. He said you should have never got together, but you got pregnant and he didn't know what to do.'

'That's a lie. I never forced him to stay with me.'

'Could you really imagine him walking out on you when you were having his baby?'

She couldn't. Even when she was leaving the clinic having made up her mind to go it alone, she'd known deep down that Oliver would stand by her.

'He tried to make the best of it,' Laura said. 'Don't get me wrong, he loved you and Charlie. But you were never what he wanted.'

'And you were?'

'I was a friend,' Laura said. 'I never asked to be anything else. I made it clear to Oliver as soon as we realised how we felt. There was no way I was going to get too involved with him while you two were still together.'

'Big of you,' Anna said.

'But he wanted to be with me,' Laura insisted. 'He kept promising he'd sort it out, make everything right. He was waiting for the right time, he said, but he kept putting it off and in the end I just lost patience.' She stared at a worn patch on the rug. Her voice was a thin thread of sound. 'If I'd known what was going to happen I would never have started that stupid argument. Then maybe he'd still be alive.'

It took a full moment for it to sink in. 'You were – with him when he died.'

Laura hesitated a moment, then nodded. 'He was driving me home after work. We started talking about you, and I wanted to know when he was going to tell you. I kept saying to him it wasn't fair to keep stringing you along. He promised he'd do it soon. We were arguing about it, and suddenly—' She closed her eyes. 'I didn't know what was happening. I must have been knocked out or something. When I woke up the car was off the road and Oliver was sort of – slumped. There was nothing I could do to help him,' her voice rose. 'I kept calling his name, trying to make him wake up. I thought he was dead.'

'So you left him,' Anna said in a hollow voice.

'I panicked. I didn't know what else to do.' Laura's eyes were huge in her thin, pale face. 'I did it for you,' she said.

'For me?'

'I knew if the ambulance found me in the car they'd ask all kinds of questions. You'd be bound to find out, and I didn't want that to happen.'

'You left him to die,' Anna said again.

'I didn't know, did I? Do you think I would ever have left him if I'd known that? I would have stayed with him, died with him if I could. Anything's better than living without him.'

They were both silent for a moment, lost in their thoughts. Then Anna said, 'Why are you telling me all this now?'

'I didn't want to tell you.'

'Liar.' Anna turned on her. 'You've wanted to tell me all along, haven't you? That's why you've been acting so friendly, trying to get close to me and Charlie.'

Oh God. Charlie. To think she'd left Laura alone with her son.

'I thought we could be friends.' Laura sounded hurt. 'I thought maybe in time I could tell you, that you'd understand ...'

'Understand?' Anna's eyes blazed. '*Understand?* What did you think we'd do, mourn him together? Go and visit his grave?'

'You never visit his grave,' Laura said flatly. 'I see Eve there all the time, but you never come.' She looked up at her. 'I suppose you don't have to bother now you've got a new boyfriend.'

Anna gasped. 'Get out,' she said.

'Out of sight, out of mind for you, isn't it?' Laura stood up, facing her. 'One boyfriend dies, so you just move on to the next, and meanwhile everyone feels sorry for you. Poor Anna.' She pulled a face. 'But who feels sorry for me? I don't get any cards or sympathy, do I? Nobody knows I exist. I even have to mourn him in secret.'

Anna looked down at her hands, her fingers clawed into her palms. She wanted to lash out, to hurt Laura.

'Just *go!*'

'If that's what you want, but it won't change anything. Oliver didn't love you, Anna. He loved me.'

If her mum was at all surprised to see her at one in the morning, standing on her doorstep with Charlie wrapped up in her arms, she didn't show it.

Anna took one look at her standing there in her yellow bathrobe, her kind, unmade-up face shiny with night cream, and burst into tears.

'Oh, love.' Her mother ushered her inside and closed the door, just as Keith stumbled sleepily down the stairs.

'Did I just hear the – oh!' He saw Anna and stopped. 'What's happened? What's wrong?'

'I'm just about to find out.' Jackie took Charlie from Anna's arms and handed him over to Keith. 'Can you put the little lad in the spare room? I'll come up and check on him in a minute.'

She took Anna into the sitting room and sat her down on the sofa. 'I'll put the kettle on.'

Five minutes later she returned with two mugs of tea. Anna couldn't help smiling, in spite of her misery. Tea was her mum's answer to everything. As far as she was concerned, there was nothing in the world that couldn't be made better by a mug of Typhoo.

Jackie settled herself on the sofa beside her. 'So tell me all about it.'

She told her. Her mother listened in silence, and it was impossible to tell from her expression what she was thinking.

'And you believe her?' she said when she'd finished.

'Why would she lie?'

'I don't know, love. People do strange things for all kinds of reasons.'

'She was with him when he died,' Anna said. That was what

hurt most of all, that hers were the last eyes he looked into.

'So she says. Anyway, how do you know he wasn't just giving her a lift home?'

'Mum, I *know*.'

Jackie twisted her wedding ring around on her finger. 'So what are you going to do?'

'I don't know,' Anna said. She wanted to scream and rage, but what good would it do? She couldn't lose her temper with a dead man. 'Can I stay here tonight?'

She didn't want to go home. She never wanted to sleep in the same bed again.

'You don't even have to ask. The bed's already made up for you. Do you want to go up now?'

She shook her head. 'I'll stay down here for a bit, if that's okay?'

'Shall I stay up with you?'

'No thanks, I'm better off on my own at the moment.'

Her mother stood up reluctantly. 'Call me if you need anything, won't you?'

'I will, don't worry.'

'Don't worry, she says,' Jackie muttered as she headed for the door.

Anna didn't know how long she sat on the sofa, not moving. She was too shocked and numb even to cry. It felt as if she'd lost Oliver all over again.

Except this time it was worse. When he died, she had the happy memories to get her through the bleak times. Even when things were at their blackest, she could remember that he loved her and that was enough to help her through.

But now she knew there were no good times, no happy memories. There were only lies.

She couldn't even lie in bed and talk to him in the darkness the way she used to. Sometimes when she lay there whispering to him, she could almost feel his warmth beside her.

This time no one was listening. Oliver was gone.

She didn't go to bed, because she knew she wouldn't sleep. She curled up on the sofa, staring at the wall and thinking.

By the morning she knew what she had to do.

It took Lynch a long time to answer the phone. His voice on the other end was groggy with sleep. 'Anna? Do you know what time it is?'

'I have to see you as soon as possible.'

'Can we make it later? I spent half the night in the police station.'

'Please, Lynch. I need you.'

He didn't hesitate. 'I'll be there in half an hour.'

'No,' she said. 'Let me come to your place.'

He was showered and dressed by the time she arrived twenty minutes later.

'So what's so urgent that you have to turn up in the middle of the night to discuss?' he grinned.

But he wasn't smiling when Anna told him what she planned.

'Are you sure about this?' he said.

'Absolutely sure.'

'I realise you're bound to be upset and angry. Maybe it's not the best time to make these kind of decisions.'

'I've made up my mind,' she insisted. 'Now, are you going to help me, or not?'

'Of course,' he shrugged. 'You're my client, I have to follow your instructions. But I'm warning you, it isn't going to be easy.'

'I understand that, but I just want it done.'

'Then I'll see what I can do.' He paused, and Anna knew what was coming next.

'Before you ask – no, I haven't spoken to Eve,' she said.

'Don't you think you should? You are supposed to be partners, after all. It's hardly fair to leave her in the dark about something like this.'

Anna faced him. 'You deal with your side of things. Leave Eve to me.'

Chapter 37

NOVEMBER

'Pistachio or Iced Coffee?' Eve asked.

They were sitting in the empty restaurant, paint charts laid out in front of them.

'Or we could just cover the walls with naked murals of ourselves,' she added.

'Hmm?' Anna looked up vaguely.

'The colour.' Eve pushed the charts across the table at her. 'What do you think?'

'Whatever you like, I don't mind.'

Eve watched her playing with a strand of her hair. It wasn't like Anna not have an opinion. She usually had a view about everything.

'So I'll just go ahead and choose, shall I?'

'Yeah. Whatever.'

Eve got up and poured herself a cup of coffee to hide her irritation. This was a big deal for her. After much heart-searching, she'd decided to take the plunge and give Oliver's a makeover.

It was a difficult decision, but she'd realised she couldn't cling on to Oliver's ideas for ever. It was time to change, to move on.

Besides, she'd had to face the unpleasant truth that Oliver wasn't always right. She only had to look at Frankie to see that. Oliver was kind, adorable, a great guy, but he made mistakes like everyone else. She'd thought Anna would be as excited as she was about the changes they were planning, but her reaction was underwhelming, to say the least.

She folded up the paint charts. 'Maybe we should do this some other time?'

'Good idea,' Anna said listlessly.

Eve frowned at her. She obviously had something on her mind.

'We can't start redecorating until after Christmas, anyway. Not with so many party bookings coming up. Which reminds me, I've been talking to Simon about the new seasonal menu. I don't know if you've got any ideas—'

'Before you say any more, there's something you should know,' Anna blurted out.

'What's that?'

'I've decided to sell my share of the restaurant.'

Eve stared at her blankly, the coffee pot still poised in her hand. 'What do you mean?'

'I want to sell my share. I don't want anything to do with this place.'

'But why?'

Anna averted her face. 'I don't want to talk about it.'

Eve came round to face her. 'Sorry, but that's not good enough. You can't just drop a bombshell like that and then not explain why.' Anna stayed silent, her lips pressed together. 'I'm waiting,' Eve said, and sat down at the table again. 'I don't understand it. I thought you wanted to be part of this?'

'That was before I found out—' Anna stopped abruptly.

'What?'

She took a deep breath. 'Before I found out Oliver was having an affair.'

Eve's hand shook, splashing coffee over the table. 'No!'

'It's true. I found out a few days ago.'

'Who was it?'

'Laura.'

'Laura?' At first it didn't register. 'You mean, Laura the *waitress*?'

'It had been going on for months, apparently,' Anna confirmed bitterly. 'Cosy little meetings after closing time. Sharing a bottle of wine, opening their hearts to each other.'

Eve got up and found a cloth to mop up the spilled coffee, trying to gather her thoughts. 'I can't believe it.'

'Why not? He did it to you, didn't he?'

'He never had an affair.'

'How do you know that? How do you know there weren't others besides me?' Anna's voice was full of hurt. 'None of us knew what was going on in his head, did we? I mean, look at what he did to this place.'

'That was different.'

'How? He lied to us about the business, why shouldn't he lie about another woman?'

'But he loved you.'

'You don't know that, and neither do I. Anyway, it's too late. To be honest, I'm sick of thinking about him, sick of going over and over it in my head. I just want to be free of him, and free of this place.'

She rubbed her eyes. Eve could see the hollowed planes of her face and guessed she must have lost a lot of sleep lately.

'What about me?' she said. 'What will happen to me if you sell up?'

Anna's face lost some of its anger. 'I know none of this is your fault, and I don't want to leave you in the lurch. Not when you've been so good to me. That's why I want to offer you first refusal.'

Eve's hackles rose. 'Why should I buy back something that was mine? I gave you those shares, remember? I thought we could be partners, really make a go of this place—' She stopped, anger choking her.

'I'm sorry.' Anna looked wretched. 'I don't want you to suffer, but you've got to understand why I don't want anything more to do with this place, or with Oliver.'

'You don't mind taking his money, do you?'

'I've got Charlie to think about. He's the only good thing to come out of all this—' Some of her icy composure crumpled and she looked as if she might cry, but she pulled herself together quickly.

'So do you want those shares, or not?' she asked.

'You know I can't buy them back. I don't have the money,' Eve said. 'Anyway, you'll never manage to sell them anywhere else. Who the hell would want a restaurant that's worth next to nothing?'

'I can think of someone,' Anna said.

'You're doing the right thing,' Spike Mullins said.

He sat with his Gucci-clad feet up on the squashy leather sofa, ignoring the furious stares of the waitresses whisking past them in the coffee shop. He exuded the relaxed confidence of a man who was certain of getting exactly what he wanted.

Anna, by contrast, was hunched in her seat, her latte going cold in front of her.

'Right for whom?' she said.

'For both of us. You get a good price for what is basically a worthless piece of crap, and I get—' He smiled broadly. 'Well, it doesn't matter what I get. The point is, you get rid of your share of Oliver's for once and for all. That's what you want, isn't it?'

Yes, that was what she wanted. Or at least, she thought it was.

'But I don't understand what you plan to do with your share,' she said. 'It's not as if you can do anything with it. Eve still has a controlling share and she'd never agree to you extending The Burger Shack.'

Spike Mullins leaned forward and patted her knee. 'There are ways and means, love. I reckon once Eve and I have been partners for a while she'll soon come round to my way of thinking.'

Anna was swamped by guilt. Poor Eve, she'd been so good to her. She wouldn't even have had the shares to sell if it hadn't been for her generosity. Her trust ...

For a moment she hesitated, ready to change her mind. Then she remembered Oliver and the way he betrayed her, and her guilt was replaced by cold anger.

'I can't see that place lasting much longer as things stand,' Spike went on. 'It's empty most nights. It's quite sad to see, really, your friend Eve slaving away for nothing.' He smirked. 'I reckon she'll soon realise she's wasting her time.'

'Who says? Bookings are up since the menu changed, and once the place has had a makeover it should do really well.'

'The only makeover that place needs is a couple of sledge-hammers through the wall to next door!' Spike laughed loudly at his own joke.

'You should give Eve a chance, see what she can do,' Anna said. 'You'd be surprised.'

'I'd be surprised if Oliver's is still open by Christmas. But then, it always amazed me how he managed to keep that place open. He can't have been making much money, that's for sure.' He shook his head. 'Must have been a real labour of love.'

'It was.' He'd been more devoted to it than he had to the women in his life, she thought bitterly.

Chapter 38

DECEMBER

'Is it just me, or does Santa look like a child molester?'

They were in a queue at the shopping centre, waiting to board the magic train that would take them to the North Pole to meet Father Christmas. They'd just spent twenty minutes standing in a tinsel-bedecked tunnel listening to a band of animatronic elves singing 'Rudolph the Red-Nosed Reindeer', and some of the shiny Yuletide magic was wearing thin.

'Shh, everyone will hear you.'

'I don't care. Don't you think there's something odd about this?' Lynch pulled a face at a whining toddler behind them in the queue. 'You spend all year warning kids not to go near strangers, then come Christmas you make them sit on some dodgy old bloke's knee. That can't be right, can it?'

'It's traditional.'

'And then you tell them he'll be coming into their bedroom on Christmas Eve. I don't know about you, but that always scared the shit out of me as a kid.'

Anna smiled. 'You didn't have to come.'

'What, and miss a magical experience like this?'

Charlie started to shift from one foot to the other. 'I want to see Santa,' he complained.

'You've got to be patient,' Anna told him.

'No, he's right. We could have caught a flight to the real North Pole by now.' Lynch looked around, sized the situation up for a second, then said, 'Won't be a minute.'

'Lynch, where are you going? Don't—' But he'd already

headed to the front of the queue to speak to one of Santa's helpers, a pretty blonde in a perky green elf's outfit. She glanced at Anna, then summoned an older, sterner-looking elf.

The three of them had a quick conference, then Lynch returned.

'Come with me and don't catch anyone's eye,' he said out of the corner of his mouth.

Anna felt incredibly guilty as they hurried past all the other harassed parents and irritable children. 'What did you say to them?'

'Does it matter?'

'Tell me!'

He sighed. 'Okay, if you must know I told them he was Posh and Becks's youngest and we were worried the paparazzi might be on to us.'

'And they believed you?'

'Apparently,' he shrugged. 'I also gave that blonde elf my phone number, so that might have swung it – ah, here we are. All aboard the famous Magic Train. I hope it's got a buffet car.' He lifted Charlie on board.

Charlie thought the clunky scenery rolling past the windows was utterly magical. Anna and Lynch were more amused by the fake reindeer grazing in the snow and the mechanical elves marching purposefully in and out of their factory.

'A few health and safety violations there,' Lynch said. 'I hope they've all got good lawyers.'

'Maybe you should leave a few business cards scattered around,' Anna suggested.

They reached the grotto, and went in through the spangly curtain. The elf outside had obviously called ahead to warn Santa's minders of the VIP in their midst. They were surreptitiously taking photos on their mobile phones. Anna cringed, mortified, but Lynch played up to it, shielding Charlie from their view with a gruff, 'No pictures, please. Mr Beckham wouldn't like it.'

'See? I told you,' he whispered as they spotted Santa. 'A kiddie-fiddler if ever I saw one. I'm sure I've seen him on *Crimewatch*.'

'Will you keep your voice down?' Anna hissed, trying to stop herself laughing.

'Either that or selling *The Big Issue* outside Woolworths on Coney Street.'

Charlie had a last-minute attack of nerves as he approached Santa's throne. Anna went to take his hand but Lynch was there before her. Anna's heart melted as she saw the trusting way Charlie went with him to meet the Great Man.

Lynch returned, with Charlie triumphantly clutching the present Santa had selected out of his sack especially for him. 'I'll tell you something else,' he whispered to Anna. 'That beard's not real.'

'You don't say?'

Outside in the bright lights, heat and madness of the shopping centre, they joined the seething mass of irritable shoppers.

'You'd never believe it was the season of goodwill, would you?' Lynch remarked, as a large woman barrelled past him, laden down with carrier bags. 'I don't know about you, but I'm dying for a drink. Is there a bar around here?'

They couldn't find anywhere but the food court, a vast arena crammed with plastic tables and chairs, surrounded by various fast-food outlets. Charlie had chicken nuggets and fries, Anna had a slice of pizza, and Lynch had a glass of red wine and looked disdainfully at their food.

'I suppose you know you're poisoning that poor child?' he said, helping himself to a mushroom from her pizza. 'Those nugget things bear as much resemblance to chicken as Santa's beard does to reality. I've a good mind to report you to the food police.'

'Says the man who lives on Marks and Spencer's ready meals.' Anna slapped his hand as he reached for a slice of pepperoni. 'Anyway, it's Christmas.'

'Really? I would never have known.' Lynch looked around. 'Do you think people actually enjoy shopping in places like this?'

'Some of us have no choice.' She wiped Charlie's chin with a paper napkin. 'I suppose you get all your Christmas shopping direct from Harrods?'

'Who doesn't?' He smiled ruefully. 'Sadly, my idea of a Christmas dinner is one of those ready meals you've just mentioned.'

Anna hesitated. She'd been thinking about it for some time, and now was as good a time as any to come out with it.

'Actually, I was wondering if you wanted to spend Christmas with us? I'm not the world's greatest cook,' she rushed on, suddenly self-conscious. 'In fact you'd probably be better off with the ready meal—'

'I'm sorry, I've already made plans.'

'Oh,' she faltered. 'Going anywhere nice?'

'New York.'

'Again? You must really love it.'

'I do.' He paused. Anna suddenly felt a chill run over her. There was bad news coming. 'There's something I need to tell you,' he said.

'Oh?'

'I've been offered a job over there.'

It took a moment to summon a smile. 'That's great news. How did it happen?'

'I met a guy from a legal firm while I was working there. We got talking, and he said they were looking for an associate to join their company. Apparently they're doing a lot of business over here, so they need someone who understands the way things work, so to speak.' He fiddled with his wine glass. 'I wasn't going to say anything until all the details had been finalised, but now it looks as if it's really happening.'

'When do you leave?'

'Next week.'

She felt winded. 'So soon?'

'I don't start the job until the beginning of January, but I thought I might as well spend Christmas over there.'

'Why not? It's not as if there's anything to keep you here, is there?' She fought to keep the bitterness out of her voice.

He looked across the table at her, his blue-green eyes pleading. 'Don't be like that, Anna.'

How am I supposed to be? she wanted to ask. He'd come into her life uninvited, raised her hopes, made her think they might have a future together. And now he was dumping her because a better offer had come along.

She picked at her pizza, her appetite gone. She was upset, but not surprised. Somewhere in the back of her mind she'd always known it wouldn't be for ever.

Lynch wasn't a for ever kind of man.

'It's only a year's contract at first,' he said. 'I'd be flying back all the time. We could still see each other.'

'Of course,' she said. But they both knew they didn't mean it.

Sitting in the office, staring at the wage packet in her hand, Eve wondered what to do.

Not surprisingly, Laura hadn't turned up to work in the weeks since she'd confessed about her affair with Oliver, but she hadn't collected her final week's wages either. Eve was sorely tempted to keep the money. It was the least Laura owed her after all the trouble she'd caused. Thanks to her, Anna was about to sell her share of the business to Spike Mullins.

Eve had got tired of his knowing looks and remarks every time their paths crossed. Her only consolation was that Anna still hadn't signed the contract, although from what Spike said, it was only a matter of time.

She hadn't seen Anna either. So far they'd managed to stay out of each other's way, which was a good thing; Eve wasn't sure she would be able to bring herself to stay civil if they met.

'All right if I take my break now, boss?' Lizzy stuck her head around the office door.

'Sure, no problem.' Eve put the wage packet down on the desk. Lizzy glanced at it.

'Can I have that, if they don't want it?' she asked.

Eve smiled. 'It's Laura's. I've been waiting for her to collect it, but I think I'll have to post it.'

'Whatever happened to her, anyway?' Lizzy asked. 'One minute she was working here, and the next she was gone.'

'She – um – decided she needed a change of scene.'

'I'm surprised you ever had her back, after last time,' Lizzy said.

'What do you mean?'

'Oliver sacked her. Didn't you know?'

She went out into the yard to take her break. Eve followed her. 'Why did he sack her?'

'Dunno,' Lizzy shrugged. 'But we were all glad to see her go, I always thought she was a bit weird.'

She took a packet of cigarettes out of her pocket and lit one up. 'Do you want one?' She offered the packet to Eve.

'No thanks.' Eve thought for a moment. 'Can you and Simon manage on your own this afternoon?'

'I expect so. We're not busy 'til tonight.' Lizzy looked at her curiously through the curling smoke of her cigarette. 'Why?'

'I thought I'd drop Laura's wages round. It's about time she and I had a little chat.'

Chapter 39

Laura lived on a leafy lane close to the university. The tall, shabby house screamed student, from the grey net curtains and peeling posters on the windows to the patches of weeds and discarded takeaway cartons in the basement area.

Someone had left the door open. The hall was littered with bikes, and from somewhere upstairs came the throbbing sound of heavy-metal music. A smell of cigarettes and stale cooking hung in the air.

Eve made her way up to the top floor and rang the bell. She expected Laura or her flatmate to answer it, so she was completely unprepared for the middle-aged woman who came to the door.

'Yes? Can I help you?'

'I'm sorry. I think I must have the wrong address.' She pulled the piece of paper out of her pocket to check. 'I was looking for Laura Morris.'

'This is the right place. I'm Laura's mother, Judith.'

'Her mother? But I thought—'

'Yes?'

'It doesn't matter.' Perhaps she was visiting, she thought. 'I'm Eve Robinson. From Oliver's restaurant.'

'Ah, yes.' The woman's thin face brightened. 'She's often talked about you.'

'I was hoping to have a word with her but I suppose she's still at college?'

'College?' Judith Morris frowned. 'My daughter doesn't go to college. Whatever gave you that idea?'

'That's what she told me. So where is she now?'

'Isn't she at the restaurant?'

'She hasn't worked there for weeks.'

Mrs Morris stared at her for what seemed an age. 'I think you'd better come in,' she finally said.

Inside, the flat was a bit dingy but spotless, which didn't stop Laura's mother from apologising for the mess as she ushered Eve to one of the sofas and fussed around making tea.

'I'm not surprised she left that job,' she said, as she put a tray down on the table, immaculately laid out with teapot, cups and a plate of chocolate digestives. 'I thought it might be too much for her, going back there after her boyfriend died.'

Eve's heart sank. 'So it's true, then? About her and Oliver?'

'Oh yes, it's true. Why wouldn't it be?'

Why indeed? Eve thought. But there was something about this whole situation that wasn't adding up.

'They were very happy together, so I gather,' Judith went on, pouring tea into the cups. 'Of course I never met him, he was always far too busy working, but I used to see him sometimes from the window when he brought Laura home from work. And then that awful crash happened.' She handed a cup to Eve. 'I was so worried for her, I thought she was going to go back to the way she used to be when—'

'When?' Eve prompted.

Judith slowly spooned sugar into her tea. 'My daughter was very ill a few years ago. Depression, the doctors said. She had to spend some time in hospital.'

'But I thought she told me it was you who'd been ill, after your husband died?'

Judith stared at her coldly. 'My husband isn't dead. At least, not as far as I know.'

'But Laura visited his grave. That's where I met her.'

'Even if he was dead she'd have no idea where to find him. She hasn't seen him since she was fifteen years old.' She sipped her tea. 'That was what made her so ill. She was devoted to him. A real daddy's girl. When he walked out on us, her whole world collapsed.'

No wonder it was easier to think of him as dead, Eve thought. But if she could lie about that, what else could she lie about?

'Mrs Morris,' she said. 'Has your daughter ever made things up?'

Judith's face fell. 'What makes you say that?'

'She told me her father was dead. She also told me she was a student, and that you'd spent time in hospital. I can't think of a single thing she's told me that's been the truth. So I really don't see why I should believe this story about her and Oliver.'

'It's the truth,' Judith insisted. 'I've seen them together.'

'You've seen him giving her a lift home, just like he's given all the staff lifts in the past.'

'She was with him when he died.'

'Maybe she was, but that doesn't mean they were lovers.' Eve put down her cup and leaned forward. 'Did Laura mention Oliver was living with someone else, or that they had a three-year-old son?'

Judith faltered. 'These things happen, don't they? Maybe it wasn't working out between them?'

'He was planning to marry her. He had the ring in his pocket on the day he died.'

Judith's mouth worked for a moment, as if she was trying to come up with the right words. Then, to Eve's amazement, she burst into tears.

'Not again. Please, not again.'

Eve moved to sit beside her and put her arm around the sobbing woman. 'It's happened before, then? Laura making things up?'

Judith nodded, her face buried in a crumpled scrap of tissue. 'Ever since she was a little girl. She doesn't mean any harm, she's just very lonely.'

'Why didn't you tell me?'

'Because I hoped this time it would be true. Laura's a kind, loving girl. She deserves a man who can make her happy, that's all she needs.' She was pleading for Eve's understanding.

'Has she made up stories about men before?'

Judith didn't reply for a moment. Then she admitted slowly,

'There have been times in the past when she's developed – feelings for certain men. They were just harmless crushes, I thought, but then they got a bit more serious.'

'How serious?'

Judith lowered her eyes. 'There were a couple of times when the police got involved.'

'She stalked them?' Eve said.

'It was never that bad. They over-reacted. Laura would never hurt anyone.'

Eve thought about Anna, torn apart by Laura's so-called revelation, not knowing who to trust any more.

'I think you're wrong about that,' she said.

As she left, Judith said, 'You're not going to tell the police, are you?'

'I don't see what they can do.'

She looked relieved. 'I'll talk to her,' she promised. 'I'll make her see sense, tell her it's got to stop.'

'It's a bit late for that. The damage has already been done.'

'I'm sure she didn't mean anything by it,' Judith said as she followed her down the stairs. 'Don't be too hard on her, will you? My Laura's a good girl, really. She wouldn't hurt anyone,' she repeated.

Chapter 40

It was the afternoon of Charlie's nursery Nativity play, and Anna, Jackie and Nana had bagged front-row seats.

'I love a kids' Nativity,' Nana said, passing a packet of Werthers' Originals down the row to Anna. 'All those angelic little faces singing their hearts out. It always brings a tear to my eye.' She nudged Jackie. 'Do you remember when our Anna made all that fuss because they wouldn't let her be Mary?'

'She grabbed baby Jesus out of the crib and wouldn't give him back until they let her,' Jackie laughed. 'I was so embarrassed.'

'I can't see Charlie anywhere.' Anna craned her neck to get a better view of the back row.

'What is he this year?'

'Seventeenth shepherd from the left, I think, but he's not there.'

'Probably got stage fright,' her mother said.

'Or needed a wee,' Nana added. 'I always get caught short at moments of crisis.'

'Here comes Mrs Wendover. You can ask her.'

The teacher had already spotted Anna and was coming over to her. 'Is Charlie not with you?' She frowned.

Anna felt the first stirrings of panic. 'What do you mean?'

'Your babysitter picked him up this morning for his dental appointment. She said you'd bring him back in time for the performance.'

Anna felt her mother clutch her hand. 'You let my son go off with a stranger?'

315

'Well, I didn't. But we had an assistant in this morning and I suppose she didn't know—' She broke off as she saw Anna's stricken look. 'I'll see if I can find her.'

Anna looked around wildly. 'Someone's taken him,' she said. 'Someone's taken Charlie. We've got to call the police.' She wanted to go in a million directions at once but her feet were rooted to the spot.

The teaching assistant was summoned. She looked absolutely terrified. 'I – I'm sorry,' she stammered. 'He seemed to know her, so I just assumed it was all right.'

'You *assumed*?' Anna said, her voice rising with fear and panic. The other parents were stirring in their seats, trying to see what was going on.

'Can you remember what this person looked like?' Jackie asked, still holding on to Anna's hand, anchoring her in her seat.

'Let me think … She looked a bit like you,' she said to Anna. 'Except she had long hair.'

'Laura,' Anna said. She felt sick.

'You know her, then?'

'Oh yes, I know her.'

An office Christmas party was just reaching its end at the restaurant when Anna stormed in fifteen minutes later. The long table was littered with empty bottles and shreds of Christmas crackers. Men in paper party hats were entertaining giggling girls by inhaling helium from the balloons and talking in funny voices.

Eve was at the bar, cashing up.

'Oh, hello,' she said. 'I was going to call you—'

'I need Laura's address. Now.'

Eve frowned. 'Why?'

'Because the mad bitch has kidnapped my son, that's why.'

The office party fell silent. Everyone turned to look at her.

Eve closed the till. 'I'll come with you.'

'I just need the address.'

'You need someone to stop you doing something stupid.' Eve grabbed her coat from behind the bar.

Eve insisted on driving. Anna sat in the passenger seat, trying not to scream with frustration every time the traffic lights turned red.

'Isn't there a quicker way?'

'Not unless you can sprout wings and fly.' Eve looked sideways at her. 'How do you know it's her who's taken Charlie?'

'I just know.' Anna stared ahead of her, willing the lights to change.

The lights changed and they edged forward into slow-moving traffic. Anna cursed under her breath.

'Before we get there, there's something you ought to know,' Eve said. 'I met Laura's mother this morning.'

'And?'

'And she told me Laura had made up the whole thing about her and Oliver.'

'What?' Anna swung round to face her. 'She was lying?'

'She suffers from mental illness. Apparently she finds it hard to tell truth from fantasy.'

Anna was silent for a fraction of a second while it sank in, then the same thought seemed to strike them both at the same time.

'And she's got my son,' Anna said.

The lights ahead flicked from amber to red. Eve put her foot down and roared through them, narrowly missing a van coming out from a side street.

There was no answer at Laura's address. Anna hammered on the door until her fist was numb.

'We're going to have to break it down.' She looked up and down the hall for something to use as a battering ram.

'What's the point? There's no one home.'

'How do you know that? How do you know she hasn't got Charlie in there?' Anna bent down to look through the letterbox. Inside, the flat was ominously quiet.

'Think about it. She wouldn't bring him home with her mum there, would she?'

'So where is he?' Anna's mobile rang and she snatched it out of her bag. 'Hello? Yes? No, I haven't found him. You've rung the police? What did they say? Tell them to get here —' she gave them the address '– and tell them to bring something to break the door down with.'

She hung up. 'My mum's called the police. They're on their way.' She frowned at Eve, who'd gone very quiet. 'What is it?'

'I think I know where she might have taken Charlie.' Eve looked at her. 'Somewhere she thinks you've never taken him.'

Realisation dawned. 'The churchyard.'

It was only three o'clock but already getting dark when they reached the church. The wind howled around the bell tower and the yew trees made weird silhouettes against the indigo sky.

'He hates being out in the dark,' Anna said, 'he'll be so frightened.' Another thought occurred to her. 'What if he's not there? We'll have wasted all this time.'

'He'll be there,' Eve said.

And he was.

As they rounded the corner of the church, Anna saw them straight away. Laura was kneeling at Oliver's graveside, arranging flowers. Charlie stood next to her, sucking his finger the way he always did when he wasn't sure about something, and he wasn't wearing his coat. How could she bring him out in weather like this without his coat? Anna thought.

Blind fury overcame her. 'Charlie!' Her scream was carried away on the wind.

Laura looked up sharply. She scrambled to her feet and gathered Charlie to her, holding him protectively against her.

'Let go of my son.' The words came grinding out between gritted teeth.

'Mummy?' Charlie's lip wobbled.

'Leave us alone. You're scaring him,' Laura accused.

'Let go of him,' Anna repeated, her eyes blazing. Laura backed away, colliding clumsily with the edging stones of another grave.

'No. You don't deserve him, just like you didn't deserve Oliver.' Her face was defiant. 'You never bring Charlie to see his daddy. You don't care about him. You never cared about him. Not like I did.'

'I don't have to listen to this.' As Anna moved towards them,

Laura clutched Charlie tighter to her, like a protective shield. He began to cry.

Eve stepped in, her hand on Anna's arm, holding her back. 'Let me deal with this,' she whispered. 'Please?'

She approached Laura slowly and calmly, like she would a frightened kitten. Laura, still clutching Charlie, watched her apprehensively.

'I like the flowers you've brought.' Her voice was carefully light, as if they were discussing the weather. 'You often bring roses, don't you?'

'I know he likes them,' Laura said with a touch of pride. 'I bring flowers nearly every day.'

She sniffed back tears. Still holding on to Charlie, she reached forward and gathered up the flowers she'd dropped when Anna appeared.

'You know this isn't right, don't you?' Eve said gently.

Laura hesitated, her eyes still fixed on the flowers. 'It isn't fair,' she murmured. 'She didn't deserve him, and now she's got Charlie to help her remember him, and I've got nothing. Why should she have everything?'

Her hand moved quickly, jabbing the roses back into their vase. She'd pricked her finger and blood oozed down her hand, but she didn't seem to notice. The sight of it made Anna shudder.

Eve reached out, covering her hand with hers. 'I know what it's like to love someone and know they don't love you back,' she said.

'He could have loved me, if he'd had the chance.' Tears ran down Laura's face. 'All he needed was time. I kept telling him I loved him, and I know he felt the same. The only thing stopping him was her.' She glared at Anna, her eyes full of malevolence. 'He felt guilty, that's all.'

She started to cry. Eve gently took the last rose out of her hand and laid it down on Oliver's grave. 'It's time to let him go,' she said.

They were all silent, frozen for a moment. Anna didn't realise she'd been holding her breath until Laura released Charlie. He ran to Anna and she grabbed him, holding him to her.

Then she realised Eve was doing the same to Laura.

'I'm taking her home,' she said to Anna.

'What about the police?'

'She needs help, Anna. Not locking up.'

Anna watched them walk away. They were almost out of sight before she realised she hadn't even thanked Eve for saving her son.

Chapter 41

Eve always knew Christmas Day would be difficult.

It was a cold, grey, drizzly morning, and she and the children made a dismal group as they made their way through the church-yard, huddled under one umbrella, icy rain dripping down their necks.

Eve hadn't expected them to come with her. She was surprised when Matt suggested it the previous evening.

'It's Dad's birthday,' he'd said, as if that explained everything.

They spotted the flowers before they'd reached the grave, a bright splash of scarlet against the washed-out greyness.

Georgia picked up the small posy, read the card and propped it against the headstone. 'Anna's been here,' she said.

Eve let out a sigh of relief. She'd been hoping they wouldn't have to come face to face. They hadn't met since the Laura incident, two weeks before.

'We haven't seen Anna for ages,' Georgia said as they trooped back to the car twenty minutes later.

'No.' That suited Eve fine. She'd already heard from Spike Mullins that he wanted a meeting in the new year to discuss their new partnership. It infuriated her that Anna had sold to him of all people. Worse still, she hadn't had the grace to tell Eve herself.

'Maybe we should ask her over for Christmas dinner?' Georgia tried again. 'She might be lonely, just her and Charlie.'

'I don't suppose they'll be on their own. She's got her mum, and the rest of her family.'

Another reason for her to resent Anna. Her own mother had

promised to come this year, but had cancelled at the last minute to go skiing with some new friends she'd met in New York.

'You have to grab life while you can, darling,' she'd trilled down a crackly line. 'Surely the last year should have taught you that?'

Eve had put the phone down. She didn't even have the energy to feel disappointed any more.

The visit to the cemetery had cast a dismal shadow over the whole day. Matt retreated upstairs to play moody music on his guitar, leaving Eve and Georgia to peel potatoes in silence.

'I don't even know why we're doing this,' Georgia said, as they stood side by side at the sink. 'I hate Christmas dinner anyway. And I hate Christmas.'

'How can you say that? You've always loved Christmas.'

'When I was a kid. It's all different now, it's changed.'

'I never heard you complaining when you got your presents this morning.'

Georgia ignored her, whittling away at the potato until it was the size of an acorn. 'It's not the same without Dad,' she said.

Don't you think I know that? Eve wanted to shout. Don't you think he's left a hole in my life, too?

'I know,' she said, 'but we've got to carry on. It's what Dad would have wanted.'

'He wouldn't have wanted us to be all depressed,' Georgia muttered, hacking away at another potato.

'You're right.' Eve put down her knife, suddenly decisive. 'Forget the potatoes. I want you to grab the phone and the address book, and tell Matt to stop playing those suicidal songs and get down here. I'm going to need him to help.'

'Why?' Georgia asked.

'It's your father's birthday,' Eve said. 'We're going to have a party.'

Maybe it was a mistake, she thought later that day, as they all gathered at the restaurant waiting for the first guests to arrive. She and the children had worked hard all afternoon, decorating the place with balloons and candles, and defrosting food. Luckily they had plenty left from some of the office-party buffets they'd

322

hosted recently. It had helped pass the time and take their minds off the grim day, but now Eve wasn't so sure it was a good idea.

'What if no one comes?' Matt said.

'They said they would.'

'It won't be the same without Dad here,' Georgia muttered.

She was right, Eve realised. It was Oliver who had lit up the room, made every party go with a swing. People gathered around him like moths around a flame, drawn to his warmth.

'It's going to be a disaster, isn't it?' she sighed.

Then the door opened and Jan and Peter walked in.

'Oh God, are we the first?' Jan said, looking around.

'At this rate, you might be the only ones.'

'No chance,' Peter predicted confidently. 'This was a great idea. Exactly what we all needed.'

'Do you think so?'

'Oliver would have loved it.'

Eve could have hugged him.

After that, people started to arrive. They seemed a bit uncertain at first, as if they weren't really sure if they were supposed to enjoy themselves, but after a while the wine and laughter began to flow and everyone relaxed.

'This is exactly what Oliver would have wanted,' Jan said when Eve bumped into her by the champagne.

'I hope so.'

'I mean it. It's brilliant.' She looked around. 'You've done wonders with the place.'

'Shame no one's going to see it,' Eve said.

Jan looked at her. 'Anna's still selling?'

'As far as I know the deal's already been done.' She looked around. 'You could call this a kind of farewell party.'

'That's such a shame. You've worked so hard.'

'That's life,' Eve shrugged.

'I bet now you wish you hadn't given her those shares.'

'I didn't give her anything. They were her shares. Oliver would have wanted her to have them.'

'Talk of the devil,' Jan said, looking over Eve's shoulder towards the door.

Eve turned round. At that same moment the crowd parted and she found herself face to face with Anna.

She stood there all on her own, marooned among a sea of people, her chin lifted with the touch of defiance Eve knew so well. She put down her drink and walked towards her. People backed away, clearing a bigger space between them, as if they expected a fight. Even Anna looked wary.

'Hello, Anna,' Eve greeted her calmly. 'Can I get you a drink?'

'Thanks.'

They went to the bar. Everyone watched tensely as Eve poured Anna a glass of wine. Then a collective sigh seemed to escape everyone when she handed it over.

'I think they were expecting you to throw it in my face,' Anna said in an undertone.

'The thought did cross my mind.' Eve replied.

Georgia found her in the crowd a few minutes later. 'You did say invite everybody,' she said defensively, before Eve could tell her off. 'Anyway, it's time you two talked. You can't stay pissed off at her for ever.'

Can't I? Eve thought.

She didn't see Anna for the rest of the party, and decided she must have gone home. Eve didn't blame her. She felt exhausted by trying to keep up her spirits and make sure everyone had a good time. Putting a brave face on was very hard.

She'd sent Matt and Georgia home and was stacking the dishwasher, when she realised she wasn't alone.

Anna stood in the doorway. 'Need a hand?'

'You could collect up some glasses for me.'

Anna gathered them up and stacked them on the draining board while Eve filled the sink with hot soapy water ready to wash them.

'Thanks again for inviting me,' Anna said. 'Although from the look on your face when I walked in I'm guessing it wasn't your idea.'

'Blame my daughter.' She put the glasses in the bowl and started to wash them. 'How's Charlie?' she asked.

'He's fine.'

'Has he got over all that business with Laura?'

'He'd forgotten it within a few hours, especially with all the excitement over Christmas. I'm still having nightmares, though. Sometimes I have to get up in the night to check no one's taken him.' Anna glanced sidelong at her. 'How is she?'

'Getting some help at last. I don't think she'll be any threat to you any more.' Laura had seemed a lot better the last time Eve visited her at the hospital. 'Maybe you should go and see her? It might set your mind at rest.'

Anne shook her head. 'I don't think I'm ready to come face to face with her again just yet.'

'I understand.' Eve couldn't blame her. Laura had tried to take away Anna's past happiness as well as her future. She doubted if she'd be very forgiving in her position.

'I never really thanked you for getting him back for me. I don't know what I would have done if I'd lost him.'

'You wouldn't have lost him. Laura was never going to hurt him.'

'All the same, you handled it a lot better than I could. I would have rushed in screaming and probably made everything much worse, as usual,' she grimaced.

Eve smiled. 'We've just got different ways of doing things. That doesn't make either of us right or wrong.'

Was that something she would have imagined herself saying a year ago? She was surprised at how much she'd changed since then. And she hadn't even realised it.

Anna looked around. 'It was a good idea to have this party. Oliver would have loved it.'

'I had to do something. The children and I were climbing the walls.'

'I know what you mean,' Anna agreed. 'I knew it was going to be hard getting through today, but I didn't realise it was going to be that hard.'

'Didn't you have your family with you?'

'They did their best, but I got tired of smiling and pretending to be fine,' Anna confessed. 'Besides, there's only so many times

I can watch *The Sound of Music* without wanting to shoot myself. Why are there so many films about love and happiness at this time of year? I would have been better off staying at home and getting drunk by myself.'

'All I keep thinking about is what I was doing this time last year.'

They were silent for a moment, standing side by side at the sink. 'Do you remember it?' Eve said.

Anna pulled a face. 'How could I forget? I always dreaded Oliver's party.'

Eve looked at her in surprise. 'Why?'

'Because I never felt as if I fitted in. Oliver would be here with all his friends and family, and I got the feeling they all hated me and didn't want me to be here.'

'That's not true.'

'You didn't want me to be here.'

'You didn't want me here either.'

'True,' Anna agreed. 'But only because I was scared.'

'Scared?'

'That Oliver would suddenly look at you and realise what he was missing.'

Eve nearly dropped the glass she was holding. 'What made you think that?'

'You looked so right together.' She sprayed cleaner on the worktop. 'It always made me feel as if I didn't know him at all. You two had so much history I couldn't share, couldn't be part of.'

'I might have been his past, but you were his future.'

Anna lowered her eyes. 'I don't know that.'

'I do.'

Eve put down her cloth. 'Wait there,' she said. 'I've got something for you.'

It didn't take her long to find what she was looking for. Anna was confused when she handed it over.

'I don't understand.' She opened the little box and her eyes lit up at the ring nestling against the white satin.

'They gave it to me the day Oliver died,' Eve explained. 'But it was meant for you.'

Anna frowned down at the ring and said nothing.

'Aren't you going to put it on?' Eve said.

Anna didn't move. Eve gently took the box out of her hand, removed the ring and held it out for her. 'He wanted you to have it,' she said again. 'He told me so the day he asked me for a divorce.'

Anna's head shot up. 'He what?'

'He told me he wanted to marry you. If things had been different, you might have had a wedding ring to go with that by now.'

Anna still held the ring, mesmerised by the sparkling diamond as if she couldn't quite believe it was really hers.

'I'm sorry,' Eve said. 'I know I should have given it to you a long time ago. But it never seemed to be the right time—'

And deep down she hadn't wanted to give it to her. She finally allowed herself to admit it. She hadn't wanted Anna to belong to Oliver the way she'd belonged to him.

Anna seemed to know exactly what was going through Eve's mind.

'I guess this makes us even,' she said.

'I suppose so.' In more ways than one, she thought.

A look of understanding passed between them. Eve was the first to turn away.

'I'd better finish this washing-up,' she said briskly, plunging her hands back into the hot soapy water.

'I've got something for you, too,' Anna said.

Eve looked over her shoulder. 'For me?'

Anna nodded. 'That's why I came here today. To give you this.'

She pulled an envelope out of her bag. Eve recognised it straight away.

'It's the shares you gave me,' Anna said.

Eve looked from the papers to her and back again. 'I thought you'd sold them to Spike Mullins?'

'He made me an offer but I decided not to take it. And it's nothing to do with finding out the truth about Laura,' she added hastily. 'I'd already made up my mind not to sell before then.'

'You couldn't do it to Oliver.'

'I couldn't do it to you.' She took a step forward, holding out the paperwork. 'They're yours, if you want them.'

Eve stared at the envelope. Then she said, 'I can't take them.'

'But I thought it was what you wanted?'

'It is, but not like this. Those shares are yours. I want to buy them from you.'

'You don't have to do that.'

'I want to,' Eve insisted. 'I want to do this properly – although it might take me a while to raise the money,' she said ruefully. 'Business is getting better, but it's not there yet.'

'I can wait,' Anna smiled.

They finished clearing up. 'There's half a bottle of champagne here,' Eve said. 'I don't suppose you'd like a glass, would you?'

'Why not?' Anna said.

Eve poured it out. 'Shall we have a toast?' she said. 'How about to Oliver?'

Anna's eyes gleamed over the rim of her glass as she held it up. 'How about to the future?' she said.

Chapter 42

When they'd finished the champagne, Anna called her mother's boyfriend to ask for a lift home.

'Are you sure we can't drop you off?' she offered, as Eve saw her out.

'No thanks, I've got my own car parked round the back. Don't worry, I've only had half a glass of champagne,' she added as Anna looked worried.

'As long as you're sure?'

'I'll be fine, honestly.' She glanced past Anna at the Mondeo that had just pulled up. 'Looks like your lift's here.'

Halfway out of the door, Anna turned. 'Thanks again for inviting me,' she said. 'And thanks for – you know.'

Eve looked at her bare left hand. 'Aren't you going to put it on?'

Anna shook her head. 'It wouldn't feel right,' she said. 'But at least I know it's there.'

They stood in awkward silence for a moment. Then, to Eve's surprise, Anna leaned forward and planted a swift kiss on her cheek.

'Thanks again,' she said. And then she was gone.

Eve finished checking around the restaurant, turned off the lights, and let herself out of the kitchen door into the yard, locking it behind her.

She'd almost crossed the yard to her car when the figure stepped out of the shadows, blocking her path.

'Before you start chucking coffee at me, I'm not an intruder,' a deep voice pleaded. 'I've had enough of a battering for one evening.'

'Adam!' She nearly collapsed with relief. 'Bloody hell, what is it with you and creeping up on people? If I'd had my pepper spray you would have been rolling around by—' As he stepped into the glow of the street lamp she suddenly noticed the bruise gleaming over his right eye. 'Oh my God! What happened?'

'Imogen and I have split up.'

She took a deep breath. 'You'd better come inside and tell me all about it.'

Inside the brightly lit kitchen, his black eye looked even worse. He winced with pain as Eve gingerly touched the shiny, swollen skin. 'We should put a steak on that,' he said.

She went to the freezer and searched the shelves. 'Fillet or rump?'

'Does it matter?'

'Probably not.'

'Aren't you supposed to defrost that first?' Adam asked warily, as she ran the rock-hard slab of frozen meat under the tap.

'What do you think I'm trying to do?' She turned up the hot water.

'You know you could get food poisoning like that?'

'You're not going to eat it, dummy.' She tested the steak with her hand. It was still frozen, but not quite so bad.

Adam flinched as she approached him. 'It's okay, I can do it.'

'Keep still and don't be such a baby.'

She moved to put the steak on his eye but he took it from her. 'I'll do it,' he said firmly.

Hurt, she said, 'Why don't you want me to touch you?'

He fixed her with his one good eye. 'Why do you think?'

She held her breath. 'I don't know.'

'Because every time you touch me, I lose a bit more of the iron self-control I've spent the last twenty years building up. Is that a good enough reason for you?' He twisted around in his seat. 'Do you have any brandy? I'm in the mood to get seriously drunk.'

'Are you sure?'

'It's not every day a man gets unengaged.'

She fetched the bottle and two glasses, still in a state of confusion.

'So what happened?' she asked. 'Did you have a row?'

'Not really. I just realised I couldn't go through with it.' He stared into the amber depths of his glass. 'We were having a wonderful Christmas Day, everything seemed perfect. Then I looked around and suddenly realised it wasn't what I wanted. So I told Imogen.'

'How did she take it?'

'How do you think?' He lifted the steak. 'For a small woman she packs a hell of a punch.'

He downed his drink and pushed his glass towards her for a refill.

'What happened then?'

'We had a big row and I got out while I could. For all I know, she's still trashing the house.'

'You'll have to go back and face her sometime.'

'Not tonight. I'll give her some time to calm down first.'

'Where will you stay tonight?'

'I can sleep in the back of the van.'

'In this weather? You'll freeze to death. Why don't you stay at my place?'

'You really don't get it, do you?' He sent her a long, level look. 'I can't do this any more, Eve. I can't pretend we're best buddies when really I can't stop wanting you.'

'Me?'

'Oh come on, you must have realised how I feel about you? I've been following you around like a lovesick schoolboy ever since Oliver first brought you home twenty years ago.'

'I never realised,' she said, dazed.

'Story of my life. No one ever noticed me when Oliver was around.'

Eve frowned. 'Were you jealous of him?'

'Only when it came to you.'

Adam drained his glass again. He seemed like a man on a mission to get drunk. 'I knew I'd never stand a chance with you,' he said. 'You were so besotted with Oliver, it was as if no one else existed.'

'You didn't look as if you were pining for me. You never seemed to be short of girlfriends.'

'I was hardly going to save myself for you, was I? Not when you were so obviously mad about my cousin. No, I was very brave about it all and wished you both well, then concentrated all my efforts on working my way through the female population, trying to find someone who could make me feel the way you did. Needless to say, it didn't happen.'

He adjusted the steak on his eye and winced with pain. 'Then you and Oliver split up. I was furious at him; I thought he was an idiot for letting you go, but at the same time it gave me a tiny spark of hope. I thought maybe, after you'd got over him, there might be a chance for me to step in and pick up the pieces.'

'I thought you were just being a good friend,' Eve said.

'Good old Adam. Everybody's best friend. But I still went on hoping one day you'd realise I meant more to you, except you never did. It was always Oliver. No matter what he did, you just went on loving him.'

'I couldn't help it.'

'I know,' Adam sighed. 'I realised that a long time ago. Just like I realised there would never be room in your heart for me.'

'Is that why you got engaged to Imogen?'

'What else could I do? I couldn't spend my whole life waiting for you. I had to move on, get over you.' He looked wretched. 'I thought I loved Imogen, I really did. I thought we could make each other happy. But then, after my engagement party, I realised my heart really wasn't in it.'

He put down his glass. 'Look, I'm not expecting you to fall into my arms or anything like that. I know that's never going to happen.'

'Who says?'

'But I can't go on being friends either. That's why I've been avoiding you lately. I just can't handle— What did you say?'

She scrubbed with her fingernail at an imaginary spot on the stainless-steel countertop. 'Who says I'm not going to fall into your arms? I seem to have been doing it quite a bit lately.'

'I'd noticed. It's taken all my willpower not to do anything about it.'

'And there was I hoping you would.'

He reached out, took both her hands in his and pulled her towards him. It was probably a violation of every health and safety practice in the book, she thought as they made love in the darkened restaurant. She'd worried that after all this time she would compare every man with Oliver, but her ex-husband couldn't have been further from her mind. Adam made sure of that.

Afterwards, he said, 'So when did you realise you were madly in love with me?'

'I didn't. It just crept up on me. I didn't even begin to suspect until the night Britney gave birth.'

'Oh God, don't remind me. I'd planned this big romantic dinner, and we ended up having an argument about bloody Frankie.'

'And then the goat went into labour.'

'Not exactly the ideal first date.'

'I didn't even know it *was* a date.'

'Obviously.'

'But something happened that night. I realised after that how I really felt about you.'

'There's nothing like helping a goat in labour to put you in the mood for love,' Adam agreed.

'It wasn't that. Well, maybe it was – just watching you made me feel kind of—'

'Sick?' he ventured.

'Safe,' she said. 'But by the time I knew how I felt about you, you were engaged to Imogen. I didn't feel as if I could say or do anything.'

'I wish you had.'

'But she seemed so perfect for you. She was so lovely.'

'You should have seen her laying into my CD collection,' Adam said. 'She wasn't so lovely then.'

'There's no chance for you two, then?' Eve knew what she wanted him to answer, but she wanted to give him the chance to back out.

He shook his head. 'I think once she calms down she'll realise we were never meant for each other. Actually, I think she's been aware of it for a while.'

'What makes you say that?'

'She's been suspicious ever since that night she came into the barn and caught me about to kiss you.'

'I nearly kissed *you*,' Eve corrected him.

Adam smiled. 'Either way, after that night she didn't want me to have much to do with you. That's why she didn't want us to come to the party tonight.'

'I missed you,' Eve said.

'I missed you too.'

'I thought you and Imogen were having a cosy Christmas together.'

'When all the time I was dodging flying crockery.'

'All the same, you've got to talk to her.'

'I know.' He sighed. 'I will, tomorrow. In the meantime, would it be okay if I slept over at your place?'

'I told you, the spare room's there if you need it.'

'The spare room?' His dark brows lifted.

Eve nodded. 'I need some time to get used to the idea of us – you know.'

'You need time? Try waiting twenty years.'

'And I have to think about the children,' she went on, ignoring him. 'I don't know what they'll think of all this.'

'They're practically grown up, they'll understand.'

'I hope so.' She chewed her lip worriedly. 'I know Matt won't mind, but it's Georgia I'm worried about. She's at such a funny age, and what with losing Oliver not long ago, and her exams coming up, I don't want—'

'Eve?'

'Hmm?'

She turned to look at him and a second later he'd silenced her with a kiss.

She pushed him off. 'Oh God, I've just thought of something. This is never going to work.'

He frowned. 'Why not?'

'Think about it. Adam and Eve?'

He smiled. 'After all this time, I don't care if we have to change our names to Laurel and Hardy,' he said, moving in to kiss her again.

Chapter 43

It was New Year's Eve at the advice centre, and they were getting ready to close early.

'I don't know why we had to open at all,' Barbara grumbled. 'No one's been in all morning. And I need to get my hair done for the Rotary Club dinner dance.'

'The Rotary Club dinner dance, eh?' Elliott raised his eyebrows at Anna. 'Sounds like a riot.'

'Oh, it is,' Barbara said warmly. 'I'm telling you, when my Bernard and I do the Pasa Doble, we clear the floor.'

'I'm not surprised,' Elliott said.

'So what's everyone else doing?' Barbara asked.

'Having an early night,' Neil mumbled, waking up briefly from where he was quietly snoozing over a pile of paperwork. He was still in the new-baby blur, where he didn't know whether it was day or night and didn't care either, as long as he could get his head down for five minutes.

'Me too,' Anna said. 'Although not with Neil, obviously,' she added.

'There wouldn't be room,' Neil grumbled. 'Ruth insists on having the baby in bed with us to bond. Most nights I feel like crawling into the cot.'

Anna and Elliott sneaked conspiratorial grins at each other. Sheer exhaustion had driven out a lot of Neil's New Man correctness. Now he would have clubbed a baby seal if it meant he got a good night's sleep.

'I'm sorry,' Barbara apologised to Anna. 'That was very tactless of me. Of course you wouldn't want to go out celebrating, would you? Not after Your Loss.'

'Have you noticed,' Elliott remarked, as Barbara bustled off to do some filing, 'she always talks about your loss now, never mine? I'm beginning to feel quite neglected.'

'You're old news,' Anna said. 'And that's the first time she's apologised for putting her foot in it in three days. The novelty must be wearing off.'

All the same, she wasn't looking forward to the new year. Not the evening itself – that could easily be got over with a couple of stiff drinks and an early night – but the whole idea of facing a new year scared her. It would be the first that didn't have Oliver anywhere in it. Her first official year on her own. It stretched before her like a gigantic blank canvas, waiting to be filled. Once she would have thought about all the exciting possibilities that lay ahead; now it just made her apprehensive.

'So you're going to be on your own for New Year?' Elliott said.

'Just me, a bottle of wine and a giant bag of Doritos,' she confirmed.

'Would you mind if I joined you?'

Anna looked at him in surprise. 'Don't you have other plans?'

'Do I look like the kind to have plans? Actually, I was hoping to join Barbara at the Rotary Club dinner dance, but since my invite wasn't forthcoming and the girls are sleeping over at a friend's, I'm at a bit of a loose end.'

'I'd be terrible company,' Anna warned him.

'Doesn't matter, I'm only coming round for the Doritos anyway.'

'In that case, how can I say no? I'd hate to stand between a man and his junk food.'

'Great. We can be terrible company together.'

It was a nice, undemanding evening. Anna cooked dinner, and even though she'd always thought of herself as hopeless in the kitchen, she was pleasantly surprised that Elliott seemed to enjoy it.

'I thought you said you were a terrible cook?' he said as he helped himself to more lasagne.

'It must be Eve's good influence.' She'd spent a lot of time hanging around the restaurant kitchen watching her cook, far more than she ever had when Oliver was in charge.

After dinner, he insisted on helping with the washing-up, then he played with Charlie.

When Charlie had been put to bed, they watched a dire 1970s disaster movie on TV and howled with laughter all the way through it.

Half an hour before midnight, Elliott put down his glass and said, 'I'd better go.'

'But it's not twelve yet!'

'What happened to your early night?'

'I don't feel like it any more.'

Their eyes met. 'Do you want me to first-foot you?' Elliott asked.

'I beg your pardon?'

'You know what I mean. Tall, dark, handsome stranger knocks on your door at midnight, carrying a lump of coal and a handful of money? Supposed to bring you good luck through the year, so I'm told.'

'I could do with some luck.' Anna pretended to think about it. 'I'm sure I can lay my hands on the change and the coal, but I don't know about anyone tall, dark and handsome—'

'Very funny.' Elliott made a face.

There was a knock on the door. They looked at each other. 'Looks like someone's beaten you to it,' Anna said. 'That's probably Tom Cruise.'

'I did say tall, didn't I?'

But it was an even bigger surprise than Tom Cruise.

'Happy New Year,' said Lynch, holding out a duty-free bag with a bottle of champagne sticking out of it. He looked jetlagged, but rumpled and sexy.

Anna did her best to cover her shock. 'Shouldn't you be in Times Square, waiting to see in the new year with all the other New Yorkers?'

'I was planning to,' he said, 'then I realised I was missing something.'

'Oh yes? What's that?'

'You.'

Elliott appeared behind her, breaking the spell.

Lynch frowned. 'Sorry, I didn't know you had company.'

'It's okay,' Elliott said. 'I was just leaving.'

'You don't have to go.'

Elliott glanced at Lynch. 'Oh, I think I do,' he said.

As Anna saw him out, she whispered, 'I'm sorry about this. I had no idea he'd be turning up out of the blue.'

'Life's full of surprises, isn't it?' Elliott seemed odd, slightly distant. Anna hoped she hadn't offended him.

'You can say that again. I wonder what he wants?'

'You'd better ask him that, hadn't you?'

She watched Elliott heading down the street, and fought an urge to call him back.

Lynch had already made himself at home. He was stretched out on her sofa, flicking through the channels on her remote control and finishing off the last of the Doritos.

'I bet you had a scintillating evening,' he said sarcastically.

'Actually, it was very pleasant. Better than being on my own.'

'Only just, I imagine.'

She took the TV remote out of his hands and turned it off. 'Can I get you anything?'

'A drink would be nice. Jack Daniels, if you've got it.'

'How very American.' She searched in the back of the drinks cupboard for the dusty bottle she knew she kept somewhere. 'You'll be humming the "Star-Spangled Banner" next.'

'Not me. But I did buy this for Charlie.' He reached into the duty-free bag and pulled out a baseball mitt.

'That's very kind of you, although I'm not sure how much use he'll get out of it. They don't play a lot of baseball in Homestead Park.'

'He'd get a lot of practice in New York.'

'I daresay he would,' Anna agreed, 'but the park's a lot closer.'

'You could come over? A change of scene might do you good.'

'We'd love to,' she said, 'but it might be a bit difficult. I've already had so much time off, it wouldn't be fair on the others to ask them to cover for me again.'

'I didn't mean a holiday,' Lynch said. 'I was thinking more of a permanent move.'

It took a moment for it to sink in. 'I'm sorry, could you say that again?'

'I want you to come and live with me. Is that simple enough for you?'

She sat back on her heels. 'I understand what you're saying, I just don't understand why.'

'I miss you.'

She listened, gobsmacked, as he told her how, two days after moving to New York, he'd realised how much he wanted to see her.

'I could hardly believe it myself,' he admitted ruefully. 'There I was, watching the Macy's Christmas parade, and all I could think was how much I wanted Charlie to see it too.'

'Are you sure about this?'

'Absolutely,' he confirmed. 'I can't think of anything else. It would be great for you and Charlie. I've got a fantastic apartment downtown, right in the middle of the West Village. It's a terrific place for kids. Charlie would love it there.'

'He loves it here,' Anna said. 'So do I. My life and family are here.'

'We could fly your family over whenever you wanted,' Lynch promised.

Anna smiled at the idea of Nana taking to transatlantic travel. It was a big adventure for her to go to Tesco.

'And it's not like you've got a career to worry about,' Lynch went on. 'No one's going to miss you at that crappy community centre.'

'Thanks a lot!'

'I mean it. You're wasted there, Anna. You could get a far better job in New York. Great prospects, great pay. You could

339

even go back to college and finish your degree if you wanted.'

'I could do that here.'

'Yes, but would you? I doubt it. Five years from now, you'll still be stuck in a dead-end job, living in this place and wondering about the life you could have had.' He leaned forward eagerly, pressing home his point. 'You owe it to yourself, and to Charlie. There are some terrific schools over there, he'd be so happy. You'd be giving him a great start in life.'

Anna frowned at him, thinking. 'And what about you? What do you get out of all this?'

He looked taken aback. 'Don't I get you?'

'I don't understand why you've suddenly got this big thing about settling down. This new job of yours – it's not the kind of place where you have to be married to get a promotion, or anything like that?'

'No!' Lynch laughed. 'God, you really don't think much of me, do you?'

'I'm just trying to work it out, that's all.'

'There's nothing to work out.' He reached for her hands. 'There's only one thing you need to know, and that's that I love you and I want us to be together. You, me and Charlie. That's not so hard to understand, is it?'

'I suppose not.' She smiled at him.

'This is your chance to get away from all the memories, to make a new life for yourself. New year, a whole new start. You could do anything, Anna.' He squeezed her hands. 'What do you say?'

Somewhere in the distance, the Minster bells chimed midnight. Ringing in the new year. She took a deep breath.

'I say yes,' she said.

Chapter 44

FEBRUARY

Her mum was trying not to cry as the 'Sold' sign went up.

'I know it's silly,' she sniffed. 'I mean, I should be happy for you, shouldn't I? This is a whole new beginning for you, a chance to start again. It's just what you need.'

'I really think it is.' But Anna felt sad too, as she watched the estate agent's board being nailed into place. This was her first home, the one she'd made with Oliver. Lately it had brought her a lot of heartache, but her memories were deep in its walls, buried under every creaky floorboard and in every plaster crack. It was so hard to walk away.

And yet she knew she had to do it. She'd made up her mind not to look back. Six weeks into the new year she was making a fresh start.

Just to make it all extra poignant, it was Valentine's Day. The day Oliver died. The day he was planning to propose to her. She twisted the engagement ring on the chain round her neck, thinking how different her life might have turned out, if only ...

But this was no time for regrets, or for looking back. And it was especially not time for dwelling on what might have been. She was determined to look into the future, which, from where she was standing, wasn't such a bad view.

She left Charlie with her mum while she headed off to the restaurant, where Eve was waiting for her. She was standing outside the door, watching anxiously as the workmen hoisted a new sign into place. There was a smell of new paint in the air, and twin clipped bay trees flanked the doorway in shiny blue pots.

'Robinson's.' Anna read the sign out loud.

Eve blushed. 'I thought it was about time I put my own stamp on the outside, as I've already put it on the inside.' She glanced at Anna. 'You don't think it's wrong, do you?'

'Why not? You've worked hard to get this place back on its feet. You deserve to take some of the credit.'

Eve smiled with relief. 'I've got your cheque,' she said. Anna followed her inside. The place was bustling with the lunchtime crowd.

She'd seen the new look when it was first unveiled a month ago, but it still impressed her. All the old dark wood and red-checked fabric was gone, replaced by a fresh, modern décor: mint-green walls, pale furniture and lots of daylight flooding in.

'How's business?' Anna asked.

'Booming. We're fully booked tonight.' Eve looked uncertain. 'I thought twice about opening, under the circumstances—' Her eyes were red-rimmed, and Anna understood why. She'd shed her own tears that morning, remembering Oliver.

'I think he would have gone mad if you'd closed this place on one of the busiest nights of the year,' she said.

'That's what I thought.'

They were both silent, lost in their own thoughts for a few moment, then Eve was brisk again. 'Anyway, here's your cheque.' She handed it to her. 'Are you really sure you want to do this? You could stay on as a silent partner, you know.'

'When have you ever known me to be silent?' Anna grinned.

'True,' Eve agreed.

'No, it's better if I make a clean break. The place is all yours now.'

'It is, isn't it?' Eve looked around in wonder.

She deserved it, Anna decided. She'd worked so hard to save the place, and to raise a loan – a proper one this time, from the bank – to pay Anna for her shares. Anna had tried to refuse, but Eve was insistent.

'I've got to do this properly,' she said. 'The place won't feel as if it's really mine if I don't. Besides, you might change your mind and sell to Spike Mullins.'

'No chance,' Anna said firmly. One meeting with him had been enough to tell her there was no way she wanted him anywhere near Oliver's restaurant.

'Would you like a drink before you go?' Eve offered. 'I've got a bottle of champagne in the fridge. I thought we could celebrate?'

Anna was tempted, she could certainly use some Dutch courage.

'I'd better not. I'm due at the airport in an hour.'

Eve saw her to the door. I'll miss you,' she said.

'I'll miss you, too,' she said, and knew she meant it.

There was a moment's hesitation, then they hugged each other. It wasn't the embrace of old friends, but of two people who'd learned the hard way to value, respect and finally like each other.

Elliott took them to the airport. He pulled into the car park and stopped, turning in his seat to look at her. 'Are you absolutely sure about this?' he asked for the hundredth time.

'I've already told you, it's what I want,' she confirmed.

'But what if you're making a big mistake?'

'I won't know that until I do it, will I?'

He looked as if he was going to argue, then changed his mind. He leaned over and planted a hurried kiss on her cheek. 'Good luck,' he said.

'Thanks.'

Her courage deserted her as she saw Lynch waiting on the other side of the concourse. She forced herself to walk calmly towards him, although her palms were sweating so much she could hardly hold her handbag.

Charlie spotted Lynch and broke free of her, running towards him.

'Hi, Chas.' She felt a pang as Lynch scooped him up into his arms. A few months ago she would never have believed it could happen.

Lynch turned to Anna, then looked around.

'Where's all your stuff?' he asked.

343

'I didn't bring anything.'

'Now that's what I call travelling light,' he laughed. But she could see in his eyes that realisation had already dawned. 'You're not coming, are you?' he said.

She shook her head. 'It wouldn't work, Lynch.'

'But we've been through all this. I told you, I want you and Charlie with me.'

'You don't, not really. We wouldn't fit into your life, and you wouldn't fit into ours.'

He looked hurt. 'I thought I was doing okay?'

'You were. You are. But if we have to try that hard surely it must mean it's not meant to be?'

'Aren't relationships all about compromise?'

'They are. But we'd both have to change too much for it to work, and I don't think we could be something we're not.' She tried to smile. 'Anyway, be honest. Could you really stand chocolate stains all over your lovely white apartment, or the jammy fingerprints on your plasma TV?'

'You're not that messy,' he joked feebly. 'Anyway, I have a cleaning lady. A Filipino. I could get her to come in every day, we wouldn't even notice the mess—'

'You could hire a whole army of Filipino cleaning ladies and it wouldn't help. It's not just the mess, Lynch. You're used to your freedom. We'd end up hating each other within a few weeks, and I really wouldn't want that to happen.'

'But I love you,' he said.

'And I love you, too. That's why I can't come.'

He looked at her for a long time, then sighed. 'I knew it wouldn't happen,' he said. 'To tell the truth, I didn't think you'd ever say yes in the first place. Then when you did, I kept expecting you to phone and say you'd changed your mind. But when I saw you just then, walking towards me, I finally started to think that maybe—' His mouth twisted. 'But like you said, it was never meant to be.'

'I'm sorry.'

'What will you do?' he asked.

'I'm selling the house. I can pay off the loans with my share of the restaurant money, and still have some left over to put the deposit on a new place. Somewhere for me and Charlie. A new start.'

'You could have a new start with me?'

Anna was still tempted. He would never know how much. Even right up until last night she'd lain awake, wondering if she was making the right decision or giving up on the best chance in her whole life.

In the end the pull of her old life had proved too much. She didn't need to cross the Atlantic to make a fresh start, she could do it just as well here, among her family and friends.

'I can't,' she said. 'My life is here. It would be running away. I know you don't think I've got much, but it's all I want. I know I've let you down, but at least try and be happy for me?' she pleaded.

'I'd be happier if you were getting on that plane with me.' He saw her face and sighed. 'Okay, I'll shut up. I never could change your mind once it was made up.'

'You came pretty close,' Anna smiled.

'But not close enough.'

She wondered if he was more disappointed at losing her, or at losing a fight.

'What about you?' she asked, as they walked towards the check-in desk.

'Oh, you know me. I'll be okay. I'll probably pick up a couple of hot babes in Club Class.'

She frowned at him. 'You're not joking, are you?'

'Maybe, maybe not.' He lifted his brows suggestively.

That was another reason why it would never work, she thought. For all his good intentions, Lynch was never going to be tamed. That was part of his charm.

'Take care of yourself,' he said, when they hugged goodbye at passport control. 'And don't forget, if Chas ever wants to practise his baseball, he knows where to find me.' He ruffled Charlie's hair affectionately, and then he was gone.

Anna watched him walk away. He didn't look back. That wasn't his style, she realised. And it shouldn't be hers, either.

Elliott was waiting for her in his car, tapping his fingers on the steering wheel.

'I thought you might have changed your mind,' he said.

'Not me.'

He regarded her carefully. 'Are you sure you're okay?'

'I'm fine,' she said. 'Let's go home.'

He was silent for a long time. Then suddenly he said, 'For what it's worth, I think you made the right choice.'

'So do I.'

'I was thinking,' he said as they joined the motorway. 'We don't have to rush back, do we? Maybe we could find a pub, stop off for dinner?'

'Sounds good to me.'

She glanced across at him as he chatted away to Charlie in the back seat, counting all the green lorries. He'd been such a good friend to her. More than a good friend, in fact.

Who knows what the future holds, she thought, as they headed back to the city together.